Mind Games and Murder

TWO

K. J. McGILLICK

Two
Copyright © 2018 by Kathleen McGillick
KJRM Publishing LLC

ISBN 978–1985600324
ISBN 978–1985600324

Interior Design & Formatting:
Christine Borgford, Type A Formatting
www.typeaformatting.com

Editing:
Amy Donnelly, Alchemy and Words LLC
www.alchemyandwords.com

Proofreading:
Judy Zweifel, Judy's Proofreading
www.judysproofreading.com

ALL RIGHTS RESERVED. This book contains material protected under International and Federal Copyright Laws and Treaties. In accordance with the U.S. Copyright Act of 1976, the scanning, uploading, and electronic sharing of any part of this book without the permission of the author/publisher is unlawful piracy and theft of the author's intellectual property. No part of this text may be reproduced, transmitted, downloaded, decompiled, reverse engineered, or stored in or introduced into any information storage and retrieval system, in any form or by any means, whether electronic or mechanical, now known or hereinafter invented, without the express written permission of the author publisher.

The author acknowledges the trademark status and trademark ownership of all trademarks, service marks, and word marks mentioned in this book. All possibly trademarked names are honored by italics and no infringement is intended. No part of this publication may be reproduced or transmitted in any form or by any means, electronic or mechanical, including photography, recording, or any information storage and retrieval system without the permission of the author, nor be otherwise circulated in any form of binding or cover other than that in which it is originally published. This book is a work of fiction. Names, characters, places, and incidents are the product of the author's imagination or are used fictitiously. Any references to historical or actual events, locales, business establishments, places or persons, living or dead, is coincidental.

DEDICATION

In memory of my grandparents Florence and William

Dedicated to my son Mark-Michael and grandchildren Rinoa and Jude

Two.
Many say, "Good things come in pairs."
Yin and Yang.
One for the money. Two for the show.
One, two, buckle my shoe.
Good and evil.
Positive and negative.
When the sun dims, your second self shall disappear.
Tick Tock.

CHAPTER ONE

ADRIEN

"I WANT HER dead. Make it happen," Avigad stated. His thick lips enveloped the rim of the fine china cup. Her death was not a suggestion. It was an order to be carried out without question. An assassination. I was a surgeon but his chosen assassin for this death. "I don't care what method you employ. Get it done."

I sat back against the black tufted leather of the booth and studied the man. Olive skin, empty green eyes, light-brown hair. Avigad was not an imposing man in stature, and he wasn't educated in the academic sense. A man of great conviction but with no conscience. His mother was from Jewish descent, and his father Palestinian. Avigad spoke with the perfect clipped British accent of a refined landed gentry from the 18th century. His command of Arabic was rivaled by none. He was as comfortable in a yarmulke as he was a kufi.

I'd been Avigad's surgeon a bit over two years ago when he needed emergency stents placed in his coronary arteries. He had suffered a heart attack and I was on call duty and saved his life.

Our physician-patient relationship led to a friendship, and then a business offer. He procured organs and I agreed to transplant them.

Over two years, Avigad had helped me amass almost half a billion dollars. Illegally earned, but all mine. He acquired the money to launder. And once laundered, opened the door to investing it in places I would have never had access. For that, I owed him a debt.

The only thing he asked in return was when he needed a surgeon to perform an organ removal surgery, I would be ready to leave at once. No questions about my assignment were allowed, and I understood and accepted his stipulations. No questions about where the surgery would be performed. A fake passport was always provided to protect my identity. To procure a steady flow of organs he scoured every hellhole on earth and made promises he could never keep. His share was far greater than mine, but as he often reminded me, without him I wouldn't have the surgeries to perform and money would not magically find its way to my bank.

I was in it solely for the money. The only mistake I'd ever made was mixing some Albanians' money with mine in a questionable investment that went bad. They wanted a two hundred percent return on their money, I promised twenty percent. We now were in a dispute and negotiations were not an option, but more importantly, I wanted to wear my wealth like a coat that no one could misinterpret. As a child, my clothes were torn and dirty. I was forced to wear them to school because I had nothing else. My mother was too drunk to care, and the bullies smelled my fear. I didn't worry about tattered clothes or bullies any longer.

The organ removals were becoming a logistical issue. Countries had been scrutinized morally and ethically, forcing

TWO

government agencies to develop regulations regarding the donation or sale of an organ consensually or otherwise. The human rights issues that had surfaced were bad for business. I thought foolishly that Avigad kept time, place, and the other people involved secret for my protection, to have plausible deniability if questioned. In reality, he was compartmentalizing his cells of people. His demands, at times, proved challenging, but the payment I received drove me to make it happen. Until now.

My income as a surgeon was adequate. I worked hard to maintain a practice that kept me in demand. The money never seemed enough for the luxury I wanted. I lived on the third floor of a luxury nine-bedroom apartment home, in the heart of Paris. My building was so close to the Eiffel Tower that we could almost touch the hourly twinkling lights at night.

My second stream of business was an art gallery I shared with Isabella, my wife. As Avigad became a silent business partner over the last two years, the gallery had sold its fair share of forgeries. I couldn't complain because it lined our pockets with millions of dollars. My success was obvious. I had a thriving practice, beautiful home, and gallery that was by appointment only.

As we sat in the café where I met with Avigad to discuss our business, I waited for the server to finish pouring a fresh cup of the Turkish coffee from the cezve into our cups. The blend was bitter and the acrid taste bit at my tongue. As displeasing as it was to me, not drinking the offering would offend my host. I compromised and drowned my cup with sugar, evoking a disapproving sigh from Avigad.

Avigad, a rigid man with rules.

"Your request is a little extreme, Avigad. I can manage Isabella." This was ridiculous. The man has been on edge for the last week. I could not have his anxiety bleed over into my profit margin or affect any part of my life. He had no reason to believe

I maintained an emotional attachment to her. She was a business connection at this part of my life, nothing more.

He watched as I stirred the coffee, tapped my spoon on the side of my cup, and placed it on the saucer. He took that as a prompt to continue.

"She is asking questions and I cannot have that, Adrien," he said.

Isabella had started asking questions, this was true. Unfortunately, she'd come upon inventory I'd left exposed on the computer server. It was my fault for not closing the encrypted site properly before leaving two weeks ago for a heart-lung transplant surgery in Iran.

Iran. I despised traveling in that country. Yes, no moral dilemma there; buying and selling of organs was legal. However, transplanting an organ from a woman into a man was forbidden by local surgeons. So, the surgery was outsourced to people like me. The generous pay after negotiations usually quelled my concerns of getting caught breaking the law. However, the consequences, if I was discovered, were deadly.

"I said I have this. You try my patience, Avigad," I said. I quickly realized I may have crossed the line when his left eyebrow raised in response. "You are not yourself lately. The art forgeries are doing well. The money laundered for the art and the organ transplants through the gallery is running like a well-oiled machine. Now, out of nowhere, you tell me I must purchase Roselov's London gallery and backdate the transaction. You requested I add Roselov under the umbrella of the gallery here. I did as you'd asked. I falsified Isabella's name without question, but I cannot just dispose of her. You don't think if something happened to her there would be a protracted investigation?"

Taking possession of Roselov's London gallery raised the hair on my neck. Something was wrong, and my internal alarm

TWO

buzzed. The Roselov gallery, like ours, trafficked forgeries with original works. At Avigad's request, we had acquired our fair share of fakes from Roselov to sell to specific clients. And those paintings always turned us a handsome profit. The fakes were of excellent quality that passed the scrutiny of the auction house specialists in London, Paris, and Abu Dhabi, and had passed rigorous testing of private laboratories a time or two. I was happy to make a profit from a venture that had little risk and great reward. Thus, dealing time to time with Roselov was acceptable.

But now we were in the thick of what could be a massive problem, if I was reading the signs correctly. In this purchase, Avigad again stayed a silent partner under the umbrella of our business. He put up the money for the new gallery purchase and took over operations. Well, *I* ran the forgeries. Isabella had no idea we owned the property at all.

The ownership in Isabella's name could present a problem if we had to maintain the gallery long term. And we had to think long term. Forgeries might soon be a part of the past. It had been rumored that a company had developed artificial intelligence that could identify forgeries by brushstrokes. We recently learned the technology was created and actively used. The technology would certainly prove a disruptive factor to forgers trafficking their canvases. Acceptance of this technology in the art world was becoming an enormous financial issue for me.

"You're a doctor. Surely there are drugs to make it look like a suicide," he said easily, as the coffee cup touched his lips again, leaving a drop lingering there.

"Of course, there are drugs that cause death and aren't easily traceable. A high dose of potassium chloride or Anectine would do nicely. But to what end? The husband is always the first one to be suspected in an otherwise healthy wife's death. The added issue is I am a doctor, with access to drugs. Not to mention an autopsy would find any suspicious drug in her blood and tissue." I ran my hand down my face. "Look, this is getting out of hand."

"Is something more bothering you, Adrien? Since when did risk stand in your way?" He read my nervous tapping of the spoon on the table.

I may as well address the elephant in the room. It was time to have the discussion.

"I agreed to perform a service, beneficial for us both. You've helped me earn money far beyond what I ever thought possible. However, I was clear the medical service was for a limited time. Everything has an end date, and my end date for providing those specific services is upon us. I have enough money, Avigad. I am comfortable in my life. I have asked you over the last months to find someone else to do the surgeries outside the European borders.

"You are aware that the government agencies that oversee these things are ramping up. It doesn't help that, in India, people are placing signs on lamp posts to recruit people. And brokerages for body parts litter the dark web. Security is being stepped up. I have no wish to be arrested in a foreign county as investigations of organ transplants intensify." I attempted to reason with him.

He regarded my logic with an understanding as he nodded his head. And took another sip of coffee.

"And now, out of nowhere I am—or legally, Isabella is—the owner of a new art gallery. A gallery that most of the civilized world whispered for years has a Russian mafia connection," I threw in for good measure, which brought a level gaze of disapproval.

I *did* have a comfortable life. I took risks to obtain that comfortable life. At some point, though, the risks started to outweigh the reward. Laws were tightening. China no longer allowed prisoners to die untreated, to harvest viable, healthy organs. Global

TWO

humanitarian groups were pressuring people to develop a conscience. With more scrutiny, it might be time to exit this lucrative endeavor. I did not want to be on the losing end of a zero-sum game.

"London, I assure you is for a limited time. Next month, I will have you transfer ownership to me through one of my holding companies. But for now, I need you in place to move the pieces on the board. There were plans that had been disrupted and I had to regroup. Now more than ever, time is of the essence.

"And as for your medical services, you shall have your wish shortly. We will alter our base of operation. However, I need you on a flight tonight at six to Cairo. We have donors from Aleppo coming through," he stated.

Aleppo. Syria. Where refugees are desperate to leave that war-torn land and start a new life. That came with a price, and Avigad was right there to exploit the needs of those poor souls. Their ticket to a new life was a mandatory kidney donation. It was rumored children were sold into slavery for a price. I was a part of that machine and wanted out now.

Egypt and India were two places I did not find accommodating for surgery. Both had their drawbacks, but the governments in both countries tolerated these operations. To be fair to Avigad, the accommodations for the surgeries were adequate and little went wrong. The donors were treated humanely, unlike other areas in Eastern Europe where I refused to execute the procedure.

"How many? What type of surgery? What is my cut?" With such urgency should come an extended gratuity.

The wheels turned in his mind, telegraphing the information to his right index finger that rubbed against his right thumb. His tell. Several moments passed, and I figured out he was weighing how he would present the information.

"More than your usual two," he countered. His carotid

artery pulsed in an accelerated rhythm as he thought his answer through. "Ten people." He let the number hang in the air. "Most of the donors are kidneys, two are donating a lobe of liver"—he snapped his fingers, as if he was now recalling the exact details—"and one is a lung."

I waited for him to correct the numbers. He did not.

I took this in. How could this man think it would be humanly possible to operate on ten people in anything less than five days. His temper had flared several times over the last week, forcing me to measure my response, not knowing how volatile his reaction would be.

"That is physically impossible," I told him quietly, and the truth was not exaggerated. Operating on more than two people a day in less than optimum conditions posed risks that events could go bad fast. No one wanted unexplained deaths. Especially in a region as volatile as Egypt.

"I want you on that plane tonight. Wheels up at six. It is a private transportation jet, and use your Canadian passport. Your travel visa will be ready for you," he said.

He removed several euros from his billfold and placed the money under the silver tray on our table, ending the discussion.

We looked at each other, as was the nature of our well-rehearsed dance, and then he stood.

"Your remuneration will be eighty thousand euros."

Eighty thousand was about half a year's income for one day's worth of work. But still impossible to achieve by myself. I would have to complete an organ removal every half hour without any breaks to ensure the viability of the organ for use. Even if I could perform the surgery that quickly, it would be impossible to clean the room between people and recover each patient adequately. Avigad was, in essence, signing ten people's death certificates.

TWO

"Unacceptable. I am the one risking everything. Even if the government officials look the other way for what I assume is a hefty premium you are paying, this is something that can go terribly wrong very fast.

"If my math is correct, after all the bribes and payment for the facility and staff, you should net about four million for brokering this deal. And you are offering me two percent of your take? I will say no this time." I was done with this conversation.

He sat down on the bench again, readjusting his left leg, and removed his phone from his jacket pocket. He tapped the screen a few times, sending and receiving a text, then placed the phone on the table.

"Will one hundred fifty thousand euros motivate you?" Haggling was not in my blood. However, it was in his. I knew I could drive it farther. These were his opening offers. He was in an obvious bind, and the economics of supply and demand held true in all business transactions.

I shook my head no. He again tapped a message and received a reply.

"Two hundred?" I could read in his body language, as he adjusted his hip, this would be his last offer. Yet five percent as my fee seemed incredulous. He was merely the broker, and without me, the process would grind to a halt.

"Yes, I believe that is acceptable. Why the rush?" I asked, although I did not expect an answer. In the end, I didn't want one.

"Not something I can discuss with you. The transportation is arranged to and from the airport, and the jet to carry the organs to their destination will be ready to leave at exactly seven p.m. You can start the surgery at nine, and that gives you almost an hour per person. The facility we are using is larger than the normal one, and I have increased the staff. I need you at your best and we need to move the organs quickly," he instructed. What normally took two hours, he expected done in one.

"I will need at least one anesthetist, two surgical assistants, and three nurses to recover the patients. Do you need a list of medications, medical supplies, and the type of blood supply to have on hand?" I inquired.

"No. All I need is for you to work quickly, so we can transport the organs in one transport," he said.

"I will do the best I can, Avigad," I assured him. "Have they been screened for problematic illnesses?"

"Of course. The recipients are paying high dollars for healthy organs," he replied, immediately wishing he could take that information back. His face revealed that he let that slip. Maybe his take would be more than four million.

"There is another matter that demands our attention. I need you to send Paul to London to arrange transportation for the paintings that are going to the Abu Dhabi auction. They are crated and marked. All he needs to do is be available for the transport and fly there for the auction, as the agent in proxy," he instructed. "I have arranged for people to move the rest of the valuable inventory to Luxembourg. He must be there to open the gallery for them."

"I'll make the arrangements. What account do you want the auction money sent to?" I asked, although I knew the answer.

"Use our Vatican connection. Leave it to him." That arrangement was unusual. Normally, we used a Swiss banker, who also was an *avocat*, to handle all the transfers. That was not my concern so I didn't protest.

"Fine. Now, as to my fee—"

Avigad waved a hand dismissively cutting off what I was about to say. "The money will be transferred to your account as you board the plane after you finish." He was annoyed I brought my fee into the equation. However, money matters had to be

TWO

firmed up to avoid any misunderstanding.

"Isabella—" he started.

It was my turn to cut him off. "I assure you, there is no need for worry. I secured the accounts with an additional encryption layer, and moved the bulk of problematic paintings from the storage in the gallery to Geneva. In the two years of owning that freeport space, she has never set foot there. The inventory is secure. And, might I add, if it had not been for Monsieur Dozier wandering into the gallery without an appointment, we would not be having this discussion. That problem arose from your end, and I handled it." My neck muscles tightened, and my jaw muscle ticked recalling how one person could have started an avalanche of chaos in our well-oiled machine.

A slight nod of the head as an acknowledgment that it was a true statement. That nod also served as a goodbye. I stood from the table after Avigad. I was irritated with Avigad taking all the money and me all the risk. I didn't particularly like the man to start. He wasn't trustworthy but his business sense was always spot on. To continue working and making the money I wanted, he was a necessary evil.

A server opened the door for our exit. Avigad looked at me once more, assessing, then turned and strode in the direction of the Arc de Triomphe. I stood there and watched one of the deadliest men on the planet stroll down the Champs Elysees, weaving through people he would mark for death without a thought.

As I turned the opposite direction, my phone rang. I pulled the phone from my pocket and found Isabella's name flashing across the screen. Avigad was right, she was a becoming a problem.

"Yes, Isabella. What is it?" I answered, trying to temper my reaction to her call.

"Adrien, shall I confirm the dinner reservations for

tomorrow, or have you already spoken with the restaurant?" I heard her clicking computer keys.

Isabella. Yes, how to handle Isabella.

"Isabella, I told you three days ago to cancel the dinner. I will be in Cairo giving a lecture at a conference. I leave tonight." True, I would be in Cairo, but as I had found this out minutes ago, the other part was untrue. She would never know, though, and it would keep her off balance.

Silence. The computer keys no longer tapped.

"What? No. No. In fact, you told me to make certain that the house was immaculate in the event we wanted to have them over after dinner." Her words partially belied her frustration.

"I have no idea what you are talking about. I specifically told you to cancel, and because of your scattered thoughts lately, I even left a note. Now, make sure you cancel the reservations. I'm concerned about your forgetfulness, Isabella. Can I count on you to run the gallery while I'm gone? Do I need to hire a minder for you?" I let that hang and followed it with, "I leave after work tonight. Have you anything else I need to straighten for you?"

"No, I'm sorry. I guess I misunderstood. I will take care of it at once," she said. With a sheepish hesitancy, she continued, "There is one thing. I can't access the storage area. I wanted to look through the inventory for a particular piece I thought I saw. Strangely, it's not in the computer database. The new client is scheduled for a consultation tomorrow. For some odd reason, the combination is not working."

Of course, it wasn't working. She wouldn't be permitted access until the paintings she didn't need to be aware of were moved. I did not need her comparing computer inventory to actual inventory.

"What number did you enter?" I asked, picking up my pace as I brushed against rude tourists.

TWO

"Eight-six-six-four," she responded.

"Isabella, that was the code last month. If I can't trust you to remember the code, how can I trust you with inventory? Who's the new client? Have you given Paul his details?" The last thing I needed was for her to become more involved in the inventory and finances.

"His name is Ben Jaager and he's relocating from Amsterdam. I have his financial information ready for you, and already sent it to Paul," she said. I was slightly annoyed Paul had not mentioned it.

"Where does he live?"

Papers shuffled, and she responded, "Off of St. Dominique."

"Acceptable, I'll see you later." I disconnected abruptly before she could query me again about the code.

My next matter was Paul, and quickly dispatched his number into my phone.

"Oui." His usual greeting.

"I need you at the London gallery to prepare some paintings for auction. You need to do that tout suite. Avigad's people will need entrance," I said.

"Of Course. Where are the paintings going?" he questioned, tapping notes into his computer.

"Abu Dhabi," I responded. "They're to be sent as a private reserve."

"I'll connect with Bashir at once," he said.

"I'll text the address and entrance code to you," I told him, walking toward the area in the train station to swipe my metro card. "Use the back entrance and I'll send you instructions what to do in the storage area."

"It will be taken care of immediately," he responded.

"Isabella said there is a new client. Do you have anything on him?"

"I'm still gathering data, but what I have so far checks out. His name is Ben Jaager, recently moved from Amsterdam. He's an investor. I'm tracking what investments in particular, but it seems venture capital. His bank balance is in the eight figures. The apartment he moved into he paid for in cash, around four million. He has expressed an interest in the Frankenthaler, Gorky, and Albers," he responded. "He's divorced and no children."

"Good. I'm ready to board a train. Leave a message if there's a problem in London once you get there," I instructed.

"Of course." I could hear the smile in his voice. Efficient and responsible were characteristics I could rely upon with Paul.

"Ah, Paul. One more thing. Move a painting from one place in the apartment to another before Isabella gets home. And move her car to another spot as well." I had to keep up the charade with Isabella.

"Why, Adrien?" he asked.

"Paul, that's my concern. And make sure the seat is adjusted back to her height." I didn't like involving him in personal business, but time was of the essence.

"Consider it done." He disconnected. I'd entered the Etoile station during our conversation.

What I had to do was to stay focused on making this trip my last. I'd never intended to get in so deep with Avigad. Every time I boarded a flight, I wondered if my arrest waited at the other end, and I'd live out my life in a dirty prison in whatever country. However, the money was like a drug, and my need for more money, like a habit that had to be fed. One that could possibly get me killed one day.

CHAPTER TWO

BEN

I LOVED MY job and it gave me the ability to use every skill I'd learned through all my positions in Europol. My job took a chunk out of my person life and I'd never married. I also didn't have children and that was something I'd started to regret. However, I was a field agent who took assignments that required dedicated blocks of time in different countries and that wouldn't be fair to a family. Over the last year I had been rethinking this issue, and maybe next year would be the time to ask for a more permanent assignment closer to home. Somewhere in the Netherlands. For now, I had to have my head in the game. Paris was the assigned city and Isabella Armond my target.

"Levi, I'm sorry, but I can't live in this apartment for another day, much less a month. This place is like living a nightmare in a Tim Burton movie. Is this some type of punishment? How could anyone live in this monstrosity?" I didn't think for one minute I was overreacting to the state of my surroundings. Europol asked a lot of me when on an undercover assignment. I'd lived in places, both shabby and even squalid, for short periods of time. But this place evoked unrelenting agitation in me.

"Ben, it can't be that bad. We were lucky to get anything in that area for this operation on such short notice. I think you can reach inside that steely resolve and tough out those living conditions for a month," he said.

I begged to differ. Levi hadn't seen this place. The creepy apartment walls appeared to close in on me, like some fantasy horror movie. I hope he wasn't implying I was being a drama queen because that wouldn't stand without some harsh words.

"The beauty of that apartment is the location. You're a mere few blocks from your target, Isabella Armond. Whatever it looks like, it's worth it to sell your cover." My boss ignored my hesitance to accept my living arrangements.

It would be one thing if I had to share this heinous nightmare of a place and be rewarded with sex for my effort at tolerating it. However, this place was pure chick repellent. What honest to God man in his right mind purposefully decorated the place like this. Clearly there would be no sex happening here and probably never had.

I heard a ping, hoping it was the pictures I texted as evidentiary proof of the atrocity. He laughed heartily which confirmed my assessment.

"Dear God, it *is* a Tim Burton set. However, I would lean toward *Alice in Wonderland*." I couldn't argue with that. "For the next month, it's your nightmare to live in. Get used to it and embrace it."

He stopped a moment and then continued, "Oh, that purple couch. Did someone kill Barney and plant the evidence right under your nose? That color, it's almost blinding. I seriously feel your pain."

"No, Levi. Trust me that's not even the worst of it," I said, disheartened that I was sentenced to living in someone's crazy

TWO

idea of trendy. Before I could continue, he circled us back to why I was staying there.

"Moving on to why you're there. What's your impression of Isabella Armond?" Levi asked. I could hear the creak of the old springs in his chair as he leaned back. I worried, as I always did, someday he would tip too far in that chair, falling backward in a horrific crash. That wouldn't be a pretty sight.

"Haven't formed one yet," I honestly replied. "I've watched her for the last week. All I can say is that physically she is a dead ringer for Charlize Theron. Easy on the eyes, takes the train as well as uses her car, so no pretentious use of a driver unlike her husband. On the surface you'd never know she was worth over a hundred million."

"What's the plan?" he asked, rapidly clicking his pen. The incessant clicking was more annoying over the phone than in person, if that was even possible.

"She's coming over tomorrow to look at the layout of the place and make some suggestions. I'm impressed that our front end was able to get my credentials in place so quickly. Seriously though, that Facebook friend who intimated I was a frequent member of a private sex club that serviced any and all kinks? A bit much even for liberated Netherland people. Maybe it will help. I didn't expect to be so thoroughly vetted. Especially because I'm supposedly paying in cash. There's no doubt that the life of Ben Jaager is being overly processed somewhere." This was a concern that went with being a counterterrorism agent. Our job carried a risk we all understood.

"She's smart and deadly. Right now, her gallery is at the epicenter of this operation. The Americans have unequivocally traced the connection of White to Roselov, and Roselov to her gallery. Once the high-dollar fakes reach Roselov, he distributes some to the Middle East, such as Abu Dhabi and Dubai. We believe she disburses the rest throughout Europe. Drugs, guns, and art are the tools of terrorists, and she is obviously in bed with them. We need to shut this down," he said, as if I needed reminding.

"Okay. I've got everything in place, and I'll chat with Jill as soon as I have something," I assured him. Our conversation had run its course, and I had work to do.

I placed my phone on silent and vibrate. Picking up the file for Isabella Armond from my desk, I wondered if she was a deadly spider like Roselov. Or a praying mantis like White? Did she fit the profile of a person adept at money laundering? On the yes side, she had heavily invested in real estate to clean her money. She had purchased her new gallery with cash at the outset—a very bold move. Arrogant and brazen, some would say, but she seemed to cover her tracks well, with paperwork and financials that had to be fabricated. Why the French hadn't investigated her by now was beyond me. She was a new gallery owner, but they seemed more interested in the tax they would mine from her sales and purchases than the untraceable funds available to her.

Add to that, the recent purchase of her apartment raised alarm bells to us. Four hundred twenty square meters; nine rooms, three bathrooms, and a cellar. What did two people need with that much space at such a steep price?

It was clear in my mind she had offshore accounts that we'd been unable to tap into, despite the new banking laws. Criminals always found loopholes, and it appeared some banks remained complicit.

The husband appeared to be a successful surgeon. He kept his nose to the grindstone and had a network of well-connected colleagues. Realistically, millions of dollars weren't coming from his work as a physician and lecturer, pointing us back to Isabella and her gallery. She had to be providing the funding and

TWO

laundering. Taking her down and seeing her rot in prison was a mission for me. Cutting off funding for terrorist activity, whether in Europe, the US, or the Middle East, meant more lives were safe.

Criminals who became paranoid over new banking regulations often hid their cash in the walls of their homes. Some hid drugs in false-bottom boats or in the heavy frames of forged art they sold. It appeared she'd chosen the route to hide her assets in plain sight. Located in an exclusive part of town, at first blush her gallery appeared to sell fine art like any other. There was nothing illegal about selling art. However, the increased flow of paintings coming from London through Roselov to her gallery, and where the paintings went after their sale was concerning.

Vatican museum pieces were involved, making this even more complicated. According to the EU's Copenhagen criteria defining what states are eligible to join the EU, a candidate state must be a free market democracy. Given the Holy See is a theocracy, it didn't meet the criteria. We, therefore, had absolutely no legal jurisdiction over them. My role as an agent for Europol, an investigatory arm of the European Union, gives us no rights to demand anything. Everything seemed to move around the globe, like well-placed chess pieces, their movements almost strategic.

I'd watched all the CCTV available from London as they surveilled the Roselov gallery. The gallery was now owned by Isabella Armond—as of three weeks ago. I tried but could not find any personal or business connection between her and Roselov. No meetings, no personal contact, and no telephone contact. There were neither email traces nor hidden social media exchanges. With no probable cause, we weren't able to put a trap and trace on her personal and business telephones. She appeared to be a skilled and clever opponent.

There was no need to watch the CCTV again. The footage

would provide no information. There was also no need to read the investigatory report or look at the surveillance pictures again; I had them memorized. Reading through the material for the third time in two days had left me drained.

As I was ready to rest my head for a brief moment, my phone pinged with a text from my counterpart at Interpol. "Americans have arrested Roselov. Holding him and a Qatar national along with two Armenian nationals."

I immediately snapped up my phone, scrolled for a phone number and hit the call button. This was huge.

"Jill, what the hell? When did this happen?" I could barely put two sentences together, this was so huge. I sat up and leaned toward my computer to search for a release to the team about this event. Nothing yet. "Start at the beginning."

"No, there's no time. Let's cut to the chase. I'll give you what you need. You'll be video-conferenced in on this in about two hours. The Americans will be online and briefing us in full." Her words were quick and terse.

"Okay, the abridged version. Go." I picked up my pen and pad.

"White was found dead. The details are all bits and pieces right now. His girlfriend had been taken, but the money trail gets murky from there because he's hidden all his funds in her name. We can't figure out why. Roselov's buyers needed her to release the funds to them. They kidnapped her, attempting to take her to Switzerland to gain access to the money. The FBI was able to secure her freedom, and at the same time picked up Roselov, Khalid Abdurrahman, Nare and Davit Tavitian." She now sounded breathless like she was walking swiftly. Most likely she was jogging.

Khalid Abdurrahman. Nare and Davit Tavitian. I'd never heard of them. Who were they?

TWO

"Are any of the people you named on our watch list?" Had we missed something important?

"Not at all. Abdurrahman was on a watch list for art theft and antiquities smuggling, but no active or suspected terrorist list. The Armenians are still being investigated and they are dark horses out of nowhere," she said.

"My God, this is an enormous break. Have they connected the group to anyone over here?" I hoped for a miracle.

"Not yet. They're all staying silent. The Americans are trying to determine if they're able to treat them as enemy combatants, or if they must process them and provide legal counsel. The computers and phones they were using are being mined for data as we speak.

"There is also a lawyer who acts as the agent banker who will be detained in Switzerland when he arrives at the airport. He was supposed to meet the girlfriend, Emma Collier, and have her sign power of attorney over to him to collect the funds White stayed hidden. He's part of this mess too. You are now up to speed, and we'll be briefed as a team in two hours. However, there's no doubt whatever has been planned is still moving forward. Removing these people from carrying out their part of the plan won't make it crumble. It would seem they're only one part of the cell involved, ready for others to continue without them," Jill advised. "You should be getting word from Levi in a few minutes with the call-in information for the video conference. I'll catch you then. I have several things to chase down. Later." She disconnected abruptly.

True to the information she provided, I received a text from Levi. "Check your email and join the video conference at the time indicated. The link is embedded."

This added new urgency to the reason I was here. The countdown had started.

CHAPTER THREE

ISABELLA

"I'M NOT DISCUSSING this again, Isabella. The financial aspect of the business is too important to have two people's hands in it." Adrien was schooling me as he grabbed items and threw them into his suitcase. The man must have a portrait like Dorian Gray in a closet somewhere. He never appeared to age, and he never ran out of energy. He remained the same attractive man I married ten years ago, and even under the stress of his profession, he never displayed a wrinkle.

"The gallery is mine," I reminded him. I stood in the door, watching him as he paid closer attention to what he packed in a two-tone brown leather overnight bag.

He stopped stone still and then stood from his bent position. He leveled a look at me that was cold and angry. These were the moments that frightened me lately. Although he'd never given me a sign he would physically harm me, and never exhibited violence, it appeared he was controlling an urge to strike me. His expression aimed hatred at me, delivering a physical reaction from me worse than receiving a slap. I watched as he took one

TWO

measured breath, then another, and after the third nostril flare, he spoke.

"Isabella, that gallery may have been your concept ten years ago. You had some idealistic but foolhardy concept that selling unknown artists' paintings would somehow turn a profit. It was an experiment and a way to find your footing in the art world. You never did. Even you must admit, at one point it had almost dragged us under.

"It was something to keep you busy, and then it became a financial burden. I breathed financial life into it. I took my money and invested it in a damaged enterprise. And I emphasize the word 'invested.' I am the chief stakeholder. I make the financial decisions. Don't for one minute challenge my place to make those decisions. I have no intention, now or anytime in the future, to share the financial obligations of the gallery operation with you."

Defeated. I felt useless and defeated. This argument would end the same way as the other arguments we'd had about the gallery. I eventually would apologize to him and take the blame for starting the conversation. Anything was better than the next step, where he would start listing off every mistake I'd ever made, and how he alone saved me from myself. Finally, he would remind me that if it weren't for his business acumen, we'd be living in a box under a bridge.

In his eyes, I was a failure. In mine, I was coming to terms he was correct.

This time was different. I had questions, serious questions, that I deserved to have answered. Paintings I didn't recognize and had zero input regarding their acquisition, were bought and sold without being placed on the documented inventory. That alone was a serious legal issue if it came to light. And why did Roselov from London, whose name filtered through at times, seem to be there more frequently? And why did we have his paintings shipped with part of our lots to auction houses? Why would Adrien not allow me to meet with Dmitri Roselov? And why was I precluded from conversing with the accountant? Why was Adrien the only one allowed access to the inventory?

My questions would never be answered. It was a circular conversation. I asked, and he would deflect. I was aware the art world could be seedy. I never wanted the seedy part to touch my life. I was a purist and wanted anything bearing my name to be synonymous with integrity.

"The new client wants to view the paintings in our inventory—" I started.

"My God, what is wrong with you? You know you have to obtain photos of his apartment first. Isn't that set up for tomorrow?"

I nodded. My hands clenched and my anger soared. Adrien was treating me as if I didn't know my own business. His manner of speech was that of self-important employer to an irresponsible employee. Need I remind him that this was a business I started and maintained for eight years before he decided to insert himself into it. Without my asking him to, might I add.

"When you have an idea of what he wants, I'll accompany you to the storage room. We'll look through our inventory and make a list of what we can offer him based on his requests and where they could be displayed in his apartment. Need I remind you, photos and making the list comes well before you need to prepare the paintings for his viewing? You have a few prospects on the tablet you can show him in a pinch. That will help determine if he likes bright or muted colors, portraits or abstract. Honestly, this is not that complex, but you chose to make it that way."

He snatched his keys with a quick swipe, placed them in his

TWO

pocket, and didn't even give me a backward glance. Normally, I had no idea where he traveled for his speaking engagements, except for the limited information he provided. His itineraries were like a closely guarded state secret. Whether he realized it or not, he had shared his closely guarded secret today when he chastised me about my memory. I had in my possession a nugget of information.

"Adrien, this is ridiculous. I need to be able to look at everything myself. Please give me the combination to the storage." Frustration was joining my anger, and I felt my skin heating.

"Absolutely not. I don't have time to discuss this right now. I'm concerned you've been scattered and unreliable lately—as a physician and business owner. When I return, we need to explore this further. Your obvious inability to handle the gallery by yourself necessitated me employing Paul. I asked you to obtain a few necessary facts about a client's ability to fund their purchase, and you inevitably are not able to take that task to completion. Do you think I want to pay Paul his outrageous salary? Of course not. But if he wasn't around to oversee things, I shudder to think the mess you could create.

"Need I remind you that you took an order from a Monsieur Dozier, totally forgetting to enter it into the computer, and never saved it? That was quite an embarrassment, having to explain to a man why a hundred-thousand-euro painting he bought could not be found. So, no, Isabella, until I'm certain you won't blunder another sale, I'll oversee the large purchases."

My heart rate accelerated, and my skin burned as if licked by fire as I absorbed his incendiary speech. He was insinuating that I was incompetent. Even worse, that I was starting to lose a grip. Are my beliefs and memories reliable? Are my feelings invalid or untrue? It was frustrating to prove I had no part in that transaction with Monsieur Dozier. But he swore I did, and there was computer evidence to prove Adrien correct.

"If I don't leave now, I'll have a problem at the airport, so we can discuss this further when I return. My decision is clear, and I suggest you get on the same page as me. Visit the apartment, take some pictures, and email them to me so we can determine the price range to offer him," he ordered, as he lifted his small suitcase.

"Determine the price range? I don't understand your insistence on putting someone's ability to pay ahead of what a client wants and will be in their best interest. First and foremost, we need to determine what will look best and be aesthetically pleasing to him. I need to know what will bring him joy." I followed him as he left the room. Even though someone may be able to afford a Picasso or Matisse, that might not be an artist they want to look at every day.

"Isabella, this is a business that we operate. A negotiated sale, if that makes you feel better. People come to us because they expect a certain level of luxury, and they find that with the fine art we sell. A client doesn't come to us for third-tier artists. They come for first and second tier, the best. I had a financial statement completed on him, and he can afford high-end. Again, take the photographs and email them to me. Can you do that?" He waited for me to cease my verbal assault and nod, so I complied.

"Call down to George and have him alert the driver I'm on my way down," he ordered.

The back of his charcoal-gray suit was all I saw as he picked up the pace and walked across the glossy white and black-veined marble floor in the hallway. His leather soles clipped along at a rapid pace, leaving me again without any resolution to my concerns. Without a goodbye wave or kiss, the door opened and softly closed behind him. I stood there, unsure of what had

TWO

happened, but I knew I didn't like it. I was no longer relevant in his life. I was feeling irrelevant in my own.

What happened to my life these last three years? Who was I? Did I have any goals anymore, or were my goals now Adrien's? I owned a business that I wasn't allowed to be a vital part of and wasn't allowed access to financial information and inventory. How insane was that idea? Paul, an employee, had greater access to my business than I did. Adrien had me second-guessing my reality because it was blurring with his. Where Adrien's stood on a gray scale, though, mine was black and white. Right and wrong and no smudging to meet a specific need. What or who he said I was, I had started to accept as truth. The portrait he'd painted of me was not flattering. And yet, I sat and let him think and say the worst things to me.

My eyes met the clock and I realized if I didn't hurry, I would be late for my dinner date with Chloe, my best friend since childhood. She was my champion and had a true warrior's spirit. Coming out of marriage number three, she was turning into a serial bride. Her own issues of trust were often tested by the poor choices she made in men. Yet in the finance department, she always came out better than going in.

I hurried to finish getting ready to leave. I seriously could use a motor cart to get from one end of this place to the other end. This apartment was far too large and ostentatious to call a home. There was nothing comfortable or cozy about it. Our apartment home in the Marais suited me just fine, and the place I'll always consider my home. It was a source of good memories to tap into over the eight years we'd lived there, and I would have gladly lived there another eight. This apartment was opulent enough that Adrien could host parties to determine who could afford our art, and who would be rejected either by their behavior or ultimately their bank balance. Who was worthy to join his inner circle and who would not be asked back became a game I played that I invited Chloe to join. An invitation to one of our parties, always a sought-after event for his colleagues, evolved into him holding court and regaling others with his accomplishments. As he looked into the pool of water at his reflection, he always loved what reflected back at him.

Which of the three oversized bathrooms should I use? Which of my two hundred unnecessary outfits should I choose? How had my life exploded into such excess when inside, I was a minimalist?

An hour later I was ready to leave. I gathered my keys and phone from the entrance table and placed them in my handbag. My eyes glanced to the right as they normally did when I picked up the phone from the charger. No picture. No picture? Where was the picture of Adrien and me in front of the Louvre? Foolishly, I started looking under the table and around the room. It was nowhere. My thoughts were interrupted as I heard Danielle coming from the kitchen.

As she crossed the threshold from cleaning in the other room, I asked, "Danielle, while you were cleaning, did you move the picture from this table?"

"No, it was there the day before yesterday when I left," she responded, placing her cleaning bucket down.

"You are certain?" I pushed, although she would have no reason to lie.

"Yes, I cleaned it with a new glass cleaner," she responded. "Is something wrong?"

"I don't know where it is," I explained, still turning in a circle, waiting for it to magically appear. "Has anyone else been in the apartment while you were here? Perhaps a delivery person, who may have broken it?"

"Perhaps the doctor moved it?" she offered with a shrug.

TWO

"Perhaps. I'm on my way out and I'll be back after you leave. If you find it, please make sure it finds its way back to the table. Would you please let Thomas know that I won't be dining tonight? If he wants, he can leave the meal in the refrigerator."

"*Certainement.*" She smiled. Danielle was pleasant enough. A bright attractive woman chosen by Adrien, who assured me I needed help to maintain our 420-square-meter home. Nine rooms with no one else occupying them. I believed I could handle the upkeep myself, but he insisted. A personal chef was an extravagance I also thought we could do without. But again, he insisted.

One more glance before I left, and still no picture.

It would be wise to use the metro to meet with Chloe. Paris traffic could be unpredictable in the evening. The upside was that the restaurant had valet parking and I enjoyed my car, a bright cherry-red BMW convertible; a birthday gift from Adrien. Decision made—I would drive the car. The elevator reached the first floor and George was there to open the heavy wrought iron gate to exit the elevator. Pleasantries were exchanged, and I exited the building's back entrance to where my car was parked. Considering it remained garaged most of the time, George received his money's worth.

Adrien had paid a premium to have a parking space close to the garage door area. I walked the twenty feet to my assigned spot and space 256 was empty. No car. Again, I twirled, similar to how I did upstairs looking for the missing picture. I hit the key fob to engage the alarm and reveal the location of my car. No bleep, no car.

It took me a moment to collect my thoughts and run through likely scenarios for a missing car. Only one was possible. Could someone have stolen it? How? This was a secure building, a highly secure building.

My breathing involuntarily accelerated to a rapid pace, followed by a tingling in my face and fingers. As if right on cue, my heart started to pound loudly in my ears reminiscent of an Edgar Allan Poe story, *The Tell-Tale Heart*. I closed my eyes. I'm not sure if I thought by doing so my car would suddenly appear. Of course, it didn't.

Again, with no other thought, I twirled in place like some dystopian ballerina. It was on my second spin that I saw George lumbering toward me with a concerned look on his face. "Madame?" He must have watched my distress dance on the cameras.

"George, I parked my car here the day before yesterday, and now it's gone. Can you call the police please, so I can report it missing?" I was certainly in no state to place the call.

"Certainly," he responded, then thought a moment.

"Do you have an app on your telephone that will locate your car? If the thieves haven't disabled it, it will show the location and we can alert the police to the location," he suggested.

"Brilliant, George. I forgot about that," I said, taking a much-needed calming breath.

Rummaging through my oversized bag holding half of what I owned, I found my telephone. I activated the app for the car and within a minute or so, it produced a grid. On it, three blue moving circles blinked around a red dot—my car.

"There it is. It's a half a block up," he offered, trying to be helpful.

Stunned, I studied the map. An array of emotions passed through me, shock was the one that settled and stayed. Could someone have taken it out on a joy ride and left it close to be found?

"What's it doing there? Is someone playing a joke on me?" I didn't know whether to scream, laugh, or cry hysterically. Should I ask to watch the security tapes? Probably. What if I was the last

TWO

one to use my car? It would appear as if I wasn't in my right mind and that I didn't remember parking my own car.

At the risk of him thinking I was inept, I haplessly shrugged my shoulders instead, forced a laugh, and thanked him for his help. What good would it do to ask him to consider the "what-ifs" and run through scenarios with me? The car was neither lost nor stolen, and not a problem he should have to deal with. I walked back through the lobby with him, my mind buzzing with thoughts.

"Madame?" He was confused why I followed him back in, instead of heading toward my car.

"I think I will take the train, George. I'll retrieve the car later. Have a good day," I stated, unwilling to share I was too shaken to drive my car to meet Chloe. This day wasn't turning out well at all. His eyes followed me as I left the building and I was too embarrassed to turn back and see the look on his face.

As I walked toward the underground station by the Invalides, I placed a quick call to Chloe and suggested she order dinner, telling her I might be a minute or two late and would explain when I got there. She'd have to drive me home but that was the least of my concerns.

My heart continued to pick up speed when I thought about how badly the day had devolved. My anxiety grew, and I stood amongst a train filled with wall-to-wall bodies, grasping the metal pole in the fast-moving train as if my life depended on it. Was my body swaying with the train or was that under my control? The lights of the train flickered now and then, and the walls of the train felt like they were closing in on me. It was hard to catch my breath, my hands tingled, and my head floated. Was I going to faint? I quickly realized I was experiencing a panic attack, and it seemed to be ready to go into full-blown mode.

Were people staring at me? An elderly gentleman saw my

distress, offering me a seat, which I gladly accepted. Others, I was certain, kept an eye on me. No one liked a hysterical woman and were probably glad to see the back of me as I exited at the Opera station. As if everyone had been given prior information about my distressed state, the people on the platform gave me a wide berth to exit the train doors. Or maybe it was only my imagination, as people simply went on about their daily lives.

THANK GOD THE restaurant was only a short walk from the station. Between my hands trembling and my weak knees, I stopped before entering the restaurant to gain my composure. Five minutes passed as I realized my breathing had slowed and my hands were stable. Pushing through the heavy glass door, I glanced around the open area. I saw Chloe's raised hand and headed to her. As I walked closer, her face grew alarmed. I must look a fright. Was everyone in the place looking at me and assessing me? I looked for judging eyes and saw none.

"What's wrong? You look awful, and your left eye is twitching." *Great, the left eye twitch.*

She helped with my coat and bag, then came in for one of her massive hugs. I probably held on a little too long, but today I needed the comfort. When she finally released me, Chloe held me steady by my shoulders. The way she examined me made my eye twitch more.

The waiter approached and waited for us to move apart, then motioned for me to sit across from Chloe at the small, elegantly laid out table. And as in all elegant establishments, he snapped the linen napkin open and placed it across my lap. I thanked him as he left to place our orders. Waiting for her to sit, I lifted my waiting glass of white wine and downed it in one shot. After I guzzled the glass of white wine, I fought back tears

TWO

because no one deserved to watch an avalanche of emotion with added twitching eye.

"Spill." She reached for one of three warm rolls from a basket situated on the table between us and the butter.

"I want a divorce," was how I led, as I poured another glass to the top. I was not fooling around. I needed alcohol to steady my nerves, and it was plentiful tonight. "But I need to beg a favor. I took the train here and need a ride home."

"And so, you shall have one," she returned, not at all phased. "Now, regarding the divorce. I am on a never-ending retainer with my *avocat* and I'll insist on a group discount for you." She nodded her head, as if the deal had already been completed.

I studied her delicate elven face and pixie haircut that suited her so well. At four foot eleven, she could easily be taken for a mystical creature that sprayed glitter everywhere, even with her five-inch heels.

"I'm dead serious. I am unhappy to the point I think I'm losing my mind. Adrien has taken such control of my life that I've been denied access to my own gallery," I told her. Chloe had never been a fan of Adrien's. It could be said she took great pleasure in plotting scenarios that would cause him such anger that he was forced to leave a room or explode. She taunted him without mercy and whenever possible, mocked him to his face. She had become more verbal to him over the discontented way she felt he treated me, and this resulted in Adrien insisting I end my friendship with her. Which, in turn, forced me into sneaking out to meet her when he was away. If she knew I had to sneak to see her, I feared a confrontation would happen, resulting in having to choose between him and her. So, it was my secret, and a difficult balancing act.

"I have been worried about you for a while, Izzy. You've lost weight, you're always on edge. I barely see you anymore because

Adrien has such a tight leash on you. And not in a good way. We used to get away once a month, but that has totally fizzled out. Shopping sprees are now a thing of the past. The only time you seem to leave the apartment is to go to the gallery or when he is away. What friends do you have with Adrien's seal of approval that are yours alone? Frankly, I am concerned about you. So, when you say you want a divorce, I'm in your corner," she said in a hushed tone. No one cared to listen to our conversation, but I know her critical analysis was something she wanted to keep between us.

"On what grounds can I divorce him?" I still couldn't believe it had come to this, much less that I was verbalizing it. "There is no violence or adultery."

Her eyebrows shot to her scalp—a sign she didn't agree. Leaning forward to make certain I heard every word, she stated, "Izzy, you have to be real and honest with your assessment of the state of your life. Dogs in this city get more affection from their owners than you do from the man who thinks he's God. If he's traveling for conferences, why not invite you along? When he's home, he's happy to have you on his arm as eye candy. Do you ever think he's taking a companion with him? And what about three weeks ago when you overheard him tell Paul he was flying to India, but you found his passport still in his dresser? Maybe he was in another city, visiting a lover. For all we know, he has *several* lovers. I'd go with several. Who'd willingly spend more than a few hours at a time with him? Even if they were handsomely remunerated? If you are serious, you need to hire a private investigator. If he is having an affair, then you will not have to wait the two years. Grab him by the balls and squeeze, Izzy."

She studied my face, measuring what to say next. She was on a roll, so this could go anywhere.

"And, Izzy, abuse comes in forms other than physical. That

TWO

man has beaten you down so badly in the self-esteem department that I barely recognize the vibrant woman who had so many dreams. The long and short of it is, he's a bully." She stopped and rubbed my hand. "I watch you second-guess everything you do and measure what you say. Please say if I'm out of line, but it hurts me to see how he degrades you."

She was right. I no longer trusted my judgment and felt everything I did he had to approve of before I did it. But was that so wrong? He was a brilliant surgeon and businessman.

"I've been down this road and it's not a difficult process, especially with a no-fault agreed-upon divorce. Or if he chooses the non-agreed route, he won't find that a pleasant experience. To appear in court would open his private life up to public scrutiny. Well, you know that would never happen.

"In the end, the judge will divide everything in half, whether Adrien likes it or not. He can fight a contested divorce, but it bring it into a public forum, and you know the man is more concerned about his image than anything else. He is anything but stupid and will know that an agreed-upon divorce is the best. I have Michelle on speed dial. Would you like me to make an appointment for you?" She reached for her handbag to retrieve her phone. She obviously wanted to strike while the iron was hot.

"But Adrien—"

I stopped as the waiter approached the table. We waited as he delivered the Caesar salad appetizer, garnishing it with freshly ground pepper and Parmesan cheese.

"Don't lose your footing here, Izzy. Yes, Adrien remains his charming, handsome, brilliant self, with no cares in the world. But what does he do for you? Does he support your wants and dreams? Does he offer you encouragement? Does he even make you *feel* wanted or loved? You want my love and support, I'm here for you. I'll guide you through the process and be by your side every minute. If you just want to vent, I'm here as well." She picked up her fork and speared the lettuce on her plate, waiting for my decision.

"I'll take her number." I was so distracted I poured too much dressing on my salad. "But not a *word* to my mother and Denise."

"My lips are sealed. Now, let's move on to another topic. I refuse to dwell on the man of the dark arts any longer. Tell me about this new client." She diverted my attention before I could change my mind.

I disbursed minimal information to her because he was her type. Attractive, charming, and more money than he needed. If she saw him, her sights would be set on husband number four.

"After we finish dinner, I have an idea. Let's go to that new club Ice. Or we can go back to your apartment and really let loose—maybe mess up his sock drawer. Your choice. I would do both. First the club, then the socks," she suggested.

I saw her eyes dart from side to side. Never a good sign. Then a smile broke across her face. She grabbed my hand to garner my full attention.

"I have a scathingly brilliant idea. A getaway for fun, and we can screw with Adrien at the same time, although he won't know it. Two birds, one stone. Let's plan a trip to Geneva, and you can inventory the contents of the freeport, and I will be your witness to the contents. It's always best to be prepared before you drop the bomb of the divorce papers. You don't want him removing or moving assets," she suggested. How her mind leaped from a fun-filled dance-a-thon to protecting assets was too quick a turn for me. She did indeed have a mercurial mind. So, I did what I did best when not ready to commit in full—I deflected.

"How about we plan a getaway to Rome and bring my mother? She wants to attend Easter service Sunday, but with the new client wanting an immediate appointment, it wasn't feasible.

TWO

Would that work?" I asked.

She thought a moment and agreed almost immediately.

"That works for me. I love Rome. Now, are you going to hire an investigator?" she asked, not letting me off the hook.

"I suppose you have an investigator on speed dial as well?" There was no doubt. Chloe was a thorough plotter, and we were back to the plotting and planning of my divorce.

"Is the Pope Catholic?" she asked.

"So I've been told," I responded.

"Izzy, under normal circumstances I would recommend approaching Adrien and trying to do this agreeably. But I have known Adrien for ten years, and I see you at the bottom of the Seine before he willingly turns loose one penny." Possibly one too many crime shows had tainted her thoughts.

"Now you are being dramatic." However, this whole conversation gave me a chill. "Your point is taken, though. I can't predict him anymore, and it's best to be prepared. What if there's nothing to hide?"

"Then you'll have to wait out the two-year separation. But I have a feeling once my guy starts digging, that will be a moot point," she encouraged. "Everyone has secrets. And, Izzy, the more money you have, the more secrets you're likely to hide."

That was my ultimate fear, and some secrets remained better undisturbed.

CHAPTER FOUR

ISABELLA

A NIGHT WITHOUT Adrien felt almost like a reprieve. No deadlines to be met, no hostile looks, no disparaging remarks, and a sleep-in until eleven. Those were the positives. However, on the flip side, I wandered alone through nine rooms, still afraid to do anything that would reflect poorly on me when he returned. He always seemed to know when something was amiss. Like a sixth sense, or someone looking over my shoulder.

I surveyed the kitchen as I tidied my papers and didn't like what I saw. Everything was sterile and in its place. Should I go room to room, that theme would be reflective in each room. No pet to foul the area, as Adrien instructed. None of the rooms felt cozy or welcoming. These rooms were tombs occupied by space and time. I was lonely and alone, and I couldn't help but wonder, was this of my own making?

I set my coffee to brew before my meeting and reviewed the information I'd collected. Adrien insisted on a portfolio for each client—part financial and part personal. Any social media

TWO

presence was collected and catalogued, along with school attended and active websites. To me, this felt like an invasion of the client's privacy. They came to us for a specific purpose: to help them choose art that would be functional and give them pleasure. Adrien treated their relationship with us like a matchmaking service rather than the consumers they were. He matched the paintings offered to the size of their bank balance and never considered the aesthetics of the paintings or the emotions of buyers.

As per Adrien's meticulous requirements, Ben Jaager's client dossier was thorough. Paul left no stone unturned. The dossier revealed a thirty-six-year-old venture capitalist from Amsterdam, moving to Paris to explore new opportunities, and the apartment he currently inhabited was bought with cash as an investment. He boasted a net worth of over fifty million, married and divorced, no children, and led a private life.

Ben Jaager owned an extensive art collection, showcased on his business website, and was a frequent bidder through an agent at multiple auction houses. He guarded his privacy to the point of almost seclusion, and that was somewhat troubling according to Paul's notes. In summary, he was an obscenely wealthy man with more money than necessary.

His physical characteristics and educational background were included, along with a photograph. I wonder if he has a dog? Probably not. His tailored suits and painstakingly groomed appearance left no room for a dog or cat.

From my brief meeting with Ben a few days ago, I decided I liked him, but I wasn't certain he liked me. Although very attractive, it wasn't his brown hair and blue-gray eyes that drew me to him. It was his quiet demeanor and dry sense of humor that made me feel at ease around him. I often strayed in our conversation and found myself revealing information about myself to him instead of obtaining information from him. He seemed genuinely interested in me, something I had forgotten was possible; it was nice to acknowledge. Maybe it was his relaxed manner or the way he was comfortable in his own skin. He exuded confidence, but not arrogance, strength, domination, or control. I suppose when you have amassed such wealth, confidence is a given.

Finishing up, I packed my computer in its sleeve and tucked it in my massive handbag. I slipped on my black Louboutin heels, probably something I would regret by late afternoon, and as I proceeded to the table to collect my keys, I noted the picture was still missing from its regular place.

Still smarting from the car incident and not wanting to address reality, I decided to walk to his home which, to my good fortune, was only a few streets away from us. Although his home was located in the seventh arrondissement near ours, the architecture of our home screamed old Haussmann while his was all young hipster. Both buildings had luxury accoutrements. There was one distinguishing similarity: the doorman that came with the building. I was greeted by the older, impeccably dressed gentleman, and ushered into the building. I presented my card to the person at the reception desk, who escorted me to the elevator after announcing my arrival to Ben over the phone. He explained that Mr. Jaager occupied the third-floor apartment, home thirteen, accessible after you exited the elevator on the left.

I ascended in the elevator and as I exited, I spotted Ben leaning casually against his doorjamb waiting for me. He was intensely studying me as if I were a puzzle with some missing pieces. But I supposed from what I knew, he was wary of people.

As I approached, he stepped aside, holding the door open.

"Isabella, welcome to my home. Please, step inside," he offered. As I passed him, I embraced a subtle waft of his pleasant aftershave. His casual attire and overall appearance said he was

TWO

a rugged man to the core, not a metrosexual man. Not what I expected at all after our first meeting, in his perfectly tailored suit, crisp white shirt, and shoes so shiny they could blind you. He seemed, different. Not on guard, but still sizing me up.

I removed my jacket. He carefully placed it in his coat closet and offered me a refreshment. After leading me to a large sitting room, I felt his attention shift to the matters at hand. It was obvious Ben was a very polite man who knew his way around manners.

"Isabella, tell me how you normally conduct this business because I have no clue what to expect." His genuine smile reached his eyes, the fine lines around them responded in kind. His eyes were bright, and pupils dilated a bit. Almost like someone sexually interested. God, what a random thought.

People's eyes are the windows to their souls was a true statement. A flashback to a Sunday sermon flitted across my mind; one passage in particular. Matthew 6:22 and 23 says, "The light of the body is the eye: if therefore thine eye be, thy whole body shall be full of light. But if thine eye be evil, thy whole body shall be full of darkness. If therefore the light that is in thee be darkness, how great is that darkness!" The verse forced itself into my thoughts and was gone as quickly.

I strolled to the seating arrangement, unsure where to sit. It's such an easy decision for most. For me, not so much. Adrien's recriminations of my bad judgment were always in my ear as I made choices. Looking at the two couches, one white and one purple, I chose the white. In the split-second decision I made for where to sit, I felt the purple couch would've clashed with the pink dress I wore. I could almost hear Adrien's voice admonishing me for my wardrobe choice, even though he wasn't there. He told me to always wear off-white or black to a meeting because neither was offensive. Always a lecture.

Snapping back to reality, I removed my computer and booted it up.

"We have already chatted about your expectations, which is a large part of the process," I said, leaning back into the soft couch and crossing my legs. Another no-no in Adrien's world of business etiquette.

"My purpose today is to photograph each room. We'll focus on the rooms where the art you're looking for will display. The goal is to weigh how the new pieces will blend in with what you've already collected. My first question is, are you keeping the furniture and decorative pieces the way they are?"

He glanced around and appeared to cringe or was conflicted.

"For now, yes. My mind is not made up if I will be a long-term resident of Paris. I may be using this apartment as a place to stay when I'm in Paris for work and maintain my Amsterdam residence as home base," he shared.

"Fair enough. That being said, this is a modern building and your décor is modern; I'd like to stay with that design aesthetic. If we could walk through and as I photograph, we can discuss possibilities using the inventory I have available. If I don't have the perfect fit, we will search until we find the best option," I said, watching him study me. "Are there any artists or art periods that you like or dislike?"

He sat forward from the purple couch and placed his elbows on his knees, leaning in as if to share a secret.

"Isabella, to be frank, I know nothing of art. I have no preference, except I don't want old masters with religious themes or grumpy old people. I don't want some eyeball on legs walking across a desert. If the colors are pleasant and there isn't too much going on, I can live with that," he said with a casual wink.

I chuckled and replied, "So, nothing even touching on Renaissance themes, Rembrandt, or Dali. I think the purple couch

TWO

threw me. It is a bit . . . out there."

"It's a bit of a nightmare, isn't it?" He sighed and ran a hand over the cushion next to him. "But yes, no art of that sort," he said, sitting back, letting out a breath of relief. "If I spend any length of time here, this will be the first to go." He slapped the back cushion of the hideous purple couch.

"I believe I have a number of paintings that will interest you," I said, as I mentally catalogued what I thought would fit.

"If you're ready to photograph, I'll lead the way."

As we entered each room, I opened the curtains to let in the light and photographed the room. I closed them and photographed them without the streaming sun as well. We studied each room and I queried him as to what he felt he wanted or envisioned in each area. Small or large, bright or muted, and if he preferred people or abstract. He was honest when he said he had no idea about art or what he wanted. Leading him through a list of questions, his final list consisted of seven canvases scattered through the apartment and two elongated photograph arrangements over his bed. We returned to the living area, where I sat on the white couch.

"Can I offer you any coffee?" he asked, and I declined as I made notes on my tablet.

"Tell me, Isabella, where do you get most of your paintings? Are they bought at auction, private local collections, resident painters?" he asked, avoiding the purple couch and settling into the chair facing the open-doored terrace.

I placed my camera next to my computer and answered. "My husband acquires most of the inventory. He is fortunate to have many connections in the art world." My answer evoked an immediate, almost indiscernible, eyebrow raise from him. "Adrien is very involved in choosing and acquiring pieces. I would say most of our pieces come from private collections, purchases, or exchanges with other galleries, and a few from auction. He prefers to keep the inventory fresh. I have a few selections on my computer that I would like your opinion on as part of your collection," I offered, turning the laptop in his direction. This prompted him to move to the couch, taking a seat next to me.

As he positioned himself, his right knee leaned against my left thigh, sending a short buzz of electricity through me. I reflexively moved my leg, but it found its way back to him almost instinctively and stayed there.

We slid from picture one to picture two, and when we reached picture three, he placed his hand on mine to stop me.

"That painting. I love it. Tell me if I am wrong, but I remember seeing it about six months ago in a London gallery. Do you have information about it?" he asked, quite excited and focused on the slide.

I right-clicked on the information bar about the Heinrich Campendonk, painted in 1912. It would go quite nicely in this room, with the red, cobalt blue, and lemon yellow complementing the god-awful purple couch.

"Let me see. Yes. Ben, you're correct and have quite a discerning eye. This painting was purchased from the Roselov gallery in London," I said, excited to have hit upon a painting he liked.

"Then I'd say it's a sign that I must have it," he said. The price was not even discussed, that's how much he loved it.

We continued and the next one he inquired about puzzled me. I read through the side notes and decided it was best not to offer it to him until I discussed it with Adrien. I hadn't noticed it had been marked private and not for sale when I originally went through the inventory and uploaded the slide.

"Ben, I am very sorry, but it appears this one is slated for an auction in Abu Dhabi, and I don't know how I let it slip into this

TWO

presentation. Usually, Adrien assists me with the offerings. He's in Cairo for the weekend; he asked I wait until after we have your photo layout of the apartment to choose what to offer. However, I went ahead and gathered possibilities, to get a sense of your taste, and missed that note. It might be better if we wait to discuss your collection choices when he returns." I felt my breath quicken and eye twitch again. Ben noticed as well.

"I am sure I can wait a few days. Is your husband a managing partner in your business?" he asked as he reclined into the couch, his knee leaving my leg.

Again, I felt like I was being studied. Almost tested, in a way.

"My husband, by profession, is a surgeon. However, he's an active partner in the business," I said.

"So, you don't personally choose the inventory?" He delved a little deeper than most clients as to how I conducted my business, and my eye twitched more. I'm not sure Adrien would want to reveal so much information. However, his questions were polite, and I felt no harm in answering.

"I have local clients. My husband has contacts all over Europe, Asia, and the Persian Peninsula, so he has a different reach. Each of us has access to a different network of agents and artists. We blend our resources to offer our clients the best opportunity to meet their needs. For instance, the painting from London is one my husband acquired. I'm embarrassed to say that somehow the other appeared on the available list, and I didn't catch it. My husband recently had a new technology company redo our inventory catalogue and the conversion must still be adjusting. Would you be agreeable to me showing your apartment photographs to Adrien? We'll collaborate, and I could prepare a new presentation."

"Isabella, I have an even better suggestion. After your husband returns from Cairo and you have consulted together, I'd like to invite both of you here to show me the paintings you've selected. I'd like to meet your husband. He appears to be a man of many talents and interests," he offered, rubbing his trouser leg, which now again rested against mine. Was he trying to flirt?

"Ben, I will certainly extend your invitation to Adrien," I said, as I began to power down the machine.

He extended his hand to stop me from completing the power down. "Would you mind allowing me to have a printed copy of the suggestions you brought today? I can study them and give you feedback. That might help you narrow down my taste and speed up the process. You can print it to my wireless printer in the corner." He pointed to the printer on the glass desk, another modern feature of the room.

"I'll do it right now." I smiled and sent the information to the printer. He retrieved the pile and placed them in a folder on the desk.

"I hope to hear from you and your husband soon. I am anxious to clothe these bare walls." He held his arm out, leading the way to the entryway hall. After retrieving my jacket from the closet, he walked me to the door, placing a hand ever so lightly at my back as he reached for the door handle with the other.

Surprisingly, he walked me to the elevator and as we parted, said, "Isabella, it was a pleasure to see you again, and thank you for your time and information. It has been invaluable. I look forward to a call in the next day or so."

The elevator door slid open and I entered as he stood with his hands in his pockets, studying me. I suppose that's what venture capitalists do. However, it was a bit unnerving and my left twitching eye continued its dance.

AFTER A BRISK walk back to the apartment and a long

TWO

afternoon, I'd worked up an appetite. I was overjoyed to see Thomas had prepared dinner and had left it warming in the oven. Although it was a little early to eat dinner, I was eager to dive in. I carelessly discarded my jacket over the chair, something Adrien pointed out was *not* the correct way to treat fine clothes. I inhaled the aroma of the food, tucked in and savored every bite.

When I finished eating, my dishes were rinsed and placed in the dishwasher. The computer once again engaged. I inserted the scan disc from the camera into the computer slot. I took my time to clean up and crop the lot, then saved them to the hard drive. When I looked up at the clock next, I was surprised to see the time. Had three hours flown by?

I made my way to the bedroom, changed into my night clothes, and after a half hour of mindless television, fell asleep. What I had intended to be a short nap turned into hours when I finally woke. As I opened my eyes, the television showed flashes of blue lights, and what appeared to be the scene of an explosion flashed across the screen. Something about a container and warehouse explosion. People were crying from somewhere that looked like Egypt. Screaming people and bodies; were they in body bags?

The report revealed that the police had not arrived in time to capture all involved in what appeared to be a massive human trafficking and black organ theft ring. Immigrants were rumored to be selling their children's organs, or their own, for a new life in Europe. It was an evolving situation. Poor souls. What monster would be involved in that type of activity? They should rot in hell.

I took my sleeping pill. Within an hour, I was back to sleep, unaware of the true misery that had been laid upon unsuspecting people thousands of miles away.

CHAPTER FIVE

ADRIEN

EGYPT. I HATE this blasted doorway to hell. Midday and the heat would kill us all.

"Where is Avigad?" Sweat dripping off my forehead onto the patient did it for me. I threw down the scalpel in disgust, clanging metal to metal on the filthy tray; a tray smeared with blood and some type of liquid brown cleanser.

There was no way that I was going to continue operating on patients under these conditions.

This was the facility that five million dollars gross bought? An abandoned warehouse with filthy grime-streaked broken windows, no ventilation, and outdated medical equipment. Unacceptable. The portable anesthesia machine barely administered anesthetic, and patients were waking mid-surgery. No, this was not acceptable under any circumstance.

It was too late to disagree with Avigad's assembly line set-up when I arrived. Faceless people with no medical history sat waiting in old rusted chairs, while two patients had already been prepped for me when I'd arrived.

TWO

Avigad's plan was one assistant would prep and open the patient for me. I removed the organ and another assistant closed the patient. The first assistant would already be opening the next, and on and on. The first problem was, the assistant who was to open the patients turned out to be a twenty-three-year-old medical student. His experience only consisted of working on cadavers. The person who closed was a twenty-eight-year-old first-year resident. Neither were the caliber needed for the intensity of these surgeries.

What use was it to argue now? The first person was opened as I walked in the room. The inexperienced way he was surgically opened foretold the future fiasco. Cleaning up his mistake, I proceeded to remove the kidney, place it in the transport container, and tie off the artery. The other assistant stepped in to close and suture. It was quite the organized production in theory, but in practice, not so much. Unsterile conditions, old equipment that barely worked, and incompetent surgery assistants proved a recipe for disaster.

The personnel who aided in the post-op recovery of the patients were untrained village women who only knew to watch for blatant bleeding. Bleeding that, once discovered, would be too late. They had never been trained how to take vital signs or watch for shock or blood in the urine. What a nightmare.

The heat from the afternoon sun beating on the uninsulated roof and walls made the room an unbearable ninety-two, possibly more. No open windows available for cross ventilation, and the only way the air entered the room was through the double doors that breached any sterile barrier. The paper gowns with an expired date were intended as a surgical barrier, but clung to my scrubs like a second skin.

Blood was everywhere, in all forms. There was fresh red blood dripping from the makeshift table, semi-congealed blood on the surgical stands, and crusted blood on the sink area. The floor was a brown sticky mess in some areas, where people had walked through the blood that flowed without end. Some areas were clumped with dried blood and vomit from reactions to the bad anesthesia. Or maybe a reaction to the noxious odor in the room. Trays which were supposed to be autoclaved and sterilized between surgeries where being hand-washed by the village women with dishwashing detergent and dried with dirty towels. We were running out of new surgical blades, requiring the use of old ones, and there was no hazard box for needles. Most of the intravenous bags were expired and there was no blood available for transfusion.

I had now lost every bit of patience that I had been holding onto and screamed, "Avigad, Avigad, Avigad!" at the top of my voice until he bustled into the room.

"What is wrong with you? Have you lost your mind, calling my name?" His face dripped with sweat—a highly unpleasant sight, not to mention the pungent smell of his body odor. He, too, had lost all patience.

Ripping my gown from my scrubs, I threw it on the blood- and dirt-crusted floor. Sickened by the metallic odor that hung in the air from the blood, I was seconds away from vomiting.

"I am done. This is not a medical team. These men are students from the university and completely incapable of assisting me. The anesthesia machine is barely administering the correct dosage to keep them under, and this boy woke while I was tying off his renal artery. That one over there has still not recovered from the anesthesia, and his blood pressure is dropping. I may need to open him again. You haven't provided me with sterile instruments and I'm certain half the people here will wind up with sepsis. There aren't enough saline bags to hydrate them and most of the bags are expired."

TWO

Having known Avigad for two years, I'd never known him to be anything but in control, and he was *not* in control at this point. His hands opened and closed in fists, and his face contorted in a frightening manner.

Waiting for a response, I glanced over at the last young boy whose kidney I had recently removed, and saw he wasn't breathing. His chest was still and there was no abdominal movement. Racing over, I assessed his vitals and with no defibrillator or emergency medications available, it wasn't even worth the effort to start cardiac compressions. The boy that was sewn up fifteen minutes ago was waking up ahead of time, moaning, thrashing, and screaming in pain. His sutures would surely burst, and he would soon be dead as well.

I was done. This wasn't what I signed on for. This was nothing short of manslaughter and a case could be made for murder. Negligence could be charged and given the dire circumstances of the immigrants, there would be no mercy on our sentencing.

"Get these people taken care of. I am done," I declared.

As quickly as I started to move, I stopped. I felt what I perceived to be a gun pressed to my ribs. Was this how I would die? In this filthy hellhole?

"Adrien, I don't want to use this, but I will. I need ten kidneys and two lobes of a liver. I don't care if every one of these people must be buried in the desert tonight. That boy over there is dead—take his other kidney. That one on the table will be dead soon. We can take his other as well. Now, get back to work," he ordered. What he was suggesting—no, what he was ordering—was to take both kidneys and get out as quickly as we could. I basically was harvesting organs from a recently deceased person and sentencing another to death. But I had no choice.

I went back to work, continuing as the night closed in. Four hours had passed, three people were dead, and ten kidneys had been packed and ready for transport. The organs had a maximum of thirty hours to reach their recipients for transplant, and were on their way to the plane, waiting at the airstrip.

As I was ready to start the procedure to remove the liver lobe, Avigad burst through the door. My scrubs, soaked in blood from the last two patients, hung off me. Parts of the clothing stiff with blood, other parts wet with blood. The acrid metallic stench hung heavy in the blistering non-ventilated air. The assistants and village women vomited. No one judged.

"Drop everything. Hurry, everyone, out now. The police have been called, and we have thirty minutes to move as far from here as possible. There is a van waiting for your transport," he yelled, opening the door and waving a hand.

Panic ensued, followed by chaos, as the village women and medical students ran for the door, the anesthesia machine left running, and garbage strewn all around. Three boys lay dead in a corner, and patients able to leave were helped by family members. Others waiting for family members to recover sat and cried. Everyone knew if they were arrested, then their immediate death was a given. "*Shurta!*" was shouted. Sheer pandemonium erupted in every corner of the building.

The staff were the first to run through the rusted metal doors to exit the building for the waiting van. As they piled in, Avigad held me back, motioning me to a black car behind the van. I removed my scrubs without hesitation or modesty, and he offered me a new set. I placed the used material into a plastic bag, which he carried with us. No DNA was to be left behind. With all the comingled blood, did he seriously think a DNA sweep would even be carried out? A wet towel would be my bath for now.

"The plane is ready to move when we finish here," he offered. "I have a few things to attend to. Get in the car. You can take a quick shower at the airstrip." I prayed the car had

TWO

air-conditioning because the sweat from my body and his would surely overwhelm the driver.

"You are leaving these people to die?" Even the thought was incredulous. Facing the International Criminal Court and being sentenced for mass murder flashed before my eyes.

"Adrien, we have a job to do, and you should not question me," he exhaled, barely able to string his words together. The body odor from him overwhelmed me, and I moved quickly to enter the car. Between the stench of blood and his musty scent, my control gave up. I turned and vomited.

People's moans and cries were blotted out by the terror I felt at being caught. I gathered myself, turned to him, and followed.

People talk of fight or flight, and now I understood. My heart pounded, my breath increased, and my instinct to survive took over. I was working on pure adrenaline at this point and did not question his instructions any further. On entering the car, he leaned forward and tapped the driver, and ordered him in Arabic to leave the area. The car engaged at once and raced away from town toward the desert as we followed the van. The desert was not a good sign. In fact, an ominous sign. Would this be my final resting place? No one knew I had left the country under a false name. When Isabella went to file a missing persons action, her knowledge of me traveling in Cairo would have no bearing. I had left under my Canadian passport and visa.

The desert became nothing more than a stream of brown against the black of night, the only lights from the car headlights. I had no idea where we were, or if we were on paved road or sand. Finally, we glided to a full stop behind the van now coated in the dust from the desert. I watched as the van's driver slid the van door open and motioned for the inhabitants to get out. Reluctantly, they stepped from the van. This was not good, and they all knew it.

The driver motioned to the people to step away from the van and form a line. Yes, they knew their fate at that moment, each probably saying a silent prayer. In an authoritative voice, the driver instructed them to kneel and, without question, they complied, but not without the quiet cries of a condemned person.

I was too shocked and frightened to ask what his intentions were and sat, helpless and motionless, watching the horrible scene unfold. Avigad casually leaned forward and reached under his seat. He pulled out a gun wrapped in a cloth, which he unfolded. A revolver. Holding the gun with the barrel toward the floor, he opened the chamber and checked his ammunition. Satisfied, he snapped it closed. Six chambers, six bullets, six people. Was I safe?

He motioned for me to remain in the car. I didn't argue. The door was opened by the driver, who wasn't the least bit alarmed, Avigad exited the car calmly, and moved toward the six people. Once they realized their fate was determined, the women wailed, one man cried, and one swore at him. They knew their fate. The desert spoke, and they listened.

I strained to hear him tell them each something in Arabic as his bodyguards looked on. While the sobbing and crying quieted and each tried to regain composure, he rounded behind them. One man made a move to get up from his knees to run and a bullet was shot into the side of his head. The others accepted their fate as he moved behind each and deposited a bullet into each person's skull. Upon completing the executions, he blessed them. His massacre was complete. I opened the door and leaned out, dry heaving, as there was nothing left to expel from my stomach.

Instructions were dispatched to the two men who drove the van, to bury the bodies in a mass grave as time was ticking. Unfazed, the men walked to the back of the van, opened the two doors, and removed their shovels. It was clear they were ready to

TWO

begin an unceremonious burial and had most likely performed this service before.

Avigad entered the car and turned to me. All I could think was six bullets, six bodies. I had been spared.

"When we arrive at the airstrip, slip into the side bathroom. Wash as best you can; the water pressure is not so good. Change and meet me at the desk. We will clear passport control and be off." He noticed my arm was bleeding, something the adrenaline had apparently masked, as I felt no pain. "Your arm. What happened?" he asked.

I looked down and it was a gaping long wound that had clotted, but still had the stickiness of being fresh.

"When one of the boys came in and saw his brother dead, he picked up a pair of scissors, charged and slashed my arm. He ran before we could restrain him," I said. This probably should be stitched, but there should be no nerve damage that I could tell.

He cursed softy. "He must be the one who alerted the police. Describe him to Abaas, and he will track him down and dispose of the problem."

Yet another death on my head.

"Avigad. This is a nightmare beyond all proportions. You realize if we are ever implicated that we would stand trial in the International Criminal Court." They were Syrians illegally in Egypt, would anyone really care?

"Who? Who are they looking for? Not a Canadian computer software entrepreneur and his investment banker. Don't be absurd." He waved his hand dismissively.

"There were others there, other refugees," I refreshed his memory. This nightmare would haunt me forever and every phone call I would worry was to alert me of my impending arrest.

"Yes, and after we left the place, those poor souls will be

caught up in an explosion. I am told there will be some type of gas leak in the area. These people, you see, were hiding from the authorities in a shipping container, which also exploded. All dead, no survivors. Dead men tell no tales, Adrien. Would you not say that is a correct statement?"

Mass murder. I had now traversed into Dante's Seventh Circle of Hell. The violent sin was murder. My punishment was to be put into a river of boiling blood and fire. I was there already, literally. My hell on earth.

From the time I entered the car until we reached the private airport, I entered a state of fugue. Nothing made sense, nothing was real. People talked, and I didn't hear what they said. Lights came into view, but I might as well have been blind. Nothing registered, and nothing processed.

We pulled up to the airstrip building. As instructed, I washed in the restroom at the airstrip building before boarding the plane. By 9:00 p.m., Monsieur LeBrun from Quebec, Canada, and his investment banker, were on their way back to Paris, having cleared Egyptian passport control. Four hours and thirty minutes later we touched down in Paris. Money had exchanged hands and the dead told no tales.

CHAPTER SIX

ISABELLA

MORNING CAME QUICKLY. I turned in bed and startled. I looked over at Adrien, asleep. He looked awful. He was unshaven and not the sexy stage of scruff, but the stage of "I am too tired to shave." His unwashed hair smelled of sweat. When mussed and styled with the products he normally used, it gave him a sort of sex appeal. Today, the remnants made him look disheveled and dirty. As if he knew I was watching him, he cracked open his eyes.

"What time is it?" His breath smelled like it came from a dead person.

"Eight o'clock. I thought your flight was later today." I was concerned I never heard him make it to bed. Anyone could have broken into the apartment and I would have been clueless.

"Our business concluded early," he groused as he stretched.

"Well, happy Easter. I'm getting up to call my mom," I said.

It had been months since we had been intimate. Time constraints, my lack of desire for him, and his irritability kept us apart. Today, clearly, it would be his hygiene.

I rolled out of bed and walked to the bathroom. As I closed the door behind me, I heard him say, "Isabella, there is no God, only science." I hope he tells that to the person collecting the tickets at the gates to heaven.

THOMAS MUST HAVE come by early to furnish us with fresh croissants, homemade butter, and jam for breakfast. The coffee finished brewing and I was surprised to see Adrien up as I entered the dining room, fresh from my shower.

"I want to go over what we will be doing today," he advised, as he retrieved a cup of coffee for himself and me. An odd gesture, since this was my normal routine of late.

"Adrien, you look awful. What happened to you? Is that a cut on your arm? My God, let me see. Look how deep it is! You need stitches. What happened?" The wound on his arm looked like some wild animal had torn through it and won whatever battle they fought. I went to touch the angry reddened area that looked a bit slick with drainage, but he pulled it back from me.

"Isabella, we have more important things at hand. I want to look over the pictures you took of Jaager's apartment. I hope you captured enough from different angles, and they aren't blurred. Presumably, you learned from the last mess you made of things. Wide-angle capture is imperative." He pulled his robe sleeve over the abraded area, attempting to hide the large wound.

"I'm catching the Eurostar to London later today. I have matters that need my attention there," he advised.

"What are you, insane? You look awful. Your eyes are bloodshot, and you just flew in from Cairo. What could you possibly have to do in London that can't wait a few days?" I asked.

He stood to pour milk into his coffee, trying his best to tune me out. When he finished, he turned his back to the counter,

TWO

leaned back, and crossed his ankles. Saying nothing, he raised his cup to his lips, and his eyes met mine and held them. This continued for three more sips. Total silence, only staring.

I could take no more.

"Seriously, Adrien, I am over the way you treat me. If it isn't clear to you, it's clear to me that we no longer work together. I walk around on eggshells, for fear something I say will set you off. You've made it clear my opinion isn't valued or welcome."

There it was, out there in the open. I'd dropped the bombshell and waited for him to disagree. He should beg my forgiveness and promise to be better, or at least to make an effort. I waited for him to respond as he continued to stare at me as if nothing came out of my mouth. So, I upped my game.

"I think we should divorce. I have spoken to Chloe and she can recommend an *avocat* who will help us divide our assets." I waited for the fallout.

I waited and waited.

Finally, he responded, while continuing to stare. "I see."

I see. That was it. I see. No begging me to stay. No offer to adjust his behavior. What did that mean?

"Let's look at the inventory I want you to share with Jaager." He placed his cup in the sink and walked to the living room.

"That's it? I see?" I called after his retreating back.

He stopped, turned, and stared again. It was quite unnerving. I'm not even sure his eyes blinked.

"Isabella, if that's what you want, you won't get a fight from me. Does that satisfy you? Right now, we have more important issues to discuss. Would you mind moving inside and showing me the photos, and let's discuss the strategy. Now."

I felt a little deflated and to be frank, somewhat scared. I hadn't been on my own in years and had come to depend on Adrien for just about everything. How would I keep the gallery afloat? I would need to find a new home. My bravado diminished with each step he took toward the living room.

"You will agree to support me until I am able to get on my feet financially?" I called after him.

"You will be taken care of, Isabella." The dead eyes that I looked into as Adrien reassured me I would be taken care of caused a finger-tightening grip around my neck. As if he was mentally choking me to death. How will I be taken care of, and why wasn't he more engaged?

"Show me what paintings you have chosen—" He was interrupted by his phone ringing. He glanced down and, without saying anything, he turned and strode from the room quickly. It appeared he didn't want to lose the call, but didn't want to take it in front of me.

I waited until I heard him close the door to the study. Should I wait here and prepare the pictures, or should I listen in on a phone call he clearly didn't want me to hear. I tiptoed across the room and stood outside the door to listen. Something I never did before. Was it a lover calling? I moved closer to the door and heard the muffled part of his conversation.

"How many dead? . . . It's all over the news . . . That boy told the authorities it was a doctor that had the name of a nut. His English was pretty good for a refugee."

His voiced raised slightly and then there was silence.

"Do not tell me to calm down." Silence again. "I want assurances there will be no blowback on me, you understand?" More silence, then drawers opening and closing. "Yes, yes, I am leaving for London, as you asked. I told you to leave it to me. After it's taken care of, Paul will return with me." Silence again. "Yes, yes. I'll meet you in front of Westminster Abbey at three exactly."

It appeared he was ending his call, so I tiptoed back to the living room and brought my tablet and computer to life. I about

TWO

had them up and running when he slid into the room, irritation rolling off him in waves.

"Show me the photos and paintings, and then I must be on my way," he said, sitting next to me. The smell was almost nauseating. The combination of sweat and blood left me fighting my gag reflex. Was that his hair or his skin that smelled so bad?

"Why London?" I asked, knowing a true answer would not be forthcoming.

"I need to retrieve something. Look, never mind about my business. Stay focused. What paintings will you suggest?" He became more agitated, so I complied.

"I chose these." I handed him the tablet with the collection opened on the screen.

As he moved from slide to slide, he stopped and started. Back and forth. Without raising his eyes, he asked, "How did you come across the Picasso, Magritte, and Freud?"

"Oh, those were on the flash drive on your desk. However, Mr. Jaager was very clear that wouldn't be to his taste. So, I thought—"

"You touched *my* property without asking me?" He interrupted me, his voice raised in unison with his body from the chair. "What gives you the right to touch anything without being asked to do so? Who knows about this?" He stood and loomed over me, arms shaking and face reddened.

"Adrien, stop. You're scaring me. I didn't know. It was sitting on the desk, and I had been unable to see the inventory properly, so I thought I could use what we had available," I offered in a whisper. I hoped to calm him down, but to no avail.

"You thought to punish me. Perhaps a little passive aggressive tactic? Did anyone else see this, Isabella?" he shouted with his arm raised, as if the wrong answer would land a slap or punch to my head. "And how did you know it had to do with art? What if it was patient records?"

"I've shown no one. Had it been patient records, I would have stopped immediately. Now, step away from me," I half yelled, half cried, trying to get up. But he leaned forward, boxing me in where I sat. Then, his face lowered, and we were nose tip to nose tip.

"You had better forget what you saw, Isabella. You never saw those paintings. Understand? Nod your head and say you understand." His soulless eyes searched mine.

Hot tears of fear and frustration slipped down my cheeks as I swore to him no one would know.

"Now, find suitable paintings for Monsieur Jaager from the available inventory. Make sure when I return there is a wire transfer into the business account for at least five million dollars. I don't care what you sell him, but the total must be five million," he said, stepping back from me.

I sat back in the chair, unsure of how to collect my thoughts. Five million. That would be nearly impossible with the order he needed. Additionally, I didn't know what his upper limit to purchase was.

"I have to get ready. I should be back later tonight," he said. "However, if it takes longer, I will spend the night and catch the first train out tomorrow; I'll drive directly to the hospital."

My mind and thoughts were scattered, and I felt unable to string together a full coherent sentence. I planned to attend Easter mass at church with Mama and Denise. We planned to attend the special Sunday mass at Notre-Dame at three o'clock. In the state I was in, they would be even more concerned for me than before. And not without cause. Mama had her health problems. She didn't need my problems burdening her. Our yearly tradition would have to be broken this year. I doubted I could hold myself together without breaking down, much less spend an hour in

TWO

contemplation of God when clearly, he had relegated me to hell.

I decided I would avoid a phone call, sending a text that explained a sinus infection that had caused a fever. That way she wouldn't hear the despair in my voice. Her text response to my text was immediate. She offered soup from Henri's—she would send Denise with some after church. I thanked her. I could control the length of Denise's visit. Mama would stay forever and drag my problems from me.

I sat and processed everything that had happened. Chloe was right. Adrien and I were done. Within a half hour, Adrien had pulled himself together. I watched from the living room as he rounded the bedroom into the hall with his messenger bag strapped to him, ready to leave.

"Don't wait up," he said. "I'll be very busy, so don't call me."

No peck on the cheek, no goodbye. As he walked down the hall, I heard him call George with instructions to have Andre bring the car around. He needed to be at Gare du Nord immediately. Then he was gone.

What did I know about Adrien anymore? Where did he go when he left the country? Did he even leave the country? Was he in a hotel room somewhere, or at some lover's home? Where did he get the money for our home? By God, I will find out, and then I am going to get access to our finances and the gallery inventory. I'll look for receipts, a paper trail, anything, to find out who I am married to.

I began a thorough search that rivaled Sherlock Holmes' relentless quests. Drawers were searched, suit jackets and pants were riffled through, and even his shoes were searched. After two hours of exhausting investigation, the only thing I had to show for my effort was a few wads of useless paper wrappers and his discarded metro tickets.

The man was an enigma. He owned a closet filled with suits

that measured exactly two inches apart, shoes two inches apart, and shirts in the drawer two inches apart. His rolled socks were two inches apart, as were his underwear. I guess you could say Adrien was a two-inch man.

"A two-inch man," I said aloud, and laughed. I said it out loud again and again. Giggling turned to hysterical laughter and laughter finally turned to sobbing tears. It seemed like an eternity before my emotions came into check. Exhausted, I threw myself on my bed. I needed a nap from the exhaustive emotional release.

As I lay in my bed, I turned the television on for some white noise. Drifting off, I heard the news report the carnage found from a burned warehouse, where people had been locked in and burned alive. The news indicated it was a possible attempt of an ethnic cleansing. A manhunt was underway for all those involved in the mass murder of Syrians in Egypt. Anyone with information was asked to step forward. As they flashed the artist sketches of the offenders, I was fluffing my pillow and on my way to dreamland. *Bastards*, I thought. Those people should be shown no mercy.

CHAPTER SEVEN
ISABELLA

BOOM. I HEARD it. Worse than thunder. It continued for what seemed forever, followed by a loud whistling noise and then *BOOM* again.

At 3:00 p.m. exactly, I sat straight up in bed and looked around for the source of the horrific noise. I leaned forward to try to zero in on and identify the unusual noise. What was that? I imagined it sounded like a low-flying plane buzzing a control tower.

Glasses I'd left on my bedside table moved an inch and a vase fell over. Paintings on the walls rattled and my perfume bottle toppled over. I remained seated to get my bearings. What was happening?

I threw off my covers with one swoop. My feet hit the floor and I stood with little support from my wobbly knees. My heart hammered so hard, it was ready to explode. The oxygen was being sucked from the room, leaving me almost unable to breathe. My legs gave way, and I found myself on the floor, crawling toward the window on hands and knees.

Suddenly, I heard what sounded like sixteen rapid pops in the distance. Was it gunfire? It was louder than what I imagined gunfire sounded like, with more of a bass feel to it. As I began to get my bearing and reached for the table to brace myself, I felt and heard what sounded like a long loud rumble. Maybe an explosion. The building; was it shaking, causing things to fall from the walls? Were we experiencing an earthquake?

Then I saw it. An enormous puff of white-gray smoke shot straight up and out as wide as a soccer field, coming from the direction of Notre-Dame and the city. If you were closer, there is no doubt the noise would cause deafness; by eardrum rupture, with subsequent bleeding another issue.

My mind, unable to process what occurred from the shock, reeled on its own.

Later, reports would have people talking about the flash, causing temporary blindness. Some would say it was a white light of sorts, accompanied by heat. If the blast from the church and buildings that sent tons of glass outward and upward didn't kill you, the rupture of your hollow organs caused immediate death. Survivors would speak of acrid and barbeque-like odors. Others would describe the feeling of ice picks being plunged into their ears. Several felt as if someone had stepped behind them and slammed a frying pan into the back of their heads, causing them to lose consciousness.

It would later be reported that few could be rescued from the carnage. The recovered remains of the victims, days later, proved horrific to the search and rescue teams.

How long I sat there in an almost catatonic state, I don't know. But I know it was the shrill scream of the emergency system warning that shocked me back to reality. I scrambled to my feet, falling over several times, and ran for the television remote. After the third attempt, I engaged the television, clicking

TWO

furiously to find a station that was not interrupted by static.

BREAKING NEWS: THE CITIES OF LONDON, PARIS, AND ROME ARE UNDER ATTACK.

That was all I could take in. Westminster, Notre-Dame, and St. Peter's were attacked at the same time in each city by what people assumed were terrorists at best, initiators of World War III at the worst. No one knew for sure. The story was fluid and evolving.

Questions posed by the newscasters remained unanswered. All they could say was, "More to follow."

As thoughts raced through my mind, I felt a bolt of electricity from the top resulting in what could only be termed a massive explosion inside my head. I recalled Mama and Denise were at the epicenter of this war.

I could not breathe. My heart was exploding against my ribs from my panic, and I ran for the telephone in the hall. As I raced down the slick marble hall in my socked feet, I pitched forward and fell, unable to brace myself with my arms. I slammed face-first, hard onto the cold floor, causing me to involuntarily drop to a lying, sprawled position. I thought I heard a crack and I definitely saw stars.

Dazed and my head spinning, I touched my face, then looked at my fingers. Bright red blood coated the tips. As I tried to lift my head, I saw a blood drip mark the perfect white marble floor in a splatter pattern. Tiny splats of blood, like a crime scene or a Jackson Pollack canvas, sprinkled the floor. Ouch. My forehead hurt, and my nose was probably broken from hitting the floor. I felt no excruciating pain, though; just a throb, as if someone had sucker punched me. I would have quite a shiner in the morning.

Taking a few minutes to even out the cadence of my breathing and let my heart rate adjust, I lay face to the floor. Crawling slightly toward the wall, I rolled to my right, onto my back, until I could finally gather myself to a sitting position. Like a ragdoll, I flopped against the wall for support. As I steadied myself, I looked down and saw blood droplets continue to sporadically hit my top. Using my hands and the muscles in my knees and thighs that were working, I braced against the wall for support as I inched my way up and stood. Once on my feet, I awkwardly stumbled forward, looking for the phone, bracing my right hand against the wall as if to steady me.

I reached my destination and unplugged the phone from the charger. I touched the speed dial number for my mama, only to be told by some robotic voice all circuits were busy. Again, and again I tried, and I still failed to connect the call. Mama had to be okay. Had to be. I then tried Denise without any different result.

Adrien. What about Adrien? I heard him say he was to meet in London, another attack site. I dialed his number. Again, my call wouldn't connect. Chloe! Was Chloe okay? Again, not able to call. Was everyone except me dead? No. No. No—

I slid to the floor, not knowing what else to do. How long I sat there, I had no idea. Was it minutes or hours? The only thing I remember was the power went out, and I was surrounded by darkness, hearing screams from the street.

I must have blacked out and reawakened. When I was certain I could walk, I stood and shuffled back to my bedroom, bracing against the wall for support. From my window, I could still see lingering puffs of gray-black smoke from the explosion and fires. Was I imagining that I could taste the acid-like smoke? People were in the streets, holding each other, holding themselves, screaming and crying. Power was out, and telephones were down. Chaos enveloped me.

I remember the last pictures and sounds from the television before it went dead. Flashes of London, Paris, and Rome; cities in

TWO

rubble. Panicked and confused people running or sitting in place, in shock. Centuries of history destroyed in a matter of minutes. Was I imagining it, or had they said early reports claimed that one hundred fifty thousand were estimated dead in Paris alone, with over half a million projected injuries. Over sixty thousand anticipated were dead in London, with over a quarter of a million injuries. Rome was a little tricky because Vatican City was involved as the main target, and two separate reports would be forthcoming, but numbers were estimated at over forty thousand dead and over one hundred fifty thousand injured. What was real and what had my mind manufactured in response to the shock?

I could see from my window, the basic life support crews clogging the area. There was no doubt additional crews would be needed from all over the European Union. The logistics to get them to the necessary places would be a nightmare. Airports must be closed, train systems at a standstill, and roads unpassable. Collapsed buildings probably stood in the way of people seeking safety and passage to their homes. All this flashed through my mind as I looked out the window. Not knowing what was happening was the worst.

In my heart, I knew my mama was dead; there was no escape from this massacre. Hysteria overtook me. I knew I was screaming inside, but nothing came from my mouth; it stayed stuck in my throat. I hyperventilated as my anguish overtook me and I felt darkness trickle around my peripheral vision. Unconsciousness soon followed.

How long I was unconsciousness, I don't know, but as I awoke, I knew my breathing had leveled out and my heart rate had regained a more normal cadence. I heard footsteps walking quickly toward me down the hall.

Adrien was right. I must have finally tipped over the edge and slipped into a fugue dissociative state. Or had someone broken in to rescue me?

Cracking my eyes open, I thought I saw Adrien and Paul entering the room. I didn't have the energy or mental ability to order my body to move. I stayed stone still, just watching as shadows approached me. Were they looters who broke in to kill, rape, or rob me?

No, as the shadows came into focus I could make out it was Adrien and Paul. Adrien was the first to kneel, and took hold of my chin between his fingers, turning my head from side to side. I suppose he was making an assessment, but I was too numb to engage. I vaguely heard him tell Paul to get a warm towel, some soap, and a bag of ice. My nose. That's right, I slammed my nose and forehead on the floor. Was it still bleeding? I couldn't tell. Did my face hurt? I didn't care. I heard the words shock and concussion. I think.

I was confused, my heart raced, shock—yes, it was all of that and more. All I wanted to do was lie down and sleep. Sleep now, and when I woke everything would be okay.

After he called my name five or six times, I snapped out of it.

"What are you doing here? You should be in London." I was barely able to put a simple sentence together.

"Isabella, let's get you to bed. I need to take your vital signs and check your nose. It doesn't appear broken. Can you breathe okay?" he asked as he indicated to Paul to put the towel and ice near the bed.

Paul did as he asked, then they helped me to my feet, and onto the bed. Blood pressure, pulse, and respirations assessed, and although abnormal, not life-threatening. I think that's what I heard.

"London was attacked, how—"

"There were problems with picked-up at St Pancras. The domino effect from that caused a mass delay on the trains. By the

TWO

time my train was rescheduled, I decided to abort the trip," he explained quickly, as he applied the ice to my face.

"Paul?" I started to ask.

"He's here—" he started.

"Adrien, did you kill someone in Cairo?" The news feeds and his phone call were jumbled in my mind. "You were in Cairo, right?" Why was everything so mixed up?

He moved back, assessing me further. No, studying me.

"Cairo? Don't be absurd. What an imagination. I have not been to Egypt since the Arab Spring movement. It's far too dangerous for Westerners to visit. Now, lie back and rest. I'll get something to calm your nerves. I'll be right back." He rubbed my hand.

But I couldn't let it go. My mind was working in overdrive. Pictures of people floated across it like an eight-millimeter movie. Why was Cairo important? Burning building, screaming people, organs stolen.

"No, Adrien, you told me you went to Cairo. You asked me to cancel the dinner plans we had. You were in Cairo yesterday," I insisted. "Your arm was hurt. Let me see your arm."

"Isabella, you are in shock, and your memory is faulty. Don't you remember calling your mother today and telling her you had to skip Easter Sunday mass because you were ill. You asked me to cancel the dinner Friday because you were under the weather," he said. "One minute—"

I did call my mother, I remember that, but why did I call her? Was I ill? And was I sick Friday and had to cancel dinner? It was blurred. Adrien wouldn't lie to me about such things. Was I losing my mind?

He walked into the bathroom, retrieving two pills and a glass of water. He placed the pills in my hand and helped me with the glass. Why was I taking these pills? What were they? I was too tired to ask.

"Sleep now, we can talk later. I am going to offer my help with the injured. Paul will be in the living room. If you need him, hit the button on the table," he said, as he placed the panic button closer.

My head was spinning and my breathing irregular.

"Adrien, the gallery. The paintings and inventory? How close was the explosion?"

Why did I care about the gallery? Mama was dead. No, she wasn't. She was in a hospital somewhere. Right?

"The target was Notre-Dame and the Hotel de Ville. I'm afraid the building probably sustained damage, but I had Paul move the most important pieces to the warehouse Thursday so we could do a more thorough accounting of it. The inventory should be fine," he assured me. He and Paul exchanged an odd look. Did they think I was crazy after the fall? Why were they looking at each other? A secret. They had a secret.

"Fortuitous," I replied. What an absurd thing for me to say.

"Indeed. Now sleep. I have some business to attend," he said. Yet he lingered and studied me, exchanging looks with Paul, holding a silent conversation, and then they walked out.

From the hall, I heard a muffled exchange between Paul and Adrien and as I drifted off, I heard the continuous wails of the bereaved on the street.

Cairo. I was losing my mind.

Paul appeared from time to time to escort me to the bathroom and offer more pills, which I took without question. Then he was gone, disappeared. When had he left? He was here for a long time but now I was alone. Confused and terrified, I let myself fall asleep, only to wake and medicate myself again. Surely, I was between heaven and earth, and waiting in line to enter the gates, like everyone else. I just didn't have the energy to take the final steps across.

CHAPTER EIGHT

ISABELLA

I WOKE, ALONE in my bed, to the droning news updates citing the various cities and the damage incurred. The television flashed images of people building small memorials near city centers. They filled them with candles and flowers. Flashes of social media reported people changing their profile pictures. Wait, when did I turn the television on?

I lay there, my head a stone on my pillow, listening and not moving. One reporter advised of food market offerings, admitting food availability looked bare, but crowds were pressing forward to buy what they needed.

Stock markets around the world were forced to suspend trading to avoid throwing the global economy into chaos. National and certain international banks remained closed for two more days to stave off a panic rush on them. But the automatic teller machines stayed available with a cut-off withdrawal of two hundred dollars. Leaders came forward and assured the public that although the state of the three cities was critical, forces and the local communities had banded together to offer some stability. Paris, London, and Rome would survive and come out the better for it. That thought was challenged on continual news feeds, by the national and international news stations.

Not ready to get out of bed, I focused on the ceiling. Once I was satisfied I could keep my eyes open with minimal effort, I glanced at the television. My brain engaged, and I realized the sun was up, streaming into the room and my window was slightly ajar.

I wanted to get up, but I was glued to the bed. I couldn't remember how I got there. My nose—wow, it ached, with some residual pain between my eyebrows. But it was my back that felt as if I had been beaten. Vomiting was just moments away. Snippets of time filtered through my mind.

Suddenly, I looked to the side of the bed. *Mama. What are you doing here?* Mama stood in front of me, reaching toward me to touch my face in comfort. But I could not formulate words to talk to her. My lips barely moved. My mind was foggy, but thoughts raced. I reached out to touch her, she was so close, and her hand hovered over my cheek. But how did she get into the apartment? How long had she been waiting to let me know she was okay? I didn't care. I only cared that she was here. She was okay. She had found her way back to me.

I closed my eyes for just a second, to quell the pounding in my head and bubbling nausea in my throat. But Mama was here, she would fix everything.

"Mama, thank God. I was so worried about you. I thought you had died in the attack. The blast was horrific. You know I saw it from my window, right after I heard the plane pass. How did you survive?" I waited for a response, but she must be too exhausted to answer.

"Don't worry, we will have time to talk later," I assured her from my mind, as if she could telepathically understand me, my

TWO

eyes still closed.

After the bite of nausea passed and I could control my arms again, I carefully pushed myself up. I swung my legs to the side of the bed to stand and tried to embrace her, but she was gone. Gone. What? My body felt out of my control. My wooden arms felt as if I waited for a marionette to lift a string, then they would move to his command. But not on their own. My vision was difficult to focus. It was as if a white haze of a fog trail had rolled across my room. Had I been drugged? That's crazy, who would drug me and how? No, I hadn't had that many pain pills. Wait, why did I think I had pain pills? I did have pain pills. Right? I thought back and vaguely remember Paul and Adrien being here. Adrien had given them to me for my fall. Didn't he? Yes, of course, I clearly remember him being here. Wasn't he? Wait, there she was again, but she looked like smoke. Why was she floating?

Believers in the afterlife say that before a person's soul ascends to heaven, they visit the ones they love on their way to God. Was this indeed her goodbye visit? No. I had to hold onto hope that she was in a hospital somewhere being treated. Perhaps Adrien could track her down. Yes. That's it. I must call Adrien, he will know what to do. But right now, my leg was aching from the fall and I need some more pain pills, and sleep. I made my way to the bathroom, God the bathroom was a mess. Did I do this in my sleep? I'd deal with it later. I took my pills with water and went back to bed.

"IZZY, IZZY, WAKE up," I heard someone yelling in a long tunnel echo. Or maybe we were underwater.

Who is that? Why are they yelling at me? *Stop the yelling. I hear you, I just can't move, yet.*

The racket wouldn't stop. Who is that and why can't they let me sleep? I slowly cracked my eyes, unable to keep the upper lids open. Chloe. What is Chloe doing here?

"Izzy, God damn it, open your eyes." Now she was shaking my shoulders.

Chloe, what the hell? Stop shaking me. Can't she hear me? I can hear myself.

"George, help me get her to sit up," I heard. George. George, the doorman, George? What was George doing here? Oh, I don't care. Maybe he can make her go away. I unexpectedly felt myself being hoisted under my arms to a seated position on the bed, and then pulled forward, Chloe's hand at my back for support. My legs swung—more like flopped—to the side of the bed, forcing me to plant my feet on the floor. My ankles bowed out. Not in a very sturdy position.

"Stand her up and shift her to the chair," she said. Why was Chloe giving everyone directions, and dragging me around like I was an invalid? Better yet, why was I having trouble standing?

"Turn her on my count of two, and get her to the chair," she ordered as my body started to crumple and then I felt myself jerked to the left by George.

What. Why was I being dragged to a chair?

"Izzy. Izzy, look at me. I need to know how many of those pills you took on the bedside table. Where did you get them? What the hell happened? You must have a broken nose and your forehead is banged up pretty bad. And God, woman, you have racoon eyes. Izzy, stay with me!" she yelled.

I was unceremoniously plopped in my oversized chair as she tried to keep me from falling forward. What the hell?

Finally able to get some brain cells firing, all I could say was, "I fell."

"No shit, Sherlock. Look at you. When was the last time

TWO

you got out of bed? When was the last time you ate or drank anything?" she asked. Was she mad at me?

I looked over at George, who looked sheepishly embarrassed. Behind him was Danielle, who did not hide her look of disgust.

"Danielle was finally able to make it over here, and found you in this state," she said. State? What state? Can't a person sleep for twelve hours? After all, a crisis had just occurred.

"She went to get George. Thank God they were able to find me in your phone contacts," she said.

Finally, I was able to move my lips enough to string a few words together. I held my head up for a period of time, becoming more and more difficult to look up.

"Chloe, you are being dramatic. What time is it?" It had to be about eight or nine in the morning, if Danielle was here. And the street had quieted down. No one was crying.

"Nine fifteen," she said, as she looked me over for more damage.

I slurred my words a bit, sounding wrong, even to my own ears. That, along with a slight head bob forward, could be taken as a cause for Chloe's concern.

"For God's sake, I slept through the night. Why are you so freaked out?" My mouth was dry and as my tongue licked the roof of my mouth, it felt like sandpaper. God, I must have awful morning breath.

"Izzy, today is Thursday. Stay with me here. How many pills have you taken? The bottle is almost empty."

That couldn't be right. It's Monday . . . could be Tuesday, I guess. Not even close to Thursday. This attack happened Sunday. She was wrong.

"Say something," she demanded, shaking my shoulders. This only caused my head to lull forward, and I felt whiplash could occur with this treatment.

"Where's Adrien?" He could clear this up.

"He's been in London since Sunday," she said, losing patience with me.

"No, he was here Sunday with me," I corrected her. "He is at the hospital, taking care of the victims. He told me so before he left. He left Paul to watch over me. Get Paul. He will clear this up."

"No, honey. I spoke to him a bit ago, and he is still in London. His phone went back into service this morning. If I knew he was in London, I would have looked in on you sooner. I'm so sorry you were left in this state all by yourself."

"Chloe, why are trying to confuse me? Paul and Adrien were here Sunday. They got me to bed and then he left to help. George, surely you must have seen him," I begged. Nausea bubbled up and sat in the middle of my chest, vomit ready to explode forward.

"I'm sorry, Madam Armond, I was not here until Tuesday," he said. "If you ladies don't need me further, I have matters to attend." Chloe gave him a nod and he left. What an embarrassing state I was in at the moment.

Even though the oversized chair was meant for one person, Chloe climbed in next to me and enveloped me in a hug. I leaned into her, and she kissed my head, just as Mama would do if she were here.

Chloe turned to Danielle. "Would you have Thomas prepare breakfast for her?" I didn't miss the way Danielle assessed me; judged me. She nodded her affirmation and left.

We sat there holding each other for a while, and then I spoke. "I've lost time, Chlo. Lots of it."

"I know. I think they have a name for it—post-traumatic stress disorder," she reassured me as she stroked my hair that

TWO

must be a sight. If it was Thursday, I hadn't bathed since Sunday and felt fortunate I had made it to the bathroom when needed. Yuck. I must be a mess. "You know PTSD. When people experience a shocking scary or dangerous event they often have flashbacks, severe anxiety and even uncontrollable thoughts about the event. Your mother and sister just died or are presumed dead as they were in the church that collapse. You heard the plane overhead as it set the bombs on Paris. Izzy, you were in the middle of a war zone."

I took a moment to collect my thoughts. Right now, my thoughts and speech would be unfiltered.

"I'm afraid to ask any questions, Chlo. I don't want any bad answers. You understand?" I needed her to gain assurance that she wouldn't tell me Mama was dead. She nodded.

"Then, let's start with the good news. Neither Paul nor Adrien are in the country," she said with a snicker to her smile. "And you know the further those men are from me, the better. You have plenty of food, and you are alive."

Yes, Chloe intensely disliked both men, and the feeling was reciprocated. But her humor was lost on me today because they were the only ones who knew what had happened. Adrien was the one who told me to take the pills. I was just following instructions. He'd left the pills and told me what to take. Didn't he? I would need him for corroboration. But if he'd said he's been in London that would be impossible.

"How do you know he's in London?" I wanted to know.

"He told me. Why would he lie? He said he'd been waitlisted on flights to get out," she assured me. "The Eurostar has been useless, with people desperate to get home."

"And Paul. You know he was here with him Sunday. He caught an early train home—" I wanted her to know I had a basis for my thoughts.

"I don't know where that weasel was Sunday. But Adrien said he is in Abu Dhabi right now, for an auction," she said. "I seriously think ice runs through that man's veins. He barely asked about you, but his mind was all business. Sorry, you didn't need that editorial.

"He also said to tell you he called a Mr. Jaager. God, what is wrong with that man? There is no heart that lies within that man's chest. He doesn't understand anything except what someone can do to make him some money. Your only family were just wiped off the face of the earth and he thinks you care about an appointment to make a sale? He hasn't spoken to you in days. Talk about cold and ruthless. But not for me to question why that hard, heartless shell of a person does what he does. He told me to tell you he rescheduled your appointment for next Monday, as he will be back by then. That's probably the most I've spoken to him in five years. I hope to go another five without having to talk to his arrogant ass. Is there really someone who cares about a business transaction in this emotionally devastating climate?" Did she expect an answer? I didn't care; my mind was still jumbled. "I may be wrong, but I think George said that Mr. Jaager had come by to check on you but there was no answer and I guess after talking to Adrien he thought you were okay."

The effect of the pills was apparently wearing off, and with the influx of fresh air, my head was clearing. What did I want to know first? What could I tolerate to hear first?

"All right then, I think I'm ready to hear what has occurred over the last three days. Three days, Chloe. But in a nutshell. You will lose me with details. Hit the high points."

I was about to full body sink into her as she explained, when Thomas appeared. The smell of eggs, bacon, and sourdough toast wafted toward me, and reminded me of my unfulfilled hunger.

TWO

Chloe carefully extracted herself from the chair to help me up. Thomas laid out the table by the window and we took our seats, looking out through the open window to the square green common area, and then to the street. Few people moved past. Unlike Sunday, when chaos had erupted, things were relatively back to the normal low buzz. Coffee was poured, and Chloe added milk and sugar to mine, still assessing my ability to care for myself. I suppose she thought my hand-to-mouth coordination could leave me scalded if the coffee made it to my lap instead of my lips.

"Okay. Bring me up to speed. But, the basics only," I said, again.

If anyone had heard from Mama, they would have volunteered that at once. They hadn't, and I wasn't ready to receive the information and what it implied.

"Three cities have been hit with massive structural damage to the churches. It was never even a search and rescue because they knew the way the church imploded it would be impossible for anyone to survive. And for that I am sorry because there will not be bodies to bury. The surrounding city areas are still being evaluated, but it is slow going due to the structural damage to the infrastructure; the bombs from the planes did enormous damage to buildings and bridges. Shipping is affected, and most businesses are closed for the week. There is a great worry about diseases bubbling up like cholera and dysentery because of raw sewerage mixing with the drinking water and animals' and people' decomposing body remains in areas where drinking water is obtained. We'll have to get you bottled water which has come into short supply. Markets have crashed around the world due to the uncertainty and parts of the UK, Italy, and France cannot export or import products so food is beginning to be an issue. Financially the devastation is immeasurable."

I interrupted her. "But Paul is in Abu Dhabi? The art sector of all things, didn't shut down? That's incredulous."

Why that came to mind, I had no idea. People were panicked and probably lost everything, and what comes out of my mouth? Paul, Abu Dhabi, and art. What the hell is wrong with me?

"Odd choice of topics, but I'll go with it. The rich must carry on with money laundering, I guess. No need to pull the plug from that scam," she said, leaning back, bracing for an argument.

"I don't have it in me to argue today, Chloe. Has anyone been by the gallery? Or that part of the city?" That should be the least of my concerns, but it was the first. Adrien would be furious if the gallery was destroyed.

"Sorry, I don't know. I do know there has been an enormous military presence, and I think the word is unofficially out, if anyone breaks and enters during this time, it's go time for shoot to maim, and killing would not be in disfavor," she said. What a surreal conversation.

Almost in a whisper, as if I didn't want to offend anyone, I asked, "Have they assigned blame yet? Anyone come forward?"

"Believe it or not, no. There is speculation that it was an extreme terrorist organization because churches were targeted. The talking heads are postulating that this could involve the Iranians or Russians. The geopolitical implications are all over the place. No one knows if it was religious-, financial-, or political-based, but everyone agrees it was an act of terror." She looked out the window; thinking of what she should divulge next, I suppose. How much worse could it get?

"I'm more concerned about you right now. You'll have plenty of time to catch up on what occurred." She eyed me with sympathy and concern, but I needed something tangible and real to hold onto. I gave her the go-ahead sign. She shook her head

TWO

and continued.

"The stock markets bottomed out, no one is shopping, commerce is affected and almost crippled. People are worried and trying to make a run on banks."

Her words come to me in a low buzz now as she spoke. I grabbed bits and pieces that I cared about and others, I just let flit by.

She continued to opine. "If it wasn't for a religious reason that Notre-Dame, Westminster Abbey, and St. Peter's were targeted then why not target other places as well? Why wasn't Germany the financial epicenter of the EU attacked? Why not Switzerland—the banker's playground of the world? Why not Asia? Taking down China would lead to a crippling effect on the world's economy. The US probably would be too difficult. They've been taking a lot of little hits by lone wolves. If they know they can get through with little attacks so easily why not a coordinated mass attack? What if this was another country trying to get us to declare war on the Muslims? Or could someone have done this to force us to become dependent totally on Russia for something like natural gas? What if we knee jerk and start targeting other countries in retaliation? What does it matter in the end? Right now we have to take care of you and get you well. Maybe a head CT scan just to make sure?"

She had three days and a clear head to have thought this through. Right now, it was all gibberish to me.

"Chlo, that isn't even something I want to think about. My brain isn't up to that level of functioning yet." I noticed I'd eaten most of my breakfast.

Sitting back, I knew it was time to ask. "The people at mass—?"

She sat silent, measuring what information she wanted to give me.

"They have not been able to ascertain the death toll between the church and surrounding area. There were so many tourists unaccounted for that they are still working with other governments to determine who was there. I guess there's a system in place where they can work through passport control and try to . . ." Her voice trailed off. She was putting off answering my question.

"Chlo?" I questioned. Was she trying to say there were too many deaths to identify people?

"As far as they can tell, no one in the church survived. The way the explosives were placed and triggered, it was rigged like they do when they want to raze a building for demolition by implosion. The preparation took months. You need to prepare yourself." She leaned forward, touching my arm.

"I can't, Chloe, I just can't," I shared, as tears welled, and I felt my breath catch.

Her eyes assessed me for emotions out of control, but I tried my best to hold back.

"Now, can I ask you how you got that shiner, and how you broke your nose?" She surveyed my battered face. Ah, the diversion tactic.

"I was running after the explosion and I did a face-plant." If I brought up that Paul and Adrien were here and could corroborate my story, an argument was likely to ensue. Because I had no evidence. Adrien would call it a dissociative vision; one of his favorite terms. Maybe I was losing my mind, piece by piece. But how would I know to take the pills?

"Well, as long as you can breathe, that's all that matters. You want me to wait while you shower, and maybe we could get out and stretch your legs?" she asked, then laughed. "And okay, that came out as a question and suggestion, but let me rephrase it. Take a shower, and let's get out of here; take a walk."

TWO

"Are the trains running?" I asked.

"Scattered ones are, so yes. Why? Are you thinking of checking on the gallery?" she asked, giving me a disproving eye.

"Yes, it will ease my mind."

Why I said that I don't know, because it didn't matter. Maybe I just wanted her to think I was still connected to the world. In the end, it was stone and just material. But it would give me comfort to see it still standing; almost like a sign that things would be okay. I don't know what I thought. Nothing was real anymore.

"I don't think that's such a great idea. Train line eleven took some damage, and the lines feeding into Chatelet are running on less trains. People are edgy and that's never good," she said. "The Hotel de Ville took some hits, but if you want my best guess, your building is probably okay because Adrien installed those metal doors across the front, to prevent glass from being broken. Let's just take a walk around, okay?"

"Okay, let me take a shower. You can help me with my makeup." God, how shallow that made me sound. People probably have third-degree burns and lost limbs, and I'm worried about a black eye and broken nose. But if I didn't put my best foot forward, Adrien would know. There were spies all around me. I didn't want to do anything that would embarrass Adrien.

I had lost my family and was trapped in a world of grief and denial. I had no physical body to bury so in my mind maybe they were still alive waiting to be rescued. But what chance of that after four days buried in rubble? I felt the pain of their loss and guilt for not being there with them. I was meant to be there with them. Had I not made that stupid excuse maybe I could have been the one to save them. Why was I spared. Anger had set in my thoughts, but the pills had dulled the full manifestation of the rage I felt inside. I would bargain with God and the devil himself to have news there were live bodies recovered. I didn't anticipate any bargaining chip I might have to bring them back.

No one wants to talk about it with me. Maybe it's me telling them I don't want to. But I do. I want to share my loss and pain with everyone. Someone should be able to make it go away.

Are they all afraid it will send me flying over some imaginary cliff into a permanent world of crazy if they talk about the deaths? Would I always have to bear my depression alone?

How do I fight my way back to a normal life? And God, was the life I lived even considered normal? Adrien controlled everything, and I had given control of my mind over to him. Was I even a living thinking person any more or some appendage of Adrien? He had me questioning my memories, perceptions and sanity to the point he has almost delegitimized all of my beliefs. I can't even depend on my own decisions anymore, completely dependent on him. Was I in the middle of a nervous breakdown? Or was it just my imagination running wild?

CHAPTER NINE

BEN

IT HAD BEEN a week since the attack. No radical groups had stepped forward to accept responsibility for a religious cause. No global economic group had touted their plan had succeeded. The attack was perfectly timed and carried out with no one claiming responsibility.

There appeared to be no viable connection between the three plots. Each cell within the country involved had acted on its own accord. It also appeared that within each cell in each country, each person had a specific job. This was always the worst-case scenario for law enforcement because no one knew enough to flip on someone else. Each played a compartmentalized role, with limited or no interaction with others.

No splinter war group had claimed acceptance either. There was low-level chatter in the halls of British Parliament that Russia was to blame. In the US, it was definitely thought an Iranian plot carried out to perfection. In the end, however, nothing was proven.

It would be impossible to interview people who had access

to the churches because, by and large, records were destroyed. The people who kept the records were dead. The churches were public places, where tourists and staff were granted unmonitored access overall. It was farfetched and highly unlikely, but over a period of three months, one person could have planted a device little by little. At some point, they could search for remnants of the detonation, but that could take weeks or months as the rubble was removed. It appeared hopeless, from a forensic point of view.

The basic idea of explosive demolition to implode a building is quite simple. If you remove the support structure of a building at a certain point, the section of the building above that point will fall on the part of the building below. Demolition blasters load explosives on several different levels of the building so that the building structure falls on itself at multiple points. Unlike private buildings, these church buildings' blueprints were open to public access. Tracking down suspects who asked for plans from a governing body seemed fruitless. Anyone with a computer could study it at their leisure. A structural engineer could plan it, and his or her minions could plant the explosives. The only thing going for us was the skill to have a building implode as neatly as it did; there were only a handful of people in the world that could perform such a feat as it was carried out. The problem was, none of them outwardly fit the model as a suspect.

Theories as to the choice of implosion carried through were just that—theories. If the explosion had been contained to the crypt, it would have done structural damage and claimed lives. It also would have sent a message what could be done on a bigger scale. By using explosives in a structure as well, it assured a maximum death toll. What was the message? High death toll? Maximum terror? Maximum damage?

The best engineers in the world were brought in to study the disaster and would probably study each of the churches for

TWO

months. The results were all the same—loss of life, psychological trauma, and financial devastation. The effects of the psychological trauma and fear were the most devastating. Depression led to an unwillingness to change due to non-motivation, and France became a nation on the verge of giving up. Times that by three, and the Western culture as we knew it was in peril.

Why the planes with bombs? To destroy a certain circle of the area outside the churches? The British Parliament building was hit hard, as was the Hotel de Ville here in Paris. In Italy, they scored a two for one hitting St. Peter's and a small area of Rome. The proximity to the Holy See assured adjacent devastation.

No one knew where the planes take-off point originated. Were they launched from a ship or land? Some postulated that they avoided radar detection by use of nanostructured coating on the planes; the coating made of carbon nanotubes infused in paints were used on stealth aircraft. This assured they couldn't be seen at night and were undetectable by radar at any time of day. But that would probably indicate government involvement. Wouldn't it? Where would a regular person or small group be able to acquire that type of plane, or the military-grade paint?

People on the ground who saw the plane for the split second before the bombs dropped, swore the plane was a Russian MiG. Others swore it was either a F-14 or F-17. The chaos of information led to conspiracy theories that the US and Russia had teamed up to take down Europe. It was postulated the European Union had grown too strong in market competition, and this was the way to level the playing field. Others opined it was an Arab conspiracy that involved the Saudis and United Arab Emirates. A few tossed around China, and some speculated it was a North Korean plot. There was an unlimited supply of where to lay blame, yet no significant information to support it.

Unlike offshore banks that saw an uptick in business,

national banks and financial institutions were still finding their footing. Stock markets continued to reel and maintained a wild roller coaster ride. The only market that kept a steady course was the art market. Auction houses stayed open for business, and a brisk business was carried out.

The amount of reconstruction necessary to rebuild the areas led to projections of a crippling budget deficit. More illegal immigrants and refugees were quietly let into the countries as government officials looked aside in favor of cheap labor. It would take years to rebuild and years for the economies to revive. Many had predicted the collapse of the European Union and eurozone over this catastrophe. It had come to the brink but stepped back.

My phone buzzed with an unknown caller.

"Ben Jaager," I answered.

"This is Special Agent Cillian O'Reilly from the FBI art crime team. I was given your name, and understand you are functioning in a three-prong position," he said.

"You have me at a disadvantage, Agent O'Reilly. I don't know what three prongs you are talking about. And call me Ben," I responded. I had assumed a different branch would be liaising with me, but this would do for now.

"Art, terrorism, and migrant smuggling," he offered. The Americans seemed to be on top of their game.

"Oh yes, sorry. I am with the terrorism unit, but this operation seems to have threads of the three you named. What can I do for you?" I hoped he was here to offer help. At the very least, to offer useful information.

"You are aware that we have Roselov in custody. I believe you are also aware that his gallery was transferred over to the Armonds who, I believe, are targets of an investigation you are involved with. This morning, the gallery exploded. From reports, it's being investigated as a gas leak. However, it has the

TWO

fingerprints of a gas leak-type incident that caused an explosion of the home where we had material witnesses tucked away." I overheard the call to board to Heathrow in the background. "I am heading to London now. I wanted to know what headway you've made tying Ms. Armond in with any of the money used to fund any part of these attacks," he asked.

"London? Isn't that out of your jurisdiction as an FBI agent?" I headed toward the window to watch for the Armonds.

"Desperate times and scattered resources means all hands on deck. Right now, none of the suspects are talking, and the possible destruction of evidence through the blast from this morning is a bit troubling. British CCTV had picked up someone tied to the Armonds accessing the gallery. Nothing illegal there, and we are still trying to tie the London piece of the cell funding Roselov and Abdurrahman. However, they laundered the money so well, and through so many sources, that circumstantial is what we have available," he said. "I'm boarding, so a quick rundown would be helpful, and I will touch base when I hit London."

"I'm meeting with Madame and Dr. Armond in a few minutes. I believe we've made some headway. Two things trouble me," I explained.

"Yes? What's that?" Muffled voices became louder as he reached the boarding agent.

"Madame Armond's mother and sister were killed in the attack. You have to be heartless to allow your mother to die. And something that still niggles at me. When I had first met with her, she had indicated her husband was in Cairo attending a conference, I believe she said. Don't hold me to the reason he was there, and I'm not totally sure why she mentioned it. Anyway, when we verified his flight information, there was no trace of him on any commercial flights. We then ran it through passport control and nothing there either," I said.

"Okay, but you lost me on why you were looking into Cairo." Of course, that would mean nothing to Agent O'Reilly. Sometimes I got ahead of myself.

"That was the weekend five refugees were found dead from what appeared to be botched surgeries for a black-market organ harvesting operation. The following week, two locals who had ties to the medical field in one way or another, were reported missing, as well as four villagers. However, the boy who reported it to the authorities said there was a doctor that spoke French and English, and a man he thought was Arab, who were not accounted for during the arrest," I wasn't sure if he understood the connection. "I know it's making an enormous leap with lots of speculation, and normally I don't work in the world of what-ifs. But I feel something here. Could he have been there? I know I have no reason to believe he was part of anything illegal, but I'm coming up empty on things and grasping for connections. I'll explore it while I've got them together and assess their reaction. Other than that, we are still feeling our way around in the dark. It's obvious big money went into planning this operation to attack three cities. And big money normally comes out of the Middle East. Rich in oil and all that, so that's where we are focused right now."

"I see. You think Armond is associated with this network of smugglers and organ transplant people? There is big money there. Making a leap, you think the wife launders the money through the art gallery? Are you putting the two of them at some position of funding, or helping in some way to fund this attack? And if so, to what end? Are they terrorists? Do they have some reason to want to manipulate the global markets? Who are they working with?" he asked in rapid-fire, as he took a moment before boarding his flight.

"Honestly, I don't know. It all seems farfetched. And when

TWO

you say it out loud, I have no connections or answers. It's bothering me. But why would a doctor get involved in such a sloppy, risky operation? And how could he slip in and out of Egypt undetected? It's not like taking a train to Germany. Where would he get documents to allow him to do so? There is nothing on paper that allows us to dig deeper, legally. He owns a large amount of property. However, that is not illegal in France. He seems to hold the reins on the gallery. I don't know. The pieces aren't fitting correctly," I said, thinking out loud again.

"Ben, we have a saying: trust the gut. Once I finish up in London, I might hop down to Paris. Would that be okay with you? Maybe we can brainstorm. After seeing the Roselov gallery, I'd like to snoop around the Armonds' place. If things work out, maybe you can introduce me as an American investor. You're still maintaining your venture capitalist cover, right?" he asked.

"It's more than okay. As you said, we're all hands on deck right now," I responded. "And as we speak, the Armonds are coming up the front path. We shall talk later, yes?"

"Looking forward to it," Agent O'Reilly responded, and disconnected.

I waited for the buzz from below and, shortly thereafter, for a knock at the door.

"Welcome, Dr. and Madame Armond. Please come in. May I take your jackets?" Dr. Armond's handshake grip appeared a little too firm, and lasted a second too long, indicating he was taking control of the situation. Interesting.

"Please, Ben, call us Isabella and Adrien," Adrien suggested, totally at ease in the situation and taking charge of the situation.

Adrien had the appearance of a man who obviously enjoyed the fruits of his labor. Dressed well in expensive attire with minimal, although expensive, jewelry on display. Not athletic, but obviously knew his way around a gym.

"Then, Adrien, can I offer either of you refreshments?" Neither accepted. "Isabella, I understand you lost family members in the attack, that your mother and sister were attending the Easter Sunday services. May I extend my condolences. I am surprised that you are able to return to work so soon after such a shocking loss. If you wanted to put this off for a bit, we could do that. I would most certainly understand your need to be by yourself and grieve this outrageous loss."

Before Isabella could respond, Adrien put his hand on her arm and spoke for her.

"Work can be a great diversion for people under stress and experiencing grief. Isabella insisted on being here and knows our clients' needs come before our personal problems." He spoke as if her goldfish had died instead of her family decimated in what might be the worst attack in history. "She is here and ready to give her all."

Rather than looking distant or unaffected as I would expect if she had a hand in the plot, she looked sad and forlorn. She chose either not to take the bait or was a good actress. She did not agree nor disagree with Adrien. I don't even know if she heard him and processed what he said. I decided to let it sit and study her further.

"Please come into the living area. Where would you feel most comfortable?" I inquired, and Adrien at once indicated the dining room, stating it offered a better seating arrangement and light. Isabella's eyes remained downcast and what I perceived as lost in thought. She certainly wasn't present in this room.

What an odd pair. Adrien was the dominant in the marriage and business. That was clear. By every standard, an attractive masculine man whom some would consider arrogant and assured, but no one would consider him charismatic. If my dossier didn't indicate I was a multimillionaire, I am confident he would

TWO

have never accepted my hand in greeting and scraped me off his shoe. Isabella was another matter. Today, she appeared quiet, nervous, and deferred the conversation to Adrien. I wonder how she felt about her gallery exploding in London.

"I am glad to finally meet with you, Adrien. Your schedule as a doctor must keep you very busy. I understand you were recently in Cairo—" I tried to tease some information from him.

He stopped what he was doing and raised his eyes, looking at me from under his eyebrows, not moving his head.

"Then, Ben, you would have incorrect information. Where may I ask did you get that information?" he clipped out, as Isabella sat ramrod straight in reaction.

She reached out to touch his hand, and he immediately recoiled from it. An involuntary action, which I could see he regretted letting me witness.

"That was me, Adrien. I had shared that with Ben," she said. Her breathing increased where her chest was visibly ascending and descending quickly. Her cadence in speech was of panic and her face winced as if she was prepared for an abusive scolding.

"Ah. Then excuse me, Ben. Isabella was mistaken," he said, regaining some composure. "I know your time is valuable, so I suggest we review some of the options we chose."

"Yes, I am looking forward to that, and want to thank you for taking the time to do this amidst what I am sure is a busy hospital schedule since the attack," I offered. *And because you want my millions to line your pockets.*

"It is our pleasure and life must move forward. Yes?" he offered. What a snake.

In the next hour, he explained the history of each painting presented, why it would be a good fit for the room, and price was never mentioned. Isabella sat with her hands in her lap, and the only part of her body to move were her eyes, as they followed one slide to the next. She offered no opinion and agreed with everything Adrien said. I had seen such things in hostage or kidnapping situations but this was clearly a normal business deal.

"Adrien, you have some exquisite treasures to offer. There are several that I'm interested in. Would it be possible to view them at your gallery tomorrow?" I asked sitting back relaxed hoping he would not read through my plan.

"We moved the majority of the inventory to our warehouse before the attack. It will take a few days to retrieve them." I noticed this caught Isabella by surprise. Surprise that turned to an expression, like she was trying to recall information.

"If you will excuse me one second, I have to answer this text. I apologize for my rudeness. Are you certain I can't offer you some refreshment?" I asked as I stood. Isabella's eyes never left her lap. Never met mine. It was as if she didn't hear me until Adrien tapped her hand.

They both declined, and Isabella excused herself to use the restroom.

I stepped into the kitchen to determine if the gas blast had made its way to the mainstream media. Indeed, it had.

We gathered back in the dining room and I led with, "Isabella. That lovely painting that had been at the Roselov gallery in London. Is that still available?"

Before she could answer, Adrien responded, "No, I am sorry, that painting has been sold."

"That is indeed my loss. And to add to the tragedy from the attack, now the Roselov London gallery is lost."

Adrien was handing me papers pertaining to the art I had just reviewed, but he stopped, looking at me as if I had spoken Latin. "Excuse me?"

"Yes, it was on all the news feeds. Tragic," I baited.

With that, he removed his phone from his jacket and googled

TWO

the story. Studying the screen, for a moment I read shock and anger across his face. But as quick as it came it left.

"Ah, yes, tragic indeed," he said calmly and replaced his phone. The man had nerves of steel. "We had, on occasion, acquired well-received pieces from him."

"Roselov. That is a loss. We have only had a few pieces from his gallery come through. But they were stunning," Isabella said in an impassive tone. Odd. For a woman who just lost a several-million-dollar investment, she seemed very detached. And effectively denied ownership of the gallery.

"I just said that, my dear," Adrien said, patting her hand, then addressed me. "Ben, I hope we have shown you pieces that will add pleasure and value to your new home. When you are ready to view them in person—"

"Adrien, I am anxious to do that immediately. If not tomorrow, as you said you need time to retrieve them, would three days give you enough time to prepare them?" I asked. Locking him in was crucial to move this along. He wanted my money and I wanted him to have it.

"You can send Paul to Zurich tomorrow, Adrien," Isabella interjected quietly. She raised and lowered her eyes quickly and then went silent. Zurich, I need to make a note of that, as I thought the report indicated the use of the Geneva freeport.

Her statement earned her a harsh look and a low, "I will take care of this, Isabella."

"Of course, Adrien," was her reply. She kept her eyes focused on her hands that rested on her lap.

"Yes, Ben, I believe that will be possible. And now, I am sure you have many matters to attend." He stood and extended his hand to say goodbye. I retrieved their coats and they left.

Cillian's flight to London still had seven or so more hours in the air. I was pretty sure Adrien was making arrangements to visit his now-demolished investment in London. I left a message for Cillian that Adrien was likely heading his way. My next call was to Jill, to advise her to alert the London Metropolitan Police of the same so they could be ready to put people in place to observe what went on at the gallery. I often referred to it as Scotland Yard and that always earned me a correction. Now about that freeport. The Swiss were a tricky lot not bound by the EU rules and remained unwilling to fully cooperate with financial investigations. They played by their own rules to their economic advantage. Jill had a way with the Swiss, so I would leave it to her to put eyes on the freeports in Zurich and Geneva to watch for Paul, Adrien's right-hand man.

This was quite an odd afternoon. Isabella was so off in her affect. An enigma. People experience shock and lived out their grief in many ways. Some replayed memories, others lived in fear, anxiety, anger, and still others buried themselves in survivor guilt and numbness. These were all ways people experienced how they dealt with death. Isabella seemed dissociated from the conversation, almost drugged, or hopeless and didn't care what was going on around her. She was in a world all her own. I supposed she could be on antidepressant medication after losing her family. She certainly did not portray a ruthless participant of a criminal network. Adrien, on the other hand, gave me a chill from the base to the top of my spine. I believe he needed to be on everyone's radar and remain there indefinitely.

CHAPTER TEN

ISABELLA

I WOKE TO the continual buzzing of the phone on my nightstand. Adrien was gone, the sun was up. I looked at my phone screen and it was Chloe's name flashing.

"Hello," I slurred out, as I put it on speaker and laid it on my chest.

"Where are you? You were supposed to meet me at Starbucks. We have an appointment in an hour with the attorney. Did you forget?" Irritation, not concern, laced her tone.

"Yes. Oh God, I forgot. Sorry, Chloe." How could I forget something so important? Why was my memory scattered and still losing chunks of time?

"No, not sorry, Izzy. I want you up and showered in a half hour. I will send a car to pick you up. I want you downstairs in forty minutes. I'll have the car drop you at the *avocat's* office. I wanted to talk about what you should discuss with Michelle, but I can do all the talking. Now get ready. Something is going on with you. You are absolutely not yourself, and I am getting to the bottom of this today," she stated, a little harshly, I thought.

"What do you mean? I'm the same person I have always been. I'm sad, and maybe a little depressed, since Mama and Denise died, but I think that would be expected." Defensive was not a good play on my part, but my only one.

"Are you for real?" she yelled, clearly having none of it. "Let's count off how you have changed dramatically. You are constantly second-guessing yourself. If Adrien disagrees with you, then his position must be the correct thinking. You verbalize, even to me, feeling confused and that you're having a hard time making simple decisions. Now when has that ever been a problem? You started your own business and have paid your way since you were eighteen. You constantly apologize, even to me, when nothing is your fault. You are unhappy and don't say it is because of your mama's death. This is something else. It's as if someone has programmed you to start hating yourself, and you are now with that program. You always, and I mean every day of your life, make excuses for Adrien's behavior. What's that all about? You give the appearance you don't think you can do anything right. You act like you aren't good enough for others. You and I know that you used to be a more confident, relaxed, and happy person. And, last but not least, you withhold information from friends and family, so you don't have to explain things. And that, my friend, is a list of personal issues we are going to address. Now get up, and get dressed. You have a divorce attorney to meet, who will be the gateway to your future happiness," she said. I could imagine her counting these revelations off on her fingers.

"Okay. But your list is wrong," I disagreed, although I knew her list was right. Something was going on with me. I felt absent from my own life at times. More often than not, I didn't seem to care about anything. How had this happened? Did everyone see it? Was everyone judging me? I was a burden to everyone.

No, that's crazy talk in my head. The first thing I needed to

TWO

do was dispense of the pills Adrien insisted I take, but they made me feel good, calm. If I could wait one more day to get things done, it would be okay. Adrien assured me I needed them, but never said why. "Just take them, Isabella. You need them to think straight." And he'd hold out the pills for me to take.

Suddenly, snippets of information started playing in my head out of nowhere. In the back of my mind, I heard Adrien talking to someone, and he was angry. I couldn't remember what it was they were saying. My recollection of so many things lately, was gone. I had no ability, it appeared, to retain important information.

"All right, all right. I'm getting up now, don't flip out. I'll be ready." I forced myself to sit up and move around.

"And don't take any of those pills Adrien is giving you. Put them in your bag. I want to see them, and I want Michelle to see them. We can get a picture of the label, and look them up on the internet. I still can't wrap my head around you taking any medication prescribed by him, with the mind games he loves to play. Now, up. The car is on its way," she ordered.

"Okay, okay, no need to yell. No pills. Put the bottle in my purse. I got it," I said, and suddenly felt a wave of emotion overtake me. "I miss Mama and Denise."

"Honey, I know you do. I miss them too. But what is going on with you goes beyond grief. I'm so afraid, with all the emotional abuse that Adrien rains down on you day after day, that you are starting to buy into what he is selling. And, Izzy, not on my watch. That shit ain't happening. Get up, and we are getting a divorce, and picking up a 'get out of jail free' card. Love you, see you in a few." She waited for me to respond.

"Love you also. I won't let you down," I replied.

"You couldn't even if you tried. Now scoot." And she hung up.

As I rolled from the bed, I saw a text from Adrien I must have missed. "Gone to London, back tonight."

London? What's in London? What about his surgeries? The man never seemed to be at the hospital anymore. Maybe he'd been at the hospital. Maybe I'm confused.

AN HOUR LATER, I was seated across from Michelle Dupont, the *avocat* recommended by Chloe, who sat to my right. Chloe's voice drifted past me as I watched Michelle acknowledge what Chloe relayed, in the only way Chloe knew how—filled with drama. Occasionally, she would look to me for affirmation, and I nodded. If Chloe said it, then it must be correct.

My mind wandered, as if visiting a palace in my mind. In and out of rooms, opening and closing doors. Suddenly, I heard Michelle raise her voice, and Chloe touched my arm.

"I'm sorry. What was the question?"

"What are the assets that you have acquired during your marriage?" Michelle asked, pen in hand to make a list.

"Oh. Let's see. The gallery and the paintings, the apartment and furniture, the cars, bank accounts," I replied.

"Let's drill down further." She smiled, tapping her pen on the desk. "Tell me about the gallery. What is the building worth, and what's the value of the inventory? What does your balance sheet reflect? What is your profit and loss?"

I thought a moment, searching my mind for information, but I had no answer.

"I am embarrassed to say I can't answer that question. Adrien bought the building, and he's the only one with access to the inventory and financial information," I replied, which garnered a raised eyebrow.

Chloe interrupted and answered for me. "Izzy had opened

TWO

the gallery to showcase up-and-coming artists when they married. It was her dream. Michelle, it was all her; her vision and her sweat and hard work that got the gallery off the ground. It was a place people gathered, for fun and inspiration from other artists, and Isabella thrived there. But over time, Adrien turned it from Bohemian to a fine art gallery. Everything was about status. Who shopped and browsed there—it was all about the money. I think it was about two years ago, he talked her into moving the gallery to where it is now. It took a while for the negotiations and funding to come through, but he got what he wanted. Now, she is in the highest price per-square-foot section in Paris, catering to the rich and famous. With that move, came some big named artists' paintings for offer. In fact, you can't even view them in the gallery without an appointment. What type of bullshit is that?" she said, and looked to me for verification. I nodded.

"We know that he has several warehouses where he stores collections, but we don't know all the locations. We know of two in Switzerland; one or both are a freeport, and that's used for a tax advantage," she continued. A proverbial Wikipedia of information. I suppose, over the years, she had absorbed all my chatter. And, as she says, she is a money person.

Taking a breath, she continued. "But let's get real. People store stolen artifacts and paintings in places like that, and there is no main inventory taken when a load is brought in. So, for all we know, he is storing an arsenal of guns or crates of drugs."

"I don't understand, Isabella. It's your gallery, but you have no access to it?" Michelle asked. When she put it like that, it did sound ridiculous.

"All right, cards on the table here, Michelle. You know I do not sugarcoat anything," Chloe started, garnering a chuckle from Michelle. "Adrien's picture can be found next to control freak in the urban dictionary. Frankly, I call him the puppet master and, lately, it feels like he is jerking Izzy's strings to do a dance, more and more.

"I mean, why can't she have access to financial information? Why can't she have the access code to the inventory? He tells her she is irresponsible and can't be trusted, but that is untrue. Izzy and I used to talk global finances and argue about things, like the value of the International Monetary Fund. And now she can't be trusted with a balance sheet?"

Michelle sat back and thought a moment.

"It's evident that Adrien will most likely not concede in what is a fair share to you. From his behavior, that is obvious. Since he has such tight control of things, I am willing to offer an opinion that he has assets you are not aware of, and will try to keep hidden." Of course, that not only made sense, but was probably true.

"Michelle, that is exactly what I told Izzy. I mean, the man earns a good living as a surgeon and lecturer. However, the money the man has access to raises questions no one seems to care to ask. The apartment cost millions, as did the gallery. Sure, there is a mortgage, but come on. She apparently is the sole owner of both, but has no idea who holds the mortgage credit," she offered.

"Wait, what? Why is it in your name, but you know nothing about this?" Michelle asked, leaning forward. "It's always good to have titled property. But with that comes enormous responsibility. Do you have any idea where the funds came from to purchase it?"

"I don't know. He brought papers home, and I signed them. I trusted him and had no reason to question him. He said that if anyone were to sue him for medical wrongdoings, that he didn't want them to be able to take his assets. He had me sign another document prepared by his lawyer that had me turn over

TWO

ownership to him. He told me it was for taxation purposes. I believe his attorney retains those papers," I replied.

Chloe's whisper broke the silence. "Bastard."

"Isabella, if he was sued, more than likely insurance from his practice or the hospital would cover it. Except, of course, unless it was of a criminal nature. Do we have any reason to believe he has committed any crimes?" she asked.

People in Egypt, dead, floated in my mind. "No," I replied.

"Okay. Isabella, if you are serious about the divorce," she started, and waited for my nod in affirmation, "then we need a plan."

Chloe and Michelle waited for me to respond.

"I'm serious and I'm ready." I didn't sound convinced because was I ready for, not a fight or battle, but all-out war?

"I don't want to tip him off that we are looking for his assets because he'll try to hide them further. Offshore accounts are naturally difficult to track, but I have an investigator who has worked miracles finding these types of assets. Do you have access to the paper you signed?" she asked. I shook my head no.

"Do you have life insurance policies? If so, I'll need those. Sometimes the application provides valuable information," she said.

"I'm sure we do, but as Chloe said, Adrien has control of all documents and finances." My shoulders involuntary tightening up around my neck.

"Okay, here is what I suggest. Your credit, I am confident, is stellar. Open a credit card in your name, and pay our fees with that card. Your husband will not be alerted by a bank withdrawal that you have retained us. I am sending my investigator, Richard, an email to meet with you as soon as possible. He worked for Europol for years and still maintains contacts—they'll be an invaluable resource to us. I'd like you, and Chloe, if you wish, to meet with him and provide every scrap of information you can. Search your memory, make notes of anything, usual or unusual. You never know where something can lead. Do you think he is having an affair?" She concentrated on her notepad, continuing to jot notes.

"Who would have that pompous ass?" Chloe popped off, without filtering her thoughts.

"Chloe, that is not being helpful," Michelle responded.

"No, I do not. How would this investigation work?" I asked.

"You'll give my investigator access to your joint funds, and since what's yours is his and his is yours, that covers a large spectrum. If we can't find something we believe he has access to, when we file the papers, he must produce it," she said. "Richard will be discrete and thorough."

"Okay, as long as Adrien does not find out too soon. He's been very irritable lately," I advised. This elicited an eyebrow raise from Chloe, but no comment.

"Normally, Richard can find information on even the most recalcitrant husband to nudge them toward an agreement instead of a drawn-out battle. He may, on occasion, follow him. So, as best you can, provide Richard with Adrien's daily schedule—he might decide to follow on random days. If he is going out of the country, let us know, and Richard has a protocol he follows. You'd be surprised at what we find when husbands are out of the country," she offered.

I suppose I would.

"I'll apply for the credit card today and will send a payment to you as soon as they supply the information to me. Should I call your secretary or you with the information?" The enormity of what I was about to do suddenly seemed real.

"Wait," Chloe interrupted with her hand in the air. "Iz, could you show us the bottle of pills he has you taking?"

TWO

I did as requested, handing the pill bottle to her.

"Michelle, Google this. Desoxyn."

Michelle was soon reading off the side effects, of which I had each and every one.

"Isabella, you need to taper off these. The prescribing information says you can't discontinue taking them abruptly. And naturally, I'm no doctor, but these pills are for people with attention deficit disorder. Unless diagnosed, I don't see why he should be giving you methamphetamines." Michelle frowned.

"He says I'm forgetful." I felt like I'd been kicked in the stomach.

"Again, I would taper off and get an opinion from someone other than Adrien. These could be the cause of the forgetfulness, and not the cure for it." Michelle held her hand out for the bottle of pills. "I'm going to keep a few pills and have them analyzed, if that's okay."

After completing the formalities and meeting with Richard—who was able to see us immediately—we left to search for a restaurant for a late lunch. The awkward silence continued until after we were seated and had ordered.

"I withheld information from Michelle. I actually do think Adrien may be doing something illegal." I opened the conversation, then wondered why I blurted that out.

"You mean, like selling drugs on the side?" Her eyebrows raised with her voice, then we both looked around quickly, to make sure no one heard.

"To be honest, I had not thought of that, but I suppose that could be a possibility. I have heard bits and pieces of conversations but can't put it all together." I had no proof. What if Adrien was right, and there's something wrong with my internal thinking mechanism? Maybe I have a chemical imbalance, or my synapses aren't firing correctly. Maybe that's why I needed the medication.

"What are you thinking?" Chloe leaned forward to maintain privacy.

"I can't be sure, but I think it is something medical. Or maybe something to do with real estate or property issues." Thinking that was crazy, I waved my hand dismissively. "Forget it. I'm just being hypersensitive as Adrien says. Let's enjoy lunch."

"Izzy, you drive me crazy sometimes. Do you hear yourself? 'Adrien says this,' and 'Adrien says that.' Not everything that asshole says is gospel. He's an arrogant, narcissistic dickwad that you'll do well to get rid of. He has gotten worse over the last two years. There has always been an intensity to him. But lately, he is wound so tight he's ready to snap.

"Think of the bright new beginning you can have ahead of you. You can follow *your* dream, not his. You will be able to blaze your own path, not follow ten steps behind him, on his path." She seemed to be revving up, and I was not in an emotional place to agree or disagree because damn it, I was ambivalent and confused. I was afraid of a new start and feared change.

"Chlo, I am desperate for the chocolate cake here. If you go off on a tear, and start raising your voice and spewing profanity, we will be tossed out. So, can you save your rant until after dessert, or ask for the check and get the dessert to take away," I begged.

"Good plan. Maybe if I make a big enough scene, they will ask us to leave and be happy to pick up the bill. That's good thinking, Iz." She smiled. Although the day she would dine and dash would be, like, never.

"I'll behave. Promise me you'll fully cooperate with the investigator. I live to see the day that Adrien must write you a check. Can't you see him wincing from the pain? I can. I, for one, live for that moment. He'll blow a gasket." Chloe was nothing

TWO

but gleeful planning the demise of Adrien.

"You're watching too much American TV, Chlo. Pop a gasket?" I questioned, with a raised brow.

"I'm diverse." She shrugged and then dug into her salad. "You didn't answer me. You promise to cooperate?"

"I promise." I didn't share my fear with her what snake or snakes would crawl out from under the rocks as they were turned over, one by one.

CHAPTER ELEVEN

BEN

I ANTICIPATED RECEIVING a call yesterday from Cillian with an update. Glancing down at the screen, I was pleased to see his name appear.

"Good morning, Cillian. I hope you're having a pleasant morning." I extended my normal courtesy, although I wanted to get right to the heart of the matter.

"Morning, Ben. And it's good except for the miserable weather and everyone's hair-trigger tempers." He chuckled. "I held off calling you until I'd gathered enough intel for an informative chat. Stop me with questions along the way." He paused a moment and I heard papers shuffling.

"Before I start, how did the meeting go with the Armonds?" It was always tricky deciding how much information to share with other agencies. I hadn't physically met this man, but because our governments interfaced, we were supposed to assume everyone shared a common goal. Get the bad guys. Unfortunately, at times, the bad guys hid on the same teams. My gut said O'Reilly was a good guy.

TWO

"I found it productive. I think my meeting will make more sense when I discuss it, if you start from your end. It's hard to gauge from news reports and departmental briefings how bad things are in other sectors. You are coming from overseas, so how about giving me an overview of how bad the damage is from an outsider perspective?" I inquired.

He blew out a breath. "London is an absolute mess, as I am sure Paris is as well. Not as chaotic as it could be.

"The uncertainty and fear of the unknown is the terror people have lived with every day starting with the IRA attacks through the radical Islamic attacks.

"From what I'm told, transportation options are better here than Paris. The subterranean level train system saved a lot of destruction and interruption of service.

"Now, getting to the issue at hand. Roselov's gallery. The gallery was blown from the inside out. It was a definite high-pressure explosion, and not a fire from some type of flammable material.

"Her Majesty's chief inspector of the fire department has been over the place, top to bottom. Or is it the fire brigade? I don't remember. The jet lag is catching up. Anyway, the fire investigation premised it was a faulty pipe, as many buildings in the area are old. They didn't find any incompetent pipes or joints. The building was new. The investigators haven't accepted it wasn't caused from a rotted pipe nor could they find a break or burst area. They could not find any type of accelerant nor indication it was started mechanically. For now, it's assumed an intentional interference with the gas lines.

"Did you know that even with a relatively small leak, let's call it about five percent, a natural gas leak is enough of a threshold to cause an explosion? If you light a match or a spark of any kind ignites, it can cause the gas to blow. Our explosives guy talked to the Brits, and it appears to be the same signature as the safe house in the US was blown. I can't tell you all the specifics because the guy was throwing a lot of physics terms at me, but the bottom line is, I believe it is the same people, and it has Russia written all over it. Although that is purely speculation."

"I'm jotting notes. An accelerant fire was ruled out, gas leak from a mechanical problem ruled out, and the working hypothesis is someone intentionally interfered with the gas lines." I stopped him to get the basics. "Sorry, Ben, I sometimes go off on a tangent. Next, and this is where it gets interesting. There was very little inventory in the place. I'm not willing to guess the value of the inventory. I know there wasn't a lot of little physical inventory based on the investigation. At first blush, it looked as if the place had been packed with inventory. But the way the explosion occurred, it blasted from the center outward, causing a lot of wood splintering. So, instead of large chunks of wood, it appeared more was around before the explosion because of the smaller fragments. There was a lot of glass around the floor from vases exploding, some of them had melted together. And there was charred debris over some paintings from the ceiling falling.

"The canvases were not as plentiful as you would expect in a show gallery. Those not blown apart were burned to a crisp. No one will be able to determine what each painting represented or who painted it. They were basically blobs of paint with holes in the canvas. You get the picture. They'll be identified from an inventory sheet by the owner. Mrs. Armond has taken ownership as of the last three months. We also have Roselov in custody. As far as our intel is concerned, she's never stepped foot in the place. Questioning Mrs. Armond should be an interesting conversation." Cillian paused the conversation.

I let the information sink in and added, "That conversation will be of great interest. Neither Dr. nor Mrs. Armond were

TWO

acting out of the norm when we met, so I decided to inquire about the Roselov gallery at the end of the visit. Dr. Armond was far more interested. When I revealed the explosion, Dr. Armond ended our meeting abruptly. I called the London team notifying them he was likely heading that way. Did you catch him up there by the gallery, snooping around?" Our people hadn't seen him around the area.

"No. But once the Metropolitan London Police got your information, they sent someone to St Pancras station to scout out the trains and watch for Armond. They identified and followed him. He went to a central London hotel. He sat at the bar area where he met with a man, possibly Middle Eastern, but could be Israeli as well.

"The Met guy thought he recognized the man he was meeting as Avigad Abed. This Abed guy had been flagged on some of the UK's registries and our agencies, so truth be told, he could have roots in the UK. Homeland Security has a decent file on him, but there was nothing worthy of detaining him for questioning. Our information yielded that he's crossed to Canada and Mexico from the US three times. Give me a minute . . . yes, here it is . . . He's on watch for possible sex and human trafficking, so he's been tagged." Cillian's information was thorough. Abed lurking on the outskirts of this investigation was suspicious.

I sat and took a few minutes to digest the information he'd provided. There were several possibilities as to why the gallery was blown up. But in the end, it left us at a dead end.

"Our trail and the evidence point to the gallery as a money-laundering front." I was thinking out loud, but making a statement. "It was necessary to destroy the evidence to conceal the paintings were fake or stolen." I tapped my spoon on the cup, an annoying habit I had when irritated.

"Unless the people blowing it up didn't know the paintings

were moved and were acting on orders to get rid of evidence." Cillian's theory held weight.

"Yes. Agreed. Also, we can't rule out insurance fraud. Although, that would be low on my list." I scratched my chin. It was something I did when I didn't agree with something, another tell of mine. I wasn't buying into this at all.

"Considering the people involved, destroying the gallery could have been to send a message. Possibly to Roselov that if he talks, the gallery is just the start of a destruction rampage.

"Throw into the mix that we have Armond meeting with a known trafficker. What does a trafficker have in common with a doctor who deals art? Why would those paths cross? I seriously doubt he is trying to unload art on this man." I pondered that for a moment. "Are you heading down to Paris?"

"No. There are no more leads to follow from my end of the investigation. I've tied up everything I came for, but I'm leaving with nothing but theories. At least when we interview Roselov further, we have some leverage to gauge his reactions.

"The Met has reams of CCTV to review. But until we can tie it to funding the attacks somehow, I don't see it needing my daily attention."

"I want to know who tipped that Swiss banker into not keeping the meet. If we could have gained access to the papers he had, that would have been the gateway to taking a look at the funds we can't connect now. Somehow, my gut says those funds played a part in the attacks."

Our conversation had veered into territory I had no control over.

"Do you know when Isabella will be questioned about the gallery?" I planned to meet with her shortly after that happened.

I heard Cillian release a breath. "No, I'm not in the loop on that, sorry. I don't know what the plan is, or who will contact her.

TWO

She will be questioned in London, but then someone from Paris said they wanted to be part of the interview as well. The company structure caused many concerns voiced by the French contingent. Since no insurance claim has been initiated, the insurance company is holding payout until the arson investigation wraps."

"Interesting. No insurance claims. I'm disappointed there wasn't more revealed. I'll let you know as information becomes available from this end," I said. "I have an appointment with Isabella to view a painting at the gallery. If anything major comes up, I'll contact you. Oh, that Swiss lawyer—can you send me his details? I think your people had more feedback on him."

"Will do," Cillian replied. "I'm making a note right now."

"Safe trip," I said, and we disconnected.

I turned to drop a bagel into the toaster, and the phone rang again. Richard Dupont's name came up. That indeed brought a smile to my face.

"Richard! I haven't heard from you in ages. Ready to give up that cushy investigator job and come back into the light?"

Richard, my partner for as long as I could remember, never fit in with the bureaucracy of a government agency. Without telling me, plausible deniability and all, he was now partnering in the private sector with people who walked the other razor-thin line and leaned toward a bit of criminal in their investigation.

"No, I'm good where I am, thanks, Ben. But considering you owe me for those premium soccer tickets, I need to call in a favor." Richard knew I would never turn my old partner down. A lot of water under that bridge. And I would not trade a day of it.

"Jesus. How about I buy you an insanely expensive dinner instead?" I tossed back at him as my coffee finished brewing. I poured a cup and set it out, ready to attempt to quietly eat the crunchy bagel and drink the too-strong coffee. The French and their French roast. I was not a fan.

"No, but thanks for the offer. We have a new client who's a friend of a long-standing client, and I need you to do a small amount of under the table investigating." I hated when he did this; it was such a waste of resources. However, a ten-year friendship must count for something.

"All right, hold on. Let me get a pen and paper." Living in an apartment that was a cover had its drawbacks. There were little things, like random paper pads that were not available. A pen and napkins would have to make do.

As I rummaged for them, he continued. "So, where are you working out of now? Brussels? Still behind a desk at The Hague? Or on an assignment?"

"Need to know, Richard. And you don't need to know. Now, what's this poor tortured soul's name?" Hopefully, a quick run-through of the name would reveal nothing in our data bases.

"Armond. Let me spell it, A-r-m-o-n-d. And not Almond, like the nut. First name of wife, Isabella; she's our client. Husband is Adrien, he's a physician." I heard him clicking his pen, one of his tells that something agitated him.

I was so stunned my head jerked. Surely, he must have found out my assignment from Jill, and this is a joke.

"Sorry, Richard, one more time, please. Did you say Isabella and Adrien Armond? And Isabella is your client seeking a divorce?" I could barely keep an even voice level.

"Right. I met with her and I have a dossier built with the information I have already. I can email that to you. Would that work?" He didn't laugh. There was no "got you" moment. This was a real matter. He was serious.

I couldn't wrap my head around this coincidence. It was a lucky coincidence. I'd hit the jackpot, the motherlode.

"Yes, of course, Rich. Give me your thoughts on the wife." I wanted some ground level information. Unless Rich had gone

TWO

totally off the rails, his assessments were always spot-on. Part of me knew this could jeopardize our friendship after he found out I was working for the other team in a sense. I was investigating his client as a potential criminal target. He was trying to capture as much in a divorce settlement for her as possible. This investigation could potentially end in the arrest of his client after all the dots were connected. Information he was giving me, I could use against her. But in the end, I had a duty to Europol; a higher duty than to Richard. Especially if she had any part in funding these attacks through money laundering.

"Let's start with preliminaries. She's a beautiful woman, and if you need a picture—"

I interrupted Richard, eager to learn what he knew. "No, that's not necessary. Fast forward, and give me the usual suspects." Pen in hand, I was ready to take notes.

"What do you mean?" He was confused by my urgency.

"Would you describe her as antisocial? Irrational, but sane? Is she indifferent to fellow humans, irresponsible, and self-centered? Maybe she is manipulative and deliberative? Is she full of guile, but outwardly amiable, as long as it suits her objective? Would you tag her as cunning and emotionless, extroverted, articulate, and highly narcissistic? Does she take great care with her physical health and appearance? Dress herself neatly, whether in business or casual attire. What's your take?" I stopped to take a breath after my exhaustive rapid-fire questioning.

There was a carefully measured silence. Then more silence. Then, Richard spoke with hesitation.

"Jesus, Ben, you're asking me if this woman portrays the characteristics of an organized psychopathic killer. What the hell? This is a nice lady who wants a divorce. From what I gather, she is married to someone who could possibly fit into that block you just laid out. I haven't met him or worked him up yet.

However, this lady is sweet. She just lost her family in the attacks. She's scattered, but from what her friend Chloe says, that's not the norm for her." I could hear him scratching his beard scruff through the phone, worried.

"Rich, you know me. I sometimes get a little intense. Sorry. You have a good feel for this lady?" I asked, now feeling embarrassed for going overboard in my excitement.

"Yeah, I do, or I wouldn't be calling you to look into the husband. Can we focus on him?" Now he was irritated.

"Of course. I'm ready when you are. Tell me what you have." I took a deep, stabilizing breath and allowed him to continue.

Richard repeated information back that I already knew. Nothing new. He stopped. "Any questions?"

It took me a minute to get out of my undercover head, and back into my helpful friend head.

"Um, no, I think I've got it. And it's all in the report you sent over?" I affirmed.

"Every scrap I've been able to dig up. We want to bury this guy, Ben. He's not going to turn loose his millions easily, and I need some leverage," he said. "This lady doesn't need to be tied up for two years, waiting for a trial date. We need to nudge him toward an amicable settlement."

"Rich, you know you can count on me to turn over every rock I can on this guy. When are you getting into the inventory?" I asked.

"This weekend. She overheard him talking to someone named Avigad Abed. He wanted him in India—maybe he's another doctor. I'm not sure if Abed is important, but I'll check around," he said.

Abed. I about shouted his name. It felt like my head would explode. My God, Abed the trafficker. Why were they going to

TWO

India?

"You think any of the paintings are hot or forgeries?" I pushed to find out if Isabella had revealed anything in confidence to her *avocat*.

"I have no idea, but we're digging into the places with a fine-tooth comb," he said. "I'll have digital and video documentation for when we need it. I'm even thinking of installing cameras in there to keep track of things."

"Okay, let me get on this after I read your report. When you have more information, shoot it over and I'll run everything through the databases." This was too good to be true. "And, Richard, I wouldn't put a guy on either of them if I was you. If the husband finds out and gets spooked, it might cause some unpleasantries." I didn't need my presence showing up in any reports, and we didn't need outside interference with our investigation.

"Thanks again, Ben. I hate imposing on you like this, but there's something about this lady I like. And something about the husband I want to break. When you're in Paris, I owe you a dinner." Rich's gut was always right.

"No worries. I'll work on this and get back to you." We exchanged pleasantries and disconnected.

Should I call Cillian or someone about the Avigad connection going to India? No, can't do that because it would raise questions for my source. I'll have to work this through and then flip the lid off, reporting I found it while digging through information. Oh, what a tangled web.

CHAPTER TWELVE

ADRIEN

"YOU DON'T TELL me what I must do, Avigad. I won't be leaving for India until several things have occurred. Which, I remind you, should already have occurred." I'd had it with his demands and last-minute requests.

The temerity of him to think I wouldn't be upset that a chunk of my fee remained unpaid. I never was anything but clear with him that the only reason I did this was for the money. Wealth is the ability to fully experience life. I was no longer the sad little boy with the drunk mother.

"First, I haven't been reimbursed in total for the Cairo fiasco. I want that money before I commit to another job. Second, I agreed to a temporary pre-dated document transfer of Roselov's gallery to our company umbrella until he returned. That, in itself, is a serious crime—document falsification. It appears he won't be returning any time soon, and now Isabella and I are in the crosshairs of the authorities. To make matters worse, the gallery is the focus of an investigation that puts me at risk. Third, I made it clear to you that I wouldn't be traveling outside of

TWO

France any longer. The only reason I entertained accepting your proposal for this India trip was the fee you proposed, with the stipulation the Cairo fee was paid immediately for the balance due. However, my new stipulation that I be paid prior to leaving the country hasn't been fulfilled. I don't see a deposit of the funds in my account. Therefore, I will *not* be on a plane to India."

"Adrien, you'll be on the plane. At the conclusion of the surgery, you'll be remunerated, as has occurred for the last two years. Cairo was an unfortunate incident. Now we have a matter much more pressing." Avigad tipped his cup of Turkish coffee to his lips.

I studied him, the man who had afforded me the opportunity to amass enormous wealth in such a small time. That wealth wouldn't comfort me if I sat in some third world jail for performing illegal organ surgery. Recent donors were getting more and more sketchy, and now we had children lined up whose parents have offered to donate their offspring's organs. Not mentioning the moral or ethical aspect, the children weren't old enough to offer their consent.

It was clear that when opportunity presented itself during these organ harvests, people were left to die purposefully for their organs, rather than attempt further resuscitation efforts. Avigad's machination wasn't a donor program, it was a death sentence. Money and nefarious reasoning aside, I took my Hippocratic oath seriously. However, money was money and it was my intention to retire this year. I was finished. My goal was to live the good life off the money I'd accumulated. If I became bored I could offer myself as a speaker. Or author a book on any topic I chose to research. I'd no longer have the need for the art gallery to launder money or need for Isabella to be my front. A sail around the world on a luxury yacht sounded appealing. The Albanians would never find me in the vast ocean.

The proposal in my estimation was unworkable. The damning part was his request that I sneak into Iran to perform a surgery using the organ of a female into a male. In Iran, that surgery was prohibited and could have resulted in my death. The risks he expected me to take lately were not worth jail or death. And now he spoke to me like I'm his employee, ordering me to perform his bidding. Who Avigad was allegiant to politically or even religiously was anyone's guess. To me, his only interest was money—whoever had the money had his allegiance and he would fly their flag.

How can I get free of him? Dare I reach across and punch him with enough force at any number of points to kill him? Searching his head and neck, I assessed my options. Which would be the most effective? The summit of the nose, the Adam's apple, the temple? Or possibly a hard punch to the chest, to throw him into arrhythmia. No, that would be too tricky. I touched the scalpel in my pocket. A swift jab and slice to the carotid would cause exsanguination quickly. We were in a secluded booth. Would anyone notice? Would he struggle and fight?

I said nothing as he leaned into the padded back of the booth. His face morphed into a medieval expression, spittle gathering at the corner of his lips. He was tense, and he should be.

"Isabella has outlived her usefulness." He waited for a reaction. I wouldn't grace him with one.

Was this the card he was playing to keep me in line? I had to admit she had become a liability and under other circumstances I would have disposed of her already, but I stayed silent. I would not engage.

"I told you weeks ago that you needed to take care of this matter. You assured me that it would be dealt with, and I trusted you. The British authorities have been trying to reach her as the gallery owner, and I cannot hold them off any longer. She cannot

TWO

be allowed to meet with them, Adrien. There is no other option. Dead men tell no tales." His eyes never left mine. I felt as if he was calculating the risk of killing me here if I disagreed, exactly as I'd calculated the risk of killing him.

I weighed how much information I should share with him. Where once we had been partners, now we were traveling into adversarial territory.

"As you are well aware, all the property I own is in Isabella's name on the public record. Robert my attorney holds the documents that confirm her transferring ownership back to me in his safe. I'll concede your point that the authorities' interest to speak to her about the London gallery could be problematic. That was a mistake on your part. If you had consulted with me, I would've suggested another route. Now we indeed are in a bind." Angry, I let that sit.

He let out a breath. "Good, then we agree. I'll leave it to you to dispose of her."

"No, Avigad, we are not in agreement. If she dies, then my life becomes the focus and I become a person of interest to the authorities. We have been down this road before, and my path hasn't changed. I'm the only one to gain by her death on paper.

"I have anticipated things devolving, and initiated a plan. With some drugs and mind manipulation, she's ready to tip into a mental breakdown. She questions everything she does and believes she's slowly losing her mind. The maid has come to me with worries over her misplacing things. The doorman has confided in me that she orders cars to pick her up and when they arrive, she argues with him she didn't order the car. The grocer has contacted me that she has, for two months, forgotten to pay his bill, and the bank has advised me she is thousands of dollars overdrawn. I have overheard her telling Chloe that packages arrive she doesn't remember ordering, and the cook has confided in me he is concerned that she's having conversations with her dead mother. I have it in hand." My words were spoken with finality.

His neck tightened, lips pulling back to bare his brown stained teeth. He leaned closer to me across the table to avoid anyone seeing or hearing him. He held my gaze with intense focus. There was no doubt in my mind Avigad was the most dangerous man on the planet.

"Dead by next week. Make it happen," he ordered.

"I repeat—On what planet, Avigad, will I, the husband, not be the one they put under scrutiny?" His demands were incredulous. "If I am under scrutiny, I will not be able to freely move about, and that includes leaving the country."

"I've thought about this at great length, and I thought you would have as well. If I believe you, and she is as you say, acting odd, then suicide is of course a legitimate outcome. People overdose from drugs, drown in a bathtub, slip and fall and hit their head. Make your choice, if you don't like suicide."

"Again, you don't think a thorough investigation would be performed? And one major obstacle to suicide is that the life insurance policy precludes payment. I will not leave five million on the table for the personal policy, and fifteen million as the key person in the business. Now, have we ended this conversation?" I tired of him trying to dictate my life.

"You'll arrange for her and her friend to take a weekend vacation, and I'll arrange her death on foreign soil. We're running out of time. The British will certainly be making a personal appearance here in the next few days. And how do you see that going?" Avigad pounded his hand on the table lightly to emphasize that last sentence.

"Actually, I see no problem with the British showing up." I shrugged.

"And how is that?" He straightened his jacked and gained

TWO

his composure, stopping to pour himself another cup of that vile coffee.

"You see, Avigad, I believe in the organic nature of life. I have arranged for psychotropic mushrooms and LSD of a significant quantity to be placed in her evening meals. However, I need her coherent to take one last meeting for an art deal—that will be her final business meeting. The client appears to like her, and I want that deal sealed.

"Once that is complete, I plan to add the psychotropic drugs to the mix she's already taking. I would say, by the time anyone speaks to her, she'll be a raving lunatic, poor woman. Or God willing, catatonic and in need of round the clock psychiatric care. I'll have documentation of visual and auditory hallucinations. I'll have enough evidence to have her committed to an institution and take over our assets as her guardian. How much of an investigation can there be when she is institutionalized? And I, of course, know nothing of her illegal activities. As a busy physician, I've left the business to her and had no idea of any illegal activities." I brushed the crease of my pants. It was a foolproof plan, with little risk.

He stroked his short beard and thought. I watched his eyes sweep the room until they landed back on mine.

"Won't the drugs show up in a drug screen at a hospital?" he asked. This was a move in the right direction, as he was contemplating the effectiveness of the plan. At least he was off the murder attempt.

"Does it matter?" I was pushing hard for this angle.

"What do you mean, 'does it matter'?" His voice was harsh and raised now.

"People dabble in drugs all the time. You are not asking the right question." I knew his mind clipped at a fast pace, but I would have to feed him the answer.

"Which is? Adrien, my time is valuable. Do not play games," he ordered. His voice raised enough for the people a short distance away to glance at us for a second.

"The question should be, would it be questionable for a woman who has anti-anxiety and antidepressant drugs in her bloodstream over the recommended dose to also use other drugs?" I knew the answer, but I waited for Avigad to catch up.

"Does she even know she has these anxiety and depression drugs floating around her body? Isabella doesn't seem the type of woman who would seek help." He was thoughtful again.

"She is taking medication I hand to her, and that's all you need to know. I have a plan. I'll execute the plan. The dosage I have planned will seriously alter her brain chemically, for a long time. My hope is that it will be permanent. She may never regain the full use of her mind after ingesting the cocktail of drugs I have planned. At the proper time, I'll file for divorce, based on her placing herself in this position from an overdose of illegal drug usage." There was the pure and simple plan.

"You must make this happen before the authorities start to pressure to see her." Avigad shifted and sat back in his seat.

"And whose fault is that, Avigad? I don't understand why the gallery had to be destroyed," I threw back. After all, he was the one who had caused the problem.

"Roselov is in the custody of the Americans and with that comes certain risks that have to be managed." He apparently felt that was enough.

"Yes, I suppose there would be questions raised when they started to examine the contents of his gallery." I knew I was close to crossing the line. "It was a fortunate occurrence that my wife had purchased the gallery from him before he left for America. Fortunate indeed, because that blocked the authorities from having a reason to seize his assets. Am I right? However, it was not

TWO

our good fortune to come under scrutiny from the destruction of it." I drummed my fingers in agitation.

"I must admit, the execution of the explosion follow-up plan was not optimal. The person involved has been removed from the equation. We must deal with the fallout now. Your plan has merit. I do, however, like to cut off all loose ends, Adrien, because just tying it off can lead to eventual unraveling." He took another sip from his coffee, while I pondered again how I could discretely kill him right now.

"We will go with your plan. However, if I see the plan wobble, there will be no more discussion. You'll fly back to India. You do drive a hard bargain, but I'll concede. What account do you want the money deposited into?" He pulled his phone from his jacket pocket.

"I want to receive my remuneration by a different method this time." With the financial watchdogs scrutinizing financial institutions after the attacks, I didn't want to raise any alarms.

"And how would that be?" Irritation laced his question.

"Gold and cash in various denominations." I followed with, "I have a list of the banks I want it transferred to, and have calculated the gold, based on today's daily value."

He stared at me, assessing my commitment, and then responded, "Done."

I had no doubt that he could retrieve the gold within hours; the cash might take a day or so.

"Why the change?" His eyebrow was lifted, making him look sinister instead of inquisitive.

"Since the attack, I would assume banks, even offshore, are tracking money closer. You have hundreds of banks to spread your money to fly under the radar, that gives you some breathing room. My choice is limited. Gold is a fluid commodity and cash spread around a large number of banks is anonymous as to ownership," I replied, not anxious to divulge too much.

"Why not art or a boat, which you can then resell?" His question was unworthy even for him, when he knew the simple answer.

"Seriously, Avigad, you insult me. A title is always traceable. And owning two galleries, I have all the art I'd ever need." I sat, my face void of emotion.

"Careful, Adrien, do not fly too close to the flame. Roselov's collection, which is safely tucked away, is mine."

The proverbial gloves were coming off. He was ready for a brawl, but this topic was a fight for another day.

"Of course, Avigad." I smiled. He smiled back, but neither of our smiles reached our eyes.

I slid, ready to exit the booth, when I caught the frosty stare of a man three tables away. How long had he been there? I don't remember him entering the café or sitting near us, but he had breakfast in front of him he'd already consumed. We held each other in a locked stare until Avigad exited the booth, and we both walked out the door.

My mind was diverted from the man when Avigad said, "Use the Canadian passport."

He left the café and walked in one direction, and I walked the other.

That Canadian passport had been used too much lately and was undoubtedly leaving a footprint. I needed to think on this a little more. Soon, no passport would be in use. This would be my last mission.

CHAPTER THIRTEEN

ISABELLA

"NOW DON'T FORGET, Isabella. I have chosen the paintings we want to sell him." He sighed and wait for me to acknowledge him as he spoke. "Look at me, stay focused. All you must do is smile at him and hand him the papers. The papers are in a black leather folder on the desk. The provenance for each painting is in there, along with the invoice for the transaction."

I sat slumped in my chair, still wearing my nightgown and robe. I was distracted by his words, but couldn't focus on what he'd said.

"Jesus, look at you. You are a mess. Get up and clean yourself up. I'll help you dress. Isabella, get it together. People are talking about you." Adrien walked to my chair and pulled me to an almost sitting position.

My mouth felt full of sand, and my limbs didn't want to obey my commands. Did I care if people talked about me? No. What were they saying?

"I'm fine, Adrien. I'm just feeling disoriented. My head feels like it's packed with cotton. Maybe I'm coming down with something." I steadied myself, climbing out of the chair with his help.

"Listen. I have surgeries lined up all day today. After you finish with Jaager, come home and have a lie-down. Tomorrow—are you listening to me, Isabella? Look at me, not out the window. Tonight, after surgery, I leave for the weekend. I've spoken with Thomas about meals. My God, can't you focus?" Did he shake me?

He was right. I felt as if I had no control over my neck. It swayed forward and down, then flopped sideways and back. Was I awake or asleep?

"Here, lie back down. I'll prepare the shower." Irritation infused his voice. I watched as he left for the bathroom and heard the shower start in the distance. Such a nice shower. So much water from so many heads coming out of the wall. And rain from the bathroom ceiling. I smiled at the thought. I only needed a few more minutes of sleep.

Damn. Torrents of wet needles were hitting my face and body. Pricks like tiny ice picks were assaulting me. Adrien was behind me, holding me up around my waist, to face the onslaught of water. In my mind, I screamed for him to stop the needles, but no sound came from my mouth. I was only able to produce a low moan. My legs gave way and we slid to the floor. Adrien held me as the water beat down on my head and body, the small pricks of pain now lower on my body.

"Isabella, Isabella. Shit. Isabella." I heard his voice, but it was in a tunnel. Finally, I opened my eyes and everything was in focus. I was back on the bed, naked, but dry. Did he give me an injection? No, it must be the water hitting me like needles I remembered.

"There you are." He hovered over me with some type of medical instrument. Was that a syringe? "Now get up, we have

TWO

little time to spare. We need you dressed and at the gallery, preparing the pictures. You feel better?"

My lips were able to form words, so I suppose I was feeling better. Did I drink anything last night to put me in this condition? Maybe those damn pills? Oh God, yes. I think he gave me three last night. I'm so confused what is wrong with me. Am I losing my mind? Is it grief taking over for my family? Why can't I put things together?

"Yes, I'm feeling better. Can you help me up?" I looked at the carafe of water on my bedside table and it was almost empty. Did I drink all the water? My mouth felt moist, so it would appear so.

"Steady. Sit up a bit. That's right. Now swing your legs over the side." Adrien pulled me forward and to the side until my legs were touching the floor.

"My arm hurts. Did you inject me with something?" I rubbed the area where I felt a slight sting.

"Don't be absurd. What is wrong with you? Are you taking any drugs I need to know about? Street drugs?" He was scolding me.

"Drugs? What are you talking about?" He knows I would never touch drugs, not after I saw what it did to my sister before she went to rehab and got sober. The pain of losing Denise and Mama came flooding back.

"People are talking Isabella, and I think we should make an appointment for you to take a little rest somewhere—" His words were cut short by the shrill ringing of my phone. The screen lit up, notifying me of an unknown London area caller.

Adrien startled a moment, then said, "Let it go to voicemail." I did as he asked. Once the phone stopped ringing, it dinged with a message waiting. He listened to the message. "Nothing to worry about. I'll take care of it." He then deleted the message.

"Now, get up. There's a fresh cup of coffee on the table by

the window. I've laid out your clothes." He gestured in the direction of the clothes. "We're all worried about you, Isabella."

I acknowledged what he said, but could not understand why he said it. Who is worried and why?

"I'm feeling much better. Leave me with the coffee, and you go on. I know you have a busy day ahead." I was eager to be rid of him. Why did my arm still hurt?

"No, I will help you dress. Make sure you get to the gallery, and that you're prepared for Ben. All you have to do is focus on collecting his signature for the wire transfer. The paperwork signing title over to him for the paintings is complete. I'll be back in a few minutes. I will use the other bathroom to dress. If you need anything, press the button." He checked my eyes with a light as if I was a patient. "Good, you look much better."

"Go ahead. I'll finish the coffee. I can dress myself," I assured him, not so convinced myself.

"Okay." He gathered what he needed, then left the room.

I lifted my phone and tapped out a text confirming lunch with Chloe after my meeting with Ben. I touched the icon for the phone, and the tab for voicemail. I scrolled to the deleted messages, and found the last one deleted from London.

I clicked to listen to the message. "Good morning, Madame Armond. This is Detective Inspector Maddox of the London police. I need to set up an appointment for you to meet with us to discuss the incident at the gallery here in London. I hope this is a correct number. We have left several messages on the other number you provided, but have had no response. Please return this call as soon as possible, so we can work toward a completion of the investigation—" He left his details, as well as the case number.

My mind raced. Gallery in London. An incident at a gallery in London. It must be a mistake, and that's why Adrien erased

TWO

it. Should I call Detective Inspector Maddox back or wait and let Chloe listen to it?

I placed my phone in my robe pocket, and decided I'd wait to call the inspector after Chloe listened to the message. After my third cup of coffee, I was ready to dress. It was a bit of a challenge engaging the hooks and eyes on my bra, but after fumbling with my useless hands, I finished.

"Ah, you look ready for the day now, Isabella." Adrien smiled as he walked in the room. He looked fresh, polished, like he owned the world. "Now hurry and put your necklace on. I have calls to make. I'll meet you in the living room in ten minutes."

Assessing me, he appeared satisfied, and left.

AFTER OPENING THE gallery, I reviewed the paperwork Adrien had prepared for Ben's acquisition.

As I dusted the glass counter, I received an acknowledgment from Chloe that lunch was on, and she would meet me at twelve thirty.

At ten thirty sharp, the bell over the door announced the entrance of Ben Jaager. He had a look about him that was wholesome, yet sexy. Brown hair neatly combed, but not overly done, as Adrien's was at times. Clean-shaven with a faint smell of linen, possibly aftershave. He wore a sharp, tailored dark suit and a teal-blue tie, with a crisp white shirt. Ben Jaager was the full package.

"Good morning, Ben. It's good to see you. I hope you're well this morning." I extended my hand to greet him.

The smile that had at first appeared on his face faded as he came closer.

"Isabella, please excuse me for being so forward, but you don't look well. Would you like to sit?" Concern etched his face.

"What? No, no. Thank you so much. I've just had a few

challenging days and odd nights. It's nothing to worry about. I have the paintings here in our showroom for you to view under similar lighting in your home. Would you care to step this way?" I directed him toward the room. I had to close this sale and complete the money transaction. That was my only goal.

"As you wish," he replied, and followed me to the room. I could tell he was still concerned. What was it? My eyes? Were they bloodshot? My posture or pallor? What gave it away?

"Have a seat, Isabella, while I inspect and appreciate these lovely paintings. Are you sure you are well?" he asked again. I nodded and took a seat in the wingback chair.

Ben walked from painting to painting. He stood before each, then closed in an inch from the canvas, studying the brushstrokes. When he reached the fourth, he leaned in to sniff the canvas. What was he doing? He leaned back, and then closed in again.

"Would you mind if I removed this from the wall to inspect the back?" He turned his head to me.

"No, of course not. We want you to have every confidence with your purchase. Would you like a hand?" I moved to the painting.

"No, I've got it." He smiled, reaching for the sides of the frame. It was a nice smile at first, but it quickly dissolved into a straight line. Then it disappeared altogether.

"Isabella, I am not an art expert, so I may be wrong. This painting was painted in the nineteen-fifties. Would that be a correct statement?" He spoke slowly, trying to choose his words carefully it seemed.

"Yes, that's correct." He had the paperwork in front of him, so it was a very odd question.

"Has it recently been cleaned or restored? Maybe it wasn't noted on the paperwork?" He turned the painting around to view

TWO

the back.

"No, of course not. Any type of chemical application or alteration must be noted," I replied. "May I see the provenance?" He handed me the papers, and I reviewed them. There was no notation of an alteration or conservation performed.

"Come here, please," he said softly, as if afraid to spook me. "Close your eyes." I obliged as I swayed a bit. "Now inhale." I did as he requested. "What is your impression?"

I opened my eyes, leaned in, and inhaled again. Paint, possibly acrylic. This canvas was at least fifty years old. There should be no residual smell of paint. He looked at me for an explanation, and I looked back at him.

"And see here on the back." He turned the painting around. My God, could this get any worse. "These nails don't look right." He carefully pointed at the nails in the frame. "Where did this painting come from?"

"Give me a moment, and—" I started toward the computer, and belatedly remembered Adrien had the systems locked down. I didn't have access to the information. "Ben, I'm sorry. Adrien has the system secured, and he's the only one that can access it. He's in surgery all day today. Unfortunately, I can't access that information. Tonight, he's leaving for the weekend, to guest lecture somewhere. It will likely be Monday before I can provide that information to you."

"I understand. And I'm not an art expert by any stretch of the imagination, but this is troubling." His fingers twitched where he held the painting. "Do you personally inspect these paintings?" He placed the painting back on the wall.

"No. Because of the initials D.A. on the bottom of the paperwork, I want to venture a guess this particular one was from an Abu Dhabi private auction. Adrien was involved in the purchase." I had no other recourse but to tell him the truth.

I began to panic. Not only did I not close the deal, but Ben is questioning the authenticity. Adrien will lose his mind.

"If that's the case, the auction house should stand behind their sales if there's any problem. I'm sorry, Isabella, but until we clear this matter up, I'll need to place my order on hold. It certainly is disappointing."

"We could possibly make another recommendation?" I asked, hoping to salvage something of this mess.

He searched my face. What he thought he would discover, I didn't know. Seconds passed before he placed his hand on the small of my back and led me toward the couch.

"I must be frank, Isabella. The provenance of the painting is very troubling. The art world is filled with forgeries, and I'm not in a position to make a mistake and purchase one. The destroyed London gallery you acquired a short time ago, had a quiet reputation for dealing in gray market paintings. So, you can see my trepidation, can't you? I certainly don't mean any insult, it's just, that makes things tricky," he said. A valid explanation, but nonetheless, it was an explanation that Adrien would not accept.

As if an avalanche of snow had broken from a mountain and buried me, I froze. I stared at him, waiting for him to laugh, touch my knee, and say "Just kidding." He didn't.

"What gallery?" My voice was barely above a whisper, even to my own ears.

"The gallery in London that you bought from Mr. Roselov. The one that has been in the news that was destroyed in an explosion." He tilted his head and looked at me closer as his brow furrowed. "Are you sure you're all right? You look a little pale."

My mind raced from room to room in my mind, looking for a door to open with information I needed. I didn't find one. I had no memory or knowledge of buying a gallery. No, that can't be right. I don't own any such gallery.

TWO

"Where did you get such an idea that I own that gallery?" I asked.

"You know, I cannot recall who brought it to my attention. Do you not own it?" His words exposed how surprised he was.

"No, that person is certainly mistaken." My response was immediate, without question.

However, why would the London police be calling me as well? What was going on? Had I lost chunks of my memory, to the point I don't remember purchasing a gallery?

"I hope you don't think me rude, but I'm a little tired. Unfortunately, I suppose our business here today is complete until I can have Adrien address this embarrassing turn of events. I want to assure you this isn't the way I conduct business, Ben. Please accept my apology for wasting your time today." I felt the walls closing in, inch by inch.

"Not a problem, Isabella. When shall I expect a call from you?" Why he would want to do further business with us, I had no idea. "I'm curious, at the very least, to find out the results."

"Monday is the earliest Adrien could start an investigation. I'll let you know when we have some results." I read the concern in his face as he watched embarrassment flood my checks with a furious blush.

He stood, took my hand and thanked me for my time, and left.

My knees almost buckled. I leaned on the desk for support, overwhelmed with questions. I'm possibly in possession of a forgery. A multimillion-euro forgery, a multimillion-euro mistake.

No, that was the least of my worries. Auction houses have errors and omissions policies, and stand behind their sale. If the painting is a forgery, they will stand behind it. My bigger problem was I was possibly experiencing blackouts. If I was losing track of time, what did I do during those blackouts? Did I own a gallery I don't remember purchasing? What would Adrien say when he found out? Where did I get the money to buy it? How did I even know it was for sale? And now that gallery is destroyed. Should I return the London police call? Maybe they have information. No, my instinct said to wait.

My meeting with Ben ended sooner than I expected. With a quick call to Chloe, we decided to meet for lunch earlier, but I didn't disconnect the call without giving her a summary of the troubling events.

"Izzy, he's probably mistaken. The man is an investment banker, not an art expert. What is the likelihood that such a fake would slip past an expert? Slim to none. And this gallery thing is just bizarre. Trust me, Richard will get to the bottom of everything. When he was investigating Michael, he found two bank accounts I had no idea existed. Do you remember that?" Chloe clicked her tongue loudly at the memory of her divorce.

Twenty minutes after I completed my call with Chloe, I left the gallery to meet her. As I left the building, I received a call from Richard. Chloe must be worried and concerned to have called him so quickly. Richard took the information for the painting and assured me he would track down the validity of the ownership.

"CHLO, I DON'T even have the first clue where to start. I was humiliated because he might be right. Can you imagine what will happen if it gets out that I had a forgery on my hands. Ben had asked where the painting came from, and the best I could come up with was a private sale through the Abu Dhabi auction house. You see where this drives me mad? This is my name on documents used for another gallery, and I can't even assure someone that my

TWO

inventory is authentic," I complained.

I was about to continue when the waiter arrived at the table. Richard was behind him. This was a surprise. I had not expected to see him until tomorrow. The waiter stepped aside, so Richard could be seated, and returned with a cup for his coffee.

"Ladies, I am sorry to interrupt your lunch, but I felt that this was time-sensitive. And not something for a telephone conversation." He looked from me to Chloe.

He retrieved an envelope from his inner jacket pocket, and removed papers from inside. Placing them on the table, he turned them toward me.

"Isabella, it would appear that you purchased the Dmitri Roselov gallery through a private sale." I drew a breath and gasped. "However, to be fair and give an honest opinion, the circumstances are sketchy. I showed the documents to Michelle, and we feel there is a possibility the date of purchase may have be falsified and backdated. Normally, once a property is transferred, it must be recorded at once with the public office. Look here"—he pointed to the date of record for the sale—"it wasn't recorded until a week ago. Why the wait?"

I picked up the papers and reviewed them, although the legalese was beyond me.

"Before I even question who or why someone would falsify a document, tell me about the gallery. The only thing I know of this gallery is that we might have bought one or two paintings from them. Or held a painting overnight before it went to auction." Again, I sorted through my hazy thoughts.

"The gallery was owned by Dmitri Roselov for eight years. From what I can determine, it did very well and has an international reach. The negative is that he's rumored to have criminal network connections, possibly including the Russian Mafia. From what I could determine, he wasn't in the market to sell legitimate paintings. His trail shows that he left for the US to retrieve some paintings, and never came back. This is where it gets foggy because the date of sale predates his trip." Richard points, showing me the date of sale and transfer deed.

"Richard, I have had no contact with this man. I would know if I bought a gallery. Money would have been transferred and my signature affixed to some document," I said, and felt I was on firm ground.

"Yes, and that is where sketchy becomes murky. The document was electronically signed. The sale terms agreed on was that the first payment be made ninety days from purchase, so the first payment was coming due. Throw into the mix the gallery was destroyed. The explosion has a whiff of destroying evidence and possible insurance fraud." Again, a measured silence fell between the three of us.

"I have no answers for you, only questions." I could feel my eyes brim with tears. Now would be an appropriate time for a full-blown nervous breakdown. I was going to jail for sure, never to see daylight again. Insurance fraud? For a building I didn't even own.

"Ladies, I hesitate to say this because I don't know how you will receive it. However, we could be heading into some turbulent waters. Your divorce may have branched into a criminal matter, with you taking a hit head-on." He waited for me to digest his words. "I'm going to share something with you and hope I'm not overstepping," he continued, cautious.

"No, go ahead, please," I replied, hoping this nightmare would end.

"This stays between us, yes?" We affirmed. "Until three years ago, I was an agent with Europol." He paused, and Chloe said, "No," loudly, bringing attention to our table. At times, her emotional outbursts reached theatrical level.

TWO

"Go on," she encouraged, now hanging on his every word.

"I know. Michelle told me, and you were there, Chloe. So, no need to act as if it was a state secret." I shot Chloe a look.

He smirked and shook his head.

"My training and skills from that job transfer to this work naturally. I'm fortunate to have the ability to tap into resources that are otherwise, shall we say, unavailable to others." He looked between us for affirmation that we understood.

"There is something not right about your life, Isabella—"

"You think?" Chloe cut Richard off, garnering a look from him, signaling her to be quiet.

"Let me cut to the chase. I've spoken to my former partner about your case. I wanted him to run Adrien through some databases. It's not common for me to ask him for a favor, but I was hoping something might surface that we weren't aware of, hoping he might find the answers we're looking for." Richard thumbed the paperwork in his hand. "Now, with this information that you own this gallery, I am getting a bad feeling. My gut says there is a storm coming your way, and we need to get ahead of it."

I was dumbstruck. My insides felt ready to explode all over the table.

"Here is my suggestion," he continued, without skipping a beat. "I would like to invite Ben to meet with us tomorrow before we leave for Geneva to inventory the freeport. He knows the backstory and may have already started researching Adrien. I suggest we lay out what we have, and ask him to start an official investigation. I think this will get you ahead of the issues that are about to catch up with you. Would you be open to meeting with him?"

I took a moment to think.

Chloe answered, "Make it happen, Richard. We need to find

out what's going on. As an outsider—an objective observer—I can say that this looks really bad, Izzy. Just do it."

"Okay, do it. Set it up." I didn't need to think about it any further.

I was worried, though, that maybe I was mentally ill and now they would find out. What if it came out that I had that—what was it called?—dissociative personality disorder.

"All right, I am going to put the phone on the table, and set the speaker on low. I'll tell him we need to meet about your case. I don't know where he is—it could be Brussels or The Hague, where the office is located—but I know he will be on the next plane or train here to meet us, once we give him the facts as we know them, and he knows you want him involved. I need you to tell him you want him there. We good?" Richard pulled his phone out and placed it on the table.

He hit the icon button for contacts and the name Ben.

Within seconds, a face flashed on the screen with the name.

A face I knew all too well.

My mind tried to process what was happening when the telephone flashed to FaceTime, and Ben Jaager and I were looking at each other.

CHAPTER FOURTEEN

BEN

OH SHIT. SHIT. Shit.

"Richard, I need you to take me off FaceTime and walk away, so we can talk," I said, with a modicum of urgency.

"Ben, is that you? Ben Jaager?" I heard Isabella. Then I saw her face take over my entire screen, looking down at me as I looked up at her. I quickly switched my camera angle, so she could no longer see me. What a fiasco.

"Who's the hot guy?" I heard from across the table, and then saw another face take over my screen. Jesus, can this get any worse?

"Richard, now might be a good time to pick up the phone, and walk away from the table, so we can have a private chat." My words were clipped, I hoped relaying the urgency of my request.

He left the phone on the table. He just stared at the phone and left the call open.

"You two know each other?" he asked like a dullard. Not his finest moment.

"Yes, Richard, we know each other. Now pick the damn phone up and walk away," I directed. At this point, denying what was obvious seemed useless. The jig was up; the operation was indeed compromised.

"Right, right. Excuse me, ladies," I heard him say as he shuffled away from the table. Then I heard him breathing heavy, shoes clipping along the floor, and, "Hold on, I'm stepping outside."

When I heard the door whoosh behind him, I blew open the conversation.

"What the hell, Richard? What were you thinking? You might have blown a six-month operation. Tell me there is a good reason that I came face-to-face with a person of interest in my operation. On your phone, no less."

Confusion was mapped across his face at first, then concern, and then it changed to anger as he spoke.

"What the hell, Ben?" he said, mimicking my tone. "You're telling me that my client is a target of Europol, and you didn't tell me?" I wasn't certain if he was going with the best defense is a strong offense, or if he truly was angry.

"Think about it, Richard. How could I tell you? You aren't read into the operation. This, my friend, is a global initiative that you may have just sunk." I had to remind him that we no longer worked together.

"You could have said you had a conflict—" Again, deflecting. I didn't even listen to his response, waiting for him to finish his rant. His training served him well, and he pulled out all the stops.

"Right, and that wouldn't have started the wheels in your head turning? You wouldn't have tried to start building up a wall around her. You wouldn't have felt obligated to share that with your client? No, I think you know the minute I said that, she would have been insulated and possibly coached to remain silent." There was no way that Richard or his boss would let their

TWO

client sink. Especially if they felt she was innocent or being railroaded.

"Oh man, what a mess. Give me a minute." Clearly, he was unable to decide how to proceed. "Man, this is bad. Did I say anything that would help you make your case? Wait, don't answer that—plausible deniability."

"Let's start with what's important to world security. Can my cover be salvaged?" I asked.

"No," he said. Without hesitation, no.

"Fuck. All right then, let's get to why you called and blew my cover wide open." I was pissed and wanted him to know it.

"All right. Here's the bottom line. There's something going on behind the scenes, and Isabella is square in the middle of it. I have limited use of my normal ability to hack into databases. After the attack, everyone was waiting for an immediate cyberattack to follow. Credible sources of intel that I could tap into not only put up more firewalls, but impenetrable concrete barriers. Right now, I have limited access to confirm information, much less track it down to a root.

"Isabella is the owner on paper of the murky Roselov gallery. She said she has no knowledge of accepting ownership of the gallery. Her claim is she wasn't a participant in the acquisition and disavows ownership. Except for her husband, who else would have access to information to authorize a purchase. Did he do it? And if he did make the purchase, why not do it under his own name? Why go through what could be considered an identity theft scheme by using her name to complete an unauthorized transaction? Unless he knows the gallery is shady and didn't want his name associated with it, but wanted a benefit," he postulated.

"Ben, she's totally freaked. I guess your visit . . . it was you this morning, right? You totally freaked her out. She wants answers, and I have vowed to get them for her. It's the reason I called—so

I could have her share her concerns with someone who has the means to get to the bottom of things." The traffic in the background was making it difficult to have a conversation.

"Look, gather your posse up and come over to my place, and we can have a full-blown argument, and then I can gather the data I need from her," I told him. "I can't promise I can give her information that will set aside her fears. And you must realize there is always the possibility talking to me can land her deeper in the mess she's already in." This was a fan-crap-tastic mess.

"Ben, that might not be a bad idea. Except, I don't know where you are!" he yelled into the speaker of the phone. He probably forgot, in his anger, I could see him holding the phone out to yell.

When he remembered he was on FaceTime, he looked at me to answer with my address.

"Ask Isabella," I said, and disconnected.

Forty minutes later, a succession of sharp rapid knocks at my door announced the arrival of the group. As I opened the door, the greeting I received was varied.

Richard immediately shot me the bird and pushed past me. He barreled in uninvited and headed for the kitchen for a beer, or likely something stronger if he could find it. Isabella had a face that Medusa would find frightening, walking past without looking at me to the living room. Chloe was the only friendly to enter. She raked her eyes from my feet to my head and said, "You're a keeper. I'm a bit of an anarchist. But for you, I'll flip." That brought a smile to my lips, and I waved her in to join the others.

The first to start the verbal assault was Richard. He looked around the living room in disgust and shook his head at the purple couch. He assumed it was my personal choice, and that offended him in some way.

TWO

"Before I lay into you, I want to know why you're living in an apartment that looks like a chick threw up all over it. This place is god-awful, Ben. Did you pick out this hideous furniture?" Ah, the old deflection again. Or lull me into feeling comfortable and then zap me right between the eyes.

"Whoa, stop right there, Richie Rich. I was about to take a picture of the Barney purple and ask my hairdresser to match that color for my hair tips. And I personally think this place is chic, upscale." Chloe peeked into the dining area. "Not loving those hideous wall murals though, Ben."

"Chlo, you have lost your mind. People will want to come up and squeeze your head to see if it will pop like a grape." Isabella had her head tilted down, avoiding eye contact with everyone. Caught off guard, Chloe's love of purple wasn't what I thought she would lead with. In fact, I thought Isabella was fond of the Barney couch.

"If everyone will please take a seat, we can start this meeting. Can I offer anyone refreshments?" I asked, hoping for a resounding no.

"This place is pretty upscale. Do you have one of those five-thousand-dollar expresso machines?" Chloe asked.

"Sadly, no. Although, I can offer you a Keurig pod."

"Pass. Let's get this started. I am dying to know the details. Should Adrien be marched off to prison in cuffs, all the better," Chloe said.

"For everyone's protection, I'll record this meeting. Does anyone have an objection?" I asked. Nos all around. I set up the recorder, read the purpose of the meeting into the record, and asked everyone to identify themselves. I then identified myself for the record, making sure to use my fake last name, and what my official status was with Europol and the matter.

"Richard, let's start with you. Would you please state how

you first made contact with me in relation to these matters?" I relied upon him to keep it succinct and on point.

"Ms. Isabella Armond contacted our firm to represent her in a divorce from her husband, Adrien Armond. I met with her and she provided details to me to aid me in the consensual investigation of her husband."

Clever. He did not say "confidential investigation."

"And at some point, did you contact me about your concerns?" I asked, to cover my ass that I didn't go fishing for answers to my work that could later be construed as attorney-client privilege or work product.

"I did. As an employee of the law firm, and under the direction of Michelle Dupont, I contacted you," he replied.

"And what did you say to me?" I asked, knowing this could get into some murky territory for us both. But I counted on him to couch the language, the way we needed it to be reflected in the record.

"I told you I had some concerns that her husband might be traveling and concealing illegal activities. I asked if you could look into it. If so, it might call for opening an investigation," he said. A little gray, but close enough.

"Today, you contacted me about information you had obtained from Isabella Armond," I led him.

"That would be correct," he responded.

"And you and your client are here to share that information?" I asked, making sure the information did not have a basis to be precluded down the road for attorney-client privilege. Or any indication that the information was coerced.

"That is our intent," he said.

"Then proceed," I said, specifically not making any promises or assertions.

"It has come to my client's attention that she's the registered

TWO

owner of an art gallery in London that she neither provided money to purchase nor signed as a purchaser or transferee. She has no knowledge how her name came to be on the paperwork. Because the gallery she now owns is under investigation, she thought it prudent to make the authorities aware of this information," he said, sitting back, more relaxed.

"Why come to me? Why not the British authorities?" I asked, looking from him to Isabella.

"Well, Ben"—Isabella said with some derision in her tone—"if that is your name. It might be because you had pointed out to me this morning that I am peddling forgeries. And this knowledge sent alarms bells off that, if that is correct, I might be looking at some criminal implications, including jail. Did you make that information up?"

"No, Isabella. I have every reason to believe, based on my training and experience, that the painting is a forgery. Forty percent of paintings in the mainstream art world are forgeries, that means where you have one, you may have more. It wasn't something I had expected to discover. However, once I did, I couldn't let it stand."

She opened her mouth to speak, but I continued. "I realize that you indicated your husband was the one who procured the painting but let me pose a question. Your name is on the gallery paperwork, the bank statements are set up in your name. Invoices and contracts have your name and signature. Exactly what proof do you have that you're not the one at fault for this, either by negligence or intent? If someone asked Adrien if he was involved in the purchase of a forged painting, what would be the likelihood he would admit that?"

Possibly a little harsh, but the truth. When the inevitable march to jail took place, people often turned, and finger pointing began in earnest. I had no doubt that Adrien would not take responsibility if he could lay blame at her feet.

"Ben, your point is taken, but I think you're being a little harsh with Isabella," Rich said, which sent my blood pressure on an upward trajectory.

"Rich, all due respect, and I mean that sincerely. I trust your judgment. However, we are not looking at a crime of omission where we could say some wealthy guy, Ben Jaager, is defrauded out of millions and could take the hit financially. We are talking about a gallery with suspected ties to a network of criminals. Roselov did business with Isabella's gallery, and he disappears. Suddenly, she swoops in and takes up the slack. So, tell me how, in your world's orbit, does that not ring of co-conspirator?" My neck was straining to get closer to him without getting up from my seat and throttling him. I was afraid spittle would fly. "You see where I am going, Isabella? Right now, Adrien has no fingerprints on anything."

"I don't know this man Roselov. Why would I want to help him?" she said. "And I can assure you, I'm not allowed to have access to my family or business finances. So how I could help manipulate a criminal enterprise, is mind-boggling."

"Isabella, I see where Ben is going. We must look at the facts one of two ways. First way, Adrien bought the gallery under your name for any variety of financial or legal issues. Possibly to own it, but highly likely to shield himself. Or, he could be setting you up to take a legal and criminal fall. Among a host of other reasons." Richard folded his hands in his lap.

"We are veering off the path and into speculation territory. At this point, it's more helpful if we kept with fact gathering. Let me ask some further questions," I suggested. "They may be compound and confusing. If so, please seek clarification." I looked to Isabella to make certain she understood. "Let's start with the basics, for the record."

TWO

She nodded her head as she replied, "Okay."

"Do you know Dmitri Roselov or have you ever met him?" I asked.

"No and no," she responded.

"Have you had professional dealings with him?" I tried to relax with this part of our question and answer.

"My gallery has, I have not," she said.

"Clarify."

"My husband, who is my business partner, is the person who knows Roselov and has dealings with him regarding paintings. We have bought some paintings from him and, other times, held paintings for him. I have never spoken to the man, nor accepted any financial payments from him. And I most certainly did not buy his gallery." Isabella huffed and straightening her back.

"Do you know if you have any of his paintings now?" I leaned forward toward her.

"That's a bit of a conundrum," she said, hedging a bit in her response.

I had expected her to say she didn't have any of his paintings. "How's that?"

"After you left the gallery this morning, I took a closer look at the painting you questioned. In fact, I looked at it with a magnifying glass. I believe that the letter we thought was an A is an R, and it was not from the Abu Dhabi auction house, but Dmitri Roselov," she said.

"I see." Thinking back, the letters were very likely Dmitri Roselov's initials.

"Where is your inventory stored? Specifically, the inventory that painting came from?" I asked. Finally, a potential break.

"She believes her husband has some in a secured storage area in the building. Others, in a freeport in Geneva. Geneva is where we are heading tomorrow," Richard interjected.

"Is that correct, Isabella?" I asked, and she affirmed.

"After her husband is safely on an airplane tonight, I have someone ready to work through the encryption of the computer system. We hope to get a crack at the inventory. I have someone else helping us gain access to the storage area. As we speak, he's working on disrupting the camera feed while we record the assets. To be honest, I don't think we'll find incriminating evidence on the computer inventory. However, the storage area might prove helpful." Richard nodded at me. "Before you ask if it's legal—Isabella's the owner. She's signed the proper documents. And no, you don't want to know who the people I engaged are." Richard raised his eyebrows at the mention of the professional participants. I had no doubt I knew who he was paying to do this task.

"Until the present information came to light about the forgery, my sole reason to gain access to the inventory list and paintings was to record the asset valuation. Now, we seem to have wandered into new territory. And trust me, Ben, I don't want to interfere with a potential crime scene like this one." Richard knew the potential implications if any possible evidence was compromised.

I still couldn't clear her as a suspect. However, I believed her. Why would she agree to have Richard access the information, if she knew there were illegal objects there that could be verified. There was always the worry, though, that she was a conspirator with Adrien, and was using this to flip on him. If so, it wouldn't take us where we need to prosecute him as a conspirator.

"If I presented a document indicating you consent to me being there in a position to search and record the inventory as potential evidence, would you sign it?" I waited for her to answer me while I studied her body language. If she hedged even a bit, I would be concerned that she was trying to play me.

TWO

Richard jumped in and said, "I'm not comfortable with that scenario, Ben. I would want to get Michelle's input on that before she responds."

"Ah, worried about culpability?" I taunted Richard to challenge me.

"Ben. I don't know what we are dealing with here. I don't know who the involved players are, and from what we are learning, this enterprise could be involved with a global criminal network. It might be some forgeries being passed, or it might be money laundering through those forgeries. It might be trafficking drugs, using the inside of those heavy frames to transport the contraband. For all I know, packets of money line the inside between the backing and painting.

"I'm not naïve. You're not here to break up some art and money laundering ring. You're here to sniff out ties to terrorism. You're trying to tie together the pieces that might implicate Adrien, Isabella, or someone they know, with funding the attacks." He was getting too close. I had to divert it back.

"That's a lot of speculation, Richard. What I want is access to the inventory spots. The gallery storage and freeports. Right now, I have enough to obtain a search warrant. However, once that request is put into the system, the element of surprise is compromised if it gets out. Either way, I will get into the gallery here. The one or two in Switzerland may take longer, plus the length of time it takes gives a criminal time to move the paintings," I advised.

He nodded and acknowledged the facts I'd laid out were indeed correct.

"If you don't cooperate with the joint search, but record the inventory for the divorce, I can obtain a copy eventually. However, then I'll have to call you as a witness to authenticate it, as well as Chloe and Isabella. In the end, you may be putting people in danger."

He sat for a moment and absorbed what I'd said. I could tell he was processing it, and evaluating his options.

"I have to first get permission from Isabella, then Michelle." That statement let me know I was in. Michelle would take his counsel.

"You can tell Michelle I give my permission," Isabella said, without hesitation.

"Isabella, that's noble. But what if Adrien has had time to cover his tracks, and it makes it look like you did it?" Rich asked.

"Then, Richard, whether Ben sees it tonight or tomorrow when he has a warrant, I am screwed. This way, at least I can see what is there and we can try to figure it out. If Ben, at some point, comes in with a team of people and removes everything, I won't have an opportunity to see it and comment. I'm the client, and I say yes." Isabella made her wishes crystal clear.

I stared at her, wondering if I'd miscalculated her. She had a well-thought-out argument. And this afternoon, she seemed clearer in thought. If Richard didn't want her to cooperate, he could have told her that the chance of my gaining legal access would be questionable. He must be fairly sure she'd come out clean.

"Then give me a moment, so I can clear it with Michelle." Richard pulled his phone out as he walked toward the kitchen.

The room was left in an awkward silence.

"So, are you always this hot, or is it part of your Europol cover?" Chloe asked, breaking the tension.

"Chloe, I can assure you I am always this hot," I responded, trying to extend the levity.

"Then I should trust you, since you have spoken the truth, *n'est-ce pas?*" she inquired.

"I believe that would be a correct statement." I watched

TWO

Isabella—her attention had started to drift to a place far away from the room. Was she starting to get muddled?

"I have several theories about Adrien, which I have shared with Isabella—" Chloe said out of nowhere, clearly uncomfortable. Suddenly, she went from playful to dead serious.

"Feel free to share with me." I sat back and left the recorder running.

"That would mean I could put my friendship in jeopardy with Izzy." That caught Isabella's attention. They exchanged a look only friends understood.

"Chloe, I don't think Ben will care that you think he's having an affair," Isabella finally said with a dismissive wave.

Chloe stood, walked to the hideous purple couch, and sat next to Isabella. She took her hands in hers.

"Izzy, I have been hiding something from you, and I am frightened to tell you." She rubbed her hands, as if trying to infuse her love into her. They stared at each other, unsure of what would be said and what damage could be done.

"Oh, for the love of God. Go on then, tell. Do you think anything you can say can stop my head from its imminent explosion?" Isabella said.

Chloe looked at me as she worried her lower lip with her teeth. She let go of Isabella, stood, and walked toward the window. It appeared she was contemplating how best to phrase what she needed to say and mitigate any damage ahead of time. She looked back, prepared to speak.

"I don't know if you remember, but a few months ago when Adrien was away, we got really drunk. You know that you are a lightweight when it comes to drinking." She nodded at me, Isabella nodded along. "She is, trust me. Anyway, I got bored when you passed out and started roaming the apartment. When I got to Adrien's office, I saw a sliver of a light coming from somewhere inside his office, but no light was lit. I could see a shadow across the floor. It seemed like it was from under the paneled area. Anyway, I walked over to the area, and yes, there was a soft sliver of light coming from somewhere. I got on the floor, on my belly, and found the source of the light. I was pretty drunk, and in my mind, I imagined a secret room. Trust me, at the time it sounded great. I ran my hand along the side and felt a slight bumpy area. I pushed it, and it revealed a door that had cracked open," she said.

"What are you talking about? That room is all paneled," Isabella said.

"No, Izzy. I think it is a panic or safe room," Chloe answered.

"And for this, you think I'd dissolve our friendship? Just because you were snooping? Don't be crazy," Isabella assured her.

"No, Izzy, because I went in and snooped around inside. I found four passports with various names, with his photo on the passports, a gun, lots of cash, and two paintings. One painting looked like a Van Gogh and the other, a Gauguin. And when I say lots of cash, Izzy, I mean lots of cash."

I jumped in. "So, this release to get into the room does not require a combination? Was it a push release?"

"It didn't require anything but pressure on, like, a button. But I tried it again a few weeks later, and couldn't get in. My thought was because the light was left on, it didn't automatically lock properly. That's just a theory," she offered.

This was huge. That's why we couldn't track him. He had various passports.

"Can we add that to our list that you allow us entry to and to investigate, Isabella?" I asked, but she was too caught up, she didn't answer.

"Why didn't you just tell me? Why would you think I'd be mad?" Isabella prompted.

TWO

"I was snooping, and the friend code says never to snoop," she replied, clearly uncomfortable.

I saw Richard approaching, putting his phone back into his pocket.

"Ladies, not to interrupt this exhilarating conversation, but Michelle said it's a go." Good, Richard had heard the last bit of conversation so we wouldn't have to rehash.

"All right, let's formulate a plan. Richard, you already have your man in place, who will remain anonymous, ready to open the gallery inventory area. So we don't compromise this unnamed magician who I will never meet"—he and I exchanged a knowing look clearly; I knew who he was—"you call me when it is open. I'll wait a block or so away."

Richard sat and took his phone out again, texting someone who responded at once.

"I don't want anyone tampering with the room in the apartment. I'll get a copy of the blueprints and have someone look at it, and then we can determine if there is anything to let us know how the panel door operates through those schematics." I made a quick note.

"Isabella, to be safe I want you to spend the night with Chloe after we inventory the gallery contents tonight. We can meet at the airport tomorrow and fly out together. Do you know where Adrien is going, Isabella?" I asked.

"No idea," she said.

"I will put someone on him when he leaves the hospital," I offered, and Richard agreed.

"Does this plan work for everyone?"

Everyone affirmed.

"I am shutting off the recorder. During this discussion, I prepared a document for everyone to sign, indicating you have done this of your own free will. That's it, folks. Isabella, I want to thank you for your cooperation."

I touched her arm and she jerked it back a bit.

"Something wrong?"

"I don't know. My arm has hurt since this morning. I swore Adrien gave me an injection, but he said I was crazy. The area has been tender all day," she said, favoring her arm.

"Let me look," I said, and she lifted her sleeve. "Something is wrong. You have a lump and inflammation. You should put some ice on it and take some ibuprofen when you get to Chloe's apartment. We'll keep an eye on it, to make certain it doesn't get worse."

Plans were confirmed, and I walked them out.

My next call was to Jill, inquiring if it was possible to run facial recognition on passports on file to check for duplicates. She didn't know, but took on the task to find out. I prepared my notes from the meeting, then took a nap, so I would be fresh and alert for the inventory search. Where there is one forgery, there have to be more. I was betting that one forgery would be the thread that led us to the epicenter of the financial mess.

CHAPTER FIFTEEN

ISABELLA

WHEN DID LIFE become so complicated? "Isabella, my guy has done a thorough sweep of your apartment, and there are four cameras throughout. It's pretty easy. He shuts the light off and uses night goggles and you can spot the blinking light. Then I suppose like dodging lasers he works his way around the area. Plus, he said you can buy some gizmo and use your cell to detect sound waves. If we dismantle them or interfere with them, it will trigger the central feed," Richard told me. "Now, this is your apartment, and we can take them down, but then you are letting Adrien know that we are on to him and he might step up his game. If we leave them, we can feed him misinformation and throw him off."

I couldn't wrap my head around being monitored twenty-four hours a day. For what purpose? Did he think I was cheating on him? Or was it to monitor what I said to people. Did he get some sick pleasure watching me? All that kept running through my mind was Chloe calling him the puppet master.

"Have they been here a while?" I'd hoped they were installed by the previous owner.

"From the schematics, they were not here before you moved in. This would be pure speculation on my part. Something felt out of place when Chloe found that room. Maybe because she was drunk, she was not careful about the way she put things back. Maybe she turned the light off, and the door didn't engage correctly. We will never know. However, two things we know. One, there are cameras recording a live stream. Two, there is a panic room you were unaware of until now. I don't want to disturb the mechanism on the paneled area as it might trip a silent alarm. We have a general idea of what is or was in there, and Adrien may have relocated the contents," Richard said.

"So, he may have installed them after Chloe found the panic room?" I asked, hoping there was an answer that would at least be plausible.

"I don't know, to be honest," he said.

"And you're sure he installed them? It wasn't some random person who had access to the place?" I was terrified by that prospect.

"Excellent question. Again, I can't confirm or deny. It's something we have to follow up on and find where it's transmitting to," he said, which made my stomach jolt. What if some stranger had gained access and was watching everything both Adrien and I did?

"Are we ready to enter the building?" Chloe asked as she snuck up behind us.

"God, you about gave me a heart attack." I physically jumped as my heart simultaneously kicked, then raced.

"Is Adrien gone?" she asked.

"Yes. My guy followed him to the gate for his flight and watched him board a plane to Mumbai, India. He saw him board, and my guy reported to Ben what number in line he was, so we

TWO

can try to get a name for the passport and visa he is using," Richard interjected.

"He left without any problems?" Chloe wanted confirmation he was gone.

"He was acting a little odd when he called to check in on how the sale went. I did as Ben instructed, and told him that he was pleased with the paintings. And that before he paid for them, he needed to add them to his insurance, which would trigger an outside appraisal. He seemed content with that, and I assured him it would be completed by next week. For good measure, Ben signed the papers as a purchase pending appraisal," I said, having felt we sidestepped a potential catastrophe.

"Did you tell him you were spending the night with me?" Chloe cocked her head to the side.

"No. With Adrien, it's better to ask forgiveness than ask permission. There was a twinge of guilt that crept in." That prompted an eyebrow raise. "He said he had asked Thomas to prepare some special meals for me while he was gone. He felt we had fallen out of touch these last few months. The meals were a gift from him."

"Poisoned, more likely. I would hire a food taster." I knew it was said sarcastically, but with a modicum of truth.

"Ladies, I have the signal we can enter. Here comes Ben," Richard advised.

Chloe was right. The man was attractive, in and out of a suit. His swagger could not be mistaken for anything but a man comfortable in his skin.

"The cameras in the storage are on a video feed, and we have an hour. One hour, and not a minute more. Adrien's flight time is nine hours, and it's an international flight without internet access to monitor, so let's get moving."

"What about the door that logs in entrance and exits?" I

asked.

"Isabella, my guy is a genius, and I mean that literally. With his genius comes an obsession with details. If he says we're clear? We are clear." Ben winked at Richard. "So, punch in your code and lead the way."

We walked through the gallery using only beams from low glow flashlights. We passed the office where a man sat at the desk, scrolling through the computer. He would leave with the history of the gallery on his flash drive. Would the information mined be legally legitimate, or would Adrien have been so arrogant to think everything he did in life was secure and left some breadcrumbs for us to follow?

The door to the storage area was ajar. We entered and flipped the light on. We closed the door, but didn't engage it to close and latch.

"We're going to treat this like an assembly line, with each person having a specific job. I have a video camera set up to tape this, right there." Ben pointed to a camera on a tripod.

"Isabella, we need you to quickly look at each painting and, as best you can, identify it either by subject matter, artist, or period. Anything strikes you as odd, you tell us. If you remember purchasing it, say so. If not, then state that as well. Then hand the painting to Chloe. Chloe, you hold it and I will photograph the front and back. Then hand it to Richard. Richard, you check it for any irregularities that might suggest anything wrong. You know the drill—if it's off-balance in weight, possibly hiding drugs, or the frame looks tampered with to hide flash drives. Smell the canvas and if it smells of fresh paint, even a slight odor, then make a note. All right, the clock is ticking. Let's go." Ben clapped his hands and we were moving.

A little less than an hour later, we exited the building with information that could close my gallery for good. Had I not

TWO

cooperated, there were enough problematic paintings that a stay in jail for six years could have been a result.

The information mined from the computer yielded no worthwhile results for Ben. It wasn't a surprise. Adrien wouldn't be careless enough to leave documented evidence. Which left us wondering why he'd allowed the fake paintings to remain in the storage. Either Adrien never intended to sell them but kept them on the books as an asset for banking information, or as Richard suggested, he was planning on selling them privately, as part of a money laundering arrangement. There was no indication that drugs were being transported in the frames. No drug residue or pills were found, and no flash disks that could transport corporate or government secrets.

As we started toward the car, a text pinged on my phone, "I hope you enjoyed your meal," from Adrien. That was a bit disconcerting. He is supposed to be somewhere in the air. Ben looked at it, and between him and Richard they deciphered it was a preset text possibly using one of those new programs like Text Magic. I remembered there was something about a business that supplied alibis for people. I suppose he could have paid a company to send them.

"Is the dinner laid out and we need to dispose of it, or do we have to make sure the cameras see you eating it?" Chloe asked.

"No, there were no cameras in the kitchen," Richard replied.

"By the way, where are the cameras?" I asked.

"Living room, dining room, his office, and your office." Thank God, they weren't the bathroom or bedrooms.

"I have what I need," Ben advised. "I'm going to transcribe all of this, then upload it to the server. I'll have Jill forward the questionable paintings to our people, and see if we can determine their origin and how many hands they have passed through."

"Good job, everyone. We'll meet at the airport at seven."

Richard rubbed his hands together and we parted ways.

My mind buzzed with information. But my mind was on the brink of exhaustion.

THE NEXT MORNING, we arrived at the Charles de Gaulle airport to board the first plane out for Geneva, Switzerland. As a child, I thought Switzerland was a magical country. When I thought of Switzerland, I thought of cows with enormous bells hanging from their necks, trudging through fields, snow in the winter, and hot chocolate with marshmallows. Now, all Switzerland meant to me was Ferraris lined up alongside the banks of Lake Geneva, secret banking, and the place we kept our lovely paintings as a tax haven.

It was surprising how easy it was to gain access to the freeport. I was sure that Adrien would have put layers of security in place, but that was not the case. This, my first visit, left a sour taste in my mouth. An ugly windowless gray stone building behind a choppy barbed wire fence that sat in the middle of a congested area was what held our collection of masterpieces. Here sat an infinitesimal amount of priceless art that was so secret, no one had any idea of what was stored, or the value.

This time, taking inventory would not be as easy. The room where the art was stored was of a moderate size. Unlike our storage area at the gallery, where paintings were stacked against the wall and covered, here the paintings were crated and had to be removed from their crates, and then expertly crated again.

"Yesterday worked out well, sorting and recording the paintings. I suggest we use the same procedure. These crates are going to be a bitch to get open, so let's get started." Ben tipped his chin at the shipping crates. He had a crowbar in one hand, a drill in the other.

TWO

One hour later, five crates had been opened, each holding six paintings. Thirty paintings were unpacked, the protective layer around the painting was removed, and all were placed around the room against the walls. However, one thing was troublesome on many levels. Two of the crates were isolated from the others. One had "DR" written on it in permanent marker, on the outside right upper corner, and the other had "ADA" written on the upper left corner. It did not take much of a leap to realize DR was Dmitri Roselov and ADA was Abu Dhabi Auction. The paintings in these crates were given a higher level of scrutiny than the others, and four out of twelve appeared to be fakes, or altered in some manner.

I was astonished at the collection Adrien had accumulated. An old master I believed to be Frans Hals, two Impressionists—most likely Renoir, a Pre-Raphaelite Brotherhood by Rossetti, Cubism, Post Impressionism, and Abstract Expressionism. All sat hidden away in the collection, housed in an ugly building in beautiful Lake Geneva, the town of the rich and frivolous.

"Izzy, the good news is you are in possession of enormous wealth if no one pays attention. The bad news is, some of this might be stolen or from the gray market, and some, we are pretty sure are fakes." As we had inventoried the paintings, and as I called out the artists, Chloe had been googling the last known or presumptive value. She also had been accessing online databases for stolen or missing property.

"That will not help me sleep at night, Chlo." Was I being unreasonable to worry about all the illegal activity I had no idea occurred under my nose?

"Speaking of—today you seem, I don't know . . . better than you have in the last few weeks. More engaged." She rubbed my arm and gave it a squeeze. I actually felt a little more reassured.

"I haven't taken those pills anymore. I stopped them when

we were with Michelle. From what I read, they have a short half life, so they should be out of my system soon," I said.

Living in what could be a drug-induced fog was not living. The depression I felt from the death of my family required a clear head to mourn, and the grief dealt with head-on. Once divorced, I'd need to be clear-minded and on my toes every moment. There would be no room for error.

"Adrien was giving you pills, knowing your history with your sister's drug addiction. What the hell is wrong with that man? Wait"—she held up her hand and shook her head—"don't answer. The list would be way too long." Chloe rubbed my arm again, sympathetically. She'd been there for me when we had to cover Denise's drug bill debt and would help me track Denise down when she disappeared for days. If my sister had not entered rehab when she did, she would have been dead five years ago. The irony is, if she had died five years ago, I would have a gravesite to visit or an urn on my mantel that I could talk to at will. Now I have nothing because she and Mama died in a mass grave, leaving nothing to bring me closure.

"I've been so overcome with grief over Mama and Denise's death. Everyone has their problems, and I didn't want to burden you with mine. I thought it would be okay to take the pills for a bit. They did seem to make life easier. But clouded judgment doesn't feel good at all. The cure was worse than the disease—"

Richard interrupted. "Isabella, we just opened this last small box, and I need you to look at the contents. Have you ever sold jewelry as part of your gallery offering?" He motioned for me to join him a few steps away.

"Richard, I don't even have to look. The answer is no. Jewelry is a very specialized sale item that takes a lot of effort to choose correctly and then authenticate. A friend of mine had a part of her inventory confiscated, as the authorities believed

TWO

she was trafficking blood diamonds. It took a year to process and finally return them to her as clean, but a nightmare for her nonetheless."

"Okay. We'll inventory it for now." Richard went back to investigating the contents.

Another hour later, after all was inventoried and repacked it was almost five o'clock, leaving us two hours to kill until our flight back.

"I have to say, I am in a quandary. There are obviously illegal objects here that should be confiscated. However, if we do that, then we tip our hand." Ben placed the last crate where we'd found it and stepped away.

"Ben, this is way above our heads. You need to put this in Levi's hands and let him make that decision," Richard offered. "This is one of those executive decision moments."

"You're right. Now, how is this going to impact your divorce, Isabella?" Ben asked.

Richard waved a hand, interjecting. "I will have to verify with Michelle, but this will be a good news and bad news scenario. The good news is, I think, once this officially comes to light, we can force the justice to waive the two-year timeline for a final hearing. The bad news is, you are now stuck in the middle of a criminal investigation."

"Obviously, she didn't know what Adrien was doing here," Chloe interjected.

"I have to agree with Richard," Ben said. "Her name is associated with everything. Going through all the documents to unravel where it started and how it unfolded could take months. Now that the Roselov gallery is destroyed, it plays out as good and bad for documentation."

"Ben, might I suggest months for you, weeks for us. We have a team of accountants that can tear through the documents in record time." Richard and Ben shared a conspiratorial smile. "Money buys a lot of cut red tape."

"I don't think Europol, Interpol, and the French authorities will agree to using a private accounting firm to secure their case. And I don't think they'll allow you unfettered access to the information we generate." Ben didn't disagree.

"Ben, Ben, Ben. We are one step ahead of you. I won't share the details, so you'll have plausible deniability. However, trust in me. My investigation will be more thorough and quicker than yours. Let's get something to eat at the airport. I think we are all starved." Richard obviously wanted to avoid an argument. He'd undoubtedly find a way to win later.

I saw Ben gear up to argue, but he folded. As former partners, I supposed they'd done this dance before.

"One last look, everyone. Check my pictures I took as to crate placement before, and make sure everything is exactly as we found it." Ben looked at the crates, at us, and then back at the crates again.

Within three hours we were in the air and on our way back to Paris.

I hadn't checked my phone all day. When I did, there was a text from Adrien. "I hope you are enjoying your meals." Again with meals? I deleted the message, similar to how I would soon delete him from my life.

CHAPTER SIXTEEN

ISABELLA

I MUST HAVE taken a small nap in the car from the airport. What time is it? My God, it was almost midnight. I woke to Chloe shaking my arm.

Ben explained how he'd process the information and Richard acknowledged we would cooperate fully. After a brief call to his boss, they decided to leave the paintings in place, so the chain of evidence would not be broken, especially since there was no active warrant in place, and the Swiss hadn't been advised a criminal investigation was taking place. For good measure, Ben had me execute an electronic request to limit access to the freeport to myself and Adrien. It was a risk if Paul tried to gain access. However, he had a plan in place for that as well.

Ben and Richard left us down the street from my apartment so George, or whomever was on desk duty, wouldn't wonder who they were, and they wouldn't be caught on any building security cameras. Chloe and I passed Nick, who was on duty if you disregarded he was high, giving him a quick wave.

Entering the apartment at night with what I'd learned

yesterday and today, along with knowing cameras were running, left me feeling uneasy. Soon, soon, I had to remind myself, this will be over. My greatest fear was living through the nightmare of a criminal investigation, and my name and credibility of my gallery tarnished. This evoked an immediate sense of guilt as I thought about all the people touched so drastically by the attacks. Some were homeless, some jobless, and many burned through their savings, as insurance companies waded through the process of delaying and supplying limited checks to them. The global markets remained skittish, but at least the EU was stepping up with infrastructure aid and workers.

"Thanks, Chloe, for everything you've done. I'm not sure I would have reached this point, if you hadn't kept a gentle hand at my back, pushing me forward." Chloe was a true and dedicated friend. I felt sick as I catalogued the excuses I'd made not to spend time with her to appease Adrien.

Coming back to the apartment left me feeling oddly disconnected. From my life, my goals, and people I thought I'd loved and trusted.

"Izzy, you have a long road ahead of you. I can't see Adrien immediately caving and saying, 'Fine, take what you think is fair.' I also know the wheels of justice move slow. Pace yourself. Before we discovered what a mess the inventory is, I thought this would be quick. What Ben alluded to concerns me. Everything is tied up in your name. As it stands, if an investigation were to blow wide open right now, you are the primary person of interest. There is nothing to tie Adrien into this mess except your word. Your name is the face of the business," she said as she walked to the refrigerator.

"I know. I just have to trust that Richard and Ben can unravel this mess. I thank God for Richard because he seems to have resources he can utilize quicker then Ban. And I think we can agree

TWO

time is of the essence. What are you doing?" I asked, as she piled several plastic containers together.

"These look yummy. I thought I would take them home. You were supposed to have already consumed them, and I can eat these over two or three days." She opened and smelled the contents of each container.

I looked at her as if she had lost her mind. Chloe was a carbohydrate only person, except when I forced her to eat a salad with me at lunch. And, like a child, she always put up a noble fight. I doubted vegetables ever made it into her body, except if hidden in a carb-heavy meal.

"Just kidding," she laughed, and gave me a "gotcha" finger. "I'll dump them in my bin when I get home. We don't want to leave any unconsumed evidence. However, this pasta salad looks edible. I'll give that a go. And what's with the labeling of which one you should eat in what order?"

"Who knows? One of his obsessive quirks, or just another reminder I'm too incompetent to even remember to eat. Leave one for me for tonight. I have to at least know what it tasted like, in case he asks," I said. "But he can always run the tapes, and see I wasn't here."

"Don't be silly. Richard has that covered, or weren't you listening? It appears Saturday through Sunday, there was a problem on and off where the server was taken down for repairs. Can you get me a tote or something? I don't want to pass the cameras with the containers. God knows, he will accuse me of stealing his food, and I don't need him on my back," she said.

"How do you think I should not act closing the sale?" I slid the containers out of my way and made us a cup of coffee.

"No coffee for me. I won't be able to sleep if I'm caffeinated. Let Ben handle that part. You already said he had to get clearance from his insurance. It's a plausible explanation. Let it sit. If you over explain, it will raise a red flag. Okay, now walk me to the door. I have to run." She gathered her containers, put them in a tote, and we scurried to the door. A quick hug and air kiss, and she was off to the car waiting for her below. No doubt he would try to flirt, she would blow him off, and there would be a dramatic tale tomorrow to be told.

After a quick shower, I was now settled in. I had my work cut out for me. The papers Ben left for me to review and sign, acknowledging the works were authentic and to avoid suspicion from Adrien, required some initials and a signature. The insurance appraiser was scheduled to appraise the paintings, and the appraiser was from a reputable company. The set of papers would convince Adrien.

It was disconcerting to remind myself that cameras watched my every move, and I had a role to play that commanded a performance. How long had they been running, and what obscenely crazy things had I done while alone? I used to sing and dance all over the house like a crazy person, but not for years now.

Walking through the galley kitchen with royal-blue cabinets reminded me I should change the color. What if someone thought of the bold cabinet color as offensive, my mind leaping to the purple couch at Ben's. At least the stainless steel refrigerator was appropriate, which had been a selling point for Adrien. Classic lines and sparkling. It was large enough to hide a body. I must be tired to let my mind wander to a place of no consequence.

Opening the massive refrigerator, I pursued my selection, and I decided on the lovely Caesar salad with mushrooms. Mushrooms. I hadn't realized that Caesar salad was made with mushrooms. Well, it was marked Saturday, so my choice was made for me.

Sitting at the small counter area, I unwrapped the meal and

TWO

placed the chicken from the aluminum foil on top of the salad, then the cheese, and tossed it all up. Ew, the mushrooms were oddly bitter. Should I pick the pieces out? No, that would be too much effort. I returned to the fridge, and after soaking the lettuce and chicken with massive quantities of Caesar dressing, I devoured it. Ten minutes later, I was looking at an empty bowl. I washed the bowl and placed it into the dishwasher, as Adrien liked. But today, I was going rogue. I decided to slice an orange, along with some grapes, and brought them into the living room where the cameras would catch my treachery.

As I settled in to review the papers, it finally hit me that if not for the appointment for divorce, I'd never know what had occurred with my business. It was alarming, the number of questionable paintings we owned. How many of these had been sold over the years? And how much did Adrien know, or had he been duped as well? If I'd been allowed access to the inventory, would I have caught the discrepancies?

My mind started to wander, and I could not concentrate. I focused on the orange slice. Plump, with drops of juice on its surface, and veined like my hand, only orange. Suddenly, my stomach cramped, and I had the urge to retch. But that urge competed for my attention, as my arms and legs started to involuntarily move a bit. My limbs were out of my control. My legs felt like Jell-O, and I could not stand. Or maybe I could, but my mind wasn't sending the correct signal to my appendages. My head felt as if someone had grabbed it, and then one finger at a time pressed into it, trying to reach my brain.

Time . . . where was time going? The clock on the wall was melting like the Dali clocks. What was that painting called? Something about a memory. And why was the orange so brilliant and glowing? Was it glowing or was it an afterburn? How did I get on the floor? Oh my God, this was hilarious. Everything was hilarious. Why wasn't someone here to share my hilarity?

Wait. Was the painting talking to me? It had to be. No one else was here talking to me. If it was speaking to me, what it said made no sense. I concentrated on the painting; my favorite painting, for its colors. Suddenly, the vivid colors from it shot forth to surround me in a circle of rotating lights, enveloping me in euphoria. My mind was moving fast, zipping through so many connections, but unaware of each other. I could see the white light as the electricity sparked through my brain. If only briefly, I heard someone laugh. Was that me?

Grasping at the couch with my fingertips, I pulled and hoisted myself onto it, then collapsed as nausea again took hold. I turned my head to the side, so that if I threw up, I would not choke. *Good thinking, Izzy*, I praised myself. But as I did, I became aware the red and green colors were arguing with each other while the blues and yellows laughed. Not just tittered, but laughed loudly. And yes, the yellow smelled exactly like lemons. I could smell it, even this far away.

My legs involuntarily jerked again, and I rolled from the couch and landed hard on my back on the floor. Did I pass out or just float away?

When I looked up, laughing to the point of almost snorting, someone was standing over me. Adrien. The melting clock said eight o'clock. That damn clock couldn't tell time. Was that Adrien standing in front of me? And who was next to him. Was that George with him? How hilarious. George was a cartoon, like Pluto, and Adrien looked like a stick figure. He was there, but not moving. Lips moving, but not talking. Walking, but standing still. Could he not see the humor in the red now arguing with the yellow? And then, finally coming to an agreement between themselves. Good, they settled on accepting the juicy orange was a mixture and blending of them.

TWO

Where did Adrien go? Didn't he want to listen to my explanation of the existentialism of this whole matter? No worries. I would sleep, and then he would understand as I giggled my way to unconsciousness. On the floor in my multimillion-dollar living room.

I WOKE TO the sun filtering in through slightly parted curtains in an unfamiliar setting. Why was I in a bed with rails? Why was there a needle in my arm attached to a bag of fluid? Why was my head elevated at a forty-five-degree angle?

Taking in the dimly lit room, my eyes landed on Adrien sitting in a small uncomfortable-looking chair in the corner. He watched me, and I watched him. Was he really there, or was he a hallucination? He spoke before I could ask a question.

"You're in a hospital, Isabella. In a medical psychiatric ward, to be exact."

I bolted up, but a wave of nausea hit me from the quick move.

"Why am I in a hospital? A psychiatric ward, you say?" I lost my breath with each word. I looked around to verify that this was correct, then down to my hands to check they weren't restrained. Unrestrained; that was good.

"George and I found you in quite a state. I wasn't sure if you had a complete break with reality. You kept telling me to stop the blue from being so abusive to the green. Laughing one minute, and then sobbing the next. When the ambulance arrived, they found you almost catatonic," he said, as he stood to check the bag with fluids.

"How long have I been here?" I tried to push my covers aside.

"It's Monday morning. Now that you are awake, the

specialists will perform some tests and we'll then determine the next step. I'm meeting with Ben and his appraiser in an hour. You rest, and I'll be back tonight after I complete my rounds. Just relax; the nurse will be in to administer some medication shortly. I don't know what has brought you to this place; I feel the death of your family was far too much for you. Leave it to me now, Isabella. I have everything under control." He kissed my forehead and stroked my hair.

"Adrien, no, you must believe me. Someone must have drugged me. Or I had a bad reaction to something." I pleaded for him to understand and investigate.

"Don't be ridiculous, Isabella. You have been heading down this black hole for months. Losing things, can't remember where you parked the car, forgetting to make or break reservations. And the books at the gallery are a mess from your inability to concentrate. Your memory is questionable, at best. I'll surely have to have someone come in and try to undo the gibberish in the books. You have ordered paintings, and then forgot you did. Give yourself time to let your mind heal. I'm afraid you're in the middle of a total and complete breakdown," he said. "Rest. Rest is what you need."

I turned to watch a nurse walk in the room with another small bag, which she piggybacked with the larger one. Adrien watched as she adjusted the wheel to regulate the amount of medication that was being infused into my body. He watched me, until I drifted to sleep. Sleep? Sleep or medication-induced unconsciousness? Either way, my questions stayed unanswered, and I was now his prisoner.

CHAPTER SEVENTEEN

ADRIEN

WHO WAS THE man that kept watching me? He didn't even try to hide that he had me in his sights. A well-dressed man of what appeared to be Middle Eastern descent, and enough muscle to snap me like a twig. He was not your normal train rider. His discomfort among the crowd was clear, and he was making me uncomfortable.

The train came to a jarring stop at the Hotel de Ville station. There were people rushing to and from the train, as well as throughout the station. With a quick step and skilled crowd dodging, I exited the train. If he was following me, I could lose him. What was wrong with me? Was I being paranoid?

First, I thought I had seen someone watching me in the café, and now this man. Unfortunately, we both left the train at the same time. As I ascended the stairs and rounded the corner to find the exit, he was behind me. As I walked to the gallery, he was always a few feet behind. He was definitely following me, but for what reason? Had I done something to him or his family, medically, that would cause this stalkerish behavior? Was it something to do with the organ transplant affair in Egypt? Had I sold him a forgery?

I remotely keyed in the code to open the metal doors to the gallery, and as I entered, I watched as he passed behind me, past the gallery, and continued down the street. Paris was still physically and emotionally traumatized from the terror events, and everyone was looked upon with suspicion. I watched as he maneuvered around the construction barrels and continued on his way. I hadn't realized how badly the homeless population had exploded until I watched him dodging and weaving around their legs that faced the streets where they sat against the remaining buildings of Paris. Unlike others who had lost a fortune with the roller coaster ride of the stock market, my investments remained level.

This meeting with the appraiser was an annoyance, and had interrupted the flow of my plan to deal with Isabella on a more permanent basis. It would appease Avigad, and free me up to be more mobile.

Flipping on the lights in the gallery, everything appeared normal. She hadn't put the paintings away, so I prepared for the paintings to be displayed in the viewing room. As I placed the last picture where it belonged on the wall, I made my way to the office. First order of business was to run the end of month profit and loss statement. My hope and expectation was that the five million for the paintings would be on this run of the P&L sheet.

I checked the time. It was exactly ten o'clock.

As my eyes lifted to the front window, Ben, and the gentleman I assumed was the appraiser, appeared, both impeccably dressed, both here to transfer money to me. I'd hoped. They took a moment, as if they were conferring, then Ben pushed the button for admittance. When I granted them entrance, he appeared both surprised and annoyed. Closing the door behind

TWO

them and engaging the lock, my eyes fell upon the man from the train. He sat casually in the café across from the gallery, sipping what appeared to be a coffee, watching me.

I tried to ascertain what the man across the street was doing as I looked over Ben's shoulder. Focusing on Ben and his guest, I extended my hand in greeting. The appraiser introduced himself and the company he represented. Monsieur Pardue. He retrieved a card from a black leather card holder he kept in his pocket, handing it to me with a tight smile. Evidently, the company paid him well to have all the proper initials behind his name. His elite standing was also reflected by his well-appointed attire.

Ben appeared a bit nervous as he glanced around, probably anxious to complete the transaction.

"Dr. Armond, as this is such an expensive collection that we will be insuring, there are steps that we must complete before the application is approved. I thank you for the time you are giving us today to complete this portion of the evaluation." The appraiser tugged on his sleeve and continued. "Might I place my briefcase somewhere, so I can remove the documents for your review?"

"Of course. Would you prefer my office or the showroom? The showroom has a small work area." I extended my hand in the direction of the showroom.

"I believe that would meet our needs," he said, and I escorted them to the work space.

As we positioned ourselves around the small round table, I chose the seat where I could watch the man across the street. The appraiser sat next to me, opened his case, and retrieved the documents.

"Here are the documents I need for you to review. It's standard information as to what we expect from you, and you from us. If you need me to go over each document, I'll be happy to do so, but I'm certain you're familiar with the process." His smile was tight, and his manner professional and all business.

"You should read it in total and then decide if you wish me to proceed. It specifies and outlines that you certify these paintings are genuine. Except for any alteration noted on the selling notes, no alteration or conservation has been performed on these canvases. You also agree that should we choose at any time before we agree to insure the paintings, we may subject the paint pigment for analysis. Or should we consider it necessary the paintings may be sent for an X-ray analysis and tests. Should the paintings leave the premises, you have the right to accompany them. We naturally will be responsible for the cost of the testing. There are times that we have found a painting not to be authentic. Sometimes we can return the painting to the gallery owner. Other times, under limited circumstances, we are obligated to hold that painting aside and alert the governing body." Monsieur Pardue smoothed his suit jacket and tie, signaling the end of his explanation.

"I'm not aware of such a stipulation under the law," I challenged and I had the best lawyers that money could buy. I demanded meetings with them every two weeks whether we needed or not just to be kept abreast of any potential problems that might be afoot.

"Ah, yes." Monsieur Pardue held up a finger. "For example, if a Chagall is found to be a forgery, the Chagall family can ask that it be confiscated and destroyed."

This settled my nerves a bit, as I had no Chagall in the offering to Mr. Jaager.

"I see. We deal in only the finest of art," I assured him. Even the forgery in the lot I offered to Ben had passed two auction house experts. I was confident it would pass the appraiser.

"We can proceed if you wish." Pardue and Jaager shared a look that made me suspicious they thought this scrutiny would

TWO

cause me to change my mind.

"Yes, that will be acceptable." No forgeries had been detected so far, and we had passed several through Abu Dhabi where expert eyes were cast upon paintings looking for any defect. Except for the right price Abu Dhabi's director might occasionally.

"Very good. When can we expect Madame Armond?" Pardue asked, sitting back as he prepared the papers. He pulled a large metal seal from his bag and placed it on the desk with an ink pad.

"Pardon?" I hoped the discomfort I felt was not reflected on my face.

"Madame Armond, when can we expect her? She's the owner and she must sign the papers," he responded matter-of-factly.

Now I was in a quandary. I couldn't disclose that Isabella was hospitalized for psychiatric issues. If pressed, I couldn't sign as an owner or partner because I had made certain my name did not appear on any documents. This certainly disrupted my plans for having her declared mentally incompetent on an expedited basis.

"She was not feeling well today and didn't want to cancel the appointment. Had I known papers needed to be executed, I'm certain she would have insisted on being here." I struggled to recover this quickly deteriorating situation. "However, I can sign and bring them to her to sign for your records, and then return them. I am sure Mr. Jaager would like to move this along."

"I'm sorry. It's impossible to proceed without her. Would you prefer to make another appointment?" Pardue asked.

"Well, if you're certain we can't make other arrangements, then yes, let's reschedule for Wednesday. If you leave the papers with me, I'll review them with her," I said.

Damn, this isn't what I'd planned. At all. My plan was to have her seventy-two-hour observation extended to a month of therapy. By then, the London gallery issue would be taken care of, and I'd be free of Avigad. Now I had to devise a plan to have her released in the next twenty-four hours.

"I hope it's nothing serious," Ben interjected, as my mind raced to reach a resolution to this dilemma.

"We hope not," I replied, unsure how to respond without raising an alarm or red flag. "I am sure she'll be available Wednesday."

"Good, I'll schedule it on my calendar." Pardue nodded and smiled.

Ben. Ben was an enigma. He was studying and assessing me, as if he didn't believe me. The sooner he was out of my life, the better. The sooner his funds were transferred, the better.

"Please send her my regards." Ben stood to leave.

They extended their hands in farewell. After we shook hands, they exited as quickly as they arrived.

I picked up the papers and walked to the office to make a copy to review and mark for notes. Should I send them to Gregory for a legal opinion? No.

As I moved from the office back to the gallery viewing area, the buzzer at the front door announced a visitor. Avigad and the man from the train were standing outside the door, waiting for admittance. Wonderful. Could this day get any worse?

I opened the door and couldn't miss the scowl on Avigad's face. The other man remained impassive.

"We need to talk. Lock the door." Avigad signaled for me to follow his command as he passed through the door. He proceeded to walk through the entrance as if he owned the building and I was a mere visitor.

"I'm not comfortable meeting here, Avigad," I said. Without waiting for me to provide hospitality I did not wish to offer anyway, he started the conversation.

"I'm here now, and we have business." It was apparent this

TWO

could turn ugly from the way he clenched and unclenched his right fist.

"Come to the show area. There are chairs in there to sit," I offered, as it was clear he wasn't leaving.

The man he arrived with didn't introduce himself. He simply turned and moved toward the front door to stand guard.

Entering the room, Avigad took stock of the surroundings. It was a feeling that sent a wave of cold water down my spine. A trickle, drop, and then stream of ice. He walked from painting to painting, examining them with an expert eye.

"How much for the collection?" he asked as he looked around the room possibly trying to assess how a deal should be struck and he was going to offer an opinion.

Although it was none of Avigad's business how I negotiated a deal and never had been, I answered. "Five million." That was all he would get. He was not entitled to an explanation.

"The money I have helped you earn has brought you many creature comforts, and given you a comfortable life, Adrien. You appear at ease in the trappings of your life." He smirked at me. Was he trying to now insinuate the silent partnership we had entitled him now to determine how the earnings I made should be structured?

I had no idea how to respond. But that was an opening that could end ugly if I didn't couch my response correctly.

"What brings you here? And more to the point, why didn't you call so we could meet somewhere else?" I hoped a slight diversion would lead us away from discussing money.

"You have truly bungled this, Adrien." He turned to face me fully.

"I have no idea what you are talking about. Have a seat and share with me what is on your mind." I directed him to a wingback chair. He sat, and stared at the paintings.

"You assured me that your wife would be dealt with." He sighed.

Yes, this would be difficult now to explain. How I now needed to have her discharged instead of admitted as a long-term patient. Instead of being tucked away, and an application of power granting me rights over the business, now I was saddled with controlling her every move again.

"Your point?" I swallowed loudly.

"It has become impossible to hold off the London authorities any further. I understand that they've now traced her real phone number and are contacting her. This could turn into quite an unpleasant situation if she has an interview with them. Billions of dollars are at stake, when all is accounted for in the end."

The London gallery. "Yes, they contacted her, and I intercepted the call." I tilted my head as I spoke. "I have it under control."

"I think not. Why wasn't she at the meeting today?" he asked.

"None of your concern, Avigad," I immediately sniped back. "We arranged for the meeting to be concluded on Wednesday. She wasn't feeling well, but I have everything in hand."

He studied me, waiting for me to change or supplement my answer. He seemed already privy to the truth, but chose to hold his cards in reserve.

"She's a loose end. You obviously don't have the ability to do what needs to be done." He stood, ready to end the conversation.

"Not so fast. Why have the funds still not been paid from the Cairo matter?" I demanded.

"Consider that debt settled. I have to take a loss on the London gallery because I can't close the books on that investigation to obtain an insurance payout." His voice rose a pitch too high, and his hand fisted where it rested on the back of the chair a bit

TWO

too hard.

"I don't think so," I challenged, leaning into a standing position to meet him head-on. "I wasn't the one who destroyed the building. I didn't sell you the building either."

"Do not challenge me, Adrien. You like your comfortable life? You want to continue to enjoy it? There will be turbulence ahead. Weather it and keep still. If you prefer a prison cell, that can be arranged," he said, schooling his temper. "Consider the Cairo payment as a debt settled for your weakness. Unless, of course, Madame Armond is tragically found dead after a mysterious accident, or a victim of a robbery gone wrong. Her demise could bring a swift conclusion to the London matter."

"I see what you're doing, Avigad. Dispose of her and set me up for the crime. Get out," I ordered.

He had me and he knew it.

"I trust you'll wrap matters up as necessary." He wasn't retracting his request.

"Of course." I gritted my teeth.

He motioned to the man at the door to move aside, and left.

This was quite the clusterfuck. I placed a call to the medical team in charge of Isabella. Surprised at my request, they agreed nonetheless. Further testing was suspended, based on the admission that I was embarrassed to say I had found drugs in the apartment that morning. Drugs, if made public, could cause a scandal. The team leader agreed to document a subjective finding that Isabella had ingested LSD or magic mushrooms based on the account. They agreed to discharge her to me, stating in the record she was hydrated and cooperative, and no danger to herself or others. I had to get her ready to complete the Jaager sale, and then determine how to dispose of my problem.

CHAPTER EIGHTEEN

ISABELLA

A STAFF MEMBER removed my intravenous line and took a final set of vitals as Adrien supervised my dismissal. Another staff member brought in papers for me to sign, and I was formally discharged. Neither of us spoke as we exited the facility nor as we entered the apartment a little while later. Adrien was treating this as if it never occurred.

He prepared a cup of coffee for me, and we sat at the dining room table, where papers were laid out.

"I met with Ben and his appraiser yesterday. We couldn't complete the transaction without you there. As the owner of the business, they require your approval and signature." He gathered the set of papers in front of him, tapping them on the table to straighten them.

"I've reviewed them and found them in order. However, we should review them together, in the event they ask you questions to ascertain your understanding," he said. "Neither of them know about your recent hospitalization, and it will remain that way. No need for them to question your level of competence."

TWO

He had yet to mention the London gallery, or address if the one painting Ben thought was a forgery was indeed a forgery. If I were to broach either subject, the entire thing could blow up in my face. I was stuck. Afraid to ask any questions, I remained silent and nodded at the appropriate time.

He finished with the documents and looked at me, ascertaining I wasn't planning to cause him any trouble.

"Do you have any questions?" He thumbed the papers.

"No. If you say it's in order and I should sign, then of course I will," I said. "Do I need to sign now or later?"

"Isabella, what's wrong with you? I told you that you need to be present to sign it. Read it over again. Make notes, even if it's so they can see you reviewed it. I have work to do. I'll check in on you later." He rinsed out his cup, and left.

I'll bet you'll check in, with all the cameras around. I need to call Chloe. Where's my phone. After a phone hunt that lasted ten minutes, I finally found it. I almost forgot about the cameras before I hit speed dial to her.

As soon as I was in the kitchen with both doors closed to prevent any sound from traveling, I hit speed dial, and was immediately connected.

"Oh my God, Izzy. Are you okay?" Her breathing was rushed and heaving. "Wait. Before you answer, I hope you didn't eat any of the food."

I stopped walking and sat on a barstool. That's an odd question.

"Yes, I did. Why?" I asked.

"Shit, do you even have to ask. That crap was laced with either LSD or some type of hallucinogenic. After I stopped tripping, I called Richard and he came by and took the rest to have it tested. By the time I called him, he said testing my blood or urine would most likely prove useless. The metabolites would be out of my system." I heard her walking around in some area that gave off an echoing sound.

"I don't want to alarm you because if you go over the edge with drama, you'll take me with you. I've spent the last day or so in a psych ward. Adrien found me in a state after eating the salad. It was laced with something, I guess what you've said was some hallucinogenic. I think the only reason I am out is so Adrien can pull the puppet master strings, and have me sign some papers for Ben. Does Ben know what's going on?" My stomach flipped with anxiety as bile clawed its way up my throat.

"I would guess not. I've only been in contact with Richard, and right now, running for a train. All I know is you didn't show up. But I think Rich would share with Ben that I thought I was doped from the food I got from you. You have any after effects?" She appeared short winded from keeping a fast pace toward her destination.

"Not that I am aware of. No flashbacks or whatever happens after you take a visit to Alice In Wonderland's rabbit hole. But how do you know it was a hallucinogenic in the food?" I knew there was no other explanation.

"I think it was mushrooms that make you hallucinate. When I was eating the salad, those fuckers were bitter as hell. But I didn't want to take the time to pick them out because I was starved. Right on schedule, I became nauseous, then it felt like I was going to poop myself—sorry, but the truth—and then the show began." Chloe sounded out of breath as she ran. "In my misspent youth, I dabbled from time to time with LSD. And don't ask why you didn't know. It was my secret."

"How soon before Richard knows if something was in it? And, more importantly, can he determine if it was intentionally placed there, or a bad batch of some real mushrooms?" I moved around the kitchen checking for anything else that could

TWO

be harmful but looked harmless. How would I even know? I barely told the difference between a portobello mushroom and a shiitake.

"Seriously? That's what you are going with? A mix-up? I don't know how long it will take him, but look in the refrigerator and see if any food is left that could be tainted," she rushed out. I was one step ahead of her. I checked the herb bins with anything that was lose and dumped it. I didn't care if it was sage, rosemary, or thyme. Anything lose, it was gone. It could be hemlock or Wolfsbane. How would I know?

I walked over and no food, other than fresh food, remained in the refrigerator. I am so screwed. What is Adrien's game? After I sign the papers, will I be back in the hospital again?

"Look, don't eat anything. I'll bring something after my appointment. You sure you're okay? No after effects?" she asked.

"No, I'm good, except I never want to go through that again. The colors arguing, I could handle. It was losing control of my legs, and feeling like I was having a seizure that was troubling." Troubling—that was an understatement. I guess Chloe thought so as well, as she gasped, trying not to make me feel bad. "I'm going to bed, so don't worry about bringing anything. I couldn't sleep a wink last night, and now I'm exhausted."

"Girl, if you had seizures that bad, it's most likely you had a four-gram dose. I would think someone not used to that could probably take a permanent trip totally out of their mind and never return. I'm calling Richard right now and see what he thinks. Talk later."

Should I call Ben? No, Chloe will get word to him. I need to review the papers again, so I know what they really say.

As I pushed open the door from the kitchen to the hall, I felt a slight resistance and pushed harder. I heard an "Ouch," and the door gave way. Danielle faltered back.

"I'm sorry, madam. I heard something, and I didn't realize you were home." She was breathless, and stepped back further.

"Why wouldn't I be home?" I asked.

"The doctor said you would be away for a few weeks. That you needed"—she struggled for the right word—"a rest."

"You can see I am here. Danielle, I'm trying to figure out if something I ate here upset my stomach. Was it Thomas who prepared the food left in the refrigerator in the marked containers?" I asked.

"I don't know. The doctor told me not to clean over the weekend," she answered with downcast eyes.

"I see. You seem to be upset or conflicted. What's wrong?" I asked.

"Nothing, madam. I'm worried for you. The doctor said your mind has been—"

"Has been what?" I demanded, now angry that even Danielle appeared to think she could judge me.

"Nothing, madam. Might I return to cleaning?" she asked.

"Yes, go ahead. I'm going out. I'll be back later." I wasn't going to chance eating anything more, and now I was too agitated to sleep.

I grabbed my purse and jacket, and walked past George, who also looked surprised to see me.

With no particular destination in mind, I decided to head toward the Eiffel Tower, get something to eat and sit to contemplate my options. Walking down the main area to the side street, I had the distinct impression I was being followed. I peered back to see a man in a heavy navy-blue peacoat, with a blue beanie covering his disheveled hair, gaining on me. Should I run, let him pass, drop back, stand and scream?

Before I could make any choice, the man was shoulder to shoulder with me. Ben.

TWO

"Go to the Eiffel Tower and find a bench by the Seine. Get something to eat and wait there." He continued walking, looking straight ahead. "I don't know if you are being followed, but assume you are."

Fifteen minutes later, I was sitting on a bench with a warm pretzel in my hand, waiting for further instructions. After he located me, Ben sat and slouched on the same bench, looking out over the Seine. We were about two feet apart. God, he didn't even look like himself with the mussed hair and the beanie.

"I was worried sick. I thought we'd pushed Adrien to do something drastic." He leaned forward.

I sat back and took a bite of the pretzel.

"Yes, I was in the hospital, admitted to the psychiatric unit. Apparently, I was given hallucinogens, with the hope of a more permanent stay due to permanent brain damage. Had you not insisted that I be there for the signing of the papers, I might have been secreted away, never to be heard from again. Do we have a plan? Please tell me you have one." I tried not to show my desperation, but failed.

He sat back, and I watched him from my periphery. He'd turned, studying the people that walked past.

"I don't want to frighten you any more than you are, but we are working an angle where we need you to stay in the game a little longer." Belatedly, I noticed Ben didn't look like he was speaking. His chin was tilted and his mouth barely moved. "This is bigger than we originally thought, and although I can't divulge why, I can't pull the plug on this. Even knowing your life might be in danger. I'm putting a man on you round the clock."

Well, that was alarming. Didn't I get a say in this? I stayed silent and let him continue.

"Tomorrow, when we're reviewing the papers, the appraiser will question whether a painting had some restoration or conservation performed on it. You will have signed the papers, and this should not alarm Adrien as it's just questioning the conservation of the painting. This means my guy will have the painting transported to a facility for testing, and we'll need you available to accompany the painting and remain with it. You understand?" He was convincing, but I could hear concern in his words too.

"I don't know. You tell me. How deep am I implicated in this circus?" I asked.

"Very deep. Adrien and the person or people working with him have you legally buried," he said honestly. "Buried deep."

As we began to speak again, people stood behind us, taking pictures. Americans who, once they surmised we were French, began to pepper us with questions. Thankfully, they left when Ben turned a dangerous vagrant look their way.

"The London gallery?" I asked.

"We're taking it off your plate. Today or tomorrow, you should be receiving a letter from the London district fire department stating they're finished with their report, and it's now being forwarded to the city structure department for review, taking it from the hands of the police. Based on the amount of backlog due to the attacks, it may be six or more weeks before the insurance company receives the final report. At that time, the insurance company may conduct their own investigation, if necessary. I assume Adrien receives the mail?" he said.

"You assume correctly." I tried to eat while mumbling, so if anyone was looking, they would have a difficult time deciphering if I indeed was conversing with the man next to me.

"He should be appeased that it hasn't been sent to any department for further criminal investigation, and now he needs to sit and wait," he said. "Don't bring the London gallery up anymore and by the time the next step is to be completed, we may

TWO

be ready to tie him into an ongoing conspiracy. That said, you still need to be cautious. I'm leaving a device on the bench next to you when I leave. Put it on your key ring. It's a sort of panic button that rings into my phone, and the person assigned to you, as well as the central office. Use it if you need it. I don't want you becoming anxious, only for you to be alert.

"If Adrien asks where you were, tell him you wandered down by the Seine. See you tomorrow." And with that, he left.

Finishing my pretzel, I grabbed the device and attached it to my key chain. Knowing that someone was watching over me, I felt lighter. Lighter than I had in a long time.

A short leisurely walk home had me trying to guess who was my tail, but it was impossible to tell. After a slight detour down the Rue Cler for a takeaway pastry and coffee, I was on my way back to what I now thought of as a prison. A prison guarded with cameras.

Walking toward the building, I concluded that once this was over, I'd sell my share of the apartment and the gallery, and move. Where, I didn't know. But I wanted to be Isabella Stone again, and reboot my life. I'd had it with the art world, and thought a massive life change was the way to go. Possibly something in cyber security. Why that crossed my mind, I had no clue. Maybe it was Mama whispering it in my ear.

I passed George, who gave me his customary nod. Once inside my apartment, I returned to the papers to review, with my chocolate croissant and coffee in hand. I might never eat anything from the refrigerator again.

As I passed Adrien's office, I heard him talking to someone.

"Yes, I received the letter today. They have referred it to the building structure people to determine if it should be condemned, or if it can be rebuilt. It says once they have determined what is appropriate, the report will be completed and forwarded to Isabella and the insurance company. But from the verbiage, it appears they are preliminarily declaring it an accident. I'm scanning and emailing to you—" he started. "Yes, I am sending it encrypted. I will burn it once you tell me you have it."

Then silence.

"Avigad, I can't be clearer with you than I have been. Under no circumstance, will I step foot in Israel or Iran." His voice filled with ice. "I am done. Our time has come to its end. Once the insurance money flows your way, that should terminate our need to have any contact with each other."

There was silence, and then he spoke in a muttered tone. The conversation was probably reaching a conclusion, so I found my way to the dining room to review the papers again. As I was about to write something in the margin, a text from Chloe popped up on my phone. "The results are preliminary and positive." She knew I would understand. The food had been drugged.

CHAPTER NINETEEN

ISABELLA

BEING HOME WAS surreal. Knowing Adrien was trying to have me committed to a psychiatric facility was terrifying and devastating at the same time. Did he no longer see me as a person with emotions and the right to exist outside his control? I needed to follow the plan to save myself, but what would be left of me when this was over?

"Isabella, I have documents that require your attention." He was going to his office before our meeting with Ben, carrying a stack of papers. Papers with Post-it notes that didn't look promising.

Moving around my desk toward me, he waited for my full attention. From the pile, he handed me the top three documents. Each page indicated it was page three of a three-page document. The document indicated my unencumbered ownership and title to a painting. It further certified I agreed to the sale of the painting from our gallery to the ascribed auction house. Once signed, I agreed all terms and conditions of the auction house were accepted by me. One was to be sent to Paris, one to London, and one to Abu Dhabi. All three set aside for a private reserve purchase prior to the auction. I studied the skimpy paperwork he'd handed me and looked at the pink strip of paper, where he indicated I should sign.

"Adrien, I am a little concerned here. I want to see the other two pages that go with the signature page, so I can review the title. I don't recognize the paintings, and these paintings don't look like they're part of our inventory," I said.

"What are you talking about? Of course they are. Now sign the pages," he demanded.

"No, I'm positive I would recognize these artists. I don't see our inventory number or when, and from whom, the paintings were acquired. It seems as if they are part of someone else's collection. Care to explain before I put my signature on here?" My tone was snide and not appreciated. There was no way I would sign something this sketchy. Had I been signing things like this before?

He straightened up at once from leaning on the desk, and moved behind my chair. He placed a hand on each shoulder, a little too close to my neck for my comfort, and massaged my neck. Massaged might be a loose term for what he did, which was dig into my muscle with each finger, squeezing it to produce pain and it stopped me from being able to move my neck freely.

"Isabella, you're in no position to be making decisions about the business after your recent hospitalization. I have everything in order, and I need your signature on the documents. These matters are time-sensitive, and if I must explain everything to you, then it may become jumbled in your mind. Sign the papers and we can be done," he ordered, still digging into my shoulders and triggering pain.

"Adrien, my name is on these papers, and if something was amiss, I would be the one accountable. I don't recognize this

TWO

inventory, and I don't understand why they are not being offered for a public auction sale. Why are they all going to a private reserve? And how much is the selling price? In what account will receive the funds? There are no accompanying transfer papers for the final sale. Because it is not clear to me that these painting were bought by the gallery, I am not comfortable signing off on these documents." Why was he being so evasive? Why couldn't he show me exactly when they were purchased, and from whom?

"They've been sitting in the freeport for almost a year," he said, squeezing my shoulders, causing me to develop a headache. "I had Paul remove them, and now they need to be on their way."

"When did he remove them? Why not ship them directly from the freeport?" His answer would be a lie; that was for certain. I knew every piece in the freeport and storage, and these pieces were not from either place.

"I just said they had been in the freeport, and he just removed them. Enough. Sign the papers so I can send them on their way. IsabellA, if you aren't able to conduct business, then my only course of action may be to have you declared incompetent, and the business transferred to me. Your actions and behavior are more than questionable. With your recent hospitalization, possibly you are having a relapse?" His threat was obvious, and his anger relayed his plan. He would have me declared incompetent.

"Adrien, I won't sign these papers until I have a valid explanation. I also want access to the computer, the storage area, and financial data," I said, ready to stand my ground.

He walked around the desk from behind, and sat in the chair opposite me. His eyes locked onto mine and he steepled his fingers under his chin.

"An important client found himself in a bit of a bind after the attacks. I had been holding the paintings for him in the freeport, and he had not transferred a sale to us until recently. Now he must sell these paintings at a lower price. They were in our facility, so it was easier this way, to move his inventory through us. Additionally, if it's released into the knowledge of the general public that the paintings are his, and anyone is aware of his financial circumstance, the value offered will be lowered. These painting are not on our books because when they are sold, the money will be transferred to a separate account we have set up, so that he will be remunerated for his portion from that account, and I keep the rest for my trouble. I have found a private buyer, and going through the auction house makes it easier to move the money," he said.

This convoluted explanation made absolutely no sense. To parse out the absurdity of what he'd said and feed it back to him would cause a circular argument. An argument I would never win. I opted for another route.

"Why can't we purchase the painting from him at a lower price, and then offer them for sale at a public auction? We are in the business of making a profit, so what's the problem?" I asked, probably not wanting to know the answer. Besides, whatever answer he comes up with would still not fit this scenario.

"Several business reasons. The person wishes to have a discreet sale. He needs an agent to facilitate the sale to bring the most profit, and that would be our gallery. Any profits to appear on our ledger would raise questions as to where the painting came from. Therefore, it is an unrecorded purchase and sale." He let that sit as he studied me.

"So, let me recap what you're telling me and summarize this transaction. You're asking me to sign my name to something illegal, never mind unprofessional and unethical. With that, I'm now implicated in a crime, and should something go wrong, my name is on the document and I would be held accountable. The

TWO

painting has no point of origin except here. If an investigation at the auction house was initiated, I would be held accountable if anything was amiss. To add even more issues to this problematic scenario, taxes and duty fall to us because the authorities think we bought the paintings, and if investigated, nothing will ever show up as paid. Thus, possibly earning me a tax evasion conviction as well. Have I got that right so far?" I asked, sitting back in the chair, placing my pen down.

He neither agreed nor disagreed. He just stared and studied. So, I continued.

"I'll ask again. If this transaction came to light and the initial transaction was found not to be recorded, and the completed transaction was not recorded, and duties and taxes not properly paid, then it would be me dropped in the middle of this mess. Would that be correct?" I said, standing up to move toward the window, with only his eyes following me.

After a few minutes passed and he did not answer, I continued.

"I'm sorry. This is just not something I can do. This is my gallery, and my name on the papers. If I'm not comfortable signing the papers, then I must go with my feelings," I said.

I'd let the entire management of the gallery fall into his hands, and in reality, knew nothing of what went on under my nose. Would I have a legal defense? That would be a resounding no. I couldn't even shift liability to him, as his name was nowhere on any ownership papers or transaction papers. I'd be marched off to jail. He would produce his secret paper of ownership of the apartment, and keep his kingdom intact.

He stood slowly and gathered the papers from the desk, tapping them to straighten the stack. This was the controlled anger that frightened me the most. The anticipation of how the punishment would be doled out was worse than the punishment itself.

I would rather have him yell and rant and the anger would eventually blow over. This cold freeze promised a worse retaliation.

"As you wish. Don't forget to be at the gallery at noon for our meeting with Ben and the appraiser," he said, and walked from the room. I was summarily dismissed. There was no doubt this battle he felt I won. However, in his mind there was never any doubt he would win the war.

From the area adjacent, I could hear the mild buzz of the news feeds on the lowered television volume, and I turned my attention to the screen. "Now, weeks after the horrific attacks, the center city area remains difficult to traverse, and businesses are being forced to close their doors, selling off inventory at a deeply discounted rate. The jobless rate has increased in the double digits. Investments are being sold at rock-bottom prices to capture enough money to pay for necessities. Economists wonder how much lower stocks and bonds can go. Car sales are off and repossessions on the rise. People wait in food lines, and sheltered areas remain overflowing." The newscaster droned on as pictures of people from countries in the European Union voiced concerns that their hard-earned money was being shuttled to other counties to help rebuild their infrastructure instead of their own.

It would appear the stress of the attacks was pulling apart the fabric of a European Union. Country was pitted against country. The euro had tanked, stocks plummeted and recovered slightly, only to tank again, and American tourists put off a trip or canceled plans until things settled. Manufacturing companies were at a slowdown, yet oil prices surged. And incredulously, it appeared the art world prospered. Not one auction was canceled, but many paintings remained unsold.

I picked up my phone and texted Chloe. "Need to meet you in an hour at Patron's."

Without waiting for a reply, I slipped the phone into my

TWO

purse, grabbed my jacket, and started down the hall. My tapping heels against the polished marble alerted Adrien to my approach. As I passed his office, he called to me from the room. "Where are you going?"

"I have a brunch appointment, and if I don't hurry, I'll be late," I answered. Not a complete lie, but an omission of who I planned to meet.

"And who are you meeting?" he asked, coming from around his desk toward me.

"Honestly, Adrien, am I not permitted to set up appointments without having to clear them with you? You come and go as you please, and never leave an itinerary. Do I interrogate you as to where you go and where you stay?" I challenged.

As I started to turn to leave, he reached out and grabbed my arm to stop me. He gripped me with a hold strong enough to probably leave a bruise, temporarily immobilizing me.

"Careful, Isabella," he warned. What I saw in his eyes was anger and disdain. "I repeat again. Where are you going?" he gritted out, and squeezed my arm harder.

Looking at my arm, with a nonverbal request for release—which went unanswered—I replied, "For God's sake, if you must know, Ben asked me to meet with a designer to discuss the paintings we are selling him. He wants to get rid of the hideous furniture in the apartment, and wanted to build his new furniture arrangement around the colors in the paintings. Now, let me go or I'll be late for the appointment. I'm certain Ben will want some feedback when we meet this afternoon." I twisted my arm away. How I ever came up with such a lie on the spot surprised—no, astonished—even me.

"Who is this person?" he demanded to know, studying my face for my twitch to indicate I was lying. He did not find one.

"You aren't to be believed. You have been pushing me to

close this deal. Now, when we are within a whisper of doing so, you are about to disrupt the finalization. I would think it a positive sign that he's wanting me to meet with his decorator to choose new furniture. It shows he's committed and all in on the purchase. So, unless you want to put the kibosh on this deal, let me go. There is nothing ruder than being late," I said, with my most authoritative voice and no eye twitch.

"I'll get my jacket and join you to meet this person." He started for the closet in his office.

"Absolutely not," I said, causing him to turn and stare with his mouth opened slightly, ready to argue.

"This woman will think you are some type of control freak. She won't want to meet with us. What man, what professional man with a busy medical practice, is going to cancel his morning appointments to meet with an interior decorator about a home that's not even his? What, in God's holy name, do you think will happen without you being there? Will I make a heinous faux pas and agree to a hot-pink couch? Or perhaps I'll tell her a lime-green and magenta chair selection would work well. What is your problem?" I demanded.

"Isabella." He drew out my name with disgust. "Only a few days ago, you were having a conversation with fruit and colors in the paintings in the living room. Can you be trusted to meet with someone of importance without some supervision?"

I felt my chest heat and the heat spread to my face. "Well, Adrien, might that be because I was drugged?"

He bristled and turned to face me, full-on. "What did you say? What makes you think you were drugged? No one said anything that could lead you to that assumption. Where would you come up with such an idea?"

Well, now I'd gone and stepped in it good. Thinking under pressure was getting more difficult. How would I know such a

TWO

thing?

"What other explanation is there? Someone must have thought it a laugh to lace a drink at some place I was at. In the old days, it was teenagers putting laxatives in hot chocolate. Today, it's drugs. What's the drug of choice, roofies or ecstasy? Yes, what a laugh, get someone high and send them out to fend for themselves. These evil people have evolved in their pranks. Either way, what happened wasn't my fault."

I had him there, and he knew it was a reasonable explanation. He turned his back to dismiss me, and reminded me once again of the appointment. With that, I left. From paranoia, or perhaps I was being proactive in the event he had me followed, I took evasive action. Instead of leaving by the front, I slipped out the side door, managing to dodge the building's hall cameras. Once outside, I took off my shoes and ran, ball of foot to cement, until I was certain whoever was waiting for me outside had given me time to disappear.

WITH MY SHOES back on my feet, I caught my breath from power walking to the café and spotted Chloe and Richard at once. Since the attacks, even restaurant business had decreased to a level where employees were sparse, and less food choice was on offer.

Good, she got my message and understood my code. What had my life devolved to, where I was sneaking away from my home and setting up a clandestine meeting with my best friend? Giving the hostess the opportunity to meet me at the station and escort me to the table, I saw Richard stand to let me slide into the crescent-shaped booth. Chloe was already pouring me a cup of coffee as I sat.

"Spill. Why the meet?" she asked breathlessly, almost causing an overflow of the cup from her distraction.

"Good morning, Richard, and good morning, Chloe," I said, remembering how important it was to my mama to have pleasantries acknowledged, and in doing so, reminding Chloe of the same.

Richard studied me, but I gave nothing away. He placed his hands in front of him on the table and waited for me to open the conversation. He was a patient man.

"This morning, Adrien asked me to sign papers that clearly were documents falsifying the ownership and value of paintings. He says he's transferring three paintings from the freeport. However, I'm absolutely positive they weren't there when we did the inventory. I asked where they came from because I didn't know. One is to stay in Paris, one is to be transported to London, and one to Abu Dhabi. The scheme of sale was so convoluted that I can't even begin to reiterate it to you. His story was so unbelievable, I lost track of what was fact and what was fiction. Look, it all sounded too wrong to me, and I refused to sign the documents because, in the end, if the paintings were questioned, it would be me going to jail," I said.

"Did you get a look at any of the original papers?" Richard inquired, playing with his spoon.

"No, he gave me the last page only of the final transfer papers, with the place to sign. And he also didn't have the regular paperwork to transfer the funds from the auction house to our account for the business. He had a special account set up for the money to be wired where he said he and the paintings' owner would withdraw the funds. So, not only could I be criminally and civilly liable for some type of art fraud scheme, but who knows if he is laundering money for this man as well."

Richard blew out a breath and pulled his phone out. "Ladies, excuse me. I'll be right back." With that, he left the area.

"While he's gone, let me fill you in on the food. The lab

TWO

must send it out for further analysis to break it down into, I don't know, nanograms or something. They only did a basic preliminary. But from the preliminary results only, they believe that the food had a mixture of both lysergic acid diethylamide and psilocybin mushroom. Richard has the report. The LSD was actually mixed with the food itself. He'll have to tell you. It was after it was cooked. The mushrooms, however, were sprinkled on it. I'm no chemist, but I think if it was heated with the food, it would take away the effectiveness. After Thomas cooked it, could Adrien have put the drugs in?" The expression on her face was somber.

"I have no idea." I don't remember seeing the containers in there at all.

"That wasn't a question, only a thought. Anyway, it appears that from the container markings, the amounts of drugs incrementally increased as each day passed. Breakfast on day one had the least and each meal after, the drugs were increased. By the end of the weekend, if you had consumed all the food, you would have gone so around the bend that no rubber room would have been needed. You would have had such traumatic brain damage that you would be in a catatonic state." She slammed her hands on the table and threw her head back, rolling her eyes back with an open guppy mouth.

It took a while for me to gather and process the information. Adrien had purposefully drugged me, or at least attempted to so that I would never be able to function normally again. I would, for all intents and purposes, be brain damaged. Possibly unable to pee by myself or feed myself.

"I can't go back to that house, Chlo. I can't. What if during the night while I'm asleep, he gives me a shot or places a drug-infused patch on me and kills me? Especially now that he knows he can't control me anymore?"

Richard returned to the table. "Isabella, I just got off the phone with Ben and after the transaction is completed today, we're placing Adrien under arrest and removing you from danger. He was going to have the paintings sent for verification with a bogus appraisal excuse, just so we have a chain of custody, but once he takes possession of the evidence by waiving the appraisal, and the money is transferred, we are arresting him," Richard said.

"We?" Chloe asked, nearly dribbling her coffee from her open mouth. "Are you actually undercover as well?"

He shook his head and smiled. What's going on with these two?

"No, sorry. Old habits die hard. He will. But that's the plan, Isabella. Once the money transfer is made, we will have him on fraud, and then we can open a larger investigation. Sorry, Ben, not we," he corrected himself, and continued, with Chloe hanging on every word.

"I'm not privy to any information about the case. But if I was looking at this, I'd want to tie this business to money laundering somehow. It's a delicate balance because Adrien and whoever he is working with might be getting nervous. It might force them to move things into position where we will never find anything," Richard said.

"You think he has a partner?" I found that hard to believe. Adrien was not one to share or trust anyone.

"Have I got any evidence? No. But the money and inventory he is moving around takes more than one person. If I was to guess, I would say that he had a partner, and his partner has partners. In other words, I think he's part of a network. Does he know everyone in the network? Probably not. However, you must wonder where he comes upon those fake paintings like the ones we inventoried. He didn't just order them from some

TWO

local store. They were good forgeries. How long has this been going on, right? Where does his money come from? Except for us looking at him with a microscope because of the divorce, he comes and goes as he pleases. No one tracks his money. How do you know how many painting are sold, if any are fake, or where the money goes? I'd put money on it that he has ample funds in offshore accounts. We'll know for sure once Ben or I am able to get full access to the accounts." He let that sit.

Whatever he said made Chloe nervous, and she started drumming her fingers on the table.

"Do you want me to come with you to the meeting?" Her presence would totally tank this whole operation for sure.

"No. I had to lie to him. I said I was meeting a designer Ben hired to replace his furniture to match the art. Richard, can you make sure he knows I used this as a cover story?" Looking at my watch, I knew I had to leave.

"I hate to break up this meeting, but I have to start back to the gallery for the meeting. Richard, please make sure Ben knows about my cover story as to why I was here. I'm stopping by Tela's shop to pick up some swatches, to prove to him I met with a designer."

Chloe studied me, and I appreciated her ability to pick up on my inner panic and not call me out on it.

"I love you, and be careful, Izzy," Chloe said, as she came in for a hug.

"No worries. I am sure Ben has it in hand," I said.

Richard rubbed my shoulder to comfort me.

FORTY MINUTES LATER, samples and catalogues in my bag, I walked through the door of the gallery. As I made my way to the office, Adrien sat behind the desk and watched me like I was his prey. He was especially quiet and neither greeted nor acknowledged me as I entered, so I sat and waited.

As we continued our staredown, the bell at the front door buzzed. Adrien looked to me to answer it, and I responded. As I walked to the door, Ben gave me an almost indiscernible head nod as he watched me open the door. Everything was going to be just fine.

We strolled past the paintings on display. Ben said with a slightly raised voice, "Thank you, Isabella, for meeting with my designer. I haven't spoken to her yet, but I'm certain whatever you ladies decide will be a relief from seeing that hideous purple. And might I add, I'm glad you are feeling well enough to join us."

"Thank you, Ben. It must have been that flu going around. I was out of commission for almost two days. And I'm pleased to say that we made some excellent selections for the living room." I smiled. "Shall we step into the viewing room?"

I started toward the room and noticed Adrien watching us from the desk, making no attempt to get up and join us. When we reached the room, the door was locked. I looked toward Adrien, who walked our way, staring between me and Ben. Not in any rush at all.

Without an extension of his hand in greeting to Ben or the appraiser, he gave a quick nod acknowledging both men. He turned the key and the lock disengaged. Pushing the door open for admittance, he stepped in and flipped the light switch to illuminate the room. However, something was wrong. Very wrong. None of the paintings were on the wall that the appraiser was to inspect. The viewing room walls were empty. No paintings anywhere. What the hell was going on?

Ben looked to me and I looked to Adrien.

"Gentlemen, I'm so sorry that you have made this trip. I must share the news I have with you. I need to withdraw the

TWO

paintings I had prepared to show you, and terminate our business," he said. Just like that, nothing more.

"I'm sorry, I don't understand." Ben shook his head in confusion. "Do you mean you have others for my consideration?"

"Sadly, no, I don't, Ben. I have run into a slight problem and have nothing to offer you." A casual shrug was all he offered, as he looked from person to person.

"What are you talking about? Where are the paintings?" I asked, twirling around, as if they would magically appear.

"Not to worry, Isabella. I have everything in hand," he said, and smiled his tight smile at me.

"Now, gentlemen, if you'll excuse us, I'm sorry to have wasted your time. Accept my apologies, but I believe our business has come to an end," he said, ready to escort everyone out of the room.

An end. What does that mean?

"Again, I'm still unclear. Are you saying that not only do you not have the paintings on offer, but none?" Ben said, with a righteous indignation.

"That's what I'm saying. If you wish, I can refer you to another fine art gallery," Adrien offered with a smarmy smile.

"Adrien, I don't want to get ugly about this, but I believe we had a contract," Ben started.

"Ben, I believe you are mistaken. You didn't accept the paintings as offered, and in effect, counteroffered by requesting the appraisal," Adrien said. He must have consulted with his lawyer to pull that one out of his hat.

"And you accepted my request. And if I might be so bold, it's Isabella who owns the gallery, and I haven't heard her withdraw the offer," Ben countered.

One point for Ben, but this was turning ugly. Adrien would never be outmaneuvered. That would be totally unacceptable.

"Then Isabella and I will confer as you wish, and give you a reply within twenty-four hours." He signaled with his left hand to the door, inviting them to leave.

Now what?

"Then I'll wait for your decision, and hope you reconsider," Ben said. Ben's eyes met mine and offered no reassurance. He was as stunned as I, and needed to regroup as well.

And with that, Adrien stood by the door, holding it open, and they left.

He turned toward me with a cold stare, offering no explanation, and I asked no questions. Waves of anger rolled off him, and I knew to bide my time wisely.

"I will discuss this with you later. I have your car in the structure next door. I need to take the train somewhere. Drive it home, and when I get home, we can discuss this further," he said.

"Is this about me not wanting to sign the documents?" I asked, scared out of my mind now.

"Don't be absurd. I said we would discuss it later. Now go. Car. Parking structure." He snapped his fingers, like I was a dog to obey my master.

I grabbed my bag and jacket, with the intent of driving right over to Michelle's office and having her file whatever papers needed to be filed to end my marriage to Adrien. I wanted my life back. By God, I would show him. This was over the line. How dare he make such a unilateral decision without me.

I stormed from the office and barreled to the structure, keys gripped tightly in my hand so hard, I thought it would make a permanent indent. I might have noticed if I hadn't been so focused on my anger. I might have noticed if I hadn't been so focused on getting the better of Adrien. I might have noticed if I had been more aware of my surroundings. I might have noticed when I reached my car, the well-dressed man who came out of

TWO

nowhere, stepped in front of me, grabbed my bag, and shot me. Burning hot pain. Searing pain. Shock. Did he just shoot me again, or was that the pain radiating out? My life flew before my eyes as I crumbled against the car, setting off the alarm, as blood dripped over the cherry-red exterior, blending in with it. If it weren't for my twitch of an involuntary pain reflex, I wouldn't have pressed the panic button on my keys that Ben had given to me.

CHAPTER TWENTY

BEN

WALKING AWAY FROM the meeting I'd so carefully planned, and the plan I so precisely executed, I was dumbfounded by the result. Confused, even angry, I had not seen that coming. What the hell just happened? Did he see through me? Had my cover been blown? Were the paintings in play for some other reason? What spooked him? Was he spooked, or did he have another agenda? I was flabbergasted, deflated, and played.

"Jason, I'm sorry for bringing you out here with no results. Just send the invoice to the office, and you will be reimbursed. When I do the daily report, I'll send it to you to sign off as accurate and authentic." I owed him more of an explanation, but I had none myself.

"Ben, I'm not a psychologist, and I'm frankly not even what you would call a people person. That's why I like authenticating. It has me acting on a limited time frame with people," he said. Yes, one would never accuse Jason of being a people person.

"Something isn't right there. That guy has changed from the

TWO

last time we saw him. It's like a switch flipped inside. His eyes were . . . empty. He's playing some type of game, Ben. The man gives me a bad feeling," he said, looking between his shoes and my eyes. "I'd rather not have to deal with him again. If it means the operation will tank without me, you know you can count on me. But otherwise, I hope my path would never cross his again."

"Jason, I understand, and that's fine. I think my time as Ben Jaager is over with him. I don't know what happened, but I . . . I'm just stunned," I told him.

We shook hands and parted.

Yes, criminals could be called bad people. Sometimes good people made bad decisions, but did that make them categorically or inherently bad? I was on the fence as to this thinking. If they admitted it, were remorseful, and accepted their punishment, then I could flush them from my mind and not obsess over their bad deeds. Somehow, I don't think Adrien was a good person doing one bad thing. Whatever deal he made with whatever devil he danced with, one thing was for certain. He had no remorse.

I retrieved my phone and hit the speed dial to Richard. Probably not the smartest idea to talk on the street, but I'd keep it short.

"Ben, what's up. Something go wrong?" he asked. Yeah, Richard still had the agent in his blood, only he was now earning twice the income. Given the perks of more autonomy and less red tape, he probably made a good deal taking the job.

"You could say that." Pacing back and forth in one place the block over from him was not a good move.

"Hold on, Chloe is here. Let me put you on speaker so I don't have her stopping me every five seconds for an update." I heard the speaker engage, and I could hear the last part of Chloe spouting profanity, and then, "Go ahead."

I scanned the street for any type of tail, though I was sure there was none. I did see Isabella hell-bent, storming out of the gallery toward the parking structure. I crossed the street and tried to slowly catch up with her, as I finished my call with Richard and Chloe.

"We weren't in there for more than five or ten minutes and he said he was calling off the deal. There were no paintings and no explanation. He said he didn't want to do any further business, and that was it. I'm still shell-shocked. I can't figure out if he is on to me and my cover is blown, or if something spooked him and he's just being overly cautious. Possibly, he's trying to sell a fake somewhere else, and is being called out on it, and he's not willing to take this risk. I need you to review the tapes from the cameras that you didn't have Dickie plant in there before we did the inventory. We need to see if he met with someone, and if he moved the paintings. You know what to look for." Mentioning Dickie could be a career ender.

Suddenly I heard a popping noise, like a car backfire, and was about to continue when my phone started vibrating and buzzing, indicating Isabella had activated the alarm.

"Was that a car backfiring?" Richard asked.

"Hold on," I told him. Switching to the map app, it showed that the keychain was down the street at the parking garage, and had just been engaged. Looking over to the two-story car park structure, I heard a car alarm going off. Beep . . . Beep . . . Beep. No, that was no car alarm accidentally activated. There was something happening, and I was afraid Isabella was at the center of it.

About to disengage from Richard, I received notice from the central desk that an emergency signal had been activated, with the coordinates of where the signal emanated.

Without knowingly ending my call to Richard, I instinctively called local emergency services, as I was on the move. Central

TWO

office would be activating them as well.

I headed toward the structure at a full-on run, emergency services engaged. Help would be here soon.

"What is the nature of your emergency?" the female voice asked dispassionately.

"Ben Johenson, Europol. I have an unknown emergency; I need law enforcement and ambulance rolling. I think I heard a single gunshot. Have the ambulance meet me on the second floor on the parking structure at the corner of Avignon Boulevard. When I get there if I don't need the ambulance, I'll cancel," I said, as shoe leather slapped the pavement.

"I'll stay on the line with you. I just dispatched the ambulance and law enforcement. Estimated time of arrival, five minutes," the dispatcher said, still remaining calm, but her voice now tinged with anxiety.

I held the line open, and with nothing but pure adrenaline coursing through my veins, I was closing in on the structure, as other people were looking upward to figure out what was causing the offensive noise. Truth be told, I don't even remember my feet touching the ground any longer, as I raced to the building. I do know my chest tightened and side began to ache from the excitement and the run. My breathing was labored as I took the steps two at a time, but I couldn't let Isabella down. I'd been careless in taking her shadow off her, thinking an arrest was imminent.

As I bounded up the stairs, Richard's name kept popping up on the screen. Dispatch was still on the line and I faintly heard her ask, "Sir, have you assessed the situation?"

"Almost there," I breathed out.

I could hear the noise at the far end of the deck, but couldn't see it yet, so I kept running. The deck was free of other people who were either hiding or had left when they realized something bad had occurred. No Good Samaritans here.

My last step and the heavy red metal door opened, and that's when I saw the bright red car in the corner of the structure, next to a door where the offender must have escaped. There she was, slumped forward over the hood of her car.

"I'm here," I relayed to the dispatcher. "She's not moving. She's on the hood of her car, give me a moment. I'm putting the phone in my shirt pocket to assess the situation." I put the phone on speaker, and slipped it into my pocket.

I heard her say the ambulance should be rolling up momentarily, that they'd hit some traffic, but I mentally blocked it out. I was Isabella's lifeline, and I had to do something.

Bright red blood soaked through the lower right part of her shirt. My feet couldn't move around fast enough. She wasn't moving, she was just stretched on her car hood. *Please, dear God, don't let her be dead. Please don't let this be my fault.*

"Looks like a gunshot wound to the right side of her body, with a moderate amount of blood loss. I'm going to move her to the ground, so her breathing won't be impeded by the hood," I reported.

I'm sure they were giving me instructions, but all I could focus on was getting Isabella from the hood to the ground of the garage without smacking her head on the concrete. An alarming amount of blood had already soaked her shirt and smeared her car hood.

"Revising my assessment. There is a large amount of blood loss. She is breathing shallow, and I can only get a faint pulse. Where's the ambulance?" I yelled.

"Rounding the corner at the light. Can't you hear it?" she asked.

Yes, I could hear the siren, but my mind had blocked out everything except what was in front of me. A woman possibly

TWO

on the verge of dying. Was this my fault?

"God, she's still bleeding, it looks like"—I tore her blouse apart to find the wound—"Jesus Christ, it looks like a gunshot. It *is* a gunshot. I see the entrance on the right side, and don't know if it's a through and through or if the bullet is still lodged. I don't want to turn her over to check for an exit wound!" I yelled to the only lifeline I had, on the other end.

Oh my God, first aid, remember first aid. Move her on her side to keep her airway clear. Should I move her, or will I cause spinal injury? *Think, man, think.* I ripped off my jacket and immediately applied pressure to the area. Shock could come from blood loss. Where is the ambulance?

I heard the wailing of the sirens getting closer and closer, until they were right on me. I watched what appeared to be slow motion as a man and woman jumped from the ambulance. Time stood still, I was frozen in time. The sudden activity surrounding me snapped me out of my daze.

The emergency service motioned me to move aside so they could assess her. My hands and pants were smeared with Isabella's blood. Her skin was pale, and her chest barely moved.

"What can I do to help?" I asked as the woman opened her case and applied a device to assess vital signs, while her partner looked for a vein to start an intravenous drip.

"Just step back. We've got this," she said, as the machine attached to her arm read 90 over 40 and a little heart sign said 110. Her partner indicated he found a vein and was in.

"Go over to Matthew, and hold the bag as he attaches the tip to the catheter hub. Stand there while he tapes it in place, so we have some liquid flow by gravity. She may be going into shock, and we need to get fluids in her fast. If I tell you to squeeze the bag, apply slow, steady, light pressure. We don't want to get too much going and blow a vein. Any idea her blood type?" she asked.

"No, I have no idea." I moved around to collect the bag from the man, who attached one end into a plastic mechanism that had been inserted into her hand. The hand that pressed the panic button that probably saved her life.

Law enforcement were exiting their car as I saw Adrien come running toward the ambulance.

"I'm a doctor and that's my wife! All of you, get away from her!" he yelled, starting to take off his jacket.

The medics looked at him and went back to work, doing everything they could to save her life. I stayed in place, holding the bag as directed.

He pointed an accusatory finger at me and said, "You! What are you doing here? Did you do this? Is this in retaliation for me not selling you some paintings?"

Another emergency vehicle, this car probably an administrative person, roared up the platform, sirens screaming, which diverted his attention momentarily.

Then he started again, "Who's in charge here? I'm her husband and a doctor. I will take over. Everyone, move away. What are her vital signs, and what have you given her?"

As he moved toward her, the emergency service person in charge pushed past him, motioning for me to remain where I was, but to pass the fluid to another man ready to assist.

"Sir, I don't know who either of you are. My name is Cleve Martone, and I am the senior person here. No one is touching this woman but us. Now, if you are her husband, report the information you have to law enforcement right there." He pointed to two people assessing what was now a crime scene.

Stepping back as instructed, I watched how one listened for lung sounds and another assessed that there was likely no spinal damage. It was a blur of activity, as they placed her on the gurney

TWO

and were moving her to the ambulance, the wheels clacking against the smooth concrete.

I heard the senior emergency responder saying something into his mic about having an operating room staff ready for a gunshot wound to the abdomen, possibly involving the liver. Adrien must have told them she was blood type A-positive, as they were asking for it to be available. It was reported she had a potential hemothorax on the right side, and possibly a collapsed lung.

"She's not breathing!"

Everything stopped. Everyone stood still, as the male emergency responder said the words no one ever wants to hear.

With that, a flurry of activity ensued, where she was quickly intubated and a plastic device the shape of a football was attached to a tube in her mouth. One of the attendants started to slowly pump the bag, over and over. Within seconds, she was in the back of the ambulance, and the screaming vehicle set off, carrying the body of a dying woman.

Adrien stood there, unsure of what to do, or who to lash out at next. He had no control over the situation, and the frustration and anger were evident. He looked at me, and I realized I would be his target. In what seemed like an instant, he lumbered toward me, his face contorted with unbridled rage, his fists ready to deliver punches. A police officer nearby quickly sprinted over, and with finesse moved him away from me.

"Sir, you were first on the scene. I need to interview you," the officer said to me. He turned to Adrien. "Step back, sir, we will get to you next."

Adrien replied, "I am returning to the gallery across the street. You can meet me there." He wasn't racing off to the hospital? What a cold-hearted bastard. Before an argument with the law enforcement agent could ensue, he took off, ignoring the man telling him to stop.

Now I had come to the proverbial fork in the road. Do I lie to law enforcement as to how I came to know she was in danger, and have that memorialized on a record for everyone to see? Or do I maintain my cover and blur the details to clean up later?

I made the split decision to blur the lines. Once my story was told and recorded, I was cleared to go.

As I left, I heard one officer saying to another, "Probably a robbery . . . no purse . . . likely a vagrant . . . but where'd the gun come from?"

As the discussion trailed off, I left and would have Jill follow up to obtain the final details. Levi would need to be briefed immediately, to liaise with the police and understand why my story lacked certain details, and why those had to be kept out of the record for now.

CHAPTER TWENTY-ONE

ADRIEN

"Gunshot to the abdomen. Purse taken. We think it's a robbery." That's all the police would give. Did I know of anyone that would want to harm Isabella? Seriously, how do I even begin to answer that loaded question? Was she involved with anything that could cause her to be in any danger? Again, how to answer that?

"No, absolutely not," was my firm answer. "However, since the attacks, we have had a vagrant problem, and we even felt compelled to move our inventory from the store to our freeport because we feared a robbery."

They indicated they would be keeping me updated. As soon as I was certain they'd left, I was on the phone to Avigad.

"Tell me you didn't do this?" I gritted out.

"Do what?" was his calm, indifferent answer to my question.

"Someone shot Isabella." I waited to hear an affirmation I didn't want to hear.

"I assure you, I didn't instruct anyone to harm Isabella. Now, we have more pressing issues," he said, quickly dismissing an issue I suppose he no longer felt a problem.

"And what could be more pressing than Isabella on her way to surgery from a gunshot wound, and the police gathering enough information to look at me for the shooting?" I tried to temper my anger by digging my nails into the palm of my hand, but I was losing the fight.

"Twenty minutes, at the café," he said, and disconnected.

Within minutes, I was boarding the number eleven train to the Etiole metro station. I despised the train system, which had become even more unbearable after the attacks. It seemed young people without jobs had nothing better to do than buy a ticket and ride the trains all day. I think they referred to it as train surfing. Was it to amuse themselves, waste time, or look for prey? What a waste of time and energy. The train's appearance had deteriorated, as did the people riding them. As more people were laid off from the transit system, safety was becoming a real concern.

As I ascended the steps to the street, I was jostled by two teenagers who, I was sure, tried to pick my pocket. For their effort, they would come away empty. I proceeded down the Champs-Élysées, into the small café where we always had our meetings. I was certain it was owned by unsavory friends of Avigad's who guarded his safety while there. Although, he probably was armed appropriately to guarantee his own safety.

I strolled in and, without an invitation, sat in the booth across from Avigad.

"Look me in the eye, and tell me you had nothing to do with what happened to Isabella," I demanded.

He continued to sip his coffee, then placed it in the saucer with a small clink of glass touching glass. Picking up a pastry from the small round bowl, he broke off a piece and placed it in his mouth, slowly chewing. Without answering my question, he

TWO

continued with his meal and once devoured, swallowed another sip of coffee.

"Were you followed?" he asked, putting the cup back into the saucer.

"Followed? No. Why would I be followed?" This was what he was leading with?

"You're sure?" He wiped his mouth with the linen napkin.

"Look, I'm not playing this game," I said, sitting back, and proceeded to spoon enough sugar in the bitter horrid coffee to make it palatable. As always, it resulted in a wince from him.

"Because the last time we met, there was a man here who raised my curiosity." Again, Avigad raised his cup to his blubbery lips.

Now I was annoyed and on the verge of leaving. I was not playing his game of throw and fetch.

"And that concerns me, why?" My irritation was not withheld.

"Because he is employed by a divorce firm. You arrived, he arrived. You left, he left. Coincidence? I think not." Avigad studied my reaction.

Then it hit me where he was taking this line of thought.

"You think Isabella is having me followed?" No way she would raise her game to this new level.

"The thought crossed my mind," he replied.

"But you have no proof?" I asked, to keep him at bay, but I didn't need a response. The way she conducted herself lately told me all I needed to know.

"I will leave you with that thought. You can assure me you will govern your actions accordingly?"

I nodded in agreement.

"So that's it? Why couldn't you tell me this over the phone? I need to get to the hospital, in the event they need me to sign

223

documents." Not that I cared what happened to Isabella. Especially now. However, there would be talk if I didn't at least pretend I cared.

"We have business to map out."

I settled back, waiting for him to continue.

"Within the next two months, all global economies, except a select few, will fail." Just like that, he said that as if it was a given. "Anarchy will reign and civilization as we know it will be no more."

Clearly, Avigad was delusional and out of his mind. Should I stop this now, or let him continue? He took my choice away from me, and continued.

"First course of business. We need to leverage the art bubble by dumping all the art possible into the market without raising suspicion." I had no idea how to respond. "Starting at once, we are going to clear out the Luxembourg freeport where Roselov's inventory is housed. I want you to contact every auction house in America, Europe, and the Middle East, and distribute the paintings around evenly. The Jude White fakes will continue to be sold to private reserve. The others with clean provenance will be sent to public auction. I have a few offered for private sale." He'd obviously thought this out and had a plan in place to leverage the most money.

"How many are we talking about from his inventory?" This was ludicrous. There was no way this could be accomplished without months of preparation. I'd seen Paul prepare the inventory and had a vague idea of what was in Roselov's collection, but to ready them for sale would take weeks.

"Seventy-five," Avigad answered. "The entire Roselov collection."

I sat, dumbstruck. How did he think he could pull this off? I'd have to wait for the specifics to my answer.

TWO

"We're also going to clear out every painting in your inventory, and you'll be closing your gallery doors. Even though my name is not on any documents outright and buried several layers deep in the shell and holding corporation, I have a silent interest in this place. Your story will be that without your wife—who breathed life into the gallery—you find it impossible to continue. Your medical schedule prohibits the care the gallery and its clients require. People will be sympathetic and not question you selling your paintings at a slightly lower than market value. And people being people will snap up a bargain." He had no guilt at all of trading on the probable death of Isabella for a sale. I had no feelings for Isabella. Her death would almost be a welcome remedy to my problems. Except I would be the prime suspect. Was his plan with her gone and me in jail for her murder that he as a partner, albeit deeply buried, rise to take ownership of his investment.

Still unable to comprehend the magnitude of sales that would have to be orchestrated, I sat and didn't question his plan. It'd better be bulletproof because it was beyond my ability to orchestrate one given Avigad's parameters.

"And how am I to move these paintings without Isabella's cooperation and signature?" A reasonable question I was certain he would have no answer for.

Wrong.

Without a thought, he reached next to him, picked up a manila envelope the sat on the seat beside him, and placed it on the table.

"Today, at four thirty p.m., you are meeting with my *avocat* and a justice, who will sign these documents. These documents give you authority to conduct business in Isabella's name, as her incapacitated guardian agent." He removed the papers and separated them into two piles.

"If you look at the last page"—he pointed on the page—"that is the *avocat* name, and you need to sign below." He removed a pen from his pocket, clicked it, and handed it to me.

Pointing to where I should sign, I did so without reading the document. What would be the use? I'd never win an argument with him. I therefore obliged, and signed my name. He placed the papers back in the envelope to return to the *avocat*.

"Now, the logistics. This preparation must be completed by the end of the week, and everything has been set in motion. Once the funds from the final sale are deposited, I've made arrangements to convert some to gold, some to diamonds, and the majority of funds will be kept in specific offshore banks. Here's a list of the offshores that are reliable to have your other funds transferred to, and I would start immediately. Sell off what you still have in stocks and move that to these banks. Do not worry over the loss you take on the stock. If you do, when the time is upon us, you will lose it all." Avigad paused, and then finished with, "You don't need any further details. Just know you'll be taken care of. You won't languish when the world comes to an end." He looked at me as he sipped his coffee.

The man had totally lost the plot, and was now barking mad. Should I take this seriously?

"Now, go visit that lovely wife of yours, and I'll text you the details regarding the court procedure. All is in place. Once the papers are signed, I can pull the lever on the auction houses. They're ready to process the sales on an expedited basis," he said.

"This wasn't something you put together overnight. How long has this been in the works?" I wasn't sure if I wanted to know, as I was starting to piece this action as possibly the shoe dropping after the attacks.

"Two years ago, but this piece was moving on the board the day before the Roselov explosion. His arrest was an unexpected

TWO

problem that sped up my timeline."

I finally understood and saw his plan without any veil of fog over my eyes. He blew up the gallery, and it had nothing to do with insurance money, but rather assurance that the tainted inventory housed there was never found and thought destroyed. There would be no need for search warrants for evidence that was destroyed. And Isabella's shooting? An obvious part of the plan, which was timed down to the hour of when I would take ownership of the gallery. He was now in a position of check. Checkmate was just weeks away.

By the end of the day, I would be in control of everything and nothing. The sale of the paintings, an obvious foregone conclusion. As long as I was compensated for their value, they could take the lot.

The next call I placed was to Paul, to ready the shipment of the lots, with instructions where they were to be sent by auction deadline date. My money stayed put until I could think more on the subject. However, I would sell off the stocks and deposit the money. The markets were a nightmare and would probably get worse, even if there was no intervention from him.

Now, what to do with Isabella and her betrayal of me? The path of betrayal and deception had been marked by her, and when she reached the end, she would die.

CHAPTER TWENTY-TWO

ISABELLA

PEOPLE SAY WHEN you're in a coma, you cannot hear what is going on. Your brain is in a deathlike state. But I am here to tell you that as I slept in a medically-induced coma, I heard people coming in and out of my room. Snippets of conversation reached my subconscious mind and I was still able to formulate ideas. And I had unending conversations with Mama, which brought me peace.

Adrien spoke to doctors, and nurses spoke to nurses. I know for certain Ben had been in several times, but how he got in without being family was a puzzle. Oh, right, he's with Europol. That in itself must be a good sign because I'm able to now make connections.

My body was not under my control. But I recall trying to scream "No!" when Adrien discussed something with another doctor about a Do Not Resuscitate order that he would bring to them. No, I never signed such a thing. Or did I? Maybe he's right. I wouldn't want to live in a vegetative state. But I don't remember having such a macabre conversation with him. I needed to

TWO

tell someone he's wrong, I changed my mind if I had said such a thing. But a tube taped to my cheeks stopped me from talking. And did he just say that if I should die while he was gone, that I wanted my organs donated to a particular Israeli hospital and my tissues to be sent someplace else. My memories were all so jumbled. But it was clear he was organizing my life to include death.

Adrien had been here. Was he leaning over me and talking in my ear? *Get away from me.* What was he saying? Was that Adrien I heard in a piece of my brain, telling me it was okay to let go, to give in and die? Was he telling me to let go and not fight the pain anymore? To float away into death? Everything was jumbled.

How long I had been like this, I don't know; there was no way to account for time. But suddenly I felt as if I was swimming to the surface of the ocean, and my face was breaking the water's surface. I could see bright light. No more wavy sounds, as if my hearing was filtered by water.

My side hurt like the devil, and I had a tube stuck down my throat. What the hell? My eyes fluttered open to find the room empty. God, not another hospital room. The swoosh of a machine by the left side of my bed indicated my breathing was assisted. A machine holding a bag regulating fluid dripping into my veins was next to the breathing machine. What's the breathing machine called? Yes, a ventilator. I could also hear the steady beat of my heart. Was that pounding in my ears my heart, or from a machine? As I rose to a higher level of consciousness, my heart rate accelerated, triggering an alarm and someone—a nurse—was quickly at my bedside, shutting down the alarm.

A face smiled down at me, telling me to be calm, not buck the machine, and she would get a doctor. What felt like an eternity, but in reality was merely minutes, produced a team in my room, releasing me from the machine I was tethered to for life support. Someone attached a syringe to the side of the breathing tube, and I felt a release in my throat. "Take a breath," he said, and the tube was out. Coughing and gasping for breath, I was helped to a semi-sitting position, and strangers' faces were smiling at me.

The head of my bed was elevated, and I was fed small ice chips with a spoon, to soothe my throat. I was indeed alive. And I wasn't brain-dead but was definitely sore as hell. I heard a commotion in the distance, and hoped it was not Adrien fighting for admittance. I was relieved to see Ben pushing the door open, rushing toward my bed.

"God, Isabella, thank God. I can't tell you how worried we all were." Ben blurted the words out in one fell swoop.

"How long have I been here?" My gravelly voice returned. "What happened? Why am I here?"

"You don't remember?" he asked, somewhat deflated.

"There's bits and pieces. I remember a man, and that is all. A man—" No, it couldn't be someone shot me. Of course, he did, and I am blocking it out.

He stood at the side of my bed, trying to assess what to disclose, and made a decision. He asked the nurses to leave, so we could have a quiet conversation, and they obliged, but only for five minutes because I needed my rest.

"You were shot at point-blank range in the abdomen. The bullet nicked your liver, necessitating surgery. That night, after the first surgery, you started bleeding and had to return to surgery. We almost lost you during the second surgery. The next twenty-four hours, your blood pressure was all over the place. The doctors were afraid you would have a stroke, then afraid of shock, so they decided to place you in a medically-induced coma, which they had been tapering off as your vital signs stabilized out," he said.

I almost died twice. Medically-induced coma. This was just

TWO

too much to comprehend.

"Ben, I want to know what happened and why. Medically, I can feel what is going on in my body. I want to know why I am lying here," I told him. I could feel the catheter, set in place to remove the urine, pulling on my leg and the fluids feeding me, infusing an almost cold sensation. The abdominal pain would be much worse without the drugs surging through my body. I just wanted the why and how.

He shifted the chair to the bedside and sat. I could tell he was horribly conflicted as to what to tell me, so I nudged him. "I have to know. I have to regain that piece of my life."

He nodded his head in understanding.

"According to the police report on file, it appears to have been a robbery. However, I cannot square that circle and until we have more from you, that's what remains the official report. Until you can give us a description of the person, if you are able, we won't know where to start looking. When you are up to it, that's our first and utmost priority. A sketch, so we know where to start. Is there anything you remember about him at all? Tall or short, ethnicity, tattoos, homeless, anything you can give us? Did he surprise you from behind a pole or do you know where he came from?" His questions were rapid-fire, like a verbal machine gun.

I lay back into the pillows and looked to the ceiling, to help me sharpen my focus and recall. God, it hurt to breathe. Was there also a tube in my lung at one time, draining fluid? I must have winced because I saw him reach for the call button, probably for medication.

"No, no medication, I want to stay clear," I said, and he nodded and sat back again.

"I'd say he was about a few inches shorter than you, brownish hair, sort of kinky or crinkled, and darkish skin, but not black.

Maybe . . . what is the term for people who are Italian?" I asked. Reaching to formulate words, and memory recall at the same time, proved a great challenge.

"Olive or Mediterranean? Or do you mean, that type of coloring more like a person with a tan?" he asked. He reached in his jacket for a pad, and started taking notes.

"I'll go with the term Mediterranean, but I don't know. Olive would suit as well." The rawness of my throat started to make it difficult to continue, so I lowered my voice to a whisper. As he leaned in to listen, I could hear his heart beating in his chest. No, that was mine pounding in my ears.

"You are doing a stellar job. While you have such great recall, can I take a moment and ring a friend of mine who does police sketches, so he can get all the details? If you're not up to it, say so. But this will give us the leads we need," he said.

The last thing I wanted to do was stay awake, much less have visitors when I looked a mess. But I needed to give them a head start. They were helping me, not the other way around.

"I'm good. Go ahead," I said. I had to have answers.

As he stepped out to place the call, a nurse came in to drain my urine bag and adjust my IV fluids. After offering me more ice chips, we tried a few sips of water, and I was able to swallow it and hold it down. Clear fluids and maybe some soup would be next.

"We are in luck. He can be here within the hour. If you are sure it's not too much," he said. The look on his face was one of helplessness.

"No, I want to do this." I grabbed his hand for reassurance. Instead of sitting back in the chair, he sat next to me on the edge of the bed.

"Ben, it was so unexpected. I wasn't even aware anyone was there. I was so filled with rage that I saw nothing but my shoes

TWO

moving forward across the concrete. But even if I'd been on my game, I wouldn't have thought him a danger. The flash I have, as I see him right now, is a man in what had to be a several-thousand-dollar suit. A man you would expect to be walking to his car, nothing more. He did not flash the danger sign at me. I met his eyes for just a moment as we passed each other, maybe even gave him a tight-lipped smile to be polite. Then *bang*. But what I do remember is seeing blood spattered on his shoes and suit because he was so close. He called me a worthless bitch in an English accent, which was surprising because I did not peg him as a Brit. All my mind could comprehend at the time, in its paralyzed state, was that he called me a bitch, as if I'd done things personally to hurt him." Now I was done, too tired to continue. "I just need a tiny break."

He was writing everything down, and I'm sure hoping for more detail. He closed his pad and put it on the table.

"Do you want some water?" I shook my head no.

"I want to see Chloe. Can you get her in?" I asked. "Adrien will stop her, but I want her."

He lifted from the bed and rang the bell tied to the rail, and a nurse appeared. I was too tired to explain to the nurse what I wanted, but he conveyed the message. The nurse assured me that Chloe would be added to the visitor list immediately. As she was ready to leave, I croaked for her to come closer, and Ben moved a bit away.

"If anything should take a turn for the worse, I want everything done to preserve my life. It's important you know that I want Chloe to have the power to make all medical decisions," I said.

Shock registered on her face. "That's highly unusual, Madame Armond. The spouse is, as we say, the de facto decision maker. And I'm not certain I should be the one sharing this with you, but the day you were admitted, your husband obtained a court order, giving him all rights and power for decisions. I am not very legal savvy, but from what I understand, due to your incapacitated state, he has control over everything, including who visits. However, now that you are alert, I believe, since he did not exclude anyone in particular on the form, she can visit."

Alarm ran through me and I grabbed Ben's hand. "Ben, you have to do something. He will make sure I never leave this hospital intact. He wants me dead, and when he finds out I am recovering, he will finish the job. I know it, Ben. Do something."

The nurse became alarmed, and her statement reverberated through my body, as if Adrien himself spoke the words, but they came from her mouth.

"Madame Armond, calm down, you are harming yourself. I will get some medication for you," she said, and turned to leave.

I grabbed the cuff of Ben's suit and would not let go.

"No, Ben. No medication." I tried to sit up for emphasis. I yelled at the nurse, "If you give me anything against my will, I will have my *avocat* here, and everyone will be sued."

"Madame Armond, I am only following doctor's orders. Your blood pressure and heart rate are elevated, and that is not good for your body. Of course, I will not force any medication on you. Perhaps your visitor should leave so you can get some rest." She smiled. Not a kind smile, but it was sympathetic.

I was certain that after Ben left and I had drifted to sleep, she would sneak back in and fill that little bag with medication to keep me docile. She and Adrien must be in on this together. Oh my God, did I just think that? Please tell me I did not verbalize that statement.

"Now, please leave. I need to speak to my friend in private," I ordered, without much bite, as my voice was barely above a squeak.

TWO

"Okay, calm down, and I don't mean that in a condescending way. I mean, calm down so that blasted machine stops beeping, like it's getting ready for takeoff. What you said about calling your *avocat* gave me a thought. Let me call Richard and see to getting that order revoked," Ben said. "You think you can lie back while I take care of that issue?"

I nodded, and Ben removed his phone from his jacket, and relayed to Richard what had transpired, hitting the most important points. Adrien had control of my medical needs and he needed Michelle to get everything reversed. Immediately. Good. He wanted me dead, and I was not about to oblige him without a fight.

"I'm sorry, Isabella. I had no idea he'd taken that step. These matters are done behind closed doors. Now that I know what is going on, I'm on it. The good news is—" He stopped to take a call, and gave me the one finger wait signal as he moved to the other side of the room. I heard him conversing in hushed tones, and he moved back over to the bed.

"It's Michelle. She needs to speak to you." He handed me the phone.

The conversation was short, and after confirming to her I was medically and mentally sound—certainly, mentally—she would prepare an affidavit for my signature, and needed it signed. She assured me by end of day, she would have my life returned to me. For that, I was grateful.

After we disconnected, Ben and I returned to our conversation.

"As I was saying, the good news is that Adrien has left the country. He flew to Abu Dhabi, then he'll be flying to London. A few well-placed phone calls gave us the information that he is selling an unknown, but large, quantity of art across the globe. My colleague in the US is tracking what is going on over there, and we have our finger on the pulse for most of Europe and the UK. The Middle East and Switzerland are a bit tricky, but we have feet on the ground, gathering information," he said, but didn't appear ecstatic about it. This could be where they could arrest Adrien for selling forgeries and he would go to prison for life.

"But you don't seem pleased. More to the point, how is he selling them without my signature?" I knew Adrien would take my life by force.

"It's complicated, and I guess that nurse just gave us the answer. He had you declared an incapacitated adult, and is in charge of the business. Once Michelle gets that court order signed, I can distribute copies to all the auction houses or private parties, indicating he does not have power to sell the canvases." He ran his fingers through his hair. "Something is not right. Why immediately sell off all the inventory? What does he know that we don't?"

"You've lost me." Was I being dense?

"Look, you just worry about getting better. I will—" he started.

"No!" I screamed in my croaky voice. "What is going on? Someone tried to kill me and now I'm not even sure that when I get out of here I'll have a business to run." Tears were welling in my eyes, but not yet flowing.

He walked over to the window, where he stood for a moment, and scrubbed his face with his hands in frustration.

"I can't, Isabella. There's a lot at stake here, and I can't tell you any more. I'll wait with you until Richard gets here to have you sign the papers, and I will witness them. Then I have to go, and I might not be able to return for a few days," he said in a measured thoughtful tone.

"Am I in any danger?" I had to know. Was this a random robbery, or was it a warning for some reason. Had I failed to

TWO

meet the expected goal—death? Did I want to know? What good would it do to know?

"The fact that you are lying in this bed should tell you that the possible answer to your question is yes," he said with a bit of caution. Did he know something and was holding it back? Or was he as clueless as me?

"Ben, I'm not up to playing twenty questions." Exhaustion from tension was starting to set in, but I wanted to be alert for the artist.

Annoyed but still sympathetic, Ben answered. "Isabella, you just woke up from a medically-induced coma and gave us our first lead. We had no idea what we were dealing with. Was it a man or woman, Caucasian or other, French or another nationality, or a hapless refugee or homeless person? Your bag is missing, so was it a robbery? Now we have a description, and it sounds personal." He was about to continue when a man entered with a black leather portfolio case. Ben turned in recognition, standing up to greet him with a warm smile. I hoped this was the sketch artist.

Ben spoke a few words I couldn't hear that made him laugh, and welcomed him into the room. A space was made on the table for him to place his venti-sized coffee and tablet. He was a laid-back man, I would guess in his mid-thirties, with a ponytail and jeans—probably not law enforcement.

"Isabella, meet Jacque. He is our portrait artist. He'll work with you to pick out characteristics. First, he'll work with his tablet on the general characteristics, then he'll sketch them out. Are you up for it?" Ben inquired, needing some reassurance.

Rest, food, and wanting the catheter removed was what I was up for, but I needed to get this done. Why the man had targeted me was anyone's guess. Reluctantly, I saved those requests for later and answered, "Yes," earning me a smile and rub of my arm form Ben, which sent electric sparks upward. I was comforted that I could please him. He'd saved my life.

Jacque picked up his tablet and opened an app. After we went through slides where I identified a generic nose, eyes, chin, forehead, cheekbones, ears, and mouth that would fit the suspect, he set about sketching while I directed changes. Small things came rushing back as he formulated a face on the paper, such as his hair was thick and wavy, his eyes were seafoam green, and lips thick and so dark, they were almost purple.

While we worked, Ben worked. He made phone calls, texted, and sent and returned emails. We waited for Richard who arrived an hour and a half after the call was placed to Michelle. Richard knew Jacque as well. They exchanged pleasantries the way people who knew each other for a long time would. There was comfort knowing these three were relaxed with each other and spoke a language only friends would know. A team to help me.

Richard removed the paperwork from his messenger bag to go over with me. The pile of documents was rather large, and the legalese was overwhelming. I trusted Michelle and would sign without question. To give us some privacy so we could execute the papers, Jacque placed his pad on the side table and indicated he would be back after he went for a refresher of coffee and pastry in the hospital café.

"Would twenty minutes be enough?" he asked.

"That's more than enough time," Ben replied, and Jacque left.

"Isabella, Michelle will come by later this afternoon after she has these papers signed by the justice, releasing Adrien as your incapacitated guardian agent. She'll go over whatever she needs to, and don't ask me what that is, because I don't know. I'm just the messenger to get these signed and over to the court, and

TWO

then I'm to meet her in the justice's room. As soon as the papers are signed, Chloe will be with her and will return here with the papers to give to the hospital administrator. Ben will also be provided copies he can distribute where needed. And that's all I have." He smiled and touched my cheek.

Ben was right, it took about twenty minutes to plow through the papers. The nurse was called in as one witness to my initialing and signing the documents, indicating I had read the papers. By signing them, I declared I wanted Adrien dismissed as my incapacitated guardian agent, and that Michelle was my legal counsel and *avocat*, and no further legal documents could be submitted without her being advised. Ben signed the papers and it was then, for the first time, I saw his legal name. I guess that's how he was able to visit and stay under Adrien's radar. He was no longer Jaager but Johenson. And Agent Johenson was probably being passed off as an agent of the local Paris police when the log was reviewed. Clever.

As Richard clipped the papers together and prepared them to be placed back in his briefcase, Jacque returned, two coffee cups in hand, one of them for Ben. Jacque returned to his seat and turned his pad over to continue sketching. Pad in his lap and pencil poised, he waited for further instructions from me.

Everything seemed to go into slow-motion time travel. Richard stopped what he was doing, his eyes fixed on the image Jacque had drawn.

At first, it appeared as if he jolted back a bit, as if someone had pushed back gently at his shoulder. Some invisible force. Gathering himself, we all watched him as he placed his papers down on top of his leather case, stepped behind Jacque, and looked over his shoulder at the portrait.

"Jacque, move the eyes a little closer toward the nose, and make the upper skin under the eyebrow a little thicker; you know, a little puffy. Widen out the nose just a touch at the bottom, but elongate it, to where it comes closer to the top of the lip. You know, lessen the space between the tip of the nose and upper lip." Jacque took his time as Ben and I exchanged glances, but said nothing.

Jacque looked to Richard for further direction, and then to me. I nodded my affirmation.

"Make the bottom lip a little fuller, and the chin a little larger, and square it off," he directed. He stood back and looked at it again.

This was causing me to involuntarily clench in my stomach. Ben moved closer to Richard as he watched Jacque work.

"A scar, like a Harry Potter lightning bolt, through his right eyebrow, and a brown spot, maybe a mole, on his upper right cheek. Shadow in the cheeks a bit to hollow them out," he instructed.

I had progressed from involuntary clenching to a fullness in my chest.

Richard placed his hand on Jacque's shoulder, and Jacque laid his pencil down. He looked to Richard, who motioned him with a chin nod to show me the finished sketch.

He turned it around, and the man who almost ended my life was face-to-face with me again. I was so shocked, all I could do was nod weakly.

Jacque ripped the paper from the pad and handed it to Ben. He gathered the tools of his trade, wished me a speedy recovery, and left—leaving his unfinished pastry and coffee behind.

Ben and Richard exchanged a look, and I thought I saw a slight nod. Some type of signal, and only they knew the code represented.

"Ben, I have to get going. Michelle is waiting for me. Walk me to the elevator." Richard turned to me. "And you, get some

TWO

rest. We've got this, and we'll have your papers signed and to the administrator as soon as possible. I promise to return with Michelle and Chloe. I am hoping in the next two hours. Shall I ask if Chloe can bring some solid food? And if not, maybe Henri's mushroom soup that she keeps saying is a favorite of yours and hers?"

He was obviously trying to distract me from asking questions because it worked. Instead of the sketch being on my mind, now I had both Henri's mushroom soup and how he so intimately knew Chloe's tastes, if she was just a client.

"That would be lovely," I said, letting him off the hook.

"Be right back." Ben and Richard exited the room together and I was left alone to think about too many things for too long as it were.

I must have dozed off because when I woke, Ben had returned and was looking out the window.

"Sorry I must have dozed off," I said with a stretch. "Are you going to tell me who attacked me, and why?"

"I'm conflicted," he said, quite honest and without hesitation.

"Okay, that obviously doesn't bode well. You know who the person is, but you don't want to reveal them to me. Why?" I asked, waiting for some type of reasonable explanation.

He cleared his throat and said, "He's someone that Richard has come across."

"In relation to my case?" I queried. This was going to be ridiculous, trying to drag the information out of him.

"Yes." Again, with a cryptic response.

"If you are wanting to hear that blasted machine start running wild again, Ben, keep it up," I warned.

He looked at me, walked to the bedside chair, pulled it closer to the bed, and sat. A good sign.

"He's an associate of Adrien's." He waited for a reactive response, and I didn't disappoint.

I don't know if the machine started beeping off the charts first, or if I yelled "What?!" first. Either way, it brought two nurses to the room—one disarming the pulse alarm, and the other racing to take my blood pressure. When they were certain I had settled down after checking my vitals the third time, they re-armed the alarm and left with a warning that should it happen again, I would be sedated.

"Christ, this is why I didn't want to get into this without Richard here to clarify." He voiced his worry.

If I wanted to gain the information I needed, I had to remain calm. I tried my best, and that took all the effort I had.

"Look, just tell me. The truth can't be any worse than my imagination. Now start." I pointed my finger aimlessly in the air, and then flopped back against my pillow.

Rubbing the arm of the chair, he took a deep breath and started.

"Richard took it upon himself to follow Adrien one day. That particular day, he met with a man, at a café. We believe it was the man that shot you. He studied the two men. He watched body language, tone of voice, and various other things, and came to a conclusion."

"And?"

"And he determined they were more than acquaintances, and appeared, at points, to argue. But at the end, they came to some type of agreement. When they left, he was sure the man had taken note of him being there, which left him feeling unsettled." He spoke a little slower as the last words came out.

"Who is he?" Certainly, I had a right to ask.

"I'm not certain, but I have sent the sketch to my counterpart at Interpol, the Brits, and an FBI agent in the US. So, that's

TWO

what I have. Nothing more, nothing less." He sat back, done.

"Motherfucker," I spit out.

This perked him up as he leaned forward. "Now, Isabella, no need to curse at me. I have told you everything I know."

"Not you, for the love of God. Adrien. Can't you see? Adrien hired a hitman, albeit an incompetent hitman, to kill me." I pulling back the sheets across my legs to get out of bed, forgetting why I was there. There we went again with the beeping. Before the team would fly through again, I put my legs back into the bed and settled, bringing my heart rate down, but not before I caught a scowl from the nurse ready to enter, then she left.

"Look. I don't have all the answers, but I'm not sure that your theory is totally correct"—I continued to calm myself down—"but it does have a ring of partial truth." Not what I wanted to hear.

"From what Richard said, it was the man who was directing the meeting and conversation, not Adrien. The other man was in charge. Before we jump to the wrong conclusion and miss an important marker or clue—or worse, evidence—let's reserve judgment. Michelle should be back in an hour with Chloe and your soup. Possibly by then, Richard or I will have identification of the man, and we can start putting things together. Do you think you might be able to catch some sleep while I stay and do some work before I leave?" He was nervous, and with good reason.

"Where are you off to?" I wanted to see if I could determine what their game plan entailed.

"I'm off to London. An FBI colleague is meeting me there for an auction. Adrien plans to bring twenty-five paintings into auction. Since it was not part of the inventory from the Geneva warehouse, I believe it's what was in the Roselov inventory that was possibly moved before the London gallery explosion. There is a huge risk with that type of bold move, and I'm not sure what's going on.

"Armed with your court documents when Michelle gets here, and your declaration stating that Adrien doesn't have authority to act under your name, after we confiscate the artwork we will have a clearer picture of what's going on. I don't know if he will be at the London auction, or at the Abu Dhabi auction, as they are scheduled within a day of each other. But I have someone ready to pull the plug at Abu Dhabi. With this document, we can pull all the paintings from an offer of sale. Cillian also has someone in New York ready to do the same, once they are armed with the document." His phone buzzed, and he stepped from the room to take the phone call.

My mind raced like the wind. Paris was obviously part of the auction. With three other auction houses, he may be trying to sell our entire inventory. But why? Even if he found out about the pending divorce, that would be property he would have to replace with money. Was he planning to close all his accounts, change his identity, and vanish? Was he coming back to finish me off? No scenario seemed good.

Ben stepped back in the room. "Good news. The justice signed the papers, and they'll be here in two minutes with soup. They are clearing the way downstairs to visit. We have arranged for you to be moved, and I have assigned someone to sit outside your door."

"I thought I had someone assigned to my safety the day I was shot, so maybe not such a reliable source," I said with an element of sarcasm.

"That would be my fault. I told the person that was assigned to you that we would be arresting Adrien, eliminating the threat. I was getting ready to reinstitute the shadow when all hell broke loose," he confessed.

"Okay, understandable. When do you leave and when will

TWO

you return?" I wanted to know. I had come to depend on his counsel and company.

"Leaving tonight. Back in four days, or sooner. It will depend if the other agencies and I have to fly anyplace else," he said. As he finished, Chloe and Michelle were walking in with soup and five manila business envelopes that she handed to Ben.

"I'm on my way to distribute the rest of these to whoever needs them," Michelle advised. "And I'll be back tomorrow to visit. I have a ballet performance for my ten-year-old tonight and can't miss it."

"Thanks, Michelle, for everything," I said, blowing a finger kiss as she left.

"Ladies, I'll leave you two to your soup. Isabella, you have my number," Ben said. "Stay safe and stay calm."

"Richard said he's out front waiting in the car, second row on the right," Chloe added.

Ben left, laughing, as I was certain he heard Chloe say, "I want every detail. Right now."

CHAPTER TWENTY-THREE

ADRIEN

THIS WAS THE first time I had stepped foot in Abu Dhabi, the capital and second highest populated city of the United Arab Emirates. A city that accounted for about two-thirds of the roughly four- hundred-billion dollar United Arab Emirates economy. Yes, I can understand why Avigad likes to do business here. Myself, I am fascinated and intrigued with the beauty of the place whose originating name means "father of the gazelle." Their museums boasted artifacts from the third millennium BC, a true epicenter of historic culture. A beautiful country flawed by its horribly incessant heat. A bit extreme for my taste.

As I took time to admire the architecture of the auction house reflective of its Arabic roots, I was drawn back to the conversation between Avigad and Habib.

"These twenty-five are set aside for B.A.," Avigad instructed Habib. "The provenance is in order, and you are instructed to finalize the bill of sale and duty, and immediately prepare for shipping. Monsieur Armond and I will travel on the same flight with them."

TWO

"You yourself will oversee the shipment? That is most unusual." Habib was surprised, his eyebrows almost touching his scalp. He quickly realized his error in verbalizing a question when Avigad flashed a disapproving look at him.

"Indeed," Avigad replied. Nothing more.

"Adrien, walk with me, so we may inspect the other lots on offer," Avigad said, indicating his business with Habib was complete.

The royal-blue carpet emulated water. Water was abundant in the large fountains disbursed throughout the area. It was peaceful walking through here, listening to the flow. Despite the conversations that surrounded us, no one seemed to be interested in another patron's chatter.

We strolled to the area replete with art on offer for the afternoon auction. Several of our pieces were there—the paintings that could be authenticated. The artwork that Isabella refused to sign her name to transfer were also amongst them.

"You want to tell me why we are going to China to accompany these paintings to the Beijing freeport? My understanding was our next stop was London, and then back to Paris."

"It was a slight and necessary detour." His statement was evasive as always.

"And why do you need me? Why can't I continue on to London?" I asked, dreading whatever response he supplied.

"Come. Let's sit in the lovely restaurant and chat over their fine offerings." It was a directive more than a suggestion. I was a bit hungry, so to argue would have proven foolhardy.

Nothing negative could be said about the architecture in the place inspired by both Islamic and Arabic designs. The flowing clean lines brought an almost inner peace, and our table next to trickling water made it all the more enticing. After Avigad ordered our meal, we set about having an irrelevant discussion until our food arrived. I steered our conversation into territory he refused to go without pointed questions.

"I am your captive audience," I started. "So again, why are we stopping in China?"

"Adrien, although the ties between the UAE and Beijing have grown close over the last years, I feel it best to oversee this transfer. Just to make certain all goes well," he said, as he ate a small portion of food.

Something was not right. I knew he was holding something back. We had been transporting pieces between here and China for over a year with no issue. Why this particular lot?

I studied him. His arrogance, his confidence, and his narcissistic psychopathy shouted he wasn't a man to be questioned.

"It seems unusual that the purchaser wouldn't want to oversee the transfer himself if he's concerned. Surely, you don't need me. I would prefer to continue to London from here. I want to tie up any loose ends with the London gallery while the temporary order gives me control over the business. At this point, no one except us knows about it being signed, and the longer it is out there, the more time lapses for someone to stumble upon it." Of course, that was true, but truth be told, I did not enjoy Beijing. The noise and overcrowded city set my teeth on edge.

"Adrien, you worry too much. Soon the temporary order will not be necessary." It just rolled off his tongue.

"Now what the hell does that mean?" I demanded, placing my knife and fork down. He flashed me a look, reminding me to take care of how I spoke to him. "Forget that. Why China and why me?"

"Lower your voice," he counseled. "There is a small job for you while we're in Beijing."

I didn't like the sound of that. "And what would that be?" As if I needed further aggravation.

TWO

"I need two kidneys," he stated matter-of-factly as he piled a fork full of meat and tomato and shoveled it into his mouth.

"You are not to be believed. You expect me, in the middle of all this, to perform what's now become an outlawed surgery, in a Communist country, where people spend the greater part of their lives in jail just for petty crimes? No, thank you," I said, without hesitation, and shook my head aggressively for emphasis.

"The circumstance is special. The client needs a special tissue typing and has been waiting for a time for the right person. We now have a father and son located that will meet the specification. It will take an hour at the most. The people will already be under and opened. All you have to do is remove the organ. You don't even have to worry about closing and recovery." He placed another forkful into his mouth.

"Cairo, and the massacre we left behind there wasn't enough?" I questioned. "No. I have to say no. I told you I am finished."

"Adrien, do not be foolish. This is a business, and neither of us can walk away while there is a special need for our services," he advised. He wiped his mouth with a stiff white linen napkin, then placed the napkin on the table. "Cairo was a miscalculation, and the people responsible have been dealt with in the proper way."

In other words, they were dead. Probably not a quick death, but a long, painful, torturous one, as a lesson to others.

"I don't like this. I'm traveling under my own passport. If anything goes wrong, it is me, Adrien Armond, who will be jailed or punished. Not a Canadian software entrepreneur or Latin American photographer," I reminded him.

"Adrien, this is personal to me, this transaction. And I must insist. Besides, I've taken precautions. We'll be traveling by private jet of a friend," he advised. The man thought of everything.

I didn't question the remuneration. There was something off about this, and to question further would only aggravate him further. The discussion was unceremoniously closed. We completed our meal and returned to the showroom area.

Moving from painting to painting, he stopped and pretended to admire several, like he was a patron deciding on a purchase, which I found amusing, as the only thing he appreciated about art was the money he could swindle people out of selling it. As we approached the last painting, a well-appointed man in his fifties, with salt-and-pepper hair and obviously of a managerial position, sidled up to Avigad. He initiated a quiet conversation, which ended with us following him to his office.

Following along to a place Avigad obviously knew well, I took in the surroundings. There was no doubt that the accoutrements were real gold, the ivory was of an elephant tusk, and the leather was the finest on offer.

"Please, gentlemen. Have a seat. Might I offer a refreshment?" he asked, giving a slight wave to his assistant.

Avigad accepted for both of us, as it would be an insult to decline. The coffee poured was thankfully not the bitter liquid infusion from hell I was subjected to when I dined with Avigad. Wonderful.

"Dr. Armond, we seem to have a problem with the paperwork you presented to us. I have invited my good friend Avigad to help me determine how we should handle the issue," he said. "I'm confident we can come to an agreeable arrangement."

He had not bothered to introduce himself, which signaled to me that I was here as a courtesy, and he would be directing the conversation to Avigad.

"Thank you, Bashir, for the opportunity to clear up any

TWO

issues," Avigad responded. "Please, advise us of what has arisen to cause you concern."

"I have made a copy, so you can review what we received a short time ago. It puts us in a dilemma, and I wanted your thoughts how to deal with this issue," he said, as he pointed to a leather folder in front of each of us.

We retrieved the document inside and my stomach revolted to the point I was certain I felt bile creeping up, ready to spill out. Surely everyone could see sweat building on my brow. I deferred to Avigad on the matter, as it was obvious they previously had similar dealings.

Avigad remained collected without a care.

"Have you a suggestion?" Avigad queried him.

"I do," the director said. He stood and retrieved a similar folder from the credenza.

"It would be my assumption that neither you nor the purchaser would like this issue to interfere with the purchase of the paintings. Would that be correct?" Bashir said rather than questioned.

"Certainly not. Everyone would be most disappointed," Avigad answered him, following his lead in their well-rehearsed dance.

"Good. Fortunate for you, these paintings were processed yesterday in a special sale. That date is reflected on the invoice in this folder. Due to the extenuating circumstances, our new fee is reflected on the invoice," Bashir pointed out.

"Of course, that seems only fair," Avigad responded, without even examining the increased number.

"Shall we have the funds transferred to the new account you set up for this particular transaction? Naturally, our three-day wait is waived, as both parties are valued and trusted clients," the director slid past us with ease.

"Yes." Avigad gave me a nod.

"I can have the package at the airport within the hour, if that meets with your approval," the director said, as if the process had been a foregone conclusion.

"Thank you. And, as always, it is a never-ending pleasure doing business with you," Avigad replied.

The director placed the document he had retrieved from the credenza on the desk and turned it toward me. The purchaser's signature was already affixed, witnessed, and backdated. He pointed to where my signature was required, handed me a pen, and I signed as well. Removing his gold seal from his desk, he placed the official witness seal with black ink next to his signature, completing the transaction.

Returning to his desk, he sat back down in his black leather chair, turned toward his computer. With a few touches of the keys, he completed the wire transfer of funds to my account. A receipt was printed and our dealings with Bashir were complete.

Further pleasantries were exchanged between Avigad and Bashir, and we were escorted to the reception area by his assistant, a young man who missed nothing.

How did she discover the temporary order so quickly? More disconcerting was, how did she know where to send it? This was a crack in the plan I had not anticipated. I turned to speak and received a terse, "Not now."

As we walked down the white stone steps toward the car, Avigad pulled out his phone and dialed a number. After a moment, all he said was, "Wheels up one hour."

"You want to tell me what's going on here, Avigad?" I asked frankly, feeling a bit panicked.

"When we get in the car," was his response, which seemed reasonable.

As we crossed the large parking area, I noticed a man who

TWO

was watching us with interest.

"You recognize that man leaning against the post in the navy-blue suit?" I asked. At this point, every person we encountered was a potential threat to me.

"No," he said, as his eyes swept that way. "Our business here is complete. I want you focused on the surgery. We'll have to move the surgery up a day. We've had a change of plans, forced on us by Isabella," he said, obviously frustrated, but more than frustrated. Angry, and that would not stand.

As we entered the car to take us to the airport where a private plane awaited, his phone rang.

Although he spoke in Arabic, I did catch that the crate was on board and ready for takeoff. Before I could ask any questions, he was on to the next call, moving up the surgery and giving instructions that the recipient for transplant would be arriving a day early, and everyone was to be prepared when we arrived in Beijing.

"Avigad, you expect too much of me," I said, hoping to slow this freight train down.

"Adrien, this time it's not about money. This time, it's personal," he replied. "I will accept no arguments."

I studied him, deciding if I should pry further, and decided to leave the matter for now.

"Here's the list of financial institutions that are safe for you to transfer money. Do so within the next seventy-two hours. After that, you proceed at your own risk," he said.

"Care to share?" I asked.

All I received was, "No," which is what I expected.

At the private hangar, we presented our passports to the agent and processed through immigration. Avigad gave a cursory look toward the crate that had been placed in the cargo area and was given the paperwork. With that, he gave the pilot a spin of his wrist, indicating we were ready for takeoff. Ten minutes later, we were in the air, heading to Beijing.

Reviewing the list of financial institutions caused a bit of alarm, as they were all in the Middle East and North Africa area.

"Seventy-two hours, Adrien," he said, and then pressed the button for service.

Tick Tock.

CHAPTER TWENTY-FOUR

BEN

NOT MUCH TO think about on my train trip from Paris to London, so my mind wandered. I'll be happy to return to the Netherlands when this job is complete. Home. After the attacks, when people were still in the stunned and horrified phase, the world pulled together. It was us against them. But the "them" had never been identified. The original leading conspiracy theory leaned to an attack on Christianity, and that theory still prevailed. No one, not even Isis, came forward to claim responsibility. This, they felt, was too big even for them to claim.

The ripple effect of the demolition of that small section of Paris reverberated throughout France. Food markets sold less food, people had less money for wine or cakes, and clothing seemed to find a new popularity with secondhand stores. Rebuilding Notre-Dame quickly, to show the Parisians weren't defeated, took a back seat to using the money to sustain people's lives and health after the attack. The once mighty symbol of old Christianity and tourist-generating activity remained in a pile of uncared for rubble. People passed it every day without a second thought. It just became part of the background. Was it the EU's fault for not pumping more money in? Were the banking leaders of the eurozone making decisions that were popular with the people in the other countries of the EU not to prioritize a swift Paris rebuild? After all, France and Germany were the locomotive pulling the Portugal-Italy-Greece-Spain train when they needed money. Yes, they were almost bankrupt and still billions were poured into their countries. Now Paris, and a great deal of France affected by general depression from the attack, was set to financially collapse.

From St Pancras, I took the Piccadilly line to the Piccadilly Circus tube station and followed the crowd out. The feel of London was different from Paris. People seemed to buzz a little more. The United Kingdom, not in the eurozone for currency, took a different tact dealing with the destruction they faced. Maybe it was because they were not old Europe and didn't depend on food markets to sell their foods, or maybe it was the fact the infrastructure of transportation hadn't been affected so badly. Who knows what it was, but it appeared Londoners had not reached the level of despair that infected France. The royals had donated money of their own toward the rebuild, which greatly boosted morale.

People had changed, and not for the better. Whether it was Paris, Frankfurt, Rome, or London, no one trusted anyone else. Each person studied the other to determine if that person had caused the ultimate betrayal against humanity. Misery, so they say, loves company. People started wishing the Americans would falter, as their economic growth ticked up under their new president. Muslims in many countries were targeted as an easy scapegoat, saying it was another terrorist attack, and the oil rich countries continued to prosper, which was not an accurate statement, as the cost of a barrel of oil went down every day, despite rumors

TWO

it went up. As people lost jobs, cars were repossessed, and less gasoline was needed.

The throngs of people that normally made Piccadilly Circus a hive of activity were indeed thinned out. Tourists were still holding back on visiting abroad and the fear of economic failure kept many from parting with the pound sterling. Glancing at the Eros fountain, he saw me before I saw him. Cillian O'Reilly and the man standing beside him walked to me.

We met in the middle, and he introduced himself and his partner, Jackson Evans, FBI, Organized Crime. The choice of restaurants was left to me. I wasn't much of a food connoisseur and opted for an English pub that looked quiet.

After a walk about a street length away, we found a restaurant that met our requirements. It had food and it was quiet. We settled in and after our order was placed and drinks served, I opened the conversation.

"Jackson, what brings Organized Crime across the pond?" Settling back against the green tufted leather, I waited for a response. I had no idea which way it would go.

"Several things, Ben. My department deals with money laundering, drug smuggling, and human trafficking," he responded, taking a sip of Guinness which, by the look on his face, was a good choice.

"I see. But you're a bit out of your jurisdiction wouldn't you say?" His job seemed to parallel mine, and other European agencies were certainly fit to handle those issues.

"We've been following leads that cross jurisdictions. Jude White, from our end—in addition to the art forgery and money laundering—has made connections to human trafficking. That information led us over here to an Avigad Abed. And this Abed character seems to be an associate of Adrien Armond." His tone was matter-of-fact, as if I should be on the same page. I was not.

"Whoa. How did you make the leap from White's art forgery to human trafficking?" We hadn't confirmed that link as anything other than speculation.

"Like I said, we're following leads. Something popped up on our radar, indicating it was Abed who fronted the financing for the purchase of Roselov's gallery, not Isabella Armond. It appears he might be a silent partner who is fronting the money for some type of ongoing operation. Pieces are starting to fall into place right now, as we're able to get more warrants now to uncover information to connect the dots. However, we haven't been able to make a physical connection between Abed and Roselov, although we know it is there somewhere. Since Roselov was an active associate with Khalid Abdurrahman, we are investigating if Abdurrahman has a traceable connection to Abed. We were starting to widen our net and the name Adrien Armond popped up in our reports. You obviously know him, so here I am. What can you tell me about him?" Jackson asked.

"Let me clarify what you are saying, so that I can connect a few dots. You believe that prior to his death, White, the art forger, expanded his reach into human trafficking. Do you have a specific area of trafficking?" I asked.

"We believe black market organ harvesting. Because of his proximity to Canada, we think he might have had sights on making that his territory, and we believe had aspirations of being the bridge between Europe and Canada," Jackson said.

"I see. Do you believe that Abed is the broker of the organ procurement and sale?" I asked.

"We have reason to believe that is a correct statement." Our meals had been delivered to the table and he was now forking shepherd's pie into his mouth.

"Because Abed has been seen meeting both in Paris and London with Adrien Armond you believe their relationship is

TWO

more a business arrangement than friendship?" I had already surmised this after Richard had placed Abed at Isabella's shooting.

"Yes," he replied.

"And Armond is a physician, connecting his possible role in the organ trafficking?" A logical assumption.

"Yes," he replied. "It would seem either he'd be in a good position to identify people who would be good candidates as donors, or actually, sellers of their body parts. He likely participates in the surgery."

"If your information about Abed being a silent financial partner that purchased Roselov's gallery is accurate, then that puts him in some type of financial partnership with Armond." That was more a question. "Could that account for their meetings?"

I sat there, tapping my spoon on the table, thinking.

"Sure, but the bottom line is, there's a connection between Roselov, Abed, and Armond now," Jackson said. "We know it's definitely art and money laundering. But is it also organ trafficking? In other words, did Roselov use his gallery to not only launder money from the fake art, but to clean the money for organ trafficking?"

"I'm a visual kind of guy. Anyone have a pen?" I asked, raising my hand to flag our server to ask for some paper.

With a clean slate in front of me, I drew a circle, and in that circle I placed Abed's name.

"Can we agree that Abed is at the epicenter of this?" I asked.

"No. I am certain he is not working alone, but I'm also not sure he is the center. So, next to him, place a circle, and in that circle put Khalid Abdurrahman, and connect the two."

I did as Jackson requested.

"Why Abdurrahman? How are you linking him to Abed?" I asked.

"For now, because he was associated with Roselov. My gut is Roselov was lower than him on the food chain. Let's go with my gut for now," Jackson requested, and I agreed.

"From Abed's circle, attach him to an upward circle, which contains Armond. From the Abdurrahman circle, attach two upward circles with Roselov and White. Since we know Armond and Roselov did business, attach a line between them. And because we know Abed put the money up for Roselov's gallery, put a line between them. At the Abdurrahman circle, put the two that were with him, that were arrested at the airport—Nare and Davit Tavitian—and in an upward line, connect them to him. So, what does everyone see here?" Jackson asked.

"Roselov connects and touches everyone in some way. Give me a minute in my mind to put everyone together. Roselov had a gallery in London and reached out to White, who produced forgeries in the US. Roselov and Abdurrahman were partners in some sense, we just don't know how but it involved the London gallery. Possibly money laundering for another source. Maybe weapons? Or drugs? White tangentially knew Abdurrahman, is that right?" I asked.

"Correct. White had been given a taste of the benefits of black market organs, presumably through Abed, and he possibly decided to double-cross Roselov and Abdurrahman. The theory is, he took some paintings belonging to Abdurrahman, plus the money owed for the sale, and tried to disappear," Cillian added. "And for that, he was murdered. Now, with the connections, possibly Abed let slip that White was moving over to work brokering organs and laundering his money, and no longer needed Roselov and Abdurrahman. Only a working theory, mind you.

"Long story short, White had transferred money to an account with an owner named Emma Collier. She was designated to cash in on their fortune. However, here's where it takes

TWO

a hard turn. There were two Emma Colliers. The real Emma, who White had used for her art history credentials to sell his paintings—authenticated. The other Emma was a woman who had her appearance altered to look exactly like Ms. Collier. We believe White formulated the idea to kill the real Emma, and the body double was to step in her shoes. Now, wait for it"— Jackson wiped his mouth with his napkin and placed it back in his lap—"the fake Emma and White were married. In the end, Abdurrahman found out about the double-cross White planned, and Abdurrahman murdered him. Having alerted Roselov to the issue, they decided to leave the country, where they were arrested. That is the short version, and all you need to understand the players."

"So, we have Roselov and Abdurrahman associated with London originally?" I asked.

"Yes," Cillian answered.

"Armond and Abed associated with the Paris gallery, is that correct?" Cillian and Jackson nodded. "But Roselov, on occasion, sent White's fake paintings to Armond to sell. This, we do know, from an inventory we did of the freeport in Geneva and his storage area in the gallery."

"But now Abed and Armond's reach has extended into London as well," Cillian supplied.

"Guys, I have to tell you, I feel like we are missing something here," I said.

"We all do. What are you thinking?" Jackson tilted his head.

"Rome or the Vatican. Both were targeted. I think we've given them a pass because people were looking at this from a religious angle. I don't know if you'll agree, but I think this is more economic," I offered. "And somehow, Rome is involved as well."

"Mary," Jackson said, shaking his head.

"Mary? Who is Mary?" I asked.

Cillian laughed, and Jackson sighed.

"Mary is Cillian's fiancée's aunt who had a theory that the Vatican bank was somehow involved in all this, and he dispelled her theory as paranoia. Now you indicate you think we are missing a connection to Rome and the Vatican, and we're back to Mary," Jackson indicated, rubbing his eyes with the heels of his hands.

"Is there a problem entertaining her idea?" I wasn't connecting the issue.

"Once you meet her—and if you do go down this road, it will be inevitable you will meet her and understand the craziness that is Mary—you will understand." Jackson sighed dramatically, and Cillian chuckled.

"Let's walk through what we know," Cillian said.

They leaned back and thought for a moment. It wasn't a new idea, but the structure of how it was done, and why, was still a puzzle.

"What does Rome or the Vatican have that could tie this together?" I pondered out loud.

"No idea yet. I've had tunnel vision on Paris and London," Cillian said.

"Let's put Rome to the side for the moment, and concentrate on Abed and Armond, since they are on the loose, and we need to shut them down," Jackson said.

"We were able get the order out to the auction house, indicating that Isabella is now back in charge of the art being distributed. It unequivocally stated no sales were to be made until verified with her. Abu Dhabi acknowledged receiving the order, but gave its regrets that sales had already occurred, and there was nothing that could be done to overturn them. Next on the list is the London sale, and that's what we are working on right now." I knew we had a better chance with the London auction.

TWO

"If Armond and Abed make an appearance at the London auction, is there anything substantial to detain them with? Anything definitive with the forgery sales or money laundering?" Cillian asked.

"Not a thing until the paintings are actually put up for sale. But then he could try to slip through the noose by saying the paintings are from Isabella's gallery, and he's only her temporary proxy and knew nothing about the fakes." Even I knew how that looked from the outside looking in.

Adrien's idea was clever indeed. We sat and ate our lunch in relative silence, thinking and processing our own theories.

"Here's my plan." I broke the silence at our table. "Adrien knows I'm in the market for paintings, and I don't think my cover is blown. How about I monitor if he shows at the art auction to sell the paintings under his temporary order authority. If he does, I can take the lead on the London auction arrest if he tries to sell the paintings. We can get him on fraud for using the order and possibly art forgery if he has some of White's paintings. If we can take him down there, then Paris and New York auctions are a moot point because everyone has the order in place."

"That might take care of Armond, but have we got a plan for Abed?" Jackson asked.

"My guy said he was at the Abu Dhabi auction. If he shows at the London auction, we can get him as a person of interest in the robbery and attempted murder of Isabella. From there, you and Jill's people will have to coordinate on the trafficking," I said to Jackson. "I have my theories that Armond was part of that Cairo massacre, and we're still unraveling how he got in and out of the country."

"Okay, your plan works. We have until tomorrow to pull this together. And then, showtime," Jackson said.

"Let's walk over to the auction house and make certain that

everything is in place," I said.

"You two go ahead. I have some leads to follow on a potential organ broker, and I'm meeting up with someone from the Met. I'll catch up with you later," Jackson said.

We paid the bill and headed to the auction house.

CHAPTER TWENTY-FIVE

ADRIEN

THE FLIGHT TIME from Abu Dhabi to China was approximately seven hours. Certainly enough time to get a decent amount of rest. The attendant asked if I wanted anything to eat and I declined, although I was a bit thirsty. I settled back into the butter-soft cream-colored leather and let my arm rest upon what I had no doubt was some type of exquisite wood. The jet screamed luxury, and I was not above taking full advantage of what was on offer. Within seconds, I dozed, then fell into a restless sleep. A restless, nightmarish sleep, encountering sleep apnea, causing me to gasp as I awoke.

I felt us descending at a rapid pace. I opened my eyes and tried to relieve the pressure in my ears without success. Looking out the window, we were barreling toward land that did not look at all like China. Checking my watch, I saw only two hours had lapsed, so definitely not China. There must be some emergency. I looked around for Avigad and saw him seated in the cabin with the pilot. Not a good sign.

The wheels lowered, preparing for touchdown, which added

a slight vibration under my feet. The descent rate slowed and ten minutes later, we were on the ground, rolling toward a large blue hangar where three men waited. One did not need to be a genius to know that the sign on the hangar was in some type of Arabic script, and not Chinese, welcoming us to wherever we were. This was an unexpected emergency stop, or our destination had changed.

Something Avigad withheld from me.

Anger, then fear, gripped me. Why the cloak and dagger? Trust wasn't my forte and Avigad had lost all my trust this last month. Crazy thoughts filled my head. Was Avigad going to force me to sign over all my assets to him, and leave me here to die? Was he going to hold me ransom and try to extort money from Isabella? What about the paintings we're supposed to be taking to Beijing? My God, was he going to steal them? That was absurd; they were worth, in total, one hundred twenty million euros. The majority of them were fakes, making them, in essence, worth nothing. But even at full market value, it wasn't a reason to steal them.

With the plane at a full stop and engines shut down, Avigad unbuckled his belt while the pilot released the stairs for our exit. As Avigad walked past the stairs toward me, men were reaching for the outer stairs, to guide them down and lock in place. This was one of those times I felt deep anger and unbridled hatred for this man. I found it difficult to school the emotions probably playing out across my face. He stood and waited for me to say something. When I made a move to acknowledge him, he sat. Assured I was calm, he spoke.

"We're in Tehran, and we're here to collect one, not two, kidneys. As I have told you, this is very personal to me, and I will share the details of this need at the proper time. Everything is set up to move us through Immigration and Customs swiftly. When

TWO

we leave the plane, walk through the private Immigration booth, and they will process our documents. No questions will be asked. My contact will walk us through the process and he'll be our minder while here. Any questions arise, he'll translate and help you give the proper answer. I'll be processed before you and will answer all the relevant questions. You will present your passport to the agent, who will ask you the purpose of your visit. Answer 'business.' Nothing more, nothing less. He will stamp your passport and return it. Your passport is under the name of Adam Zay, and you are traveling under a Swiss passport. Visas are in place. Adam Zay is a professor of mathematics, here for a meeting at the university. There should be no question about that, but if there is, your invitation is in the envelope with the documents." He pushed himself from his seat and stood, discussion closed. But I stayed seated. I wanted, and deserved, answers.

"Why?" I asked, giving him the opportunity to allay my fears about the subterfuge and secrecy.

He looked at me, deciding what game he should play. Deep in thought about how much to share with me, he answered in a measured cadence.

"Time is of the essence, and if I had shared my plan, you would have argued unnecessarily," he said.

That was all he gave me. Fair enough. I definitely would have argued. And most likely refused to go. Iran was well-known for people disappearing within the country once they breached the boundaries. I wouldn't be one of those people willing to put my freedom at risk.

"Why Iran?" I asked, not in an angry or surly tone—because that wouldn't get me an answer—but one seeking information.

"The kidney recipient has been given a short window of time to acquire a healthy kidney. If the transplant is not accomplished in a timely manner, the consequence could be dire. The recipient has a rare tissue type, and the only match is a female relative here in Iran. There is consent to the procedure and in one hour, you will be removing her kidney, and we then will be off to St. Petersburg with the kidney." Avigad seemed restless sharing that information.

He needed discretion and skill, and that is what I always provided. However, panic gripped me, and it was nearly impossible to breathe. Russia.

"No, absolutely not," I stated, knowing I had no choice in the matter at all. Avigad knew it as well. He smiled.

"Come. Let's make our way to our minder, who shall process us through and take us to the center where your patient awaits." Avigad clapped his hands together softly, rallying me to get up and get moving.

He knew full well that although selling or donating an organ was not a crime in Iran, it was prohibited to transplant a female organ into a man. A grave sin under Muslim religion and law. So that necessitated the secrecy. The recipient must be a man, and it must be kept a secret. I understood the Iran connection, but not Russia.

"Why Russia?" I asked, and didn't expect a true answer.

I watched as he collected his thoughts. Anxious to leave, he still took the time to answer.

"Because Russia is an ally of Iran. Taking a kidney to a Western country would be impossible without proper protocol being followed. It would never make it past Customs. As it is, there were enormous payouts to ease the way out of here and into Russia, but it was accomplished. If it was destined for London or Canada, without a doubt the kidney would be confiscated. In short, the delicate cargo won't be searched when we leave Iran or when we enter Russia. Adrien, we have powerful friends in Russia that I need to keep that way. The Roselov name is

TWO

well-connected," he said, and let that sit.

Roselov. Will that man never leave my life? My fate was still not certain. He needed me for the kidney removal, as doctors here were prohibited from removal of a female organ without jumping through procedural hoops. And not many, I am certain, were willing to put their life at risk for whatever money he offered to pay. But once removed, did he need me to implant it in Russia?

"Who is the recipient?" I asked.

"Soon, Adrien, soon," he said. He turned his back, and took the steps one at a time down the narrow staircase, careful not to trip.

We passed through Immigration and Customs with ease and were picked up by a well-dressed Persian driver. It was clear they were not strangers and Avigad commanded great respect from the young man.

Leaving the airport was like leaving an airport in any other major city. Tehran revealed itself to be a noisy, youthful city. It was a smoggy metropolis with a population easily over ten million. Buildings were everywhere. Tall skyscrapers and short buildings—all mostly new, but some older with a limited amount of green space—made the city seem almost friendly. Yet, a city was a city.

The lack of traffic lights and the wild drivers at first put me in fear of my life, as people raced around, barely missing pedestrians. However, it soon became clear the drivers were experts at keeping things moving and pedestrians were experts at staying alive. Still, I checked that the belt across my chest was secured, just in case. For extra measure, I held onto the door handle as I watched traffic flow in every direction. Chador-covered women flooded the streets and sidewalks as they engaged in affectionate conversations. Children ran alongside their mothers, and men sat and enjoyed coffee together. And unlike Saudi Arabia, women were seen behind a steering wheel. Iranians, I had to remember, were not Arabs. An Iranian is a Persian whose language is Farsi, and not Arabic, although the majority of youth spoke English. A theocracy and modern youth; what an enigma.

The landscape was littered with fanciful buildings, but also hosted murals of propaganda against the United States painted on some walls. It was clear that the United States and Israel were its common enemies, and I was thankful nothing indicated they harbored ill feelings about my newly-acquired Swiss nationality.

Avigad explained we were headed toward northern Tehran, a suburb of luxury, where one inhabitant was always wealthier than the next and flaunted it. As we entered the area, I gathered that the flashier, the better was the norm in northern Tehran. Teenagers drove cars worth almost a quarter of a million dollars, and I wouldn't even begin to assess the property values. Opulence was on full display as we approached the building where I was to perform the surgery. A far cry from the warehouse in Cairo. But still, the nausea I felt in such a foreign country persisted.

The driver drove to the back of the large modern green, glassed building, where we were greeted by what I assumed was another minder. However, I could have been wrong. Avigad and the man who greeted us wearing Western-styled clothing, seemed to have a personal relationship. They warmly embraced each other, and called each other names that could only be considered a nickname in Western culture. Introductions were exchanged, and the man to whom I was entrusted once we entered the building, was named Farhad. He would navigate us to what was to be the surgical suite and would stay with us during the procedure.

The new immaculate building appeared to be technologically advanced as well, beyond what I was accustomed to use. It

TWO

wouldn't have surprised me if they'd built this building for this one operation, although that probably was my imagination running away with itself.

A glass elevator carried us to the third floor, which emptied out into a large area with stark white walls and red couches and chairs. A man in medical scrub attire, about my age, approached with a chart. He advised that the CT scan was set up in the room for my review, and all tests, including renal function tests, were normal and in the chart. Handing it to me, he excused himself to return to the surgical suite to oversee the final surgical setup.

After a quick review of the chart, I was taken to an area where I studied the CT scan for a few minutes. Between the chart and scan, I deduced my patient was a woman, age twenty-six, in excellent health. She had no history of drugs, alcohol, or tobacco intake. Well-developed and well-nourished, it appeared she lived a life where she cared for herself, and I wondered what it would take to make her donate or sell her kidney. But alas, that was not my concern. Checking her scan, she presented with no anomalies or problems anatomically. I finished with the preliminary review and scan, and was ready for surgery. The team waited for my nod to start the pre-op anesthesia process and surgical preparation to open the patient. By the time I'd changed into scrubs and performed the scrub of my own body, the patient was ready.

I moved toward the room to put on my gown, when Avigad took hold of my arm. "A word, Adrien."

We moved to a corner of the room. He struggled with what he wanted to tell me, so I gave him a wide berth.

"That young woman in there is my daughter, and you must do everything you can to make sure this is a success," he said, leaving me stunned and not able to ask more questions. However, questions did stumble around my mind, that I knew would remain unanswered.

I touched his arm and assured him I would take care of her, silently cursing him for dragging this girl into this scheme. His moral corruptness knew no bounds, and it took me but a second to realize, neither did mine.

Scrubbed, now gowned, I walked into the room to the steady sound of a machine monitoring her heart and blood pressure. A mask was over her face, administering anesthesia, and she was being monitored by two people for anesthesia and to watch her breathing. Another person was administering medication into an intravenous bag, also monitored by two people. The surgical tray was prepared exactly the way I liked it.

Within minutes, an incision of twelve inches was made, and we were ready to begin. Muscle, fat, and tissue were cut and moved, and the tube that carries urine from the kidney to the bladder, along with blood vessels, was cut away from the kidney. With skilled determination, the kidney was removed, placed in the transport container, and ready for transport. In under two and a half hours, a record time for me, the kidney was removed. The surgical area was closed with staples, and the patient started into the recovery phase. Unlike Cairo, no assistant touched this woman.

Her urine bag was checked for blood. Blood pressure was monitored and fluids from her intravenous line were adjusted. I watched as Avigad stroked the cheek of this stunningly beautiful woman. His daughter. Long thick brown hair, slender perfect nose, and full lips; a true classic beauty. He kissed her forehead and said a few words in her ear, then turned to me.

"She's in the best of hands. Now we need to leave," he said.

"You don't want to wait for her to recover and say goodbye properly?" I asked.

"We don't have that luxury. Russia is on Russian time," he said.

TWO

"What the hell does that mean?" I said. None of this made any sense. Avigad had a daughter in Iran, and some relative waiting in Russia who needed a kidney. Had the whole world gone mad?

"No time to look back, Adrien. Only time to look forward and change the world in our favor," he said.

I was guided to the shower and changing area, and told to be quick. Exiting the dressing area, I watched as people buzzed around the woman who appeared to be recovering nicely. Yet another illegal surgery to worry could come back to haunt me.

I noted Farhad distributing envelopes to the staff, probably containing a remuneration for the high risk they all took to make this surgery a success. Ready to depart, I waited for Avigad, who studied his daughter, and placed a hand on the deadliest man in the world's shoulder, letting him know I was ready. Did he want me to check on her again? His response was no, my part was done.

The conversation was now closed. We exited the building and he once again warmly embraced the man only known as Farhad, and we left. Our next stop: St. Petersburg. Having been to Russia only once before as a tourist, it was a place to be visited once and never again by choice. Dread crept up my spine, as if ice had been applied to it. I hated Russia, and more than the concept of Russia, I hated the soulless eyes of its inhabitants that reflected back in mine.

CHAPTER TWENTY-SIX

ISABELLA

ADRIEN AND THE man who tried to kill me knew I was on the mend and that necessitated new plans. Was there ever a time in my life where I worried my life was in real danger before now? No. However, the threat was real, and I didn't know how many enemies I had, ready to pull another trigger.

I was moved from my room to a secured area in the hospital, with law enforcement at my door. What had I done to bring this upon myself? Absolutely nothing. Could I do anything to change what was happening around me? Possibly. By giving up all ownership of the gallery, I could have stayed under Adrien's radar. However, at some point that would have led to more people getting hurt from whatever plan Adrien and this man had put into motion. Without the drugs Adrien had been giving me, my mind was back in focus and my judgment keen.

Lost in my thoughts, Michelle touched my arm and brought me back to the here and now as she leaned forward, handing me a paper.

"I'm sorry, Michelle, I got lost in my thoughts. Could you

TWO

please repeat that again?" I asked.

"This paper is the document that will be filed with the court to set the divorce in motion. I need your signature right there in the bottom right, indicating everything is true and accurate to the best of your knowledge." She handed me a pen and the paper. I reviewed it and as ugly as the allegations appeared, they were indeed all true.

"Now, this document is a bit tricky. Pared down to the basics, it states that you, Ben, and Richard, after performing an inventory of paintings, have reason to believe these are paintings that could be forgeries. And I refer you to Exhibit A-1. You will allow Ben to take them into custody when they are returned from the auction houses, and perform the necessary testing to determine if they are forgeries. Initial here." She pointed at a box.

"If determined that they are, then you consent to any painting authenticated as a forged or faked painting to be held for evidence in an investigation, sign there." She pointed at where I should sign. "And right there, indicating you had no knowledge these paintings had been in the inventory, and you had no part in their acquisition."

I signed as requested, with the hope and assurance that cooperating would remove me of any criminal implications.

"This document is the forensic accounting of your assets. Through Richard's magic, we've been able to track down three offshore accounts belonging to Adrien. You can see there is a significant amount of money there." She handed me five documents with line after line of deposits over the last twenty-four months. What I saw was a whole bunch of zeros. I would agree the amount was significant.

"When I file the divorce papers today, I will have the justice place a freeze on his ability to access these accounts until further order of the court. We can only assume he has hidden these funds to limit your access. Do I know if the funds are from a criminal operation? No, I don't. At this point, I am not obligated to notify any authorities about it. However, if it comes to light the funds are part of a criminal operation, we need to full disclose that to the proper authorities. Once the order is signed, I'll forward it to the financial institutions and by five p.m. tonight, his access should be limited. On the business accounts, I've already removed his name as a signatory and he's not on the corporation papers, so there's no further action required. I've cancelled his ability to use the business credit cards and, trust me, if I could, I would change the locks on your apartment home," she informed me, continuing to hand me papers for review.

Reviewing the documents, it boggled my mind that he had access to so much money. He probably could buy a small nation with the funds. I signed as requested and returned them to her.

"And you are sure he had something to do with me being shot?" I asked, wanting her to say no so desperately, but even if she did, I still had my suspicions.

"Isabella, I cannot say that with any amount of certainty at all. It's an ongoing investigation." She leaned forward and rubbed my hand. "However, that the man you described is a known associate of Adrien's, and drugs were found in food he had access to. It doesn't take much of a reach to say he probably did."

"For money? I would sign over every penny we own to him. I want to control the things I own, not them control me. Who is this man? What drives him? You know what, don't answer those questions, because we would never get it right. Just tell me what to do to break my bond with him permanently, and let's be done with this mess," I said.

"You've signed all the documents. The only thing left is to place a phone call to the New York, London, and Paris auctions, making certain that the lots are pulled from the sale. Ben is in

TWO

London and can make certain that is done, Richard can oversee the Paris lots, and I will take responsibility for New York," she said.

"What's next?" I asked.

"There is a police officer waiting outside, and he has some papers for you to sign, indicating you have made an identification of the man who shot you. You will need to sign the sketch Jacque made, and he will take some further information. That's it. You should get some rest. I know Chloe will be dropping by later with some food." She gathered her papers. "Isabella, I'm so sorry you've had to go through all of this, especially after losing your family in the attacks. I will not say I know how you feel because I don't, and it would be disingenuous to say so. What I will say is that I think you are a very brave woman, and I'll do whatever it takes to get you a divorce, so that you can start your life over. Have you thought about what your future might hold?" she queried. It was a question I'd asked myself over and over.

"I've thought about nothing else," I replied. "The first thing I'll do is sell the gallery when I can. The gallery was my dream once, but Adrien took it over and made it into something I don't want. Next, when the assets are cleared away, I'll take my share from the apartment and move back to the Marais until I find my footing. I haven't formulated a plan yet for a job, but I want to make sure it's something I'll always have complete control over. Other than that, I'm open to suggestions. My only want is a minimalist lifestyle."

She stopped and reflected a moment before she continued.

"I've been in this game a long time. I've seen it all and dealt with my share of surprises. I think something you should prepare yourself for is that Adrien may be involved in some type of dangerous criminal activity. I'm not pointing fingers at all. However, with that kind of money in offshore accounts, I think you need to start gathering your thoughts that this shooting may have had something to do with his possible activities. If he has partners who know that you have access to his money, I worry you'll be in danger. It's early days, but I would give some thought to legally changing your name and moving from France. I know it's an enormous step, however, we don't know the reach of his associates," she said.

My mind went blank. I suddenly felt the need to take a vacation from life. How could that be? Someone would continue to target me to get at Adrien? Or worse yet, Adrien would target me?

Unaware of my mind checking out, her voice continued as tunnel echo in my mind somewhere.

"We know from Chloe, he has passports and lots of cash in a secret room. We know he travels out of the country, a lot. Ben and Richard are trying to track those trips. But add in the money, and I smell something very foul," she said.

Studying me, she said, "Maybe too much right now? The doctor said you are healing well and should be released in a few days. We'll talk more then. Yes?"

I agreed, and she gathered her papers and left. Upon her exit, the police officer entered and posed pointed questions and I gave vague responses. I signed his requested documents and he left, not giving me much hope that the man would be caught, but they'd do their best. After a dressing change, bathroom run, and pain pill, which I accepted so sleep would find me, I decided to give my conscious mind a rest. However, the nightmares didn't get the message.

MY EYES FLUTTERED open, and Chloe and Richard were relaxing in chairs by my bed. Well, Chloe was relaxing with her

TWO

feet propped up on my bed, and her body slumped in the chair, stuffing fries in her mouth.

"Took you long enough." Chloe tried to sound annoyed, but I knew she wasn't.

"How long have you been here?" My breath felt thick and grimy. "I need a toothbrush."

"Don't mind her," Richard chirped in. "We have some food for you. And . . ." He hesitated a beat too long.

"I'll gladly take the food, and gladly take the rest of the sentence," I said, reaching for the box that smelled of garlic and Italian goodness.

"Richard, could you not wait until she ate?" That didn't sound good. "You want to brush your teeth before or after you eat?"

I had a feeling my mouth yuckiness would have to wait.

"If Richard has information, I want that before food," I responded.

"After you eat, we are packing you up and moving you from the hospital," he said, not giving me a chance to change my mind. Obviously, he'd eaten and didn't care if this caused me to lose my appetite.

"Would that be with or without a doctor's approval?" I asked, pretty sure of the answer.

"With," he shot back. Hmm. *That* was not what I expected.

"Why?" I volleyed.

"Don't you want to eat first?" Chloe asked, as she slid her fries in mayonnaise and shoved them in her mouth. My expression gave her my answer.

"You already know about the Abu Dhabi sale. Before London could process the documents, Adrien was one step ahead and pulled the London and Paris lots. We don't know where he shipped them," Richard said, standing and grabbed a few fries as he paced to the window.

"New York?" I asked.

"Same. And he can't be physically found either. The last place we have him is Abu Dhabi, and then nothing. Not on any commercial flights out of the United Arab Emirates," he said with some hesitancy.

"The money in the accounts?" I inquired.

"Michelle has them frozen; he can't access any funds." Richard leaned against the window ledge.

"So why do I need to leave the hospital?" As if I needed a reason.

"For your safety, we think it would be better if we could keep a finger on your pulse. Literally," he said.

"You think he might try to harm me?" I asked, alarmed now that my fear had been verbalized.

"I don't know, Isabella. However, that man he associates with is ruthless and unless Adrien is in my sights, I want you out of his." He waved his hands around, indicating the hospital. "So, either eat up and we can get you dressed and out of here, or get dressed and you can eat later."

"I've lost my appetite," I said. "And, Richard, Chloe is right. Always give food first, then bad news."

Richard smiled.

Within the hour, we were headed toward a hotel room they had booked me, where a nurse waited to monitor me. Could my life get any more complicated?

CHAPTER TWENTY-SEVEN

BEN

"I'M SORRY, BUT all I can tell you is that Dr. Armond called and said that he was withdrawing the lots he had for sale. He was very specific that it was everything, including the private reserve." The London auction house director, Christopher Wray, was cooperative and unhelpful.

"Can you describe the man that came and retrieved the lots?" I was aggravated that Adrien was one step ahead of us. I was positive Abu Dhabi helped him perpetrate a fraud but had no available proof. Yet. And even if we could prove it, would the United Arab Emirates do anything about it? In the scheme of their political agenda these days, it was highly unlikely.

"I can do better. Come. I will have Mark cue up the tapes and Toni will pull the paperwork," he said. My brain must be fried to have failed to ask such an elementary request.

Cillian and I followed the director to the security room where a bank of twelve monitors were filming for security purposes. He asked the technician to obtain the tapes from yesterday and cue up to where the Armond lot was removed and placed on a truck.

The truck ended up being a regular white truck with no markings and an obvious fake license. It appeared to be a dead end.

We were able to determine that it was Paul, Adrien's employee, who picked up the lots and had them loaded onto the truck. At least there was one person to interview, if we could locate him. With the magic of CCTV positioned throughout the city, and the help of the Met, we followed where they were transported and eventually unloaded.

The place that held the lots was an obscure gray block warehouse in an industrial part of the city, surrounded by a twelve-foot fence and three layers of barbed wire. The question was, how long would the inventory remain there? Would the paintings stay there until they sent them back to Paris? Until Adrien could find some way to put them back on offer? Or until he shipped them to a private buyer.

Not wanting to take the chance of losing track of the lot, we determined it best to seize it while in London. However, that proved a bit difficult.

We arrived at the warehouse with Detective Inspector Morse from the London Metropolitan Police, armed with the order Michelle had prepared and the French justice had signed. Our intent was to procure the paintings then secure them on the truck we had with us, and let the Met take them into custody until we could sort the fakes from authentic.

The place was an enormous dirty concrete building with no windows. It was poorly lit inside, but appeared to be very secure. The area was heavily guarded by twelve men with automatic weapons, all at least six foot four and built. Was it a coincidence that every one of them had a heavy Russian accent and tattoos?

We were greeted and escorted to the dismal utilitarian office

TWO

of the warehouse director, reflecting what was obvious about the building. No one cared about it. We sat on old plastic green couches with splits and stains, as he briefly reviewed the order we presented. What he said was he would consult with his legal counsel. What his body language said was we were wasting our time. A fax of the document to his legal counsel was necessary, and fifteen minutes later, we had an answer.

"Gentlemen, it appears there is a problem," the director said. "After an exhaustive search, I find I have nothing stored here under the name of Armond."

"You must," I insisted. "We tracked the truck by CCTV all over the city to this place yesterday. We watched as it parked right in the back and appeared to unload some cargo. Look again."

"I am sorry, but I have nothing here under that name," he replied, as if this was finished. "I have also had our legal advisor look as well, and we do not see that name, or any variation of it, in the event it was misspelled."

"Then please, read me the list of people who brought items in yesterday, and the time they were logged in," the British Detective Inspector Morse interjected.

"I cannot do that. We have a confidential arrangement with all our clients," he returned, as he minimized the screen and sat back.

"This is incredulous. You have property that is owned by someone else—that someone being Mrs. Armond—sitting in your warehouse without her permission. I would say, if you do not cooperate with its return, now that we have asked for it, you could be charged as an accessory to a crime," the DI said. He was mistaken if he thought this would cause the man any alarm.

"Is it DI or DSI?" he inquired.

"DI," he responded.

"DI Morse, I'll repeat, I have no package that was delivered yesterday, or any day, under the name of Armond. I have no reason to believe any crime was committed on the property or any reason to believe we are harboring what you insinuate are stolen items. I am under no obligation to provide you the names of clients, without a warrant directing me to do so." In essence, he was correct. If we were alleging Adrien had stolen property, we would first have to prove intent that he stole it, and then that this man had the property owned by Adrien, knowing it was stolen.

"And further, every person who stores property here is assured that their confidentiality is secure, and that is incorporated in our contract," he advised, sitting back and crossing his arms.

DI Morse was barely holding onto his temper, as this person was obviously well-versed in the law and had him by the balls.

"We'll see what a justice says about that. I'll return with a warrant for the list," he said. "And at that time, you will be handing over that package."

"Until then," the director said, unaffected.

Not bothered or worried in the least, he wanted us gone. He rose from his creaky leather red chair and led us out, wishing us a good day.

We gathered by the car to formulate a plan, but with little evidence, we were screwed.

"Gentlemen, I spoke with a lot of bravado in there, but we are on shaky ground. I can probably convince a justice that the paintings are in there, by explaining the chain of custody that we saw on the CCTV. However, we don't actually know if it was unloaded, because it went into the bay under the building, and we did not see it physically removed. I think if we ask the justice for the list of people who deposited something during that period of time, he might feel it is not invasive, and will grant us that one limited thing. I may be able to stretch this to make it appear that a crime of theft is imminent based on the facts, and stretch

TWO

it to us being able to search the containers that have the size and dimension of ours that came in exactly at that time. But I'm not hopeful," DI Morse said.

"Great. Let's get cracking," Cillian interjected.

"You Yanks, always in a hurry," he chuckled, then continued, "You did notice that everyone in there was Russian?"

We nodded; it was impossible to miss.

"You do see that sign in Russian on the warehouse?" he pointed.

Again, we agreed.

"More than likely, the building is owned by some Russian enterprise. Or even possibly a branch of the Russian government. This could prove quite complicated," he offered.

To our delight, two hours later we found that the company who owned the building was a British holding company. The justice issued a limited warrant to obtain the list of people who had placed items in storage yesterday, at that time, with those dimensions. At least that was one hurdle overcome. It did not give us authority to look inside the container. An additional warrant would be needed for that.

Now armed with a warrant and our order, we returned to the building. We were invited back to the director's office. He was to provide us the name and contact information for the owner of the crate, along with description of the crate, and storage slot in the facility with any crate that arrived within the fifteen-minute range we gave him.

This time, his high-dollar Russian legal advisor was physically available to review the warrant to produce the list. He nodded at Wray, who found the property in the computer and printed out a list. Only one container had arrived during that window. This was indeed looking up.

As he handed the list to us, I felt my heart rate accelerate.

We soon would have the name of the owner of the container.

DI Morse was the first to see it.

"Shit."

I was the second, and Cillian last.

"You are certain about this?" Morse asked.

"Gentlemen, I am an employee here, and I have no interest in who decides to store their possessions here. I only record what is presented to me as identification of the owner," he said. And he couldn't just leave it at that; he clearly was having too much fun with us at our expense. "Shall I expect you back?"

Morse returned a glare and we stood to leave.

"Good day, gentlemen," he said, and we did not return the sentiment.

In the end, we knew we were at a stalemate. The crate was under the ownership of the Islamic Republic of Iran, and not only under Iranian ownership, but marked as a diplomatic pouch. It might as well have been marked as radioactive material. We could not touch it. It was as good as being on Iranian soil. Only if the contents were removed from the specially-marked wrapping and exposed away from it would we have a chance at it. We could make an appeal to the Iranian Embassy, but that would be a waste of time.

"Unlike Britain, who re-established relations with Iran in 2014, we don't have an Iranian Embassy in the US. However, there is an Interests Section of the Islamic Republic of Iran in the United States, which is located in the Pakistan Embassy in Washington, D.C. I'm going to assume that when I place a call back home, I'll find we have run into a similar dilemma," Cillian said.

"Let me summarize this clusterfuck. We have a French corporation—Isabella's gallery—that owns a building and inventory in Britain, and that would be the old Roselov gallery. Paintings, that although they belong to the gallery under the ownership

TWO

of Isabella, are still a marital asset. Adrien, the husband, cannot be charged with stealing the paintings, as they are joint owners of property as far as the marriage, for now. However, a French court has now given her the right to direct what happens with the paintings. But Adrien, or someone associated with him, has secreted the lot of paintings into a British-owned warehouse, run by Russians under an Iranian diplomatic immunity. Do I have it about right?" I asked, seething. "Because this is my worst nightmare. Unraveling jurisdiction and ownership could take years. And you know those paintings will be on a boat, and there is nothing we can do because we can't even prove they ever left that white van, or that they were ever in the warehouse."

"Yes, it would appear so," Cillian responded.

"Gentlemen, it looks like we are truly and royally fucked." I had never been more frustrated, having been outsmarted by a person who was not some government agent.

"It would appear so," said Morse.

Perfect.

"We can keep a watch on the warehouse through CCTV, but we all agree, it can leave in another crate," Morse reminded us, though we didn't need reminding.

"I suppose our job here is done," I said.

"Ben, I have a few loose ends to tie up with Jackson when he completes his investigation, then I'll meet you at the hotel so we can head to Paris," Cillian offered. "DI Morse, thank you for your time and resources. We will be in touch."

Goodbyes were exchanged all around, and I made my way to the hotel to check out. Once Cillian joined me, we were on our way back to Paris. I had hoped for a quick detour home to Amsterdam, but there was still work to be done, and I was convinced we were now working under an abbreviated timeline.

We had to track Adrien and Abed.

CHAPTER TWENTY-EIGHT

BEN

"I APPRECIATE YOU letting me stay with you," Cillian said. "As the kids say, this place is sick."

"Saying it that way, I think you mean it's amazing. However, considering it has a Tim Burton feel to it, I'll go with the original meaning of sick," I said, showing him to the guest room. "I know it's really late, and you are dog tired, so feel free to crash. I want to go through some emails, and I've been waiting for some information to come through. If you get hungry, the kitchen has your usual stuff, so feel free to help yourself."

Moving toward the window, he pushed the curtain to the side, so he could open it. "This is like living a dream. My fiancée would love it here. It's quiet, well-maintained, and I can see the sparkling of the Eiffel Tower. I don't even want to think how much this place costs," Cillian mused.

I stood beside him and looked out as well. Yes, it was peaceful, and yes, it was beautiful, but it was all make-believe. A curtain ready to be lifted, and the reality might be ugly.

"Indeed, the city is beautiful, and it breaks my heart to see

TWO

what has become of it," I said.

"Do you have a plan?" He changed the subject and refocused us.

"Based on the information I receive in the emails, I'll let you know," I advised.

He continued looking out. "This wasn't a religious statement."

"I agree." Although neither of us had a foundation to challenge the popular thinking.

"However, it has the fingerprints of some type of Middle Eastern or Arabic actor," he went on further.

"I agree." Only because no synagogue or mosque was targeted, but that was not my thought to share; simply an opinion I had formulated.

"It's got something to do with teaching us a lesson," he said, leaning on the sill. "And I don't think we've learned the lesson yet. We have another one coming, and we won't see it until it's too late."

"Cillian, here's what I think. It's a two-part plan. We've seen the first part, and as we are getting up from our knees and not quite standing, the second part will be delivered. But I don't think this is a lesson. I think it's more about power—acquiring it and keeping it."

"In bed at night, I think about it because there is no doubt part two is coming to our own shores, and can you ever be ready? What if part two is a nuclear attack? Or a nuclear and *biological* attack? The emotional devastation could cause people to mentally surrender. Please don't judge me for what I'm about to say," he said with a grin. "But I'm beginning to believe this might be Nostradamus predicting World War III and, soon, we'll be able to identify the enemy."

What do you say to that? I was not up on Nostradamus, but

at this point, anything and everything was on the table.

"He believes in the Antichrist or some such thing, right?" I asked. Why was I even having this conversation? "And the third Antichrist would lead the world into its own self-destruction?"

He laughed and shook his head. "Forget it. In desperate times, when there's no answer, we start letting our imagination run wild. I'm just frustrated. It doesn't feel like this is a North Korea or China plot. Russia maybe, but to what end? It seems Arab because of the churches, but again, is that a red herring?" He paused, looking over at me. "Well, I'm beat. How about we continue this in the morning?"

"Sounds good. If you need anything, see that black round thing there?" I said, and he nodded. "That's an Echo Dot that acts as an intercom. Just start talking and Alexa will find me."

He made his way to the kitchen. About five minutes later, he left with a sandwich and beer in his hands, while I worked at my computer.

Christ, how could such a short time from my last log in cause such an influx of emails?

I opened Levi's first, who indicated there was a video conference at one tomorrow. Next, one from Jill that relayed things had gone eerily silent on chatter again, like right before the attacks. There was nothing on Twitter and nothing on any other social media. Dead silent, and it didn't bode well. After several more emails that could wait until morning, my final email was from Richard, and this one made me want to puke.

"When you get in, call me. All of Adrien and Isabella's accounts have been hacked and emptied. I need you to get working on it from your end right away. I have Jesse working on it round the clock as best we can, using our resources, and I've put out a tag to Jill, but I'm not sure if she will get it right away. We have no idea where the money has gone." I stopped reading and picked

TWO

up the phone.

He answered immediately.

"When and how?" I offered no greeting or pleasantries.

"A half hour ago. All the banks can do is put a freeze on the funds because it's a marital asset, with a court order. Someone tries to move it by request, then they can stop it. This was a worm or something; we don't know yet. Every penny gone, and we have no idea where it went," he said.

"That's impossible. It had to go somewhere. Once it hits the wire, the signal has to go somewhere." I was not a cyber geek, but electronics was pretty basic understanding; energy moved from point A to point B.

"I've got Jesse working on it. Michelle has put a call out. But until the morning, not much will be done, because it's not being tagged as a matter of national security. So, any way you can do anything?"

"Every last penny, you say. Vanished. What kind of skillset would that involve? All the offshore accounts as well?" I asked.

"First to go. But when I say first to go, I mean, the dominos fell within seconds."

"Assuming it's Adrien behind this, he's not planning to come back." That would be the logical assumption. "Any fingerprints?"

"Not even a little bit," he answered.

"Any luck scooping up the paintings sent to other places not in the auction houses?" I asked.

"No. And we need to find out how he stayed one step ahead in London, and who their inside man or woman was." Richard sighed into the phone.

"I don't think you need to tell me my job. I've got it covered. I want to know how the hell Iran came into the mix. That was a dark horse no one saw coming. But the place was run by Russians, and Roselov is a Russian, so is he possibly connected with

Iran?"

"You have any more on the Abed guy?" he asked.

"No, just that he's pretty much a ghost and leaves a faint trail that he covers well. I would like to know where the man lives and banks and parties, but according to our database, he owns nothing and lives nowhere. He is like Jaqen H'ghar from *Game of Thrones*. He is No One. Is Isabella doing okay?" I knew the meaning was not lost on a fellow GoT fan.

"Yes, she is amazingly calm about this whole thing, and I've yet to tell her about the money. At this point, I don't think it will phase her. For all intents and purposes, her business is defunct. But for now, she has a place to live. And my thought is, if he's wiped her clean financially, except for the real estate, there's no reason to want to do her any harm. Let's face it, that albatross of an apartment would take forever to sell, and even if she sold it for what is left on the mortgage, banks are skittish to make loans. I hope this means she is free of that viper. We just have to find some way of getting her divorced at some point. Because I don't see him coming back to be served the papers." His speech was starting to get a little slurry, and I would probably soon lose him to sleep.

"Your point is taken. The French banks will be cooperative on tracking down the emptying of funds. But as most offshores are on the sketchy side, I'd say they will do a cursory sweep, but won't put much effort into it. Not much more we can do tonight. I'll get with you tomorrow. Right now, I'm beat. So, sandwich, bed, and sleep."

We disconnected, and the information spun in my head. I believe I totally underestimated Adrien. Obviously, he or possibly Roselov, somehow even in FBI custody, had partnered with Iran to have the paintings put in a diplomatic pouch. Did Paul know he was delivering storage for his boss under Iranian diplomatic

TWO

immunity? We had to track him down. It was in a Russian-run warehouse and the paintings were from the Roselov gallery—that was no big leap to what Paul could deduce. But how did he get to the money from the accounts? This put him in a whole new league. What a conundrum.

My phone buzzed, and I looked down at it to see Jackson Tate's call coming through.

"Jackson, you need me to get Cillian?" I asked.

"No, it can hold until morning, and it's you I wanted to touch base with anyway."

"What's up?" I asked.

"It appears the Syrians got someone to flip on the organ donation fiasco in Cairo," he said.

"How did you get the information, and what's the story?" This could be the break we were waiting for.

"It came via a Russian organ broker, who got burned in the deal and never got his cut. He did something stupid and got swept up in an operation. I'm not read into the whole thing yet because they are still tracking things down. But the reason for the call is that the guy who flipped said that Avigad Abed is the guy who set that whole mess in motion, and your boy Armond was the doctor." He tapped some computer keys, and I heard some video footage of people screaming and crying.

"How reliable do you think this is?" I asked.

"Very, and that's all I will say. Tell Cill to call me when he gets up."

"Will do." I ended the call and my thoughts went 'round the bend again.

About to plug the phone into charge, I saw Isabella's name popped up.

"Evening, Isabella," I answered.

"Good, you're still up. I wanted to make sure you got back

okay. I heard that Adrien slipped through everyone's fingers." Her voice was soft.

"That would be correct. I have to tell you I didn't see what happened coming. I figured that once they pulled what they did in Abu Dhabi, that we would catch up with him in London. Had it not been for our guy with eyes at the Abu Dhabi auction, our lead that he moved the paintings there would have had about a twenty-four-hour lag time. We wouldn't have known he was onto us. I'm sorry we lost Abu Dhabi and the London inventory." I sighed before continuing. "What else is going on?" I asked, not sure how much she knew.

"No need to walk on eggshells. Richard told me the banks were emptied. What I have left is real estate and, honestly, the minute I can, I am selling both."

"Have you got any cash that you can tap into?"

"I have something better. A crack financial advisor. Have you met Chloe?" she laughed. "That woman told me two years ago to put away a little bit here and there, and I sold some of my own paintings along the way. I'm good."

"Isabella, that is excellent news," I said. "You must be worried about something to call, so what's bothering you?"

"I was wondering if maybe tomorrow, I could get permission to go back to the apartment and get some things. I am going to move in with Chloe for a bit. And I wanted to make sure the cameras are off. I don't want Adrien seeing me in the apartment," she replied. "I'll have to let Danielle know that I have to terminate her services, and I want to move my car. Can you get someone to disable the GPS, so Adrien can't find me or my car?"

"Not a problem. The cameras are already disabled. And, to be honest, if he's moved all that money, I don't see him coming back." I hoped to reassure her that, at some point, her life would be her own.

TWO

"God, Ben, who knows with Adrien?" She had a point. He probably would find some way to capture the real estate funds.

"There is another issue with him that I can't talk about right now. But I think he's got more on his plate than he'll be able to handle. My guess is, he'll never step foot here again." It wasn't much, but it was all I could offer.

"And that's all you can give me?" she asked.

"For now. I'll meet you tomorrow at nine a.m. at the apartment, if you are up to it. Or you can send Chloe with a list," I suggested.

"No, I need to get out," she said. "I'm still a little sore, but the doctors said I have to use my muscles or more issues could arise, like blood clots."

"You have a restful night and see you tomorrow."

"Thank you for all you've done, Ben. I know this is your job. But I also know you and Richard have walked me back from a cliff several times."

"Isabella, I only wish I could have done more to catch him and give you peace of mind. And the fact we are still chasing down Abed, it must worry your mind. Having just lost your family, and a husband playing mind games for financial gain, almost destroying your brain, makes you one awesome lady to still be here and thinking about the future." I meant every word.

"Thanks, Ben. I've got a plan and I'll be fine," she assured me.

"See you tomorrow. You and Chloe wait until I get there."

"Will do."

Please God, let this be over. We are so close to bagging this guy. Why can't he just walk into our net?

CHAPTER TWENTY-NINE

ADRIEN

RUSSIA. RUSSIA REMINDS me of The Who song "Won't Get Fooled Again," with the new boss being the old boss. Nothing history-wise in this place has ever changed, even with the fall of the Soviet Union. Sure, they went through a time they thought was a move toward a quasi-democracy and bastardized form of capitalism. But, in the end, all it appeared to be was a five-year period of some people getting obscenely rich, then stripped of their wealth when Putin took control.

If you are in Putin's good graces, you are allowed to acquire limited wealth. But it must be in the service of Putin, and to advance his agenda. The Roselovs fit that description. A family with a longstanding reputation of being tight with the government. This much I had learned from my research. A silent arm of the government sent to London to open the gallery. As Avigad said, the Roselovs remained a powerful force in Russia. Dmitri Roselov wasn't just some dealer of fake art, but a strategically placed Russian. Was there a benefit to the Russian government in him being there? I had absolutely no proof of this, except for

TWO

the pieces that started to fall into place.

My mind continued to put the pieces together, as Avigad broke into my thoughts.

"Russia is a riddle wrapped in a mystery inside an enigma," Avigad opined as he sat deeper into his chair content in his position in life. The same could be said of him.

"So, I've heard." I tapped my finger on the arm of the seat, keeping time in my head to "Won't Get Fooled Again."

When someone shows you who they are the first time, believe them. I knew Avigad from the first time I met him when I operated on him. An intense self-absorbed man. A man who revealed himself to be a ruthless and driven killing machine. With that in mind, I would never trust him, ever. And never let my guard down. Ever.

"Your daughter, tell me about her." It wasn't difficult to figure out I knew nothing about Avigad.

He studied my face and thought about it for a few moments. What he said would reveal to me my fate. I read on his that my fate had been determined, and I would never leave Russia, so why not answer my question.

Reaching into his pocket, he produced a picture of a stunningly beautiful woman, who would be at home as easily in New York, as Rome or the wealthy northern Tehran suburb we had left. A chameleon. Flawless skin, large almond brown eyes, flowing thick dark hair, red nails, and painted red lips that weren't smiling. A slender but athletic build, with all the right curves.

"Azar Abed," he said, looking out the small portal window of the plane.

I held the picture and studied the magnificent beauty in front of me. As I raised my eyes to his, he continued.

"I will not bore you with the indiscretions of my youth. I am not proud of the way I behaved but not ashamed either. I was a man of many appetites and I indulged them. Suffice it to say that when Azar reached the age of five, I became aware of her existence in a small town outside Rome. Her mother one of my early indiscretions. Azar came to live with me as I was building my business and has had the best that life can offer. I am proud to say that I had a hand in her becoming a brilliant, shrewd businesswoman. She graduated within the top five percent at Oxford University, and in the top two percent at the London School of Economics and has used her knowledge to help me in my endeavors," he said, with immense pride but no beaming smile. It was as if she was an investment that had flourished under his guiding hand.

"Her mother?" I asked. Her fate might be telling of the inner workings of the man.

"Irrelevant," he answered. His lips moved, however his facial muscles remained static.

Irrelevant indeed.

"Might I ask why she is in Iran?" I tried tiptoeing into an area probably forbidden. Women were not highly looked upon in Iran, and a woman with obvious Western upbringing even more so.

Again, he regarded me, trying to determine if he should answer, and if he did, I knew my fate of death was sealed.

"I sent her there on a month-long business endeavor, and she will return home to Rome as soon as she has recovered from the surgery," he offered. He reached out for the picture, and put it away in his wallet. He neither implied that she was aware that surgery was on the agenda for her trip nor that her consent was given. My speculation led me to believe she went there expecting to create some business deal and would be horrified to return home to Rome minus a kidney.

"This is quite a surprise. She lives in Rome, but working on

TWO

a business concern of yours in Tehran?" I asked, as this appeared ludicrous, which gave me some hope he was disguising the truth.

"Ever the curious one, Adrien. You want the full story? Why not, my friend?" he said, as he reached across and slapped my knee with affection.

I sat back. My stomach revolted as I now knew I was a dead man walking.

"Although not of the Jewish faith, you could say that Azar has been a wandering Jew. Born a child of Christian faith—I might add her mother kept that from me, along with her existence—she spent the first five years of her life in a small area right outside Rome. When I became aware of her existence, naturally I came to claim my child, and we have been a family since. Azar is an integral part of my life and my business," he shared. Instead of engaging my eyes he clasped his hands across his midsection and looked down at them.

"And yet you took a kidney and put her at risk?" I had zero to lose at this point. "I'm fairly sure, Avigad, that if I was to ask her now if she consented that the answer would be no. If it was yes, I am fairly certain that a legal operation could be performed on someone other than a nation of terrorists and religious zealots. People who don't take no from a woman."

He closed his eyes and thought for a moment.

"I've found myself in a precarious health position, Adrien. I myself am in need of a kidney. I searched the world over for a match and told my tissue was so rare that my fate was for certain sealed. Death would come as my renal chemistry values changed at a certain point. A close family member they said would be my only match and I saw her as a viable chance to continue living. I was able to obtain a sample for testing and she matched. She was my only match and my ticket to future life. There was no choice when the time came with or without her consent I would need her kidney.

"I have known the need was coming for about two years a little after you operated on me but it was recently that my left kidney went into acute renal failure. Looking toward the future when I became aware of the intensity of the disease I became a broker of kidneys to search for a match other than her. However, I was ever the one to make lemonade out of lemons, so I developed a lucrative business as well. Without finding a match, and earning a fortune doing such, has been bittersweet. I have more money than I ever will need, but I might not live to enjoy it. The choice was clear and without regret," he said. Yes, for him, a win-win situation. Nothing ventured, nothing gained.

Me? I felt punched in the chest. I was being spirited to Russia to operate on Avigad. The government was surely involved and as they eased the process of entry sanctioned the operation.

"You are the kidney recipient?" I verified without needing to but felt some misplaced obligation to ask. The man was deranged. Was it from his kidney failure affecting his brain. Urea buildup during kidney failure can indeed damage the brain.

"Yes, I am. And in your most capable hands, I will recover." Not so much a statement, but a veiled threat, implicit in his tone. As long as I was needed to keep him alive I myself would live. Or was that wishful thinking? A qualified nephrologist could do what I was about to do. Or perhaps one was there and ready. Perhaps he was only placating me and telling I was the surgeon to make our arrival easy for him. And once in Russia I would be quickly dealt with through death.

"What's in it for me?" Yes, dead, dead, and dead. Where that came from, I have no idea, but I blurted it out anyway. Probably a mistake, but I was dead already. Why not let my thoughts fly unfiltered?

He sat up, and looked at me with such shock in his eyes, I

TWO

thought they would pop from his head. Then he laughed, and the small laughter turned to a full-on body shake.

"Good for you, Adrien, good for you. Always the negotiator. Some things though, need no negotiation. Wouldn't you agree?"

"I would," I said, and left it at that. "You daughter." I was still intrigued.

"Ah, my little flame. What of her?" he asked with a smile. I was formulating a plan and needed more information about her.

"She is Jewish, Muslim, and Christian. Quite a compilation," I inquired. My hand I found reached my chin reflexively as I stroked it and thought.

"Yes. It has served her well to meld where she needs, and has caused mild opposition for her in areas as well." He didn't exactly give me an answer, but did reveal a small window into her life with Avigad as a father.

"And she lives in Rome?" I asked, seeing how far I could go in information gathering. What business did he have in Rome? This was the first I heard of it.

"She does," he responded.

"And she works for you in your business?" Why not try to put every piece of this puzzle together.

"Her position is an associate curator with the Vatican Museums, and is reflected as such on her documents. But I would agree she works for me," he said with a smarmy smile.

I was about to ask more pressing questions, however I began to feel the plane slow and the wheels drop, as the pilot's voice came through the system. We were on the descent into St. Petersburg airport. Seat belts fastened, he leaned forward and gave me the information he felt I needed.

"Your passport remains of a Swiss national. However, you are here to attend a conference at the Hermitage. I do not believe I have to lecture you on any subjects, as your knowledge of art will gain you entrance at Customs and Immigration if asked any questions." He nodded at me.

"Do we have a minder here, as we did in Tehran?" I inquired. Although a country not receptive to Western people in general that did tolerate tourists who were allowed to move freely about unlike Iran.

"Well, yes and no. We are being met at the airport and escorted by Dmitri's brother, Ivan. He knows my circumstance and has the ear of people in the Kremlin, and has eased our way into the country. As I said, the Roselov name is powerful. The facilities you will use to operate are the best that money can buy, and the surgeon most skilled," he offered with a knowing smile. He indeed has this well planned and the plan well executed.

"Tell me about your illness," I said. Possibly there could be an organ failure during surgery from hypoxia of another organ. Or an anesthesia mishap. Depending on what medications were available I could possibly slip him an overdose of heparin. My mind ran through all the possibilities.

"All you need to know is that it is not infectious." He kept his answer succinct and what he felt was on point.

"Tests and CAT scan?" I asked. This might point to other defects like possible liver failure where I could manipulate the organ during surgery to put stress on it further and it would develop necrosis. Or if his blood sugar was on the low side I could tip him over into hypoglycemia.

"At the facility, waiting on us."

"When do we arrive at the center where this will be performed?" I inquired.

"Within the hour after we exit the airport. Less, if the traffic is in our favor. Well within the window of time to maintain the viability of the kidney," he said as if he believed that was why I inquired. "I have neither eaten nor drank anything for twenty-four

TWO

hours, to be safe. Once we arrive, I will be ready to undergo pre-operative procedures."

"Indeed," was my only reply. "Anything I need to know? Allergies or medications that may be a problem?"

"My nephrologist has been in contact with the anesthesiologist. I am drug-free and I have no allergies."

Sitting back in the chair as we came closer to the wheels hitting the ground, he gave me a speech similar to the one I received at Tehran, except this ended on a more upbeat note.

"St. Petersburg is more touristy and Western-friendly than Moscow. Therefore, unlike tourists or other business people we should be able to move through Immigration and Customs with ease. If asked about the purpose, respond with, 'Business for a conference at the Hermitage.' Russian men are ingrained to feel a man involved with art as a living poses no threat to mother Russia."

"Where are we staying while in Russia?" I wanted to factor that into a plan I was formulating for my survival.

"The State Hermitage Museum Hotel," he responded after a thought.

As we passed though Immigration, we were asked if we had contacts in Russia. Of course, the Roselovs. Did we have anything to declare, coming into Russia. That's where Ivan Roselov appeared out of nowhere, with official papers and a wad of cash.

"Welcome to Russia," the Immigration agent said in broken English. He stamped our passports, and we proceeded through the crowded area. Ivan collected us after we passed Customs, and we were shown to the exit, where a car was waiting.

Driving through St. Petersburg, you would believe you were in a Western city, only with a high Russian population. Even Paris has Russian Orthodox churches, much like St. Petersburg, so with the onion-domed churches it felt strangely familiar. People appeared reserved and not angry, like the Muscovites. I could make eye contact with a St. Petersburg resident, and they would look away. In Moscow, they would look me in the eye out of arrogance and anger, and for good measure, spit on my shoes. On balance, I felt rather safe in St. Petersburg. Until I remembered I would never leave here after the surgery, if Avigad had his way. Of that, I had no doubt.

Would I be spirited away to the infamous Siberia? Or would I be part of a slave trade network, forced to perform operations for the wealthy of Russia. Or maybe I would be put to death the moment Avigad asked for my account numbers, to transfer my wealth to him. And when would that occur? After I operated, and he was healed under my guiding hand. Living under such worry brought bile and fear to my throat.

As we passed an area that appeared somewhat industrial, yet maintained a well-manicured greenspace appearance, I watched as the onion domes became less and less. Was this a signal that we were entering a more government-controlled area? Finally, a modern building came into view, very similar in structure and lines as the one in Iran. There was no doubt this would be my home for the next few days, as Avigad recovered and I ministered to him.

If he lived through the operation, surely I would die. My question was how vested were the Roselovs in Avigad's wellbeing? If he died during the operation would I be punished for allowing him to die. Or had he paid them a fee to get him here and he was but a business transaction. Did they really care if he lived or died once they received their money?

"How will us never checking into the hotel be handled?" If I were to die here in Russia, who would ever know we were ever here. And that was actually a pointless worry since I was traveling under a Swiss passport. I was true and royally fucked. But I could

TWO

not give up.

"Ivan has arranged for men of similar builds and facial characteristics to check in and be seen about," he said staring out the window in thought. "There will be a sighting of the Swiss art professor and his investor friend at the conference."

We pulled in front of the green glass building, where two large men in black suits waited. If they had been in front of a night club, they would easily be characterized as bouncers.

Ivan's driver exited the car, came around, and opened Ivan's door. Ivan walked around the back of the car to obtain the container with the kidney. As he was retrieving the container, the driver opened Avigad's door, and then mine. Sunglasses precluded eye contact; I suppose to prevent me from reading his unpleasant thoughts.

"If you gentlemen will follow me, I will escort you to the surgical suite," Ivan said.

We followed Ivan across the pristine white marble floor, past the white soapstone reception desk to the glass elevators. The building was architecturally identical to the one in Tehran, down to the suite being on the third floor and red furniture.

"Dr. Armond, I will take you to the surgical suite, and, Avigad, I will take you to the preparation area," Ivan continued in excellent English with a slight Russian accent. Clearly he had spent years outside Russia. Nothing more, nothing less. Everything appeared regimented and awaiting our arrival.

"So, this is it?" I asked, looking around at a place which, like the one in Tehran, boasted luxury and the best technology had to offer.

"Yes, until I see you right before the anesthetist puts me under," Avigad said.

"Any instructions?" I asked.

"Bring me out the other end alive." And then the final blow.

The Judas kiss was laid upon me with everyone watching, and everyone understood. Of that, I had no doubt. To others not in the inner circle, he might be showing them that I was a trusted friend. I knew different. I knew Avigad.

"You can count on me," I responded, barely able to hold it together.

I was escorted to the surgical area, where I changed into purple scrubs and began the surgical scrub. My plan ruminated and started to fall into place.

I studied his kidney scans and all the X-rays, as well as blood and urine tests. Yes, Avigad was right. One kidney was already grossly deteriorated and in fact in failure. The other heading toward failure sooner rather than later. Without a transplant, his death was possibly months, maybe only weeks, away.

As I walked out, Ivan glanced at me. "Would you like to inspect the surgical tray?"

"Most definitely," I said. "I also want to look at the medication cabinet." In the event something went wrong, I would certainly want to know where the medication was stored. The tray was perfect, but the medication cabinet, not so much. I asked for a moment to acquaint myself with it, he stepped away to give me room to view the organization of it. Checking each drawer and medication swiftly, I was ready.

The anesthesiologist administered the intravenous medication to lull his muscles to relax but was in the state between consciousness and unconsciousness. He moved his finger for me to come closer. I approached, and he spoke in a hushed, almost indiscernible, tone.

"Azar is the flame, and the flame must never be extinguished," he said.

Gibberish, but understandable.

The face mask over his face for oxygen and then the

TWO

intubation tube inserted, he was totally under, no coming back. The machines very regulated and the heart monitor beeped a steady sinus rhythm. The ventilator bellows whooshed up and down delivering oxygen to his lungs and keeping them inflated.

It was now or never that my plan would be executed. I turned to everyone as they took their place for the surgery, and said, "I want to thank you all for your help, but Avigad had requested that no one remain in the surgical suite during the operation, except for me and the anesthetist."

The place was so silent, a pin could be heard bouncing from the floor if it dropped.

"Impossible," said one of the team's doctors. "Who will hand you instruments and hang the fluids as they are needed?"

"Avigad and I have operated under much more utilitarian circumstances. I do not know if it's his religion which precludes women being in the surgery and touching a man, or if it was a cultural request. All I know is that he requested no women in the room, and that I was the only one to touch his body. Possibly for modesty, he also asked all men to leave as well," I said. These people did not know Avigad but if they did they would know he would demand all hands be on deck to minister to his every need. If he survived I certainly would be killed for putting his life in further jeopardy. This was a risk I had to take.

Arguing in Russian ensued, and finally, they began to leave one by one.

As the last doctor walked out, he showed me where the alarm button was placed, so that should I need help, it would be seconds away.

I thanked them, then checked the IV bags and made certain the blood was properly stored, if needed. It wouldn't be. I reviewed my tray. All the surgical instruments were in their proper place. I eyed the medication laid out on the table. When the anesthesiologist turned his back to turn the dials on the anesthesia flow coming from the walls, I reached in my pocket and took the first medication syringe off the table and replaced it with the one from the chaotic cabinet. I reached in my other pocket and substituted the one in my pocket for the one on the tray. Now everything was in place.

Intubated and all vital signs good, we proceeded to do the surgical pre-check. Checking that his level of sedation was adequate, and the monitors held steady on the beats, I moved to the first IV bag. Looking at the anesthetist, I indicated I was preparing to fill the IV chamber with medication and adjust the drip rate to administer it over a half hour period. He nodded. He neither asked what it was, and I did not tell. He assumed I would record it accurately on the chart. He was wrong.

I took the syringe from the table and wiped the yellow plastic cover of the drip chamber, punctured it, and put pressure on the plunger to empty the contents of the syringe into the eight-inch chamber half filled with fluid, and readjusted the drip. A syringe filled with air injected into his vein would have been just as effective to cause an embolism, but much riskier with possibly not the results I wanted.

I kinked off the tubing delivering the fluid to his hand and attached a syringe to the cannula and pushed the fluid from the small syringe into his vein to be distributed through his body. I nodded to the anesthesiologist and he nodded back.

"I'm ready to begin. Is he ready?" I asked the man whose job it was to suspend him between life and death. He nodded.

His vital signs remained steady and the anesthesiologist was lulled into the zone when the surgeon was the most important and he became bored. If he had been alert he would have noticed the blood now leaking into the urine bag or blood streaming along the side of the table. But he would never know it was from

TWO

a massive dose of heparin given with the intent to anticoagulate the body's blood. Every organ in his body would be affected and his brain would not be spared.

Since he did not notice, I yelled to him indicating he was bleeding but there was no indication from where. This could easily be explained as an anticoagulation defect from chronic kidney disease.

As he scurried to look around with me for the site of the bleeding we were forty minutes into the surgery, when suddenly the monitor showed a significant slowing of his heart. He was torn between searching for the site of the bleed and treating the bradycardia that had set in and finally asystole. He hit the alarm button, which brought the team of physicians and nurses charging in. One administered a shot of adrenaline straight into his thick-walled failing heart, another shocked him with the paddles, while yet another opened the IV fluids wide, to bring as much hydration to him as possible. By opening the IV full force, the remainder of the massive dose of potassium chloride I had put in the medication chamber was pushed like a bolus into his system, finishing him off.

Avigad would have loved to know that in the end people buzzed around him trying to save him. He would be pissed to know they never had a chance at reviving him. The dose of heparin I administered assured his blood would never coagulate and thus never allow the kidney to take if I had attached it. But more important medication I gave him, potassium chloride, would assure heart failure. With his compromised kidneys and history of heart failure it was a risk anyone would suspect. I didn't see an autopsy in his future where the vitreous humor of his eyeballs would be studied for an overdose. It was him or me, and I chose me.

Poor Avigad's abdomen lay open, with his kidney removed

and the other waiting to be implanted. Here he lay, lifeless on the operating table, dead of an apparent heart attack. All agreed his kidneys were just too far gone to save him. Cause of death? Heart failure; most likely a myocardial infarction from advanced renal disease. No need for an autopsy. And so what if they *did* do one? Potassium is released from the cells at death, and with his poor renal function, which showed potassium elevation in his pre-op work, no alarms would be raised.

Rest in peace, Avigad, you bastard. You will never get your hands on my money, or exile me to some fucking place in this hellhole called Russia.

"Ivan, this kidney is still within the thirty-hour window. Perhaps you should look into returning it to its original owner." Why I cared about returning the kidney to the young woman rang even odd to me as it came from my lips. "His daughter I am certain would be grateful."

Ivan looked at me, studying my face. "Thank you for your thoughtfulness, Adrien," he replied, a small smile on his face. "I'll look into it immediately, to see if it can be accomplished."

Arrangements were made to have Avigad's body shipped to Belfast, where he hailed from in early life. Belfast? Unlikely. But what did I really know about the man? It was apparent they wanted this mess out of Russia as swiftly as possible with no trace and no blowback. Ivan expressed he would be in my debt if I would accompany the body until we reached Northern Ireland, where his men would give him a proper burial. Of course, how could I refuse such a heartfelt request. Although in my heart I worried I would be sharing a grave with Avigad.

I gathered my paperwork to leave St. Petersburg and as I was shrugging on my coat waiting in the center lounge to be escorted to the car to take us to the airport to board the private jet a rough-looking burly man approached me. His English was

TWO

broken but I understood enough that he wanted me to follow him. We crossed the pristine marble floor and entered the elevators to the third floor. Odd, why are we returning to the surgical area? The man never turned to converse with me and I followed him as I assumed he wanted.

We passed through two metal double doors and then traveled toward the surgical suite. Had I forgotten to sign something? Now side by side we entered the operating room where Ivan was sitting on a surgical stool and another man dressed in surgical scrubs stood next to the surgical table where a tray of instruments lay open. What the hell?

Ivan stood and walked toward me and when he reached me he put his arm around my shoulder and moved me toward the table.

"Adrien, we want to thank you for your surgical performance last evening. Avigad had become a bit of a loose cannon over the last few months and put us all in jeopardy. His work had become sloppy and he left too many breadcrumbs that inevitably could lead back to us. His part in blowing up Dmitry's gallery, that I might add was not sanctioned by us, put us in shall I say a precarious situation. His short-term goal to collect insurance money jeopardized our long-term goals. The domino effect of that misstep forced us into reaching out to Iran to safeguard art works that if they became available to the authorities would have eventually revealed how we were receiving state secrets from multiple and varied governments. Those painting are safe, and the information retrieved. However, Iran is now also in possession of those secrets after we did all the work and paid an enormous amount to obtain that information.

"The slaughter of those people in Cairo after an investigation brought our Middle East brothers knocking at our door with questions that put us in a very bad position.

"You, my friend, were involved with both these debacles and for that you must receive some type of punishment," Ivan said as he walked toward the man in scrubs and the burly man who escorted me in took his place by my side.

Panic, sheer panic was what I felt. I was going to die. My knee started to wobble, I could not catch my breath and my heart pulsated in my throat.

The voice that came from my throat was the stuttering of the scared little boy of the drunken mother who had been bullied by his betters.

"Ivan, I can explain—" I struggled to get out. Actually, no, I could not explain how greed drove me to help kill all those people. And state secrets? Where were they hidden? The frame, in the paint, the canvas? Who could have known?

"Adrien, my friend, no need for an explanation. Now if you would please step forward," he said motioning me forward while the man I now presumed a surgeon retrieved a stand-like contraption from under the table. It appeared to be a flat mental device with ten mental loops.

"Now be so kind as to place your right hand on the table and the good doctor here will administer a nerve-blocking agent to your hand," he said as he smiled what I interpreted as a sadistic smile. "Don't be shy, step forward. Here, right here."

"Why, what are you needing to do that for?" I asked with an obvious stutter and panic in my voice.

"If you don't do as I ask, Lazar next to you will be happy to assist," he said now with a more serious tone. A threat.

I stepped forward and lay my right hand on the table. The surgeon then picked up an alcohol swab and cleansed the area around my second knuckle of my index finger. He then retrieved a syringe and proceeded to administer a nerve-blocking agent around the joint area where my index finger met my hand.

TWO

"Now the left," Ivan motioned.

After the procedure was repeated again he took my hand and slipped my fingers through the loops of the device and secured them in position.

"Are your fingers numb?" he asked. I nodded. "Good. Now don't move or there will be complications you will not enjoy."

As if in a dreamlike state, I watched in a state of shock how first my right and then my left index fingers were amputated to the second joint. I heard someone scream in shock and realized it was me. I felt my body start to slump and was steadied by Lazar and another man I had not realized was in the room. They confined my body and cocooned me into a space where I could not move and they could control me.

There was no surgical incision, no teasing of the fascia and muscles away. No. It was chopped right off and cauterized. In reaction, I turned and vomited all over Lazar's shoes and I think I peed my pants but was so shocked I could not tell if there was wetness. And if I did, the urine smell was overpowered by the vomit fumes.

"Now, one more thing and we are done," Ivan said as he picked up what appeared to be an ink gun used for tattoos and proceeded to mark the skin between my index finger and thumb on each hand with a Russian symbol.

As the surgeon cleansed and wrapped the stumps while Ivan turned to me and said, "See, not so bad."

I felt the need to vomit again and swallowed it back. My heart must have been pounding out a beat to over one hundred twenty or more beats per minute.

"Now let me explain. Avigad was a pain in our ass. But it was not your right to be judge, and jury, and executioner. There had to be some punishment for your actions and, this, how shall I say, seemed the most fitting and humane. We have packed a small bag with supplies for changing your dressings and several bottles of pain pills. We wish you luck. Now the plane is ready, and I have a fresh suit and shirt for you if you want to change in the scrub area. There may be a time we call upon you again and you should answer our call. Have a good life, Adrien," he said and clasped my shoulder.

With the pressure dressing applied, I started in a shock-like state toward the room to change. I was stopped by the doctor who administered a shot of antibiotic and shot of pain medication. I briefly heard him tell me more antibiotics were in the bag with pain pills.

Robotically, I walked to the surgical scrub area and changed with Lazar's assistance. Indeed, I had urinated on myself.

I don't remember the walk to the car nor the ride to the airport. However, that morning, Avigad Abed—Jew and Palestinian Arab from Northern Ireland—and I were on our way to Belfast. The kidney of Azar, the flame, was on its way back to Tehran, with the hope it could be replanted without issue and she would be forever in my debt. Possibly even offer me a reward. My mind, still in shock, could not as yet formulate the consequences of my missing digits or the new life I would need to adapt to so I reverted to old habits, muscle memory habits. Checking my funds for comfort.

I settled into my seat as the pilots performed their preflight check. I clumsily tapped into my Swiss account, to transfer money to my European account for living expenses to stay under the radar. When the account page became visible, my heart thumped and my mind blanked. There was nothing but zeros. I scrolled through the transactions and saw where the money had been moved but there was no way to find out where unless I did a personal visit to the bank. Security was a priority to them. With no passport as identification and no money to travel, that would

TWO

present a challenge not to mention missing fingers covered in bloody bandages.

As I opened and closed each of my four accounts offshore and my national accounts, I realized they all were empty, and all but one closed for all intents and purposes. Just left with a nominal amount to remain open to taunt me. In that one, a sum of ten thousand euros remained.

Isabella, like Avigad, would pay. In so many ways.

CHAPTER THIRTY

ADRIEN

A MONTH PASSED, and the world had not slid into an Armageddon as Avigad predicted. My finances, on the other hand, had reached that point. It was imperative I return home to retrieve my hidden emergency funds, gun, and passports, to start a new life.

Getting to the building and inside was simple, gaining access to the apartment, another matter. At this juncture, I had to make the decision: do I go in or not? Nick would be high and asleep, so getting past him was not a problem. But the door to my apartment. Had she changed the locks? Would hall cameras pick me up and alert Nick at some point?

Making my way through the back entrance, past Nick who indeed was passed out, and taking the stairs up to the third floor was easier than I imagined. Still, my heart thumped, and breath came out in short wheezes. Probably no need to hug the wall to avoid the cameras in the hall, but why take the chance? My appearance was so drastically altered, there was no way anyone would recognize me—now, or on a review of the security

TWO

footage later.

Standing in front of the door to the apartment that cost me my life to possess, I slipped the key into the deadbolt lock, and without any effort, the tumblers disengaged. Unblocked and unfettered access. Could this be so easy or was it a trap. The logical part of my brain kicked in and I told myself they probably thought I was dead.

I stood inside the entrance hall for a moment, to allow my heart to slow its rate back to normal. I took some deep breaths and was able to control the panic I felt building. Placing my duffle bag on the floor, I removed my night-vision goggles and began my journey down the hall and through the bedroom, which would end in the master bathroom.

They say that the journey of a thousand miles begins with the first step. As I stepped closer, I heard the low din of the television. Shit, Isabella was here. What in the hell was she doing here? The apartment was sold. What was she still doing here? Why not stay with Chloe until the furniture was removed? Well, I had not come all this way to give up what I came for. And this might prove, in the end, to be a bonus. The element of surprise was on my side and once I retrieved my belongings, if I planned well enough, I could force her to turn over the money taken from the accounts. Well, this had turned into a win-win for me.

Removing my shoes, I walked barefoot into the kitchen to retrieve a knife. No need going into battle unarmed. Which one, long or short? Did it really matter? In the end, it was for scare tactics. Unless she forced me to use it, then it would be self-defense. Right?

Armed with the knife and duffle bag in hand, I continued to my destination. Anger mounting at the thought of all the time and money lost for the work I did for Avigad and now my home sold for pennies on the euro. Approaching the bedroom, I could hear the low white noise effect of the television she used to sleep. Her body was bathed in the eerie blue glow of the television light. Look at her, sleeping peacefully in my home that I'd paid for with my money. And yet, she was not satisfied with that; she had to steal it all. All my money. Before the night was up, she would be returning every penny. Or, if she chose the wrong way and tried to keep it, she would not live to enjoy her life.

Maybe Avigad had been right. She'd become a problem I should have taken care of, and if I'd listened, I wouldn't be here, sneaking into my own home. Should I let her live? What would one more death be in the scheme of things?

I made my way to the bathroom and placed my duffle bag quietly on the floor. I removed the screwdriver, and opened the cabinet door next to the bathtub. I went to work, removing the vent which allowed air flow from the jacuzzi tub motor and, *voilà*! Right where I left them. Gun, money, and passports. Only two hundred grand, but enough to get me by in a pinch.

Placing the money and passports in my bag, I kept the gun out.

Knife or gun? Which would be more effective? Never bring a knife to a gunfight. With that age-old wisdom, I placed the knife next to the money and passports, and zipped the bag up. I was ready to interrogate Isabella, and before I left, I would have my money. All of it.

Should I chamber a round and risk her hearing it? No, the sight of the gun would have her frightened enough.

Placing the bag on the bedroom floor outside the bathroom, I carefully walked over to her, lying on her back in bed. Such a beautiful woman. Had my plans come to fruition, she would be on the road to hell, for a permanent stay in a psychiatric facility, unaware what day of the week it was. With her tucked safely away there, medicated and supervised, I wouldn't be in this

TWO

position. My plan had seemed flawless. But now was not the time to review where things went wrong. Now was the time to restart my life because of her. Anger started to take over and cloud my judgment. I had stopped loving her long ago; now she was just a speedbump in the road.

I bent over her, within inches of her sleeping body, and placed the barrel of the gun to her forehead, right between her eyes. Her eyes fluttered open at once, as the cold metal of the barrel bit into her skin. Alarm enveloped her face.

"Adrien," she whispered. She didn't move, frozen in place. A good sign.

"Yes, Isabella. Adrien." I moved a little closer so she could see the fury and hate in my eyes.

"We thought you were dead," she said, not moving a muscle.

"Good to know. What would make you think such unpleasant thoughts?" My anger at her was about to unleash itself.

"Someone stumbled across that man who shot me. His body was found in a shallow grave outside Belfast, and we thought you were dead as well, having last been seen with him," she said.

"I see." Sloppy work on those Russian thugs' part. Or maybe they wanted him found on British soil. Who knows.

"Isabella, I'm not here to discuss my miraculous reappearance. I'm here to retrieve the money you stole from me," I asserted, and leaned over further to press the gun a little harder into her head, as incentive.

"Money? I have no money. You stole it. After Michelle put a freeze on it, you stole it. Vanished. Poof. No one can find it," she bit out, sounding angry. "What game are you playing?"

"Then how do you explain how you are maintaining your current life standard?" I asked again, pressing the gun into her head with a little twist of my wrist.

"Seriously? You are going to deny leaving me with nothing? Get out. You have the money, and I have nothing." This woman was not to be believed. Was she trying to run a game on me? Obvious she was recovering from my manipulation and mind games. Almost back to her old self.

"Answer me," I demanded. "How are you staying here and running the gallery if you have no funds?"

"Adrien, over the years as you became more controlling and abusive, with Chloe's help, I started to put money aside for the day that I might need an emergency fund. A little here, a little there—it will give me a year to get on my feet. The apartment is sold, and in a week, I will be gone. The gallery building was also taken in foreclosure when I couldn't pay the upkeep. All the inventory confiscated. So, Adrien, if I had your money, why would I be selling everything off?" she yelled at me, raising her body suddenly as she shouted.

In that split second, when I lost focus, is when I felt the knife slice into my side and, with all the strength she had, she twisted and pulled it. The pain was quick, and had I chambered that bullet, I would have reflexively shot her in the head and we would both be dead. Neither to enjoy whatever money was out there.

The searing pain was suddenly replaced with the alarming amount of blood I was losing. Where did the knife come from? Had she been sleeping with it? How could I not have planned for all contingencies?

I stumbled back and slumped as I fell against the wall with my back against it. I started to feel a cloud passing over me, like a cold vapor. In a tunnel of darkness, I saw her grab for my phone that had slid from my jacket.

As I lay there, trying to figure out how to save myself, I saw her tap the phone. Hopefully, she was calling for help.

"Ben, he's here and I stabbed him. Call an ambulance," she

TWO

said. He must have acknowledged her statement as she threw the phone back into my lap, deciding her next course of action.

"Adrien, I'm getting towels to put some pressure on the wound. Hold your phone and answer it if it rings. I'll be back in a second." And she was off to the bathroom for towels. If it was me I would have gladly let her die and watch how the light snuffed from her eyes.

I knew all the signs. Cold clammy skin, rapid shallow breathing, nausea, dizziness. I was slowly slipping into shock, awaiting Isabella's return. What did life matter anymore anyway? I'd while my life away in jail. Back to how I started. Dirt poor broke. The rise and fall of Adrien Armond.

A text pinged on my phone and I glanced at the screen, hoping it was an acknowledgment that help was on the way.

"It's come to my attention you were the one that made arrangements for my kidney to be returned to me after helping my father steal it from me. I am returning a million euros of your funds back to your account. Spend the money wisely."

The End

ABOUT THE AUTHOR

K.J. MCGILLICK IS an author of psychological thrillers and draws from her background in the law, medicine and art history to engage her readers in her fast-paced thriller series, A Path of Deception and Betrayal. She draws upon her legal knowledge as a practicing attorney and experiences as an avid international traveler to produce page turning books filled with mystery and suspense.

CONNECT WITH K. J.

Official website: *www.kjmcgillick.com*

K.J.'s Facebook Page: *www.facebook.com/KJMcGillickauthor*

You can email her at *kjmcgillick@gmail.com*

OTHER BOOKS

A PATH OF DECEPTION AND BETRAYAL

THREE: Deception Love Murder (Book 1)

ONE: Enigma (Book 3) ~ Coming May 2018

Made in the USA
Columbia, SC
13 June 2018